PRAISE FOR THE NOVELS O

"Harper writes characters you can't he

—RT Book Reviews

"Tons of heart, lots of laughs, and of course, kooky locals."

—Harlequin Junkies, on *Sweet Tea and Sympathy*

"Warm and cozy and full of Southern charm."

—Dear Author, on *Sweet Tea and Sympathy*

"This sweet tale of the city girl finding a home in the country launches Harper's latest series and will go down as easy as honey on a deep-fried Twinkie." —*Library Journal*, on *Sweet Tea and Sympathy*

"Margot is a terrific lead for Harper's supporting cast of quirky characters. This is a promising start to Harper's Southern Eclectic series."

—*Publishers Weekly*, on *Sweet Tea and Sympathy*

"Harper's assemblage of ghostly residents sparkles."

—*Publishers Weekly*, on *Witches Get Stuff Done*

"Amid magical shenanigans . . . this book might just have you laughing out loud." —Hazel Beck, on *Witches Get Stuff Done*

"An adorable yet hard-hitting paranormal romance, *Witches Get Stuff Done* is an absolute must." —Culturess

"Harper's tight and twisty plot revs up to a satisfying climax, while her characters charm throughout. . . . This will have readers on the edge of their seats."   —*Publishers Weekly*, on *Big Witch Energy*

"Hysterical laughs are the hallmark of this enchanting paranormal debut. . . . Harper keeps the quips coming without overdoing the sarcasm."

          —*Publishers Weekly*, on *Nice Girls Don't Have Fangs* (starred review)

A PROPOSAL TO DIE FOR

MOLLY HARPER

BERKLEY PRIME CRIME
NEW YORK

BERKLEY PRIME CRIME
Published by Berkley
An imprint of Penguin Random House LLC
1745 Broadway, New York, NY 10019
penguinrandomhouse.com

Copyright © 2025 by Molly Harper
Penguin Random House values and supports copyright. Copyright fuels creativity,
encourages diverse voices, promotes free speech, and creates a vibrant culture. Thank you
for buying an authorized edition of this book and for complying with copyright laws by
not reproducing, scanning, or distributing any part of it in any form without permission.
You are supporting writers and allowing Penguin Random House to continue to publish
books for every reader. Please note that no part of this book may be used or reproduced
in any manner for the purpose of training artificial intelligence technologies or systems.

BERKLEY and the BERKLEY & B colophon are registered trademarks and
BERKLEY PRIME CRIME is a trademark of Penguin Random House LLC.

Book design by George Towne

Library of Congress Cataloging-in-Publication Data

Names: Harper, Molly, author.
Title: A proposal to die for / Molly Harper.
Description: First edition. | New York : Berkley Prime Crime, 2025.
Identifiers: LCCN 2024024359 (print) | LCCN 2024024360 (ebook) |
ISBN 9780593817322 (trade paperback) | ISBN 9780593817339 (ebook)
Subjects: LCGFT: Detective and mystery fiction. | Novels.
Classification: LCC PS3608.A774 P76 2025 (print) |
LCC PS3608.A774 (ebook) | DDC 813/.6—dc23/eng/20240604
LC record available at https://lccn.loc.gov/2024024359
LC ebook record available at https://lccn.loc.gov/2024024360

First Edition: April 2025

Printed in the United States of America
1st Printing

The authorized representative in the EU for product safety and compliance is
Penguin Random House Ireland, Morrison Chambers, 32 Nassau Street,
Dublin D02 YH68, Ireland, https://eu-contact.penguin.ie.

For Natanya,

who brings so many wonderful things to my life.
Without you, Jess would just be one of my weird
"middle of the night" index card ideas.

A
PROPOSAL
TO DIE FOR

THE EMERGENCY

Jessamine Bricker thought spas were supposed to be relaxing. So far, her stay at the Golden Ash had left her creeped out, covered in mud, menaced, and forcibly bridesmaided. (Bridesmaid'd? Bridesmade?)

Jess was going to need therapy to deal with all this "relaxation."

Her solo session in the spa's thermal suite had started out so well, soaking in softly scented steam showers and floating in silent, tranquil pools. But now she was standing in the sunlit hallway, listening for . . . she wasn't sure what. Despite being surrounded by heated white ceramic tile, she shivered and drew her plush Golden Ash robe closer at the throat. Something was off. Some primal atmospheric disturbance was closing in around her.

Jess turned to look for dangers hidden in the long empty corridor. She was alone, save for the harp music over forest sounds pumped in from some hidden speaker. She should have found comfort in it.

But . . .

What was that smell?

The sour, moldy stink had Jess gagging. She clamped her hand over her mouth to prevent that offensive fog from creeping into her respiratory system.

The smell seemed to be coming from the Alpine Steam Room. She closed her fingers around the handle and pulled. The overripe cheese-scented steam billowed out over her head, making her groan out her displeasure.

Jess flicked on the light switch. A rumpled mass of person lay splayed across the sauna's aqua slate floor.

Is that who I think it is?

The irritatingly familiar person-mass in question was face down, like they'd been clambering toward the door before collapsing into a thin puddle of what she was pretty sure was vomit.

Ew.

"OK, get up," Jess huffed at the prone form, a pit of apprehension forming in her belly. "This party-till-you-pass-out nonsense was embarrassing when you were twenty. Now it's just sad."

Jess laid a hand against the mottled skin, which was cold to the touch, even with the steam curling around them.

No. No no. Nononononononoonononono.

Not hungover.

Dead.

Jess let loose a strangled yelp, scuttling back until she felt the wall.

Death had checked in at the Golden Ash Spa and Wellness Resort, and it smelled like expired dairy.

Why couldn't she yell? Why couldn't she *move*? Her hands seemed to be frozen at her sides. Everything in her was cold, numb weight. The warm air current flowed over her face, but she was *freezing*. Her hands slipped ineffectively against the tile. Why couldn't she push up?

Jess forced herself to look away from the empty eyes, the graying skin, but she couldn't seem to get her brain to concentrate on one thing, anything, that would get her out of this mess. A large, red, round shape came into focus, and with great effort, she homed all her attention on that bright spot—a plastic circle, inside a closing case, that read **PRESS IN CASE OF EMERGENCY**.

Jess was the kind of girl who followed directions.

CHAPTER 1

SEVERAL WEEKS EARLIER

One never knew when a comically oversized resin clam was going to come in handy, and Jess Bricker happened to know a guy who could procure one for her on short notice. That was why nervous prospective spouses paid Jess top dollar to find rare items like this—items that were somehow vital to their marriage proposals—and then get the hell out of the way.

Standing outside the largest tank at the Appalachian Seas Aquarium, Jess waved at the dive supervisor as he gently placed the faux shell in the tank's seaweed bed. Glittering clouds of fish swarmed around Dive Shop Dave, clearly expecting some sort of food. Dave double-checked that the precious package was inside the shell and flashed Jess a thumbs-up. Those frustrated fish jetted away, unfed.

Shaking her head, Jess stepped back to appreciate the visual scope of her evening's work. She chewed on a full bottom lip that had bid goodbye to its coat of nude rose gloss after her fourth coffee of the day. The aquarium was home to one of the few whale-shark-friendly exhibits in the world. Tonight's (human) guest of honor,

Samantha, was an avid scuba diver. Her longtime boyfriend, Gage, had gotten certified on the sly just so he could gift her a private birthday dive with the gentle giants—a big unchecked box on Samantha's bucket list.

The tank's shadowed viewing room was cleared after closing, giving Jess and the aquarium staff time to stage this romantic tableau for the future Mr. and Mrs. Gage Hallidon. Maintenance workers had meticulously scrubbed fingerprints from the tank's thick acrylic, removing all evidence that hordes of elementary school students had herded through only hours before. A sweetheart table for two stood near the tank's front, centered in a pool of rippling blue light. The effect was dreamy and ethereal, enough to make any mermaid's heart go . . . swish?

How did mermaids' hearts go?

"This is not the first time I've said this, but that is a weird question to be asking yourself at ten o'clock on a weeknight," Jess muttered under her breath. "Also, it's a little sad how often you talk to yourself."

The picture was almost perfection, but she hadn't become one of Nashville's best-kept matrimonial secrets by creating *almost* perfection. Jess picked up her Bluetooth earpiece, careful not to knock any element of the teal and silver tablescape aside. She murmured into the attached lapel mic. "Hey, Bob, the lighting feels a little cold. Anything we can do about that?"

The earpiece cheeped and the aquarium's facilities supervisor replied, "Sure thing, Jess."

Jess smiled as the overhead lights shifted ever so slightly to a warm peachy glow, thanks to colored gels meant to imitate a sunset over the ocean. She closed her eyes, imagining she was the birthday girl and a man like Gage loved her enough to set something like this up for her.

"Jess, Jess, Mermaid is in the cave," Bob murmured over Jess's earpiece. "Repeat, Mermaid is in the cave. Over."

She snorted softly to herself. Bob was really embracing this whole "secret mission" aesthetic. Of course, he was earning double overtime thanks to Gage's generous private rental fee, which bought a lot of goodwill.

"Got it, Bob. Mark this setting and then cut the lights outside the tank so Mermaid can't see the table," she said. The lights clicked off immediately, leaving Jess bathed in the otherworldly marine glow. She smiled, retreating into a recessed alcove near displays that explained the feeding habits of all the animals in the Swimming with Legends exhibit. The angle to see into the tank's overhead maintenance space was spot-on, so she could see Gage and Samantha in full scuba gear. "Countdown to splash-in?"

"Splash-in imminent. Over," Bob responded, just as the couple dropped into the water in a profusion of bubbles.

"And . . . showtime," Jess whispered into the lapel mic, her wide gray eyes tracking Gage's and Samantha's descent through the water.

The next few minutes ran like clockwork. After initially skittering away from the intrusive splash, the fish edged back toward the happy couple as if they'd always been part of the ecosystem. Samantha whirled around like a mini-typhoon, trying to see everything at once through her bright pink scuba mask. And while whale sharks couldn't be trained, technically, the enormous dark silhouette glided through the water behind them as if on cue. Jess signaled Andrew Daysong, a local photographer Jess regularly hired to shoot her clients' events. He stepped forward, discreetly capturing the moment that Samantha practically vibrated with joy under the water. It would be the perfect photo for their future mantel: Gage and Samantha perfectly framed by the tank walls with a whale shark hovering peacefully behind them.

The gargantuan shark turned to avoid swimming directly into the tank wall. Samantha put her hand out and, under the careful supervision of Dive Shop Dave, let it slide gently along the whale shark's side. As the whale disappeared into the recesses of the tank, Gage pretended to notice the clamshell and motioned to Samantha to follow him to the bottom. Samantha fluttered her fins, frequently glancing up to follow the whale shark's progress. Gage reached for the fake giant clamshell and Samantha seemed to panic, motioning for him to stop. Jess assumed Samantha didn't want to be kicked out of the aquarium for harassing marine life.

Samantha's hands froze as Gage lifted the resin lid and a seahorse-shaped foam case floated to their eye level. Gage plucked the box from the ribbon tethering it to the clamshell.

Samantha's hand started shaking in a whole new way as Gage snapped open the case and presented the tasteful diamond solitaire. Andrew dashed forward to snap a series of photos as Samantha nodded frantically, then tried to kiss Gage. Their face gear clacked together almost audibly, even through the thick acrylic tank wall.

Andrew's camera went into rapid-fire mode, and he flashed a grin at Jess. In all the proposals they'd worked together, it was rare to find a spontaneous moment that charmed them both. It was possible they were becoming a bit jaded. Gage and Samantha kicked toward the surface, even as Samantha seemed to forget how her legs worked.

Within five minutes—as long as Gage followed the carefully timed plan—the happy couple would emerge from the tank, swath themselves in matching bathrobes, and sit down for dinner for two, serenaded by a string quartet playing soft instrumental selections from *The Little Mermaid* soundtrack. The musicians—each dressed as a different aquatic creature—appeared from a side door. They quietly took their seats, having tuned up in the Gallery of Jellyfish. Andrew moved into position so that he could capture Samantha's face as she realized that Gage's surprise wasn't limited to the tank.

Jess's cell buzzed in her pants pocket, the vibration echoing through the silence of the exhibit room. Huffing out an annoyed breath, she pulled the phone out to see **UNKNOWN CALLER** on her lock screen. Jess pressed the "Ignore" button. Even if her beloved grandmother called during a job, Jess wouldn't take it. Distractions at this stage only led to chaos.

Besides, barring a hip-breaking, ambulance-necessitating emergency, Nana Blanche knew to text when Jess was working, not call. The messages were fully punctuated, and each and every one was signed "Sincerely, Blanche Bricker." But she texted.

The number calling was local. Jess frowned at the screen. Could it be the Anellos' lawyers? Anxiety, sharp and cold as December well water, flooded Jess's belly.

Jess shook her head, swallowing the lump gathering in her throat. She'd thought she had more time. Losing her snug matchbox of a rental apartment over the TonyCakes bakery would mean she also lost the adjacent upstairs storage room, which served as—under the strictest of descriptions—the offices for Bricker Consultants, Inc. Upon the death of their patriarch, the Anellos told Jess a few developers had expressed interest in buying the building and turning it into a condo/retail center. Tony Anello's kids were reluctant to further gentrify their little neighborhood and said that ideally, they would like to sell the building to "someone" like Jess. While Bricker Consultants was doing well for a two-person operation, Jess didn't have that kind of money. She couldn't dream of making an offer. The Anellos told Jess it would take the lawyers weeks to work through the estate details if she wanted to think it over. But it wasn't as if a few weeks would magically make "real estate money" appear in her accounts. Maybe the family had reached a decision about selling?

"No. You might evict me, but not today," she muttered, choosing to focus on the positive. Jess was sure she could find some other kindly septuagenarian to offer her a sweetheart rental deal on a comfortable, conveniently located living-slash-workspace in a safe building that felt like home. And always smelled like cake.

Yeah, she was doomed.

Just as Jess shoved her phone back in her pocket, it rang again. **UNKNOWN CALLER** screamed at her from the screen again. She pressed "Ignore" *again*, then opened her call list to block the number.

Jess had a job to do. She wasn't going to give Gage and Samantha anything less than her best just because she was suffering a minor "Nashville's nightmare real estate market-related" panic attack. She made a decent living, but increased rent was the sort of expense that could crush her business over time.

Shaking off her cobwebby angst thoughts, she whispered into her lapel mic, "OK, Bob, Mermaid is leaving the cave. Bring up the table lights to the previous setting."

Jess signaled the lead violinist, a lanky man who bore playing in a full lobster costume with good humor. He nodded to his fellow musicians. A pleased smile spread across Jess's face as the violins' warm notes filled the darkness.

When Jess came up with the idea for her "consulting firm" years before, this bliss by proxy was the feeling she'd been chasing. Jess had survived three grueling years assisting one of the city's most feared wedding planners before she realized she wanted more.

"Feared" might seem like a strange way to describe a bridal industry professional until one considered how many florists Angenette Ellis had made sob into their gardenias over the years. Being mentored by that woman had been like Navy SEAL training, but with more buttermints.

Even as she watched Angenette conjure lush, elegant magic from nothing, it seemed to Jess that so many of these events started with uninspired proposal stories. Jess decided to break out on her own and give her brides (and grooms) a story that showed how loved they were, a story they would tell their children. She used the observational skills Angenette had helped her develop to create grandly romantic moments on a much smaller scale. She picked up details from a couple's story or a photo or conversation and turned them into a scenario that made a proposal perfect. The professional stress levels were still there but seemed less dire when she was controlling her own schedule and workload.

Jess had carved this business out of nothing, creating a network of contacts and word-of-mouth referrals from sheer determination—all while appearing pretty and pleasing to the country club set. It certainly hadn't been easy, and occasionally, the returns were thin, but smiling while swanning through a shitstorm was where those private-school comportment lessons came in handy.

And the results were worth it. Her refusal rates were less than four percent, and according to social media, most of her couples remained married. Just look at Gage and Samantha, starting their life story. And Jess had been able to get in on the ground floor of what should be an epic and adorable tale.

Jess's cell rang. Again. Gritting her teeth, she opened the block feature on her phone—again—and noticed that the tiny print under the number read **TILLARD PECANS**.

Weird.

While Georgia might produce the most pecans as a state, the Tillard family had made use of hardy pecan species that grew in western Tennessee and maximized their proximity to interstate connections for distribution. Tillard Pecans graced the shelves of every grocery store in America. They were used in holiday dishes and trail mixes and anywhere pecans could be pecan'd.

"What the?" Jess frowned at her screen. She'd never done business with anyone from Tillard's. How did they get her business line number? It could be a telemarketing thing, but she had no idea what they would sell her. It wasn't as if Jess bought nuts in bulk. Sure, she'd attended Harrow University with the heir to the company. Anyone enrolled there was aware of the Pecan Prince, whose family had built the Tillard Stadium, the Tillard Amphitheater, and the Tillard Commuter Parking Lot.

Yes, really.

So while she was aware of Trenton Tillard the Fourth, and they'd shared some business classes, Jess wasn't sure she'd ever spoken to him directly.

Gage and Samantha interrupted this tree-nut-based train of thought by gamboling through the door, dressed in their matching teal bathrobes, embroidered with the aquarium logo for the occasion. They were giggling and kissing like a pair of lovestruck teenagers. Jess signaled the rest of the costumed string quartet, who began playing "Under the Sea." At the sight of the table and the musicians, Samantha squealed with delight and threw her arms around Gage.

"Everything is just so perfect!" Samantha sobbed into his neck, the diamond flashing on her finger. Andrew dutifully recorded this reaction for the custom hardcover album Jess would create as part of

Bricker Consultants' Tulip Package. "You must have been planning this *for months!*"

Jess never got tired of hearing that. Or, rather, overhearing that. She was usually tucked somewhere out of the way to observe her work unfold, uncredited.

Jess quickly blocked the pecan company's number from her phone. As Papa Burt would say, Jess wasn't going to worry about making tomorrow's money today.

As the couple settled at the table, Jess whispered into her lapel mic, signaling the caterers to deliver dinner. She lived for smiles like Samantha's. The look of absolute unfettered joy on Samantha's face as she threw her arms around the person she loved the most, in the moment that she knew his commitment to her was concrete.

Jess breathed deeply, wallowing in this moment of professional fulfillment, however brief.

Sometimes it made Jess a little sad that she didn't have any such occasion in her near future. Marriage wasn't an end-all, be-all guarantee of happily ever after, but it could be pretty nice from what Jess saw in her grandparents. Then again, Jess worked too damn much to have time for dating. And frankly, the men in her social circle were . . .

Nana Blanche hadn't exactly raised her to hold her tongue, but it seemed like a waste of perfectly acidic internal dialogue to describe Jess's feckless, emotionally lazy, self-obsessed potential dating pool. Doing her job felt like she was rewarding people who had managed to strike gold in a manure pile.

So her current life's path boiled down to a single entry in a carefully organized planner that only existed in Jess's head called Jess's Big Book of Life Plans. One of the first plans was *Just keep working until you figure out the rest.*

Hours later, with the lovebirds safely betrothed and their dinner debris packed away, Jess bid good night to Dave and Bob and exited through the staff door. A stuffed sea otter she'd snagged from the gift shop—leaving cash, plus tax, behind—was tucked under her arm. Yes, it was a little silly, but Otter Chaos needed a good home.

Now that Jess had run out of details to fixate on, thoughts on the disruptive series of phone calls earlier crept into her head. What was that about? She could write off the Tillard call as a mistake, but the unknown number called twice . . . Was it the Anellos' lawyers? Did lawyers work this late? The vicious taskmaster that was her anxiety urged her to unblock both numbers, call them back, and find out. But Jess needed to climb into her ancient Ford sedan and mentally prepare for the brutal gauntlet of a nighttime Nashville drive. The Music City was a beating heart of traffic flow, an urban microclimate surrounded by suburban neighborhood bubbles, each with their own flavor of Southern. Then there were the outer rings of farmland, plus woods deep enough to maintain a healthy supply of ghost stories. It was the world's biggest small town, where everybody knew everybody in their little corner. Jess had never lived anywhere else, and had never had the urge to.

Just as she unlocked her car, a shiny blue Tesla came roaring into the parking lot, braking a scant few feet from Jess. For a moment, Jess had a metric ton of empathy for headlight-bound deer.

"What the hell?" Jess shouted as a tall redhead climbed out of the driver's seat.

Even in her panic, Jess knew she *should* recognize this woman's face, a pearlescent oval crafted for magazine covers, framed by coppery waves. But it was the eyes that finally sparked a shiver of dread down Jess's spine, the deep brown eyes that *could* be warm and friendly but Jess knew to be capable of spotting every weakness, every flaw, every secret.

She was the specter of all Jess's schoolgirl insecurities, clad in a designer minidress.

"Jessieeeeeeeee!" Diana Helston wailed, her distress adding several extra syllables to Jess's name. She threw her arms around Jess's stiff form as if they were siblings long separated by war as opposed to, say, distant former classmates who'd listlessly kept track of each other's lives via social media. That was part of the reason Jess didn't recognize her right away—the damned filters.

"Diana?" Jess extricated herself from the toned Givenchy-scented arms. "Um, are you OK?"

"*No!*" Diana cried. "I need you to fix this, Jessie, please!"

"It's Jess," she reminded her. "And what—what is happening right now? What do I need to fix? How are you even here?"

Was this a prank? Maybe Diana was being catfished by someone pretending to be Jess. Some former classmates could have set this up as an elaborate joke. Jess could imagine some of the girls from her old gym class giggling at something like this.

Diana hiccuped and stepped back. Somehow, her carefully applied makeup wasn't even smudged. Her molten-penny mane was still shiny and effortlessly beach-wavy. Meanwhile, Jess's own dark hair was a fright just from standing near a *fake* ocean environment. "Your grandma told me you were here. We tried calling, but you didn't pick up. I even called you from Trenton's work phone and— Did you *block* us? Is that how you treat potential clients?"

Suddenly, the call from Tillard Pecans made sense . . . but didn't.

Diana's posts frequently popped into Jess's feed, thanks to some hellishly ironic algorithm. Trenton had made regular appearances on Diana's Instagram account for years now. She loved dragging Trenton to events for her employer, a country-club-wife-turned-custom-jewelry-designer who seemed to specialize in shiny brag pieces for her equally rich friends. Diana and Trenton were definitely exclusive, and given the way Diana wound herself around his arm when they posed, she planned to keep it that way.

Jess's business depended almost entirely on referrals. The problem was that no one could *know* how Jess contributed. Her clients *loved* that they got full credit for her efforts. It was half the reason they hired her. It was why her company had such a bland name, so her proposal targets wouldn't ask questions if they saw charges on the credit card bills. So . . . how did Diana know she was here?

All of this consideration gave Jess time to come up with, "When I'm helping my actual clients? *Yes.* I wasn't here for fun. I was *working*."

"Nice otter," Diana said, then sniffed, chin-pointing at Jess's newly acquired stuffy.

Jess barely restrained the embarrassed urge to tuck Otter Chaos behind her back. "What can I do for you, Diana?"

"Trenton proposed." Diana was suddenly sobbing into her left hand, freshly manicured to match her peach-pink dress. Jess couldn't help but notice those long, delicate fingers were pointedly unadorned—not so much as a Ring Pop.

Suddenly, Diana dragged her into another awkward hug. What was happening? And why was the girl who had terrorized their entire high school class throwing herself into Jess's arms? Honestly, Jess's shirt was starting to get uncomfortably damp at the collar. She could not seem to process everything flying at her. Or damn near running her over in a Tesla. "But that's great!"

"No, he *ruined* it," Diana sobbed as Jess gently peeled Diana's arms from her shoulders. "It was so awful!"

Jess was going to get crow's-feet from all these confused faces she was making. From social media, Jess *knew* Diana had been posting inspo hints about color, cut, and carat for months. Trenton didn't come across as particularly bright, but even he could pick up on hints that sizable. And Diana had obviously taken care with her dress, makeup, and hair that evening, preparing for the perfect engagement photo opportunity.

The survival instinct in Jess's entrepreneurial reptile brain was triggered, sensing an incoming opportunity. She asked carefully, "Did he send it over text or something?"

"Noooo!" Diana wailed, prompting Jess to step back. For the first time Jess noticed that Diana was holding a glittery pink phone in her right hand. "He took me to that sushi place, Blue Ginger. We had our first date there. I should have known something was up when he'd rented out the private dining room, but he likes to do showy things like that, you know?"

"Well, that's pretty thoughtful," Jess suggested, even as her "confused" frown lines shifted to "dubious" frown lines.

"Yeah, and he said all this nice stuff about how beautiful I am and how sweet I am and how he wants to spend the rest of his life with me, but he had to write it down on an *index card*!" Diana sniffled, dabbing carefully at her eyes so as to not smear her mascara. "Like he couldn't even remember why he wants to *marry* me!"

"Oh, honey, maybe he just wanted to make sure that he got everything out right," Jess told her, taking Diana's hand. She wasn't good at this kind of thing, never had been—not even when drunken grooms and resulting bridal rage had demanded it of her. Logistics, the minutia of dealing with dozens of details at once, and the feeling of accomplishment from checking items off a to-do list had always made more sense to her than people—at least, people her own age.

It's why she'd stuck to the *planning* side of wedding planning, back in her other life.

"And he didn't even have someone there to take pictures!" Diana dabbed at her eyes carefully with a monogrammed handkerchief as she hissed, "Don't *you* always have someone there to take pictures?"

"Most of the time," Jess admitted. "So what did you say?"

"I told Trenton I would have to think about it! That if he was gonna make such a *thoughtless proposal*," Diana yelled the last two words as if she were making a point. Jess glanced around. Was Trenton in earshot somewhere? Jess's eyes landed on the sports car's trunk . . .

Jess couldn't believe she was asking herself this, but . . . was Trenton in the trunk?

Diana lifted her sparkly phone near her face and added, "He obviously wasn't ready to make a commitment to me. Especially if he's talking about a *Christmas* wedding! I'm gonna need *at least* a year to plan my dream wedding!"

Just then, Jess realized that Diana's phone screen was live and apparently mid-call with the contact listed as **TrentyBear**.

"Has Trenton been on speakerphone this whole time?" Jess asked.

Diana threw up her free hand as if Jess were asking a ridiculous question. "Of course."

"Hi, Jessie." Trenton's sheepish voice sounded from the phone. "Nice to, er, talk to you again."

Jess supposed "awkward speakerphone" was a better position than being in the trunk.

"You didn't talk to me at Harrow," she reminded Trenton. "We were in, like, three business classes together. And the not-talking-directly-to-me thing really screwed me on an econ group project, by the way."

"Well, it looks like I'm going to be fixing that soon," Trenton mumbled. "Besides, I knew who you were. Everybody always said how smart you were—"

"Trenton, she doesn't need to know what people said about her back then," Diana said. "I mean, I didn't pay any attention to rumors about her in high school."

"OK, this is getting really weird." Jess rubbed at her temples. "How do you even know about my business?"

"Oh, Lally Shoemaker got it out of her fiancé after you helped him book that hot-air-balloon thing," Diana said, waving her off. "I thought it was a little tacky. Too simple, honestly, but *Lally* was happy with it..."

Jess lifted a brow. It hadn't been *simple* at all to arrange a five-course sunset picnic at a thousand feet. And the pictures the photographer had taken from another hot-air balloon were absolutely stunning, which was what Jess suspected had drawn Diana to her business.

"So you *have* to fix this, Jessie! How am I supposed to tell all my friends and family such a lame engagement story? *Without* pictures? How is that supposed to build my brand? I'm the face of Helston LuxeGram! My lifestyle philosophy is centered around luxe positivity—external attentiveness and internal affirmation. 'Luxe' as in *deluxe*, exclusive, extravagant, luxurious, *luscious*."

"Please stop saying 'luxe,'" Jess told her.

"I can't even scrape together a decent post with this basic bull-shit!" Diana spat. "Trenton is willing to pay any price to make this right."

She paused to glare down at her phone. "Aren't you, Trenton?"

Jess heard what she assumed was a muffled affirmative response.

From what Jess had seen of Diana's social media platforms, they were ... respectable, but not exactly influencer-level. Her "Helston

LuxeGram" had no sponsorships and no paid posts. It did, however, have plenty of duck-lip photos and a lot of "fit check" reels of Diana showing off that day's outfits. While not outright offensive, there was nothing special about her content, no hook—just a privileged, pretty girl doing privileged, pretty-girl things. Diana only had a few hundred followers to show for it. And that was why Diana was willing to throw a perfectly decent proposal aside? For the likes?

"Parking-lot confrontation" was not Jess's normal method of acquiring clients. She'd never done a job where both parties of the proposal were aware she was arranging things. But could she really afford to say no to Diana freaking Helston?

Fifteen years ago, Jess and Diana had been the only students to have *family members* drop them off at the Wren Hill Day School for Young Ladies, as opposed to household staff. Because neither of them had household staff. Wren Hill was the premier preparatory academy for the city's old-money princesses. Or at least, the princesses whose families still had old money and the daughters of security-conscious country music stars. Jess had only gotten an admission interview through a collision at the intersection of fate and good manners. Nana Blanche had clipped coupons like a fiend so their decidedly blue-collar family could afford the outrageous tuition.

How Diana's family had afforded the tuition was the real mystery. Rumors swirling Wren Hill were that the Helston family coffers had run dry several generations ago, long before they achieved the financial or social status they desired. They lived in what, in a BBC drama, might have been called "genteel poverty." They were held at a distance by matriarchs who could smell new *or* depleted money from a mile away. (By contrast, Jess they never even let close enough to sniff.) The trick about getting access to those circles was that one could never appear to *want* to join them. Diana's family wanted it. A lot. So invitations to the Junior League and the charity boards were not forthcoming due to decades of Helstons trying a little too hard.

And since graduating Wren Hill and the equally tiny and posh Harrow University, Jess had heard rumblings of what the Helstons were willing to do to maintain their carefully polished appearance. The family was plagued by whispers of embezzlement and financial shell games to stretch one more year out of a country club membership committee, to convince a creditor that *they* were the problem by expecting a payment every month. Nana Blanche thought the Helstons were proof that one should never trust a family made up entirely of redheads, but people around town seemed to look past the stories and extend the Helstons at least the appearance of grace.

Marriage to the Tillard pecan fortune would be Diana's chance to change her family's financial fate. And if Jess could wrangle the sort of fee that Trenton's cowed tone implied, she might scrape together a down payment on her beloved TonyCakes building. The fabled pecan coffers were rumored to be deep.

On the other hand, if Jess failed to help Diana achieve her dream proposal . . . she didn't want to think about what that might mean for her reputation. Or her physical safety. She'd seen what Diana was capable of when upset. So Jess needed to plan the most spectacular but subtle, sophisticated but internet attention-grabbing, proposal ever.

Right.

"OK, I'll do it," Jess said, watching as Diana's whole body seemed to relax. A pleasant grin spread slowly over her lovely face, in a manner that made Jess distinctly uncomfortable—a predator temporarily sated. "Come by my office on Monday and we'll start planning, Trenton. But you should know that my fee is going to be exorbitant."

"All right," Trenton agreed. "Anything you want, just to make my DeeDee happy."

"Thank you, baby," Diana cooed, suddenly all peaches-and-cream sweetness. "This is a good start."

"Diana, can you come pick me up now?" Trenton asked. "I really need my car back before work tomorrow. Dad and I are taking the snack-cake people golfing."

"Oh, all right," Diana huffed, pressing "End Call" on her phone screen.

"Did you steal his car and leave him at a sushi restaurant?" Jess asked.

"I didn't steal it. I *borrowed* it." Diana scoffed, as if semi-grand-theft-auto were a perfectly normal response. "I needed to get to you, and he would have just slowed me down." She clip-clopped effort-lessly to the driver's side door and waggle-waved her fingers. "Talk soon! I'm sure you'll do a great job."

Jess watched, her mouth hanging open slightly as Diana peeled out of the parking lot.

What had Jess just agreed to? This job sounded like some sort of grim future a Dickensian ghost would have used to scare teenage Jess into better life choices.

Maybe working and living out of a studio apartment wouldn't be so bad?

No. No, Jess Bricker was not a girl who resigned herself to defeat. She would coordinate this "re-proposal," which she had never done before, and she would do an amazing job—even if she didn't know how she felt about re-proposals. It seemed sort of anti-romantic to pull a mulligan on a request to spend a lifetime of love together. Trenton's effort had sounded thoughtful and sweet to Jess, but she wasn't a woman with Diana's tastes and ambitions. And even when

Jess didn't necessarily agree with those ambitions . . . yeah, she didn't know where to go with that.

Jess didn't have a plan for this. She wasn't sure what to do without a plan.

Well, that wasn't true.

Her first thought was *Jess's Big Book of Life Plans: Delete all posted evidence of Trenton's well-intended but half-baked proposal.*

It didn't sound great, even in her head.

This was definitely not going to be a Tulip Package job. This wasn't even going to be Orchid Package level, which was as expensive as Jess's proposal packages got. She was going to have to invent a fake flower to describe the cost of this proposal package. The Extinct Blossom Preserved under a Hyperbaric Glass Dome Package.

Jess opened her phone to tell Nana Blanche she was heading home. She found a text consisting of several solid paragraphs already waiting in her Messages folder.

Hi, sweetheart, I got a very strange call from an old school friend of yours, Diana Helston. I know the two of you weren't close, but she just sounded so frantic that I told her you were at the aquarium. I hope she's all right. Let me know when you're coming home.

And then, as almost an afterthought, Nana had added, **Sincerely, Blanche Bricker.**

Jess rubbed at her temples and took a deep breath.

"Any advice?" she asked Otter Chaos as she dug in her pocket for her car keys. Otter Chaos only stared back silently, its glass eyes shining under the fluorescent streetlights. "Not helpful."

CHAPTER 2

Weeks later, Jess sat in a god-awful Humvee limo, recalling the series of questionable decisions and incremental boundary adjustments that had led to her accompanying Diana on a weeklong "pre-wedding planning retreat." Jess just had to keep reminding herself that the reason for her discomfort was—as with most things—money. Specifically, the Tillard Pecans money, the same money that paid for the aforementioned god-awful limo carting them up the winding mountain from Chickenhawk Valley's tiny regional airport to the spa.

The sleepy, incongruously named town at the edge of the eastern Tennessee mountains was somehow home to one of the most exclusive, luxurious spas in the country. Dubbed "Appalachia's Hidden Holistic Gem" by several snobby travel critics, the Golden Ash offered indulgent treatments like customized salt baths and sound baths and mud baths—baths in every substance except water. Then there were the sumptuous villas, Michelin-Star-level food, and decadent wellness programs that drew the wealthy and privileged to this strange Tennessee backwater. And Trenton had managed to book a last-minute weeklong package for *four* people. Well, Diana had needled Trenton until he booked it. Jess was fairly sure there had been a Faustian bargain involved.

Diana seemed like the type to sell her soul for a seaweed wrap.

That wasn't fair. Diana could probably wrangle a facial out of it, too.

"Jess, honey, you might want to run a comb through your hair," Aubrey Porter called from down the bench. "You're looking a little . . ."

Instead of finishing her thought, Aubrey just pulled her lips back at the corners and made a face like she smelled spoiled seafood.

Jess tried not to glare down the length of the obnoxiously flashy vehicle at the official planner for a wedding that hadn't even been made official yet. In an effort to further placate Diana after the sushi-proposal disaster, Trenton had hired Aubrey's firm, Joyous Occasions, to treat this week as a wedding brainstorming session. And Trenton decided this meant an invitation for Jess to be included as well.

Ostensibly, Jess was supposed to spend her time at the spa gathering details to plan a perfectly personalized, showstopping proposal in a few weeks. In reality, Trenton wanted Jess to spend her spa time arranging those thoughtful details involved in launching the *perfect surprise* proposal at Diana immediately upon the group's return from the Golden Ash. It was a risky move on Jess's part, but she thought Trenton deserved to have some secrets.

The pair of them had made it sound so reasonable, for Jess to put all her other clients on hold while she worked to realize Diana's vision on fast-forward—to make sure the proposal Diana accepted (whichever version that might be) would set the right tone for her lavish wedding. Diana was intent on using this time to create her "comprehensive matrimonial strategy," like this was some super fancy corporate retreat. Jess supposed she had to admire the work ethic. And, well, the fee that Trenton was paying Jess was substantial enough to justify the subterfuge. Diana had made sure of that. And Trenton was willing to pay her one-third up front, so yeah, Jess felt the need to humor Diana, even if it meant spending a week in the mountains with these people. From what Jess saw in Trenton, this was as devious and sneaky as he got. Unlike Aubrey . . .

Aubrey Porter, whom Jess knew by reputation from her own wedding planning days, seemed to deeply resent Jess's presence. She was making this clear through the age-old Southern classics of unrelenting passive-aggressive bullying and backhanded "compliments," all done in a saccharine sweet tone that made one question one's sanity and belief in a greater good. Since her arrival at the airport that afternoon, Jess had coped by keeping count of the "observations" Aubrey had made about Jess's shoes, her "cute little business," her lip gloss, and now, apparently, her entire person.

One would think that having attended a girls' school that resembled something out of *Jane Austen's Game of Thrones*, Jess would be accustomed to this sort of interaction. Jess had a tendency to shy from these machinations, keeping a low profile at Wren Hill *and* Elegance by Ellis. She did not like the idea that she was headed to a secondary location with Aubrey or Diana, but there was very little she could do at this point. She was in the car. This was her life now.

Jess thought that Diana would want to spend this week celebrating her victory over Trenton's good sense with her *bridesmaids*, relaxing and enjoying the spa. Surely someone who had clearly spent so much time visualizing her wedding had a full roster of bridesmaids already measured for dresses, ready at a moment's notice. But when Jess had arrived at the Nashville airport, the only people waiting for her were Diana, Aubrey, and Diana's cousin, Kiki. This struck Jess as . . . odd. At school, Diana had her choice of followers, who weren't friends, necessarily, but people who were scared of what Diana might say behind their backs if they didn't accept her version of friendship. Years later, she seemed to have a similar array of "besties" willing to pose for selfies with her. But while Jess was scrolling through Diana's social media in preparation for this week, she realized she didn't see too many of those girls appear more than once.

That seemed to bode ill for the wedding party count overall.

"Do you need to *borrow* a comb, Jess?" Aubrey asked pointedly from the other side of the limo. She released a long exhalation through her nose.

The wedding party was Aubrey's problem, and Jess was going to let her handle it. Jess took her hair elastic out of her shoulder bag and put her thick dark hair in a ponytail with practiced ease. It wasn't her most impressive look, but it was neat and functional. From across the limo, Aubrey perked her own full mouth into a sympathetic moue. And that girl's Kylie Lip Kit *never* wore off.

There certainly weren't many distractions in the tiny town of Chickenhawk Valley to keep Aubrey from picking at Jess. The town was more of an Appalachian tourist trap, half Branson, half Orlando, all moonshine and bizarro amusements. But Jess did not anticipate Diana wanting to venture to the Pancake Palace or the Museum of Murder Miniatures this week, so she thought she was probably safe.

"I still can't believe we had to fly commercial," Diana complained, scrubbing at her hands with a sweet-smelling hand sanitizer. The label on the travel-size bottle was written in Italian. Diana had used it multiple times just since they'd stepped off the plane, as if it would ward off the "middle classness" of the people around them.

The future Mrs. Tillard had spent much of their morning complaining about Trenton's failure to secure the Tillard company jet for their trip. His father, Trenton the Third, was using it to fly to DC for some sort of agricultural lobbyist meeting. Trenton had at least had the wherewithal to book the whole party into first class for the ridiculously short flight to Chickenhawk Valley—or at least what passed for first class on a plane that seated only forty people.

So basically, the front row.

"It happens to everyone," Aubrey assured her as Diana pulled a lip gloss in a shiny rose-gold tube from her handbag. Aubrey gasped, her own lip gloss suddenly forgotten. "Is that the new LipStinger? Didn't I see Chanterelle carrying that on last week's episode of *Housewives?*"

"Isn't it adorable?" Diana grinned conspiratorially. Despite her family's fervent worship of old money, it was Diana's dearest dream to have her own reality show and diet wine label. It said so, right there on her LuxeGram TikTok profile. Diana's influencer aspirations were an incongruous contrast with the old-money values of her family—and her future in-laws, for that matter. People born to money tended to let it work under the surface for them, with subtlety. It prevented inconveniences like kidnapping attempts. But Diana couldn't seem to resist flexing Trenton's money in the most obvious way available. Just look at this giant limo. Jess couldn't think of a single proper Wren Hill princess who would have taken a car like this to prom even as a *joke*.

Meanwhile, Diana was still extolling the virtues of her lip gloss, which appeared to contain synthetic bee venom. "Plumps your lips so much, it's practically a nonsurgical filler. A fraternity brother of

Trenton's is running the ad campaign for LipStinger. He snagged a tube for me before it's even released in stores. Trenton surprised me with it this morning."

"Trenton's going to miss you *so much*," Aubrey assured her. "You know, I see engaged people all the time at work, and I have a sort of gift for knowing when couples have *it*. You know, that thing that is going to keep them together forever? And with some couples, I just think, why are you even bothering with the wedding? I give it six months, at most. But you and Trenton definitely have *it*."

"Aw, thanks," Diana cooed. "You're so sweet!"

Was Aubrey laying it on a little thick? Most wedding planners *did* develop a sixth sense for when couples had "good energy." But a properly trained wedding planner knew better than to give *any* opinion about what they'd seen. Ever.

In fact, obsequious behavior like Aubrey's was part of what had driven Jess out of the wedding planning business in the first place. That and some fairly awful coworkers, constantly competing for their boss's attention, plum assignments, promotions. It had sucked the joy out of what was supposed to be a *joyous occasion*. It was right there in Aubrey's employer's name.

The very first entry in Jess's Big Book of Life Plans was *Step 1— Quit job to achieve distance from things that ruined what you used to love about it, use life savings to start small business. Step 2—Work, work, work, then work more. Step 3—Profit.*

Spending the day with the likes of Diana and Aubrey was sending Jess into an emotional retrograde, and once again, she felt like the weird, gangly girl who was known to have no money and no mom. Telling the other Wren Hill girls that her mother was simply "away" led to a lot of prison rumors, but Jess hadn't known what else to say. Her mother was a one-woman hurricane season, blowing into Jess's childhood about once a year, causing chaos, and sweeping back out a few days later, leaving only relief in her wake.

Jess reached up and worried her pearl necklace. Despite Diana's wardrobe expectations (clearly outlined in an email Aubrey had sent earlier that week), the most expensive things Jess had packed were her great-grandmother's pearls. Jess wasn't even entirely sure they were real, despite Nana Blanche's assurances. Jess had gotten into the habit of wearing them when she needed a confidence boost.

To distract herself, Jess pulled out her cell and dialed the landline for her office. Mavis Kenner, who was technically one of Nana Blanche's bridge friends, answered on the third ring. In her opinion, answering any earlier came across as "desperate for business." When Jess opened Bricker Consultants, Mavis offered to help Jess get her office set up. A former New York City paralegal, with a loathing for retirement, Mavis just never bothered to leave. Bricker Consultants started off with a broad range of packages, including those for grooms who could barely afford to have Jess stick a ring in a piece of cheesecake in a mall food court, but over the years, Bricker Consultants' service packages had become more and more pricey. Sometimes Jess felt guilty about it, but Mavis insisted that humanitarian efforts had no place in a business plan. And as usual, Jess had to admit she was right.

"I thought you weren't supposed to be using your phone in the fancy mud baths," the sixty-seven-year-old chirped.

"We're not there yet and my phone is barely getting a signal," Jess replied. "I'm just calling to remind you that for the next few days, I may not be easily reached. You're going to have a lot more on your shoulders in terms of communication with clients."

"Like they're kicking down your doors." Aubrey snorted and tried to hide it with a cough. The witch.

Jess ignored her and continued, "So it goes without saying, be nice."

"I'm always nice," Mavis groused. "Even with Jeff Laudermilk, who is being really stubborn about his baseball-game plan."

"Respect the sign, Mavis," Jess said, sure that Mavis was sitting at her desk next to the well-worn placard on the lilac-striped wall that read "Management Maintains a No-Jumbotron Policy."

This time, it was Mavis's turn to snort. Typically, Jess went along with whatever the client wanted. She'd planned proposals by fireworks, proposals by Scrabble tiles, and even a proposal via a customized bowling ball. But she'd seen way too many public Jumbotron proposals go terribly wrong at sporting events to do one herself.

"I know. I'm leading him to our less traumatic sports-based packages, but he's just *sure* she'd love for their favorite team to be part of their big moment. I'll keep you updated," Mavis said. "Speaking of which, I got the latest group itinerary for your kelp rubs and whatnot. Woo! Diana made that boy shell out for the *pricey* stuff. She better not let his mama find the receipt."

"That's his concern, not mine," Jess insisted. "Also part of the reason I got out of wedding planning. Mama conflict."

"Yeah, *that's* why," Aubrey snorted from her end of the limo softly, which Jess dutifully ignored. What in the *hell* was this woman's problem?

Jess's Big Book of Life Plans: Finish this limo ride without going to jail.

"I've got it all under control. Now go plan what remains of that awful girl's proposal and try to relax. But don't let your guard down around those harpies," Mavis informed her. "Keep your eyes on the prize."

Jess snickered. The "prize" was the final payment Trenton's contract guaranteed, which would be deposited in Jess's account after the proposal was accepted. If the Anellos were being honest with her, she would be able to buy the TonyCakes building. (With the down payment on a rather terrifying loan. But with the referrals Trenton was sure to give Jess, she would have the business to pay it back.)

The Anellos were happy to sell the building to her, even if it meant they had to wait a bit for her to arrange financing. They knew that their dad had had a soft spot for the girl who had always been short on family, but they wanted a fair price, and Jess respected that. Life didn't hand stringless gifts to people like her. She would pay her own way.

"Yes, ma'am." Jess glanced over at Aubrey, who was literally braiding Diana's long, carefully maintained hair at the moment. "It'll be fine. Call the spa's main office if something happens with Nana Blanche."

"Your contact at the spa, uh, Poppy? She sent me a list of situations that constitute an emergency and what definitely does not," Mavis muttered. "I don't think you'll hear from me unless your grandma decides to get hitched to a card sharp on the riverboat or some such nonsense."

"I don't know what old ladies get up to on bridge-themed river cruises," Jess snickered. "I'm just sorry you couldn't go along with the group."

"Good Lord, no. One night a week is fine, but being stuck playing cards with those biddies in a small space for days at a time? I'd rather toast my buns in the seventh circle of hell." Jess could almost hear Mavis's shiver over the line. "I'd think you'd take a page out of my book, but you're locking yourself away in the mountains with those girls."

"It'll be fine," Jess replied as the limo came around one last curve, exposing a sweeping view of the entrance to Golden Ash Spa and

Wellness Resort. Her breath caught at the way the trees seemed to protectively embrace the series of low-slung, squarish stone buildings. Water crashed down a nearby hill over tiers of natural rock and into a tranquil fountain. The water flowed down an in-ground trench to frame a courtyard centered around an enormous tree whose leaves were so uniformly and perfectly golden, they didn't seem possible. Extending beyond the tiny village of bungalows stretched a forest patchwork of fiery reds and golds. The afternoon sun glinted off the nearly silver slate bungalow roofs, giving the place an otherworldly, almost Olympian appearance. Otherworldly, and insanely expensive.

It felt a little bit like . . . home, which was ridiculous. Jess had never been to this part of Tennessee before. But it felt like she could breathe easier here.

It was probably just the fresh air, she told herself. Or the altitude.

Jess swallowed the lump in her throat and murmured, "I'm gonna go, Mavis. You've got this."

She pressed the "End Call" button and let the image of the Golden Ash's front gate wash over her. She wanted to commit this moment to memory, the first time she could take in this view of the property. It felt important, monumental.

Yep, Jess was definitely having altitude issues.

The limo rolled to a stop in a gravel cul-de-sac in front of the stone entryway, as if the spa didn't want something as modern as a motor vehicle setting its tires on the actual property. The grounds centered on a series of green tiers, each occupied by a river stone cabin, reaching up toward a majestic main lodge. The whole of it blended into the landscape as if it had always been there. A team of gangly young people in Golden Ash uniform shirts came rushing out, reaching to take the group's bags.

Diana slid her sunglasses down her nose and checked her carefully curled auburn hair in the limo's pull-down mirror. Jess stepped out of the limo—which was *not* easy in heels on gravel—from a relatively weird angle from the seat. She had a lot of leg to negotiate after all.

Jess forced her eyes away from the stately stone building to the willowy brunette woman standing just inside the gate. Instead of the white-and-gold uniform, she was wearing a long-sleeved maxi dress in dark forest green, perfect for the relatively cool autumn afternoon.

"Hello there!" the woman called, the slight Southern accent lilting her musical voice. "You must be the Helston wedding party. We're so happy to have you here with us!"

Diana preened, giggling with Aubrey as if they'd just won a game show.

"I'm Poppy Osbourne, one of the many Osbournes you'll find running around here. I manage operations here at the Golden Ash."

"So nice to meet you," Diana said, shaking Poppy's hand. "I'm Diana Helston, and this is my bridal party, Aubrey, Jess, and of course, my little cousin, Kiki."

Wait, what? Aubrey and Jess exchanged uncertain glances. Did Diana mean wedding party as in "a physical party of people here to plan my wedding" or . . .

Jess turned to Kiki. Diana's cousin was staring into the distance through oversized sunglasses and not responding at all to being introduced. So she wasn't any help. While she shared the trademark Helston red hair, Kiki had slightly more squarish features than Diana's delicate lines—not to mention an interpersonal detachment that Jess envied.

Aubrey, having apparently shaken off Diana's bizarre announcement, passed Poppy a matte coral-colored folder from her leather attaché case. "Now, as discussed, the branding language for the Helston-Tillard wedding is the very essence of the Diana Helston brand itself. To maximize Ms. Helston's experience, we need you to focus on the words 'lavish,' 'romantic,' and 'innovative.' Oh, and 'genuine.'"

Jess stared at Aubrey, slightly agog at her ability to switch conversational lanes. Jess had frequently concocted bridal vision boards, distilling them down to *theme* descriptions like "contemporary rustic elegance" or "opulent beachy splendor." Still, she'd never heard of *branding language* for a wedding.

"I thought your brand was 'luxe positivity,'" Jess said as Aubrey pulled poor Poppy aside to go over Diana's expectations for her stay.

"No, my social media persona is centered around 'luxe positivity,'" Diana told her. "My wedding brand is 'lavish, romantic, and innovative.' And 'genuine.'"

"Can't forget the 'genuine,'" Jess agreed, but Diana didn't pick up on the sarcasm. *At all.*

Jess herself felt a little disingenuous, as she knew exactly when Trenton was going to propose. Diana was fully aware of the impending second proposal; the only power Jess (or Trenton) really had was the timing. She didn't even have the usual protection of secrecy because Aubrey and Kiki knew exactly who she was and what she did.

To preserve some semblance of showmanship and surprise, Jess had arranged for Trenton to meet their returning party at the airport with a limo when they returned from the Golden Ash. The group would deliver Diana to a botanical garden, which would make for beautiful pictures. Trenton would lead her down a path toward an oversized gift box that, when opened, would release butterflies into the garden, where the little pollinators could live out the rest of their limited days comfortably. Andrew was already scheduled to take photos with a special high-speed lens to perfectly memorialize the butterflies' flight around them while Trenton plucked the ring from the bottom of the butterfly box and issued his second matrimonial offer. Jess had even hired a special lighting coordinator to help the photographer capture the colors most effectively.

This spectacle would be witnessed by more than one hundred of their closest friends and family members. It was basically a lavish engagement party that Jess was having a hell of a time getting Trenton's family to RSVP to, but he swore they would be there.

But what would Diana wear to the party? How would Jess guarantee Diana's favorite (gluten-free, low-carb, calorie-free) foods would be served? Who would style Diana's hair, and where would they do it? Those were all details she would have to settle this week, under the cover of busywork.

"I'm just trying to stay ahead of the curve," Diana assured her. "My wedding *will* be the only one anyone talks about this year, just you wait. Aubrey has a whole plan in place."

Jess was suddenly very grateful that Aubrey was the one stuck with that particular plan, and not her.

"Aren't you worried that the Tillards won't like this attention?" Jess whispered.

From the two meetings she'd held with the couple, Jess knew that Diana's Insta aspirations were amongst many arguments Trenton's family had against the match. Her interest in online clout cemented Diana's place on the "not our kind, dear" list. To Trenton's credit, he had managed to ignore his mother's attempts to set him up with much more desirable, though less attractive, selections from families on "their level." His resistance only fueled Diana's belief that she could have both fortune *and* internet fame. Maybe even her own line of lash extensions.

"Well, that was before their son botched his proposal," Diana said, giving her shoulders an uncharacteristically inelegant jerk. "It's a fine line for me to walk, but they're going to have to adjust. I'm just glad that you're going to help him give me the most beautiful proposal anybody's ever seen!"

Jess considered that for a moment. Well, it was not her job to protect Diana from irritating her future in-laws. It was her job to order butterflies and shut up about it. Poppy, who seemed accustomed to demanding guest behavior, finally sloughed Aubrey off with a final, "Well, we're just happy to have you."

She nodded to the staff hustling bags into the courtyard. Another staff member moved toward them with a tray of tall glass flutes filled with water and paper-thin green apple slices.

"This is water from the spa's private spring," Poppy said. "It will always be available to you, no matter where you are on the property. It's very important to stay hydrated during your stay. Now, we don't want to overwhelm you with details in your first few minutes. We want y'all to simply *enjoy* the view and the quiet and one another before sinking into your treatments tomorrow!"

To Jess, that sounded like heaven, but she was still working this week. It was laser-focused work on one client, but technically still work. Also, she wasn't sure how much she was going to "enjoy" Aubrey. Jess just wanted to get through this job and retain a little bit of her dignity in the process.

Diana paused to take a selfie in front of the gate's logo, using a kelly-green selfie stick. Her head bent instinctively at her best angle, beaming. Diana immediately began tapping on her screen, obviously eager to post this affirmation of her entrée into the Golden Ash on the nearest social media platform. But after a few taps, Diana frowned. "I can't post. I'm not getting any signal."

"That reminds me," Poppy said, clearing her throat. "We encourage our guests to engage in a digital detox during your stay. Cell phones are pretty much pointless here at the Golden Ash. Due to the mountain's topography, we just don't get a signal. You will not be able to make calls or send or receive texts. None of your apps will work. Your posts simply will not post. We ask that you leave your phones in your villa to avoid the frustration. Relax, unwind, enjoy the natural beauty around you. If you need anything, the house phones connect to the main lodge, which is staffed twenty-four hours a day."

Jess palmed her phone inside her purse. Knowing that it would be a useless brick of plastic for the week had made sense to Jess on an intellectual level back in the city, but now, surrounded by this ocean of trees, it filled her with an odd feeling of foreboding.

Diana, however, seemed to dread life away from screens more than unknown threats lurking in the forest. Her eyes narrowed at Poppy and her lip curled back as she asked, "And if I don't *want* to leave my phone in the villa?"

"Well, it would be very rude to your fellow guests, whose privacy you could be violating, if you're filming in areas where they might be undressed. Plus, burying your face in your phone while your technicians are devoting their time to taking care of you is a blatant show of disrespect I'm sure you'd want to avoid," Poppy replied frostily. All traces of her charming "down home" accent had disappeared. It was more than a little unnerving. Diana stared at Poppy as if spa etiquette violations as a philosophical concept had never occurred to her.

Poppy continued, "Not to mention the potential safety hazard of wandering around a mountainside searching for a signal. I'm sure you would want to avoid those perils at all costs. If not, we're happy to cancel your reservation and charge you for the full length of your planned stay."

Ooof.

Considering how much Diana wanted access to the Golden Ash, Jess knew this could get very ugly, very quickly. If the owners were willing to eject their party over phone use, what would they do if Diana broke some of the very expensive-looking Edison fixtures Jess saw through the front glass of the lodge? Jess could almost see the wheels turning in Aubrey's head. Aubrey, who would probably see her wedding contract evaporate if Diana freaked out and caused a destructive scene at the Golden Ash, giving Trenton's family enough ammunition to talk him out of the wedding.

However, Diana's only response to this masterwork of blithe verbal redirection was an angry red flush creeping up her cheeks. Jess was suddenly reminded of an incident in the school chem lab sophomore year, when Jenna Turley mysteriously lost the blond fringe bangs that were her signature look. Jenna Turley, who happened to be running for class president against Diana. It was the first preelection concession speech in the school's history. And Jenna was allowed to wear a hat to school for the rest of the year, in direct violation of the school's dress code.

Diana asked, "Surely there has to be some sort of private Wi-Fi network I can connect my phone to, you know, for *special cases*? I mean, I think I need my phone more than the average person. What will my Helston LuxeGram followers think if I can't post for a *week*? They'll think I abandoned them!"

"We encourage our guests to engage in a digital detox during their stay," Poppy said again, smiling at Diana in an unflinching manner that Jess found a little unnerving. She wasn't sure if Poppy was trying to make a point or annoy Diana. Maybe it was both? Maybe Jess had accidentally joined a cult?

Jess wasn't sure that Diana's hundreds of followers would notice the absence, but she didn't think that was a helpful thing to add to the conversation. As if she sensed an opportunity for solidarity, Aubrey's eyes narrowed at Poppy. Her pink-painted mouth thinned. "Surely you can make an exception for such a high-profile guest, Pippa."

"It's Poppy," the woman reminded her cheerfully. "And this is a blanket policy for all guests, to keep things fair. We encourage our guests to engage in a digital detox—"

"During our stay, yes, I know!" Diana seethed. "I just want to do the digital detox while using my phone!"

Jess opened her mouth to ask how Diana thought the two things would be possible simultaneously, but closed it again with a click of her teeth. She wanted to side with Poppy, but Jess had problems of her own, meeting Diana's demands. She had to focus on that.

"We don't want to make you feel judged, Ms. Helston, we only want you to get the most out of your experience here," Poppy assured her.

"How am I supposed to relax when I'm faced with a total collapse of content?" Diana asked, her face turning an unhappy puce. Jess swallowed heavily and thought of Jenna's singed bangs.

"And how is *my fiancé*, Trenton Tillard the Fourth, of Tillard Pecans—the man paying your overpriced room fees—supposed to contact me if I don't have a signal?" Diana demanded, looking down her nose at Poppy. This was a common tactic amongst the well-to-do ladies of Wren Hill, and frankly, Diana's neck posture was giving Jess flashbacks. "He's going to be very upset if he doesn't hear from me regularly."

"Our office landlines are always available," Poppy assured her. "And Mr. Tillard can leave a message for you with our front desk, if needed."

"Do you really feel comfortable intentionally isolating your guests like this?" Aubrey asked.

"Considering how much Mr. Tillard was willing to pay for a short-notice booking? I'm comfortable with our choices," Poppy retorted with just enough sass to remind Aubrey of the pecking order. Poppy had the commodity *they* wanted, not the other way around. And it was an impressive strategy, going on the offensive with Aubrey instead of Diana. Jess was going to have to watch Poppy Osbourne. Maybe she could pick up some Diana-management tips.

Diana's expression relaxed, her mouth quirking up at the corners. Apparently, she liked being reminded that Trenton was willing to outlay outrageous sums of money to keep her happy. Jess supposed this was the whole point of the trip, to push Trenton to show how much he was willing to spoil her, to chase *her* while he persuaded her to accept his ring.

"Trenton's going to be very upset," Diana said again, but her voice was smaller, sadder . . . fake. It was completely fake. Jess had seen enough brides play the sad, precious little girl act to wheedle a bigger cake out of mommy and daddy. She knew a faker when she saw one. While she gave Diana an internal side-eye, Jess kept her face neutral.

"You did sign your digital check-in forms, acknowledging the expectation that you will leave your phones in the villa," Poppy reminded her a bit more gently. "But, as I mentioned, if it's a deal-breaker and you're happy to forfeit your reservation, we can ring for the shuttle and your whole party can be on your way. But you might want to decide quickly because the drive down the mountain can be risky after dark."

"We're going to be all right," Aubrey said, rubbing Diana's shoulder in soothing circles. "It's going to be rough, but it might be good to give Trenton a chance to miss you. Remind him of why he needs you in his life so desperately."

Diana chewed her (quickly becoming un-LipStinger'd) lip and considered the Golden Ash gate. After a long pause, she rolled her eyes, opened her phone, and tapped her screen several times before powering down.

Jess showed her own blank, unpowered screen to Poppy and dropped it into her purse.

"I know y'all probably hear this all the time, but I'm supposed to be working this week," she whispered to Poppy. "I'm Jess Bricker. I think my assistant, Mavis, contacted you."

"Mavis!" Poppy grinned. "She's a firecracker, that one."

"I am aware," Jess told her quietly. "And I hope she explained that I am working on a very limited timeline to prepare a surprise for Diana and I will need to contact the outside world pretty regularly."

Poppy grimaced. "I still can't believe Miss Helston brought you on a relaxing retreat so you could work."

"I'm more support staff than a guest," Jess said. She pressed her lips together and nodded. "I believe Mavis arranged for me to use your office equipment?"

Another woman, tall and sturdy with what were apparently the Osbourne cheekbones and delicate, long nose, rolled up on an oversized white-and-gold golf cart. She was dressed more casually in barn boots, jeans, and a dark purple angora sweater. Jess wished she had the confidence to pull off the dark pixie cut that emphasized the depths of the newcomer's dark blue eyes.

"Come visit me at my office, we'll work something out. We just can't let the other guests see anything," Poppy murmured to Jess before approaching the newcomer. "And this is my cousin, Sis, which I know sounds a little funny. Just don't call her Narcissus."

Jess wondered if maybe this lovely woman's mother hadn't liked her to name her after the most self-centered flower in Greek mythology, but thought it wouldn't be very nice to ask.

"Not to my face," Sis snickered, waving at the group. "Hey, y'all. Welcome to the Golden Ash. I am the resident yoga instructor. We'll take you on a bit of a tour of the grounds as we drive up to your cabin."

"It's a villa," Poppy reminded her.

"It's a cabin," Sis retorted. "Calling it anything else is just putting on airs. Anyway, we're winding down toward the end of our season, so we have a light crowd. You should have plenty of peace and quiet. Hop on."

Jess glanced around at the grounds, silent and only occupied by a handful of guests wandering the paths in fluffy white robes. They did appear to be considerably more relaxed than Jess felt, so that seemed promising.

Diana said, "I didn't realize you closed for the season."

"Oh, absolutely. The roads are too dangerous during the winter to have guests travel here, and we appreciate a little break," Poppy said cheerfully. "It takes a bit of work to shut everything down. We like to give ourselves time."

"And of course, limiting your calendar for the year makes you that much more exclusive," Aubrey said, smirking.

"Well, you don't have to worry about that because all of our facilities and services are available to you this week!" Poppy chirped as Sis carefully drove the party over the smooth stone paths that wound around the villas. Jess glanced up at the Golden Ash Lodge and spotted a tall, broad-shouldered man in black chef's togs hauling crates of produce out of a white van. He was a few years older than her and, well, a little unkempt—longish walnut-dark hair and cheeks that needed a shave. His dark eyes met hers and something twisted inside of Jess like a living thing, something that she hadn't felt in a long time. *Want.*

An urge to hop off the cart and run to that man to . . . she wasn't sure what. Probably something involving nudity and some of those out-of-season strawberries. But given the way he looked away from her the minute they made eye contact, she doubted he would appreciate any fruit-based advances. And she didn't know why, but Jess averted her gaze, like she didn't want to violate his privacy while he worked.

"You all right, Jess?" Kiki asked. Jess nodded, breathing deeply through her nose. She hadn't had a reaction to a man like that in . . . she wasn't sure she'd ever had a reaction like that before. This went beyond her normal "just waiting around for the unsolicited dick pic" phase of cautious initial interest. This was visceral . . . and felt more than a little dangerous out here, so far from home.

How thin *was* the air up here anyway?

Kiki's bag fell open as she shifted on the gold vinyl seat and Jess noticed what looked like a gray plastic eyeglasses case stamped with "Helix BioResearch Lab." It was probably some giveaway from her employer. Diana had said something about Kiki working for a pharmaceutical lab in Raleigh's Research Triangle.

"So, you took off all week for this?" Jess asked. "Sort of a big ask for a nonofficial wedding event."

"Well, it's not exactly a hardship." Kiki shrugged. "I've got the vacation days saved up, and I'm used to the bridesmaid thing. I've done it, like, ten times."

"Really?" Jess marveled at her.

"All of my cousins," Kiki said, lowering her voice as she glanced over her shoulder at her cousin. "Well, they're older than us, so Diana and I were flower girls for some of them. And then Diana decided she didn't want to do that anymore. It was just me as a junior bridesmaid and then bridesmaid. It's kind of a family tradition. Helstons showing up for one another. At least for the public occasions."

Kiki gave her a wry grin. Jess shook off the lust fog for Strawberry Guy and resolved to be a little nicer to Kiki. Diana's cousin was just trying to survive this bridal bonanza without hearing the words "always the bridesmaid" multiple times per day. If anything, Jess owed this girl her patience and a little kindness. And possibly a truckload of improbably flavored vodka.

The golf cart rolled past tiny palaces constructed of river stone and rough cedar, each marked with little signs that read "Stillness Villa" and "Placid Villa." There seemed to be a theme there. On the porch of Stillness Villa, a tiny blond woman was sitting in the lotus position, holding what looked like an egg-shaped quartz up to the sun, staring at it intently . . . like, with a weird amount of intent.

"Do you think that's one of those yoni eggs?" Kiki asked, her lips creeping back into a grimace.

"Oh, why would you put that in my head?" Jess demanded, making Kiki cackle.

This was nice, Jess decided, giggling with someone over something silly instead of stressing out over temperamental marine life and hot-air balloon safety procedures. Maybe she could enjoy this week. Yes, it was going to be a lot of work, but maybe without her phone constantly dinging in her ear, she might be able to unwind a little bit.

"What a beautiful view," Diana said with a sigh as they took a curve and the expanse of the valley unfolded in front of them. For a moment, Jess wondered if Diana was being affected by the wonder of their natural surroundings. Suddenly, her client turned around in the cart's seat. "Jessie, be sure to remember that I'll need a professional lighting coordinator to make sure I have the best possible photographs, no matter where Trenton proposes. Take note."

So, that would be a no to the transformative power of nature.

Sis hit the brakes with expert gentleness in front of Tranquility Villa. At Harmony Villa, a middle-aged couple in matching plush white robes stood on the front steps. Unlike the Yoni Egg Queen, they did not seem to be embracing the whole "Harmony" vibe.

"Why do you always have to ruin our vacations with this bullshit!" The man was all indignation, his craggy face flushed red to his thick salt-and-pepper hair.

His long-limbed brunette partner was pointing her finger in his face, yelling, "It's a *pattern of behavior*, Jeremy Treadaway!"

Jess had witnessed enough "I *saw* your hand on that bridesmaid's ass" arguments during her wedding planning days to recognize accurate whisper-hissed accusations of infidelity when she saw them. This couple thought they were pulling it off without being heard in a very quiet environment.

"Harmony Villa, huh?" Kiki murmured.

Jess said, "I don't think they saw the sign out front."

Kiki and Jess simultaneously winced as the woman stalked into the villa and came back out in record time, tossing her partner's suitcase onto the tiny lawn. The suitcase bounced impressively and, unfortunately for the man, landed on its patented easy-gliding wheels before quickly descending down the hill.

The man shouted, "Susan!" before chasing after his runaway luggage.

"What do you think they were like before they came here to relax?" Kiki pondered, making Jess giggle.

Apparently, the giggle was much louder than Jess realized. As over at the Harmony—DisHarmony?—Villa, Susan looked up at her and glared with the force of a thousand frustrated, wounded wives.

Jess sat back a bit in her seat. While she did feel a flush of guilt at finding some humor in this woman's hurt, Jess also knew *she* wasn't responsible for Jeremy's shit behavior. But . . . she wasn't entirely sure Susan was aware of that. Jess looked away, temporarily distracted by their arrival at their villa, Tranquility.

As they climbed the stone steps to Tranquility Villa, Jess wondered whether there was enough lavender salt scrub in the world to soothe you from the stress of your husband cheating—or constant suspicions that he was looking for an opportunity to cheat on a getaway that was probably intended to save the relationship.

Lavender salt scrub could only do so much.

A plan outside Jess's usual organization system popped into her head, and suddenly, this isolated, beautiful place felt eerily silent. She glanced over her shoulder to see that Susan was glaring at her.

Jess's Big Book of Life Plans: Stop making eye contact with people who look like they want to remove your face.

Jess turned away from their obviously unhappy neighbors as Poppy announced, "Our cousin and resident herbalist, Jonquil, has written a personalized agenda for each one of you to meet your wellness goals."

Aubrey held an arm out to prevent Kiki from following Diana too closely as she walked up to the villa's rustic wooden door. Poppy continued, "Since this is a bridal function, we've obviously included more group sessions and activities. But we've worked to make sure that each of you gets some alone time. We know that weddings can be stressful. Y'all need time to decompress."

Diana's brow furrowed for a moment, as if she didn't appreciate the suggestion that her wedding was a burden. Jess supposed that was fair, but she wasn't quite sure that Poppy understood that Jess and Aubrey weren't the cherished guests in this situation. They were employees, but pointing this out to Poppy in front of the others seemed inappropriate.

"These are your Golden Bliss Keys," Sis said as she handed a gold-and-white plastic key card to each of them. The front was stamped with the spa's logo. Jess's name and "No known allergies" were printed on the back of her card. "Please keep this with you at all times, on the lanyard included in your welcome packet. The cards serve as your room key and your payment method at our gift shop. And they help us track your key swipes within our facilities. You'll be asked to turn your keys over at the front desk when you check into the treatment and thermal suites. This serves as a safety precaution, reminding the staff members of your presence inside the more private areas of the building. You'll receive your card again when you sign out."

Poppy used her own staff key card to open the villa door with a flourish, prompting a happy gasp from Diana. A low fire burned in the enormous river stone fireplace, giving the room a cozy, decadent feel. The sheer number of peachy-pink blooms occupying their villa was almost enough to distract from the dizzying panoramic view of the mountains. It felt like their deck opened out onto the sky.

Diana squealed with delight, reaching into her tiny purse and pulling out the little collapsible green selfie stick again. Poppy frowned as Diana worked to get the full scope of floral arrangements behind her in the shot.

"You did say phones were allowed in the villas," Diana reminded her, her smile just short of a smirk.

Poppy's lips were pressed together in a tight line before she agreed. "Yes, I did."

Diana tapped on her screen, frowning.

"And I told you that there is *no* signal here," Poppy reminded her, also barely short of smirking.

"Yes, you did." Diana grumbled, detaching the selfie stick from her phone and tossing it on the granite counter next to a little coffeepot and clear glass electric kettle near the branded, custom-blended Golden Ash tea.

Diana pouted a bit as she minced over to the window. Jess guessed she was going to try to prove there was some magical signal spot near the glass. She glanced down at the selfie stick, a weirdly artificial, too-bright intrusion in the more organic slate gray stone decor. The plastic was printed with the logo for the Sportsman's Lodge Motor Inn, a below-budget motel off Route 9.

Weird.

As far as Jess knew, hunting tourism places like that used bottle openers and fridge magnets for marketing. Good for the Sportsman's Lodge management for their open-mindedness, Jess supposed. It was equally odd to see Diana holding a souvenir from such a "rustic" place, because it felt like she would also fail to acknowledge they existed.

Jess shook it off. With Aubrey around, she needed to keep her head in the game.

"As you can see, the villa has two double rooms," Poppy said, waving toward two rooms beyond the airy, well-appointed kitchen.

"Your agendas for tomorrow are right here on the kitchen counter. Every evening, housekeeping leave personalized updates—which we call a 'Daily D-Ash'—on your beds. You can use the house phone to contact the front desk if you need anything."

Jess turned to study the villa's spacious living area, crowded with lovely floral arrangements in a warm peachy pink. In fact, there were splashes of that same peachy pink all over the villa—in accent pillows and comfy blankets apparently added just for their arrival.

"That is a lot of pink," Jess murmured.

"*That* is Diana's signature color—Cameo Coral," Kiki told her. She handed Jess a glass of what Poppy called a rehydrating smoothie. "It's a rare shade of pink that looks universally good on redheads, *and* it's the exact color of an heirloom cameo that Great-Grandmother Helston left to her in the will, much to the collective envy of all our aunts and girl-cousins. Personally, I think it's a little tone deaf to style yourself in a shade of dead microscopic sea-creature material, but she doesn't ask my opinion of these things."

Jess snorted into her purple smoothie, which tasted of summer berries and coconut water. Now that Jess thought about it, Diana had been wearing a "Cameo Coral" dress when she'd shown up at the aquarium. Most likely, she'd picked up on Trenton's no-doubt highly telegraphed intentions to propose that night and dressed for the occasion. Sadly, Trenton hadn't lived up to Diana's expectations. Jess wasn't sure who would, without someone like her to help interpret those nuanced, detailed, and almost entirely internalized demands.

Jess glanced down the hall, into the guest rooms, where she could see yet more Cameo Coral waiting for them in the form of welcome bags, flowers, and soft cashmere throws across the beds. Jess wondered how much Trenton was being billed for these special add-ons, but she figured that was his problem.

Kiki added, "Diana chose her sweet sixteen dress and her prom dress to match it—even though she didn't actually wear the cameo on either occasion. She just loves how the color brings out the rose tones in her complexion. Anyone involved in the Tillard-Helston wedding needs to understand, anything inanimate will be coral—flowers, stationery, table linens. The works."

Jess was again glad she wasn't going to be involved in the Tillard-Helston wedding. She was already sure "dead microscopic sea-creature material" wasn't her color.

The sleeping space coup that followed happened so quickly, Jess had barely processed the machinations before Aubrey ushered Diana into a room marked with a custom coral "Bridal Suite" sign. Aubrey had smirked at Jess, catlike as Diana practically floated, before announcing that she'd had the staff unpack their suitcases—Aubrey with Diana, Kiki with Jess. "I need face time with Diana, so we can plan her big day. Besides, Jess, if the bags under your eyes are any indication, you're a total insomniac. And it wouldn't be fair to Diana if you kept her awake all night, reading or sad-journaling or whatever. Can you imagine, having the gall to deprive her of sleep right now?"

Jess merely blinked at her. Thanks to a healthy supply of melatonin gummies, Jess usually slept well. She did have the occasional nightmare about headlights slashing through rain and her mom's too-loud cackle. Sometimes those nightmares made her yell in her sleep, but that was none of Aubrey's business.

"OK, then." Eyebrows furrowed at Aubrey's continued fucking weirdness, Jess turned away into what was now her room and found Kiki already stretched out on a bed.

"I don't mind if you stay up late reading." Nodding at Jess, Kiki pulled a tiny wireless bud from her ear. "My college roommates were pretty intense about their all-night study sessions."

"What the?" Jess gasped as Kiki tucked the earbud into a special carrying case, whisper-hissing as she closed the door. "Do you have some sort of high-tech spy phone that gets a signal up here? Is that what you're really working on in your mad scientist lab?"

"No. I was secretly listening to a true-crime podcast for most of the day with a practically undetectable earbud." Kiki sighed. "I have a bunch of them downloaded on my phone. It's the only way to survive family dinners. I couldn't very well take it out in the limo and blow my cover."

"I could not envy you more, you diabolical wench," Jess said, marveling. Kiki giggled.

Jess glanced around the room, which somehow managed to look cozy despite the gray tones and rustic slate finishes. She supposed the Cameo Coral throws and flowers helped—plus the little gas-powered stone fireplace, already burning low. Between low-key bullying and the luxurious surroundings, Jess felt the familiar sensation of her middle-class roots creeping up, wrapping her in discomfort and shame. What was she *doing* here? She didn't belong in a place like this.

Jess reached up to touch the pearls at her throat, frowning slightly. She supposed she shouldn't judge Diana about the Cameo Coral, since Jess was also technically wearing dead sea-creature material.

"Jessie?" Diana called across the hall. "You should really consider some different shoes for dinner. You're representing me when you're here. Remember, the essence of luxe positivity is 'external attentiveness, internal affirmation.' Your shoes are neither."

Jess's mouth dropped open. What the hell did that even mean?

Turns out, she was perfectly comfortable judging Diana.

CHAPTER 3

The spa's enormous golden tree was no less impressive on second viewing, the vibrant yellow leaves rippling overhead as they were ferried up to the main lodge. The silvery slate square foyer was flanked by two longer wings that flexed back toward the mountains. The building seemed to serve as an all-purpose hub for the spa's services—front desk, administrative offices, and Sated, the on-site dining room. Jess wasn't sure how "sated" she could be by a menu focused on wellness, but she was too hungry to argue about branding. Diana was already focused enough on that particular subject.

A porter helped Jess dismount from the back of the golf cart. She smoothed the long-sleeved ocher knit dress that had only made it through Aubrey's outfit inspection before they'd left the villa because Kiki had lent her a pair of cute black half boots that looked nice with it. Kiki had cemented Jess's loyalty, offering up her much more stylish footwear when Aubrey found fault with Jess's "lumberjack shoes"—comfortable, utilitarian, unlikely to leave her toes smashed while moving a giant resin clamshell. Aubrey, annoyed that her weirdly unprovoked criticisms of Jess were curtailed, turned her laser gaze on the necklace Jess was wearing. "Nice pearls."

Jess's eyes narrowed. She worked to keep her voice civil but cold as she said, "Thank you. They were my great-grandmother's."

Diana's head seemed to whip toward her at that. Jess recognized a series of expressions she'd seen quite frequently on the faces of Wren Hill girls—envy, avarice, a silent complaint that an unfair universe was denying them. Heirloom pearls were significant, especially to families like Diana's. A treasured cameo was one thing, but a good string of pearls was a standard-issue signal of gentility—a traditional graduation gift that the Wren Hill girls wore with their caps and gowns. Jess's grandparents hadn't known about the tradition, and it became yet another small, incomplete ritual that separated her from her classmates. Jess had received her great-grandmother's necklace the morning of her college graduation, an attempt on Nana Blanche's part to right the "wrong."

Aubrey must have recognized the look on Diana's face, too—the pure *want* of it—because she simply turned on her (expensive designer stiletto) heel and walked out of the villa, grumbling thanks that Kiki's feet were just as "oversized" as Jess's.

Diana, of course, had required no outfit inspection, resplendent in a fitted teal dress that wouldn't have been out of place at a country-club dance. After the accessory stare-down, she'd simply walked out and waited for her entourage to join her and for the "princess carriage" to whisk them away to dinner—if a princess carriage could be powered by a marine battery.

Now the porters ushered their group through the heavy oak doors on a cloud of warm, herb-scented air. The dining room matched the villas' upscale rustic aesthetic, balancing sumptuous ivory table linens with floor-to-ceiling windows and rough wooden beams spanning the high ceilings. As they trooped past the gift shop—tucked away behind frosted glass, as if the Osbournes didn't want to be so crass as to ask for money—Kiki glanced around the dining room with a disappointed expression on her face.

"Everything OK?" Jess asked her as they waited while the seating hostess tapped several tablet screens to register their party in the dining room's reservation system. Diana looked distinctly annoyed at being expected to wait for *anything*, though they'd only stood in front of the hostess's rough stone "podium" for a few seconds. Jess's stomach rumbled at the scents of rosemary and basil sauteed in . . . some form of cooking fat they probably weren't supposed to have. She was surprised the growling noise didn't echo off the high ceilings.

Kiki waved her hand at a room that felt almost abandoned. Most of the tables, given the illusion of privacy through some strategically placed banks of tall potted plants, were empty. It only added to the "shutting down" pall that hung over the Golden Ash. It made Jess feel a little guilty, like they were keeping the staff in a restaurant past closing time.

"I believe I was promised that the rich and moderately famous regularly checked in to the Golden Ash," Kiki said, chin-pointing to the handful of occupied seats. "Diana might be the most famous person in this room, even if it's in her own head. And that's sort of sad."

"I didn't know you cared about that sort of thing," Jess retorted.

"Everybody cares a *little* about that sort of thing," Kiki muttered.

"Think of it as Diana enjoying the spa at its most exclusive," Jess replied. "Which is only going to make her happier."

Kiki grumbled and gave Jess a sidelong glance.

"Expect Diana to be weird about you wearing those," she said, nodding to her necklace. "The Helston family pearls were pawned back in the nineties—by Diana's mother, by the way. She needed to pay for her first boob job. Left a bit of a wound, that we haven't been able to afford a replacement."

Jess's mouth dropped open. Had Diana been wearing pearls at their graduation ceremony? She couldn't remember. Jess had focused on walking across the stage without tripping.

"It was part of the reason it was such a big deal that Diana got the family cameo," Kiki told her. "Some of the bolder cousins argued she shouldn't have it when her mother sold off one of the few remaining family pieces. But as Aunt Birdie pointed out, Neely was no different than previous Helstons who sold off the family signet ring, family engagement ring, family silver—including the baby spoons."

Jess suppressed a shudder. Kiki and Diana's great-aunt, Virginia "Birdie" Helston, was the self-appointed matriarch of the family. From what Jess had observed during Birdie's occasional visits to Wren Hill, the eldest Helston ran the family with her primary weapons: "guilt trips" and "subtle insults about your intelligence and/or face."

"Wait, your family had actual silver spoons?" Jess asked.

"They were the first things to go," Kiki replied. "Along with the silver baby rattle. In the end, Diana is Aunt Birdie's favorite, and she made sure Diana got the cameo."

"I would think, with the family history, that, as her cousin, Diana would insist that you bunk with her."

Kiki shrugged, shifting the square neckline of her pewter-gray A-line dress. "It's OK, I'm used to it. I'm sort of the add-on cousin. Added on to Diana's birthday parties, added on to Diana's travel plans, added on to the wedding party, because otherwise the tenuously balanced family political system would collapse under its own weight. Plus, my mama would pitch a hissy fit. My expectations are carefully managed."

Jess had always pined for a larger family—aunts, uncles, cousins, who might have helped when things went so sideways with her mom, helped Jess support Nana Blanche, or just helped make their holidays a little livelier. Jess was starting to rethink her regrets.

The seating hostess, a short, compact woman whose name tag read "Carol Lee," asked their group to follow her. Aubrey shot both of them an arch look, which kept Kiki and Jess a few paces behind her and Diana.

Kiki cleared her throat, lowering her voice even further to whisper, "So, Aubrey is pretty intense. Why does she hate you? Did you shave her head in her sleep at summer camp or something?"

"I don't *know*," Jess whispered back, attempting to keep her boot heels from clicking too loudly across the mirror-shiny floors. "We've never even worked together that I know of. She works for Joyous Occasions. I used to work for Elegance by Ellis." Jess paused to wait to see if Aubrey had overheard, but she was too busy chatting with Diana as if they were the best of friends. Kiki also didn't show any recognition of either company name, which wasn't surprising given that she had a job in the real world that didn't involve mail-ordered butterflies.

"Are you sure?" Kiki asked. "Her comments seem awfully personal."

"Maybe she's friends with my former coworkers," Jess said, shrugging. "I wasn't super popular at the office. The owner put a lot of pressure on us to book events. I put my Wren Hill connections to good use. Every time one of the girls I knew from school got engaged,

I would see it on social media, contact them to congratulate them, and . . . next thing you knew, I'd hand my boss a signed contract for their high-profile, expensive wedding."

Of course, Jess hadn't been allowed to *handle* weddings for those contacts. Without fail, Angenette Ellis immediately took them over. But it did mean that Angenette bragged about Jess's connections to anyone who would listen, which didn't exactly endear Jess to the other planners at her level. It had resulted in talk behind Jess's back, exclusion from drinks after work, being conveniently left out of the office Secret Santa. She supposed she couldn't put it past her former coworkers to bad-mouth her to whoever would listen, including Aubrey. Wedding planning was a fairly close-knit community. Viciously competitive and gossipy as all hell, but still, close-knit.

"Honestly, I'm glad I'm rooming with you," Jess told her. "You seem to be the least exasperating option available."

"Thank you. Likewise," Kiki said primly, her lips twitching into a smile as they passed the residents of DisHarmony Villa. They'd apparently carried their disagreement over to their dining table. While Susan was ignoring her carefully plated salmon, Jeremy was devouring a large helping of pasta.

Susan, stylishly coiffed and still vibrating with anger, was pointing her fork so emphatically at Jeremy that her long chestnut bob bounced with every syllable. "You cannot keep acting this way and then treating me like I'm hysterical for saying something about it, Jeremy. Honestly, this is exactly the sort of thing Dr. Petersen and I try to talk to you about every session."

"Susan, please, it's just a little harmless fun. Networking is what I *do*," Jeremy told her. "It's your *reactions* that are the real problem here, not my behavior."

"Networking isn't 'what you do,'" Susan shot back, slapping her hand on the table between them. "We never should have come here. I should have known you didn't give a damn about 'reconnecting' with me. You promised me you were going to let this restaurant thing *go*. You're not an *up-and-coming restaurateur*. You're a glorified bank teller."

Jeremy slammed his hand on the table with a *clang* of rattling silverware. Jess kept her gaze trained on Kiki as they walked to their own table. She was *determined* not to make awkward eye contact with Susan again. She could only be glared at as proxy so many times in one day. Jess couldn't even blame Susan for being unhappy. Jeremy seemed like a willfully oblivious creep. She made a mental note to avoid him at all costs.

"Ever since my promotion, your behavior has spiraled out of control. I swear, I could just *kill you*," Susan seethed. Their party moved away before Jess could hear anything else, and she was sort of grateful for it.

"I could deal with seeing them a little less," Kiki admitted, making Jess hum in agreement.

The Helston party was escorted to a table close to the panoramic window, directly across from the open kitchen door. A partition kept them from seeing the inner workings at the stove but allowed them to hear the clank of pans and utensils. In fact, that seemed to be the only noise in the dining room, aside from the bickering from the DisHarmony table. The other guests, limited as they were, seemed to respect the food too much to talk over it.

It struck Jess as odd that she and Kiki had instinctively chosen the side of the table facing away from the view—as if they were falling into their "ranks." Jess tried not to think too hard about that. A server approached their table with a friendly smile. Before he could even speak, Aubrey handed him the breadbasket she'd swiped off the table. "We're not going to need this."

The poor server, whose name tag read "Max," raised his eyebrows and carried the basket away from the table without a word.

"Wasn't that the guy we saw carrying boxes into the kitchen before?" Diana turned and craned her neck to get a better look at the kitchen door. Jess's seat might not have had a view of the landscape, but thanks to the kitchen view, she did have a pretty good eyeline toward the Strawberry Guy. He was standing in the kitchen pass-through, wearing a chef's jacket and polishing a knife with a dishcloth. When Jess dared to make eye contact, he was staring at her intensely—well, OK, the guy seemed to do everything intensely. But damn, being indoors didn't make him look any less compelling.

A large middle-aged man appeared behind the chef in the kitchen door. He had extensive food-related images covering his golden-brown skin from wrists to elbows. Jess had never seen so many fork tattoos. Or any fork tattoos, really. Maybe Jess had lived a sheltered life.

Unlike his surly coworker, the older man smiled warmly and waved at the table. Oddly charmed, Jess lifted a hand to wave back, but Diana caught her wrist and pressed it to the table firmly. "We don't make friends with the help, Jess, not even when they look like the knife-wielding chef there."

"Exactly. I don't care how cute he is, he is not going to be making pasta, potatoes, or any sort of complex carbohydrate for anyone at this table," Aubrey said. "And Kiki, forget the fruit and cheese course. We agreed you were off dairy until after the wedding."

Kiki frowned. "When did *we* agree to that?"

"Diana had your aunt Birdie talk to your mama," Aubrey insisted.

"It's no big deal," Diana assured her airily. "It's just that the bridesmaid dresses are very body conscious."

Jess watched Kiki's shoulders go round, as if she were trying to shrink into something less . . . Kiki. Jess pretended to scan the narrow menu sheet, evaluating the merits of herb-roasted chicken and couscous with red pepper coulis spheres. She noted the name "Dean Osbourne, Executive Chef" printed at the bottom of the menu. Under the table, Jess touched Kiki's arm, which seemed to bring her back to herself. Kiki's shoulders rolled into a less defeated posture.

"In my experience, bridal shops will alter bridesmaids' dresses to make them as flattering as possible," Jess told Aubrey. "I'm sure Kiki will look lovely in whatever dress you choose."

"Well, your experience really isn't that applicable anymore, is it?" Aubrey snarked back. Jess wondered if Max the server had alerted Poppy to the rebuffed breadbasket, because she appeared at their table within seconds, dressed in an elegant black cocktail dress.

"Oh, good, you're here." Aubrey turned to Poppy. "Why would your staff put a breadbasket on this table? Ms. Helston only chose this facility because she *thought* you encouraged a gluten-free, paleo-friendly diet plan."

Even Jess knew that was a blatant lie. Diana chose this facility because she wanted to prove that Tillard money could pry open doors thought to be sealed shut for "regular people." She wanted to be able to brag about Trenton loving her *so much* that he sent her to the Golden Ash and paid an exorbitant last-minute booking fee to make it happen. She wanted to experience life as the future Mrs. Tillard.

Poppy shook her head but kept her shopkeeper's smile. "I'm not sure where you got that impression. If you have a goal of becoming healthier, we can help with the education aspect of that. But really, the point of visiting the Golden Ash is to find peace, relaxation, healing. We don't serve alcohol because, in general, we've found that hot tubs, winding trails, and inebriation don't mix well. But this isn't a lockdown facility. Your choices are your own and you know your bodies."

"If I promise not to go into town and get a bottle of chardonnay, can I have access to a Wi-Fi network?" Diana asked. "I'd rather have Wi-Fi than bread or cheese."

Just then, Sis appeared near their table. Her only concession to evening attire was black pants as opposed to barn jeans and boots. Was it a bad sign that their table was getting attention from two Osbournes? Were they the "problem table"? Even with the disharmonious Jeremy and Susan in full force next door?

Poppy said, "I consider our society's inability to function without digital stimulation to be far more dangerous than enjoying a good goat cheese. Which you should try because it's made in-house by our very own Sis. When she's not leading yoga sessions, she's running our on-site farm."

"Goats are nicer than people," Sis noted, giving Diana a pointed look.

"The phone rules are meant to prevent you negatively impacting your own safety and the experiences of other guests," Poppy noted. "In the same vein, if you somehow obtain alcohol and your behavior negatively impacts the experiences of other guests, the same rules apply."

Sis's smile was razor thin as she said, "You and your entire party will be asked to leave the spa, and you will be charged for the full length of your planned stay."

"Wow, you guys really know that one by heart," Jess murmured. She wondered what Sis's role here was exactly, other than yoga-instructor-slash-goat-cheese-monger. Was she Poppy's enforcer? Could goat-cheese-monger be a real job?

"Is that 'digital stimulation' quote available on a throw pillow at the gift shop?" Kiki asked, making Jess snicker. Diana shot both of them an exasperated look, making Jess bite her lip. Kiki nudged Jess with her elbow and smirked. Jess covered the ensuing giggle with a cough.

They probably were the problem table.

Poppy winked at Kiki and made her exit, dragging Sis along with her. Diana nodded to Aubrey, then said, "This week *is* about detoxing, but not from our phones. Because this week is only the start of making you a single-file line of happy, smiling, *glowing* bridesmaids. Years from now, when I look at my wedding photos, that's what I deserve to see."

Jess glanced at Aubrey, wondering why Diana was using the word "bridesmaids," plural, when, as far as she knew, Kiki was the only bridesmaid present. Diana was giving Jess a look that gave her a panicked feeling that seemed to be dragging her stomach through to her feet.

Like Jess, Aubrey looked completely confused for a moment, but then notched up her smile and replied, "Well, of course you do, Diana."

That seemed to satisfy Diana and order was restored, however briefly. Jess looked to Kiki, wondering if she could explain what the hell was happening here exactly. Jess didn't have to wear a body-conscious dress. Was she expected to adhere to some Draconian cheese-free diet out of solidarity? Why didn't Jess just bail out of this increasingly weird situation?

Oh, right. Money. She needed money to buy the TonyCakes building. She needed to put up with Diana and her weird diet demands so she could keep her home. Hell, with the kind of loan Jess was considering, she might even expand into the bakery floor, renovate the whole building. Hire more people. She could make Bricker Consultants into something *special*.

That was why.

"OK, so obviously there's a little bit more pressure on Jessie than Aubrey this week, since Jessie's part of the job comes first," Diana said. "If we could spend at least the first two days cementing what you see as the ideal proposal mood palette, we can use that to lay out a vision board for the wedding."

Jess had been doing this job for years, and she had never heard of a mood palette. What in the Pinterest hell was that?

"Oh, Diana, I don't know whether it's a good idea to put extra pressure on Jessie," Aubrey said, smirking at her. Something about the tone of Aubrey's voice made Jess's hackles rise. This was a trap. "Everybody knows what happens when she reaches her stress limit."

"What is she talking about?" Diana asked.

Jess turned to Aubrey. "What *are* you talking about?"

Aubrey poked out her bottom lip and shot her a pitying look. "Honey, the entire Nashville event planning community talks about the Pepperfield-Cooper wedding debacle."

Jess's jaw dropped and she was overwhelmed with the simultaneous urges to cry *and* slap the taste out of Aubrey's mouth. Fortunately, her sense of financial self-preservation kept her from doing either. She simply stared stone-faced as Aubrey laughed. "Is it true the bride's family sued you personally for the entire cost of the wedding?"

"Why would the bride's family sue you?" Diana demanded. "Is there something I should know, Jess?"

Kiki's focus ping-ponged between them. "What is happening?"

"Jess was fired because a bride caught her doing the groom a little favor in the rectory right before the ceremony," Aubrey said, shaking her head.

Jess's Big Book of Life Plans: Fuck it. Mavis has bail money in petty cash.

"What?" Diana cried.

Jess stared at Aubrey in horror. "What? Is that what people are saying?"

"Yes, every time I go to lunch," Aubrey told her. "Isn't that why you had to start your little business? Because you couldn't get a job at any decent wedding planning firm in town?"

The urge to slap Aubrey was replaced by the urge to spill the entire *correct* story, so Jess supposed that was progress.

"Jess, is that true?" Diana demanded.

Stop.

Breathe.

Plan.

Jess took a deep breath in through her nose. She would not lose her composure. She didn't have to be friends with anyone in this group to do her job. Feelings didn't matter right now, results did— even in a profession that was mostly based on feelings.

Jeremy chose that moment to amble up to their table and loom over them with a predatory grin on his face.

"What a lovely collection of treats," he said in what Jess was sure he thought was a smooth tone. "I could just eat you all up."

The way his voice rolled over "eat you," all oily and rasping, made Jess's skin crawl.

"Please move along," Diana huffed. "I would hate to report you to the management for harassing us. Do you even realize who you're talking to?"

For the first time in her memory, Jess was in total agreement with

Diana, even if it was a tragically cliché "I'm going to speak to the manager" moment.

"I happen to know the chef," Jeremy continued as if Diana hadn't spoken. "If you'd like me to put in a good word, I could negotiate a few *extras* for you."

"We'd like you to leave," Aubrey said, her own voice flat and final. "Before your wife catches up with you."

As much as Jess would have liked to join Aubrey in ejecting this rude man from their space, she was too busy managing her anger, her embarrassment. Aubrey didn't have a personal stake in Jess's arrangement with Diana, so could this be an effort to undermine Jess's standing with Diana and get her fired? Maybe Aubrey thought that she could do both jobs? What was her angle?

"Oh, I guess you heard our discussion earlier," Jeremy began, his cheeks flushing. "It was just a little misunderstanding. You know how some women are. We have an arrangement."

"I'm familiar with your discussion style and we'd like you to leave before it ruins our evening," Aubrey told him, her tone as clipped as a newly shorn poodle.

"Your loss," he replied, wiping at droplets of upper-lip sweat with the back of his hand, then strolling away. Jess noticed that Susan was not at his side.

The disruption had, however, brought Jess back to a more calculating frame of mind. Jess knew herself. If she tried to explain, it would sound like a string of excuses, punctuating the world's least likely wedding story. So she wouldn't bother.

New plan.

Jess's Big Book of Life Plans: Walk out and resist the urge to strangle Aubrey with her own hair.

P.S. Don't write these plans down where anyone might see them. Avoid prosecution.

"Excuse me," Jess said, standing up and moving away from the table, then carefully sliding her chair back into place. She would not storm off.

"Jess, are you OK?" Kiki called after her.

Jess continued walking, her frustration propelling her out the door, past other tables.

"Oh, Jess, come back!" Aubrey called as Jess turned on her heel and walked down the hall. "All that Pepperfield-Cooper stuff was just a *joke.*"

As much as she wanted to be a professional and not react like a second-grader bailing out of a sleepover, Jess wanted to go home. She wanted to run back to the TonyCakes building and pull the covers over her head. Did people really think she was caught in flagrante with a groom right before a wedding? Her jobs brought her into contact with wedding industry types regularly—musicians, caterers, photographers. And none of them thought to call her and tell her.

She knew she couldn't expect that sort of grace from her former coworkers because they didn't like her. They were probably the ones who'd spun a fairly harmless incident involving a reluctant groom into this awful rumor in the first place. And somehow, Jess was going to be stuck dealing with their gossip echo all damn week.

Jess was trapped. Trapped in this situation. Trapped in this . . . very, very opulent cage, depending on Diana's goodwill to keep a roof over her head. Now Jess was left wondering what mean girl trick Aubrey would spring on her next. Why did Diana look slightly more gossip hungry than appalled at the idea of Jess having a not-quite-sketchy past?

Yeah, if she wanted to, Jess could move back in with Nana Blanche, but the woman deserved some peace and privacy. When Jess's teenage mother had abandoned her, Nana Blanche and Papa Burt hadn't been able to spend their retirement years traveling or puttering around their adorable little house. They'd had to keep working just to keep up with Jess's expenses.

Nana Blanche had tried so hard to make up for the lack of a mother. It was part of the reason she'd pushed so hard for Jess to attend Wren Hill. While Papa Burt's construction bid on Wren Hill's pool house project wasn't the lowest, Headmistress Dawson took a liking to the scrupulously polite, well-read girl waiting for him out in the hall. She'd invited Jess to interview for a spot on Wren Hill's venerated roster. Papa Burt thought it was a hilarious joke, the idea of a Bricker attending a private hoity-toity girls' school, but Nana Blanche had practically tackled him to grab Headmistress Dawson's phone number and schedule the interview. What followed were years of scrimping, improvising, and switching to generic tuna to afford the exorbitant costs of a luxury education—and that was *with* several stipends granted by the alumni committee.

Now Burt was gone, the retirement mobility sweet spot had passed Blanche by, and her grandmother's most exciting-slash-affordable travel option was a heavily senior-discounted riverboat bridge cruise with her friends. Jess wasn't going to take that from her.

Jess stopped, suddenly realizing that she was outside, in the dark. At some point, she had made it out of the lodge building toward a little garden area off the path, a trellis with a pool of herbs planted around it.

It had gotten darker faster than Jess had expected, the shadows stretching into the trees with a will of their own. In the distance, beyond the lodge building, she swore she could see a light moving between the trees, like some too-bright, oversized firefly dipping up and down in the distance.

What the ...?

She drifted closer to the bobbing light, her head tilted, following it toward the woods. After a few seconds, it blinked out of existence and Jess wasn't entirely sure that she'd really seen it. She took an instinctive step back toward the lodge building, as if the people under that roof would protect her from a rabid squirrel, much less a paranormal threat.

Jess saw a gray shape moving in the trees, slipping noiselessly like a shadow over fog. She couldn't tell whether the shape was male or female, but it certainly looked human, as opposed to, say, a bear ... or a ghost bear.

"Ms. Bricker? Are you all right?" a voice behind her asked.

Jess didn't scream, but that was only because she inhaled sharply and nearly choked on her own spit. Great, on top of tonight's other humiliations, she was going to die because she couldn't operate her own esophagus.

"I'm fine," Jess wheezed. "Just needed a little air."

The fact that the air couldn't make it to her lungs due to her deficient esophagus use was nobody's business.

"I got the impression things were getting a little tense at your table," Poppy said, stepping closer. Jess could barely make out her lovely features in the shadows. "Is there anything I can do to make your experience at the Golden Ash more comfortable?"

Jess took a deep breath—without choking—and changed the subject to something she could handle. "I mentioned before that I'm going to need the use of your phone and an office computer linked to the outside world."

"Oh, well, that's work stuff. When I said the office landlines are available to you, I meant it," Poppy assured her, waving toward a little stone bench nearby. "Even if I don't fully understand your job. I think it will be fascinating to watch."

Jess sighed and sank onto the bench, despite the discomfort of turning her back to the woods at night. The stone was freezing cold against her thighs. "It should be—this is an unorthodox situation for me, staying with the potential bride for any amount of time, the potential bride knowing that the proposal is coming. I can usually rely on a little bit more 'cloak and dagger.' Honestly, I could use a little space from her . . . and it's been less than a day."

"I'm happy to provide that. In fact, if you need anything, we're always on-site. We have an honest-to-God compound here. Behind that tree line, there's a whole row of houses that belong to our family. So, if you need anything at all, just call the front desk and I can be at your door within minutes," Poppy told her, smiling gently. "And sometimes people go a little wild in the wedding planning stage. Trust me, I've seen it, running this place. Your friend probably doesn't mean half of what she's saying, and when she comes out of the bridal fog, she'll fall over herself to apologize."

"Well, for the record, she's a client, not my friend."

Poppy pursed her lips. "During our preregistration calls, Diana described you as an old high school friend. She said that the two of you used to be really close and had only recently gotten back in touch."

Jess was gobsmacked. In her years of wedding planning, Jess had never been caught bad-mouthing a bride, and she wasn't about to start now. She didn't know how much she could trust Poppy just yet, and she didn't want her opinions repeated, or her recollections of how, much like everybody else at Wren Hill, Diana had treated her family's paycheck-to-paycheck status like it was contagious. At the same time, she definitely didn't want to be painted with the Diana brush.

"High school? Yes. Friend? No," Jess replied. "She's using me to get social media clout, and I'm using her to get, well, money. I like money. It pays for things. Speaking of which, is it ethical for spas to let clients pay extra to book at the last minute? Isn't that kind of . . . well, I'm thinking of the word 'shady,' but that seems rude."

Poppy gave her what probably wasn't *meant* to be a patronizing smile. "Umm, Ms. Bricker? It's a spa, not a waiting list for a kidney."

"I accept your point," Jess said. "And you can just call me 'Jess.'"

Poppy smiled brightly. "Jess, then. Please call me or any other Osbourne by our first names. Sis, in particular, bristles at being called 'Ms. Osbourne.'"

Jess nodded. "But she also bristles at being called 'Narcissus.'"

"My aunt Iris was . . ." Poppy paused and frowned. "An interesting woman."

"'Interesting' as in 'unique' or 'interesting' as in 'avoid her social media posts at all costs'?"

"Both." Poppy breathed deeply through her nose. "It's both."

CHAPTER 4

Jess had to stop wandering around in the dark while being funny and only moderately attractive. It was a classic horror movie blunder.

Following their conversation, Poppy had insisted on ordering Jess what she called "an emergency omelet." Poppy pushed Jess into a comfy wingback chair near her office's picture window and practically force-fed her fluffy cheese-stuffed eggs studded with bell pepper cubes. Then Jess spent two hours with her head in her hands, explaining the mechanics of her job to Poppy, her background in wedding planning, her history with Diana, Aubrey's weird microaggressions, and why she needed Trenton's money very, very badly. While the eldest Osbourne didn't seem to think Diana deserved Jess's efforts, she pledged the entire family's help to make Jess's job easier—"because, good Lord, somebody should."

Poppy even offered to drive Jess back to her villa, but Jess had felt weird occupying more of her time when she walked into the dining room and saw the staff sweeping the floors and re-setting the table linens. Oh no, she *was* the customer bothering the staff past closing time. So, Jess accepted a bottle of spring water from Poppy's office minifridge and began the long walk down the hill to the villas. She could only hope that Diana would be asleep with some sort of gel mask over her eyes before she got back.

The grounds of the spa seemed so much emptier now, with only the wind for company. The constant rustle of the leaves reminded her of that feeling she'd had arriving at the Golden Ash—of being surrounded by an ocean of trees, with possible monsters lurking in the unknown depths of the woods. From the corner of her eye, Jess spotted the same light she'd seen before, bobbing and weaving in the trees. That was . . . weird. She trailed after it, walking the length of the lodge's porch and rounding the corner near the kitchen.

It was a little late in the year for fireflies, wasn't it?

She followed that light, past the entrance to the kitchen and a wide, flat patch of land marked with an "H." Jess assumed it was a helipad for people too posh to drive through Chickenhawk Valley. Jess was grateful Diana hadn't known that was an option.

After a few more minutes of trailing that meandering light's progress, Jess found herself standing next to a sign reading "Meditation Hollow." That was just one more indication of the spa's fanciness. Normally in Tennessee, or even Kentucky, a depression in the landscape surrounded by craggy rocks would be called a "holler." Which was way less elegant. The far side of the holler was marked by a convergence of creeks, flowing gently down a rocky slope to form a pool under the lip of a cave. Jess wondered if this water feature occurred naturally or if the Osbournes had moved those boulders here to create a place so peaceful, she'd temporarily forgotten she was alone in the woods. As far as she knew, the boulders were from Home Depot.

The moving light was getting smaller, fading into the trees beyond the rim of the holler. The high full moon *almost* lit the stepping-stone path to the holler's "floor"—a wide bed of pea gravel. The bed, maybe forty feet across, hosted a double-layer semicircle of flat stones centered around one round raised stone. Jess carefully stepped down the path, even though the hollow sign clearly stated "Guests must be accompanied by staff."

Probably should turn around, then, Jess. Obey the signs.

And yet she stayed. Passing the thick glass water bottle between her hands, Jess considered the space. The rock ridge formed a sort of amphitheater over the class space, shallow enough that Jess could see the entire expanse of the cave. The pool's rock basin seemed too round and perfect to be real.

Poppy mentioned guided meditation sessions. Were the raised stones meant for seating? Jess sniffed, sure she smelled something green and medicinal, rosemary and . . . parsley? She moved to step off the path, toward the cave, but before her foot could even touch the gravel, she heard a twig snap behind her.

"Hel—" She bit off the syllable before she fully formed a word. Calling "hello" in the dark was how semi-starlets were tracked by axe-wielding murderers in those horror movies. Not that Jess considered herself starlet material. But she was definitely "wise-cracking friend who dies" material.

Jess pressed her lips together, breathing deeply through her nose. Spending time with Diana was really messing with her brain.

"What the hell are you doing out here?" a voice barked at her, making her jump. Before she could even process her surprise, Jess turned and flung the water bottle in her hands dagger-style toward the voice. She heard a faint clatter at her feet, but was focused on the bottle, flying with horrifying precision toward the tall, masculine shape standing on the path. It only occurred to her after the bottle left her hand that the shape was Strawberry Guy.

"Ow! Fuck!" he shouted as the butt end of the bottle struck his chest.

"Oh my God, I'm so sorry!" Up close, Strawberry Guy was even more devastating. The shadows emphasized the sharp angles of his features and the depths of his eyes. She could see now that they were a smoky blue, eerily reflecting the moonlight.

She'd thrown a bottle at a staff member and was now openly ogling him. She was sober, but did that count as "impacting other people"?

"Um, hi," she said, waving awkwardly. "I'm a guest at the spa?"

Why was she making it sound like a question?

"Yeah, I saw you earlier," he rumbled, rubbing a hand where she'd hit his sternum.

Jess didn't know if she should be flattered by him noticing her. Probably not. He didn't sound impressed.

"You know, you can't just go wandering around any-damn-where you please, especially in the dark," he told her, his voice growing harsher by the word. He bent to scoop up her bottle, which somehow had remained intact in its collision with his chest. "Do you have any idea how dangerous this is? There are fifty-foot drops out here. There are sinkholes. There are *bears*, for God's sake. How do you think it's gonna make those friends of yours feel if you disappear and they never hear from you again?"

"I know. I know. Well, they're not my friends, and I don't think my disappearance would bother any of them. Anyway, I'm sorry. Wait— what are you doing out here? It's kind of far from the kitchen, isn't it?"

"These are my woods," he told her.

"Got it. You're doing a whole Chef Mountain Man thing. Fine," she retorted. "Now, if you're done sneaking up on me, I'll just head back to my villa."

"It's Dean," he told her. "I'm Dean Osbourne."

"I guess male flower names are a little harder to come by. I'm Jess Bricker." She paused, biting her lip. "Unless hitting you with a bottle will get me kicked off spa property, in which case my name is Aubrey Porter."

His frown, which was starting to feel pointed, deepened. He made a gesture for her to follow him. She did what he asked, careful not to stare at his jean-clad ass as they moved up the incline and turned toward the rear of the lodge. She wondered how he was able to move around so confidently like this at night. Was it because he was used to walking by moonlight or because he'd taken the path here so many times?

"I thought the villas were that way," she noted.

"Yeah, but this way's shorter and has more lights," he told her, gesturing to a well-worn footpath marked with little black shin-high lamps. "Think of it as a frontage road. It lets the staff move around the property unnoticed. Gives the appearance of this place running itself."

"So, walking into the hollow was too dangerous, but following a man I don't know into the woods is OK, got it," she muttered. She stopped when she saw that alien light again—too blue, too bright, to be natural, this time off to her right.

Dean paused, turning to her. "Hey, I thought I made it clear how important it was to keep up."

Before she could even point at it, the light winked out. Jess rubbed at her face. Maybe she was just tired. "I saw something, I thought."

"Probably a will-o'-the-wisp," he told her.

"Huh?"

Dean groaned like he was annoyed with himself for continuing this conversation with her. He walked on, and she scrambled to follow.

"It's an old story our granny used to tell us," he told her. "Ghost lights that float through the woods to lure travelers off the safe path to their doom. Most mountain ghost stories are about luring people out of security to their deaths . . . and yes, this is what I would call 'a pointed hint.'"

"Well, I followed one into an abandoned meditation hollow, so I guess that's fair," she muttered. "I didn't mean to go down there on my own, or to stay out so late. I was angry and I needed someone to talk to, and your cousin Poppy was kind enough to listen. I kind of verbally threw up all over her. I'm wondering if it's some sort of unprocessed adolescent trauma—probably rooted in my mom leaving—that's keeping me from standing up to the cool mean girl or the other cool mean girl, or if it's my current financial dependence on keeping the first cool mean girl happy. Either way, I don't think it speaks very well of me as an emotionally evolved adult."

"I'm sorry, why are you telling me any of this?" he demanded. "Even if you tricked Poppy into listening to you complain, *we* are not friends. If whoever you're staying with made you so mad that you damn near wandered off the side of a mountain, you should just stop hanging out with assholes. I swear, you people come up here thinking this place is some mystical universal force going to fix something in you. It's not magic. It's only mud."

"Wow, your cousins should really put that on the brochure," she muttered.

He stopped before she even registered the movement, and she found her nose buried between his shoulder blades. He smelled nice, like warm spices and black tea, but also *ow*. He turned and gently put his hands on her arms to steady her so he could step back. Jess rubbed at her stubbed nose.

"They're not all my cousins, OK? Sis is actually my sister," he said. "And everything about this place is hard work for my family. It's even harder when I come off a dinner shift only to be dragged back into the kitchen by a last-minute room service order from a guest who *just ate dinner*, and find another guest wandering around a dangerous place with uneven wet surfaces, loose gravel, and dim lighting. And have I mentioned the bears?"

"Yes, you did," she murmured.

His hands, warm and ridiculously large, were still on her upper arms. She glanced down, and he snatched them back. This had to be a weird position, a staff member alone in the dark with a guest. The version of herself who purchased liability insurance for her own small business cringed inwardly for putting him through this.

As they walked along the footpath, she expected to see the bank of guest villas, but Dean led her through a fiery leaf canopy to a . . . temple. There was no other way to put it. The square stone building looked like some mystical space devoted to ancient vainglorious gods. The tall windows were inlaid with alternating clear and gold and pearlescent-white stained-glass panels, which loomed tall and stately in the moonlight, drawing Jess in, even if she was a little afraid of what she might find.

"What the . . . What is this?" she asked, marveling.

They seemed to have arrived at a strange new corner of the grounds. How had the Osbournes managed to make a hidden footpath putting her on this undiscovered side of the spa property so quickly? Would she have managed to get back out of the hollow safely without Dean, given his dire warnings of all things bear-related?

Oh, who was she kidding? She probably would have fallen into a ravine or something and her remains never would have been found. Aubrey would have given the *Dateline* producers the worst reference photo possible, and her episode would have been called "The Woman Who Disappeared . . . along with Her Dignity."

"Your group arrived too late for the full tour. That's the thermal suite," Dean said, like this monument to stone elegance was nothing impressive. "It's where Jonquil built all these hot tubs and special showers and saunas and stuff. Kind of like a grown-up water park. I don't see the point in it, but if guests want to turn themselves into people soup, who am I to judge?"

"Can I express, as someone somewhat trapped in a remote location with you and your industrial kitchen, how uncomfortable I am with you using the phrase 'people soup'?" she suggested.

Dean stared at her. Hard. But she got the feeling he wanted to laugh. She wanted to believe that, anyway, given the "people soup" thing.

Instead, he huffed out, "Look, just don't go back to the hollow alone, OK? Stop spending your time with people who make you mad enough to put yourself in a stupid amount of danger."

"That's reasonable advice," she conceded as he led her over a little rise in front of the thermal suite building. She could see the villas down the hill, which apparently kept the thermal suite hidden from the guest quarters. It made sense, giving guests the sense of being tucked away from the aesthetic business of facials and steam showers. Compared to the imposing thermal spa, the guest villas looked like Hobbit cottages tucked away in endless nature. An enchanted smile curved Jess's lips. "It's like the Shire, but for grown-ups."

"Your villa is that way," he said, chin-pointing toward Tranquility.

"Thank you for getting me back," she told him. "Enjoy the rest of your broody, misanthropic evening."

"Likewise, and check yourself over for ticks," he called after her.

She whirled around, glancing down at her legs as if she could spot them in the dark. "What?"

"Yes, this is reality, not a sterile environment," he said, sweeping his arms toward the trees. "There are bugs out here."

"Clearly, they've been biting you on the ass for a while," she grumbled under her breath as she walked away.

"What was that?" he called, sounding amused.

"Good night!" she yelled back.

She crept quietly toward Tranquility Villa, hoping to avoid the notice of anyone who might be out this late. She noticed a room service cart parked outside DisHarmony Villa. Inside, she could hear them arguing, again, clear as day. Jess wondered if they thought nightfall made them undetectable or something?

"I heard you! I heard you tell her, 'I know where all the good bars are in town if you want to sneak away some night. I know where all the secret spots are—the ones only locals know about,'" Susan rumbled out in a pathetically eager bass timbre before switching back to her more natural strident tone. "Really subtle, Jeremy."

"I wasn't implying she should 'sneak away' with me," Jeremy practically whined back. "I was just trying to be helpful! Jesus, Susan!"

"She *is* a local, you *dumbass*. She doesn't *need* you to tell her where anything is," Susan shouted. "You have *got* to stop being so weird around the staff! Slapping cash into every hand you come across. Ordering room service every night when we've already spent *hours* in the dining room! Dean Osbourne isn't going to come work at your 'restaurant' just because you order that disgusting pasta over and over!"

"The tagliatelle was his signature dish when he worked at Sazio," Jeremy protested.

Susan yelled, "It smells like old gym socks!"

"I'm trying to let him know I recognize his history!" Jeremy cried. "He's the *only* chef for the restaurant, Susan. He's the whole reason we came up here in the first place."

"I thought we were here to spend time together," she retorted. "Jeremy, you have got to let this stupid, half-assed dream go. You've been 'perfecting' your plans for this restaurant for more than ten years! You're embarrassing yourself. You're embarrassing *me*, trying to prove you're the big man, like your brothers—"

"I don't have to listen to this!" Jeremy burst out of the villa's door, dressed in dark gray joggers and a long-sleeved black T-shirt. Silently, Jess ducked behind an oak tree between their villas. She did not want to be caught up in the marital dysfunction unfolding here. She had her own dysfunction to deal with in *her* villa.

Jeremy saw the room service cart and snatched a plate, silver cloche and all. And then, after a few steps, he came back for a napkin-rolled set of silverware.

Jeremy stomped toward the golden ash tree, waiting until he was safely away to shout, "I can't deal with you when you're acting this crazy!"

And then he stormed off. It was really hard to storm off effectively while wearing bright red rubberized athletic sandals. The *smick-smack* sound of his steps sort of ruined the exit.

Jess stepped out of the shelter of the oak tree, covering her mouth with her hand to smother her laugh. Susan followed Jeremy out, chest heaving. Jess froze. She'd been in enough raging, stressed-out bride scenarios to know that any movement would attract Susan's attention and, therefore, her aggression. But paralysis also kept Jess from ducking into the shadows of her own villa's porch. So, when Susan, who seemed to have snapped out of her anger long enough to scan her surroundings for witnesses to this scene, inevitably looked toward Jess . . . she was just standing there, like the ghost of a Victorian child, creepily staring into the depths of Susan's domestic tumult.

Susan's eyes narrowed angrily. She muttered something under her breath before striding into her villa and slamming the door. With Jeremy out of her reach, Susan let loose a guttural scream only slightly muffled by the villa's walls. The sound of anguish and rage and deep, festering hurt made Jess flinch, her chin drawing into her chest. The motion felt wrong somehow. Jess paused and realized she couldn't feel the rounded weight of pearls against her throat.

Confused, she reached down and patted her neck. Her great-grandmother's necklace was gone.

The clasp, while solid silver, was about as dependable as a drummer ex-boyfriend. Where could Jess have lost them? She remembered worrying them on her angry march out of dinner. But she also recalled the faint *plink* of metal against stone when Dean had startled her at the meditation hollow.

Oh . . . shit.

What if she'd lost her necklace in the one place where she'd promised Dean she wouldn't return alone? Obviously, Jess couldn't go back and look for them now, in the dark, after defying the wise-cracking best friend movie odds thus far, but when it was light out tomorrow . . . yeah, those pearls were the one heirloom her family had. The Brickers didn't have baby spoons to sell.

While she mulled over the safest way to find them, Jess turned toward footfalls in the distance. The *clip-clop* sound was different than Jeremy's undignified sandal smacking.

Who knew there would be so much late-night traffic at a spa?

Jess watched as a curvy dark-haired woman in a bright aqua

sweater strode to Stillness Villa on an adorable pair of chunky tan booties. The Yoni Egg Queen yanked her door open, scowling at the newcomer. The visitor glanced around, as if she didn't want to be observed, and handed the Yoni Egg Queen a brown paper lunch bag. She snatched it from Lunch Bag Bearer, then turned and slammed the villa door.

Lunch Bag Bearer didn't seem offended by this display, shrugging and walking back into the darkness. Who was that woman? She wasn't wearing a spa uniform but she . . . well, she didn't seem to be a guest. She didn't seem to be trying to impress anyone with her ripped jeans and casual saunter. Even Jeremy and Susan dressed like they were trying to impress *someone*, with their flashy jewelry and designer loungewear. Jeremy's impractical sandals were the latest luxury signature product from a nineteen-year-old basketball phenom.

So, what was this strange outsider doing, delivering mystery bags door-to-door after midnight?

It could be drugs. The Yoni Egg Queen looked pretty crunchy granola, but she also seemed to be the type to only smoke organically grown hydroponic special reserve weed sold by her favorite bud-rista, not some random strand clandestinely delivered in a sandwich bag.

This . . . felt weird. What if the delivery wasn't weed but something worse? Was Dean so agitated about Jess being out at night unsupervised because he was protecting a clandestine drug operation? The spa could be a front. The entire Osbourne family could be Breaking Bad.

It was possible that she was spiraling due to extreme emotional tension, she mused.

Jess's Big Book of Life Plans: Stay away from potential drug dealers, even if they have super-cute taste in shoes.

"The Big Book of Life Plans probably isn't a healthy coping mechanism," she muttered, jerking her villa door open.

I t was possible Jess's frayed nerves were preventing her from accurately gauging threats, because waking up in unfamiliar surroundings to a virtual stranger staring at her had her scrambling back until she nearly fell out of bed.

"Morning," Kiki said, sitting up in a twin bed that hadn't seemed so close the night before. She scooted until she was sitting against the headboard, a wry smile on her face. The wide neck of a bright yellow sweatshirt reading "Girls Just Want to Have Fun . . . ding for Their Academic Research" fell off Kiki's shoulder while she slid on a pair of black-framed glasses.

"How are you doing this morning?" Kiki asked gently. "You got back awful late, and that whole thing with Aubrey last night was, again, weirdly intense."

"It was not great," Jess agreed. "And I'm trying to figure out my place here."

Kiki gave her a speculative look. "So that whole story Aubrey was telling about the Pepperman-Copperfield wedding?"

"Not even close to the right names," Jess told her, making Kiki laugh. "And Aubrey's version was *not* what happened. Forty minutes before the *Pepperfield-Cooper* ceremony—one of the few weddings that Angenette let me plan entirely on my own—there was an incident. The whole process was sort of a nightmare because the bride was overanalyzing every little word and gesture from the groom for signs that he was ready to bolt. It didn't help that the groom could not have been less enthusiastic about getting married because he was in love with his former roommate, Tiffany, who he'd sworn up and down was just a friend."

Kiki frowned. "Oh."

"Who he'd asked to be an usher."

When Kiki's brows winged up, Jess added, "It was a very awkward wedding. Anyway, he disappears right before the ceremony and I find him in the rectory, having a panic attack—because he's not ready to be married, or at least, not to the bride—but he thinks somehow crawling out of the church window using a rope made of knotted choir robes would be less hurtful than saying so to the bride's face."

When Kiki's eyes went wide, Jess added, "Men have a deep-seated misinterpretation of what makes them look like 'the bad guy.' Anyway, I try to talk the groom through the hyperventilating but he passes out. In his fight with consciousness, he drags me down to the floor and falls right on top of me. I'm pinned under his dead weight and he is a surprisingly bony guy, all elbows and angles."

Kiki winced. "Ow."

Jess nodded. "I don't have the upper body strength to move him. When the bride came in, all she saw was her groom on the floor on top of me."

Kiki frowned. "And she thought . . ."

"Yes, she did," Jess said, nodding. "And she yelled loud enough to attract quite a few of the vendors and early guests. Fortunately, one of their grandmothers was able to calm the bride down while one of the uncles revived the groom. We explained the whole 'not cavorting with the groom' thing, which, fortunately, the bride mostly believed. But I think the fact that she believed he would cheat so easily—with someone who was actively trying to help them get married—made her have second thoughts. And he was already having second and third thoughts. So, they decided to just call the whole thing off, fairly amicably, but all that the guests and vendors knew was that they were told to go home. The groom married the usher lady a year later. But by the time the gossip made the rounds—thanks to those aforementioned sucky coworkers, I'm guessing—the story was that *I* was the reason they canceled."

"Did you leave the wedding planning business because of the story?" Kiki asked.

"No, I left the business because it was time for me to do something different," Jess told her. "The sucky coworkers didn't help."

"Yeah, Diana is never going to believe this less exciting version," Kiki told her.

"There's nothing I can do about that," Jess sighed. "Changing the subject, I have a question about the Helston bridesmaid tradition. Why aren't any of your other cousins serving their tour in Diana's wedding party? Or, you know, physically present?"

Kiki winced. "As I said, Diana's the family favorite amongst the *older* generations. There's a laser focus on her, with not much attention paid to anyone else our age in the family. And that favoritism hasn't exactly made her popular with *our* generation. All the cousins found reasons not to take part—knee surgery, pregnancy, vertigo, broken foot, 'It's inappropriate for me to be a bridesmaid at forty-seven.' Aunt Birdie is incredibly frustrated over it. She's never been able to *not* guilt the cousins into doing something."

Jess pushed her unruly hair out of her face, wincing when her fingers caught in it. "Your aunt came to school sometimes, for parent events. I never spoke to her directly because she seemed like a genuinely terrifying person."

"She is." Kiki pursed her lips, plucking at the gray duvet. "You know, I was accepted to Wren Hill, but I didn't get to go. The family didn't see the sense in scrounging together tuition for a girl who wouldn't take advantage of the school's social opportunities. I had to make my own way—public schools, merit scholarships to STEM-oriented universities.

"Diana may be the favorite. She may have gotten to go to Wren Hill, *but* she's also under their thumb in a way I'm not. She didn't get her pick of colleges. She made some noises about going to Millsaps to major in business, but Aunt Birdie wouldn't hear of it. The 'right type' of man wouldn't want a woman who could *compete* with him. How was this hypothetical man going to feel if Diana got opportunities or—*gasp*—a job that he wanted? Better for her to stay local, go to Harrow, and major in marketing. That was much more aesthetically focused, less threatening, and would train her for the right sort of charity board memberships. The job for the custom jewelry lady? Diana only got that because Aunt Birdie thought it would bring her into contact with people capable of buying expensive pretties."

Suddenly, Jess remembered the math awards Diana had won on Wren Hill's parents' days. Diana had been a legitimate academic threat in freshman and sophomore years, but then she'd sort of drifted away from it. Jess supposed she was replaced by girls whose potential suitors wouldn't be intimidated by long division skills.

"Diana tried to argue that she could major in international business, where she had the potential to meet financial highfliers. But Aunt Birdie was afraid it would take her too far away for the family to benefit. So, Diana's wants got lost in the shuffle. They want her to be successful, but not in a way that benefits her only."

Jess's nose wrinkled. "I don't know if I'm emotionally prepared to feel sorry for Diana."

"Trust me, I get it," Kiki told her. "My aunt Neely didn't even get to pick her own daughter's name. Aunt Birdie named her, after *Princess* Diana. That's the expectation Diana's had on her shoulders her whole life, to aspire to that sort of notoriety and to drag the whole family up with her. It's on her to help us recapture the former Helston glory."

Jess supposed this was why Diana was the only Helston considered to inherit family jewelry, but she figured it would be pretty awful to bring it up.

Kiki murmured. "I mean, I don't even know if Diana *likes* Trenton. But she's going to marry him because the family wants that pecan money. I mean, it's been made clear to me that no one expects anything from me, but at the same time, *no one expects anything from me.* There's a certain freedom in that."

"You have a PhD," Jess reminded her. "I mean, for all they know, you could invent the next ibuprofen, and they've spent all these years backing the wrong horse. It would serve them right if you did the 'new private island, who dis?' to the whole bunch of them. All this archaic patriarchal bullshit about marrying Diana into wealth . . . Did no one in your family see any movie made about Anne freaking Boleyn? None of those movies ended great for Anne. Or the Boleyns. What do they think marrying into Tillard money is going to do for them?"

Kiki shrugged, piling her dark russet hair into a messy bun on top of her head. "Cash infusions for failing businesses. Investments in our properties all over the damn state that are basically falling apart. Funding for whatever harebrained scheme will lead to their next chapter eleven filing. They want an easy life, minimal effort, guaranteed security. Without the risks involved in some of their more 'creative' financial maneuverings."

"Wouldn't buying lottery tickets be a little easier?" Jess asked.

"All that scratching off and the math," Kiki scoffed. "Look, Trenton has a very large, very rich, very clueless circle of friends who are going to need you to organize their proposals when Diana's engagement blows up Instagram. And Trenton is a trout-mouth, so he *will* tell everybody. You just have to find it in you to get through this week and you'll be able to write your own ticket."

"Trenton does seem to have the subtlety of a sack of hammers," Jess said with a snort as Kiki opened the curtains that overlooked their balcony. "But how are *you* going to profit from all this? Where do you fit into the family's plan?"

"Oh, I have plenty of ideas." Kiki winked at her. "So, change of subject, do you want to talk about why you came back from your night hike looking, well, *flushed and bothered?*"

Jess couldn't be sure whether her flustered state had been the result of Dean's vampire cheekbones, witnessing the breakdown of the DisHarmony guests' marriage, or what appeared to be a secret drug deal, so she just said, "Nope. What's on your treatment schedule today?"

Kiki pouted briefly but responded. "Some punishing form of yoga and then we're rewarded with facials and body wraps. I'm gonna take the bathroom first, if you don't mind."

"Sure, go ahead," Jess told her. She got up and closed the bedroom door, noting that across the hall, Aubrey and Diana's door was still firmly shut.

"I wasn't 'flushed and bothered,'" Jess muttered to herself.

Kiki called from the other side of the bathroom door, "Yes, you were!"

True to Aubrey's word, the breakfast delivered to their villa was a selection of fresh fruit, fresh-squeezed juices, and plain poached eggs. Aubrey had sent back a tray of croissants and the hollandaise with the room service attendant, along with strict "no pastry, no sauce" instructions for the rest of the week.

Jess set about making herself jasmine tea in the villa's electric kettle, with an extra pot of coffee to supplement their breakfast selections. She had a feeling she was going to need the caffeine.

"I don't want to admit out loud that I would fight somebody for a croissant, but I think I could take her," Kiki whispered, nodding at Aubrey as she directed the staff in setting out their breakfast on the dining table. Jess snickered, only stopping when Diana glared at her.

Diana was wearing head-to-toe prestige-brand yoga gear in her signature color. Aubrey was wearing a near clone of the outfit—down to the off-the-shoulder sweatshirt and crisscrossed sheer-panel workout tights, but in heather gray. By comparison, Jess was decidedly more relaxed in jeans and a sweater. Kiki was wearing an old, faded Vanderbilt T-shirt and jean shorts.

"You're not seriously considering *wearing* that, are you?" Aubrey asked eyeing Kiki's attire.

Apparently, they were going to just pretend that Aubrey hadn't acted like a complete jerk the night before. Fine. Jess was lady enough to engage in abject denial first thing in the morning.

Aubrey continued, "I mean, there's a certain standard here, and you're representing Diana's *brand*. Remember, luxe positivity is all about 'external attentiveness, internal affirmation.'"

Again, Jess took a moment to appreciate the absolute concentrated banality of that brand statement. Because . . . damn.

Jess couldn't help but notice that despite hauling a professional wedding planner up a mountain with her and all her talk of "branding," Diana hadn't mentioned a lot of specific details about her wedding dreams. She'd mentioned a dress, but not a special location or food or even music. She didn't seem attached to a particular look or feeling. Was it a lack of creativity at work, or would Diana simply choose the most expensive option at every turn?

"A ratty T-shirt doesn't imply attentiveness, Kiki," Aubrey continued. "And Jessie, I'm gonna need to see your selection for the day."

"Not likely," Jess retorted. "Also, I'm not wearing yoga gear because I'm going to the office to contact some vendors for Diana's proposal."

It wasn't a *total* lie. Jess could use the phone access to call vendors for Trenton and Diana's botanical garden extravaganza, but it would also allow her to contact Mavis and possibly work for other clients. It would also allow her some space from Diana and Aubrey. And since temporarily moving Jess's room to another mountain wasn't an option . . .

"Well, I'm glad to see you making some effort," Diana noted. "You ran out of the brainstorming session last night."

"Super unprofessional," Aubrey told her, shaking her head.

"Yeah, almost as unprofessional as spouting completely untrue rumors about a colleague in front of a client," Jess retorted.

"I mean, did you really believe the Pfefferman-Copperpot wedding story?" Kiki scoffed, giving Aubrey a withering look. "So gullible."

"I appreciate the support, but you're getting further away from using the right names," Jess whispered from the side of her mouth.

"Do you still believe in the Easter Bunny? Do we have to have the Santa talk?" Kiki asked Aubrey, her eyes wide. Jess snickered. Yes, it was kind of immature that they'd basically broken down into whispering slumber party factions. But it was reassuring, having someone else who was just trying to survive this week without a stress rash.

"OK, I don't care about this anymore," Diana said. "Are you girls ready for yoga? We need to clear our minds of this static before we get down to work."

"As I said, I'm going to the office to make some calls based on some details you've mentioned," Jess said. "I thought that was the whole point of me being here."

Diana frowned, seemingly caught between being pleased that Jess was forwarding her proposal plan and displeased that Jess was disobeying a direct order. Her eyes narrowed at Jess. "I guess so."

"Thank you," Jess replied.

Aubrey gave her a withering smile. "It's probably better that you *try* to do something productive anyway, Jess."

Diana flounced back into her room with a "Kiki! I'll find you something more flattering to wear!"

"Good luck wrangling all that once the wedding planning starts," Jess told Aubrey, waving carelessly after the bride-to-be.

"Some of us are professional enough to handle the challenge," Aubrey said with a sniff, following Diana through the door.

Jess leaned over and told Kiki, "I think you could take her, too."

CHAPTER 5

Though she'd promised Dean she wouldn't go back to the meditation hollow, she had to at least *look* for her lost necklace.

She'd decided not to try to take the hidden frontage road path through the woods. While it was safer and better lit, walking through the woods alone (again) seemed ill-advised. Didn't that count as being sensible? She guessed that Dean would not see it that way.

The hollow looked completely different in daylight—warmer and more welcoming, even if the air was crisply cool. She was surprised that she'd managed to negotiate the incline toward the cave in heeled boots the night before. She could see now why the staff limited the use of the hollow to supervised classes.

The boulder seating situation made much more sense in daylight. And now she could see herbs growing in random patches amongst mossy tiers that closed around the space like a bowl, forming a sort of frame around the front of the cave. It was very theatrical.

Jess supposed this garden was what kept the kitchen supplied with garnishes. Or maybe the spa used them, too, for the required lotions and potions. Between the golden light and the music of bird-song drifting through the herb-scented air, it was … perfection. She grinned. The Osbournes were freaking magicians. This was one of the most intentionally perfect places she'd ever seen.

And yet her necklace was still missing.

Carefully, she stepped off the path and walked through the gravel to the back row of seating boulders. She kept her eyes glued to the pea-sized pebbles at her feet for some glimmer of silver amongst the white rocks.

She'd been standing on the footpath when Dean had startled her, so she kept close to that area. She broadened her search area, closer to the seating boulders. But it turned out that looking for small, round, pale objects in a sea of small, round, pale objects . . . was pretty damn difficult.

"Well, shoot," she said. She sank down to a sitting position on the nearest boulder, setting aside the file folder full of contact numbers Mavis had prepared for Jess.

Maybe she could ask one of the female Osbournes to take her around on the hidden path? Then again, all the Osbournes worked so hard up here, just like Dean said. She didn't want to add one more thing to their plates.

How was Jess going to tell her grandmother she'd lost a huge piece of family history? She might as well have taken a Sharpie to the family Bible. Jess scrubbed a hand over her face. The Brickers should have replaced the necklace clasp years ago, but no one in the family had the heart to do that, as the original Jessamine's initials were engraved on it.

She blew out a long breath, watching the water ripple down over the rocks. She tried to concentrate on the memory from the previous night so she could remember the moment the weight of the necklace dropped away.

Jess had never *tried* to meditate before, but she could see herself trying it in a place like this. She felt so far away from the potential loss of her home, far from whatever was happening in Diana's head, far from everything. She closed her eyes and inhaled the fragrant breeze. She thought of where she'd been standing on the path when Dean had barked questions at her. She tried to focus on the sound she'd heard, the faintest metallic *ping*, in the darkness, which had felt so insignificant at the time.

She listened to the water burbling until she could almost pick up on its pattern. She remembered Papa Burt and the way that his gray eyes disappeared into the crinkles of his bearded face when he grinned. She thought about Nana Blanche and how she always smelled like lilac and sang June Carter songs, and how it made her feel safe. Jess could almost feel the muscles of her neck start to unclench . . .

However, her butt was going numb. The rock she was sitting on was *really* cold and it was seeping through her jeans. And with her frigid butt feelings creeping into her mind, all those faraway thoughts clawed their way back into her brain. The bills she had to pay. The boxes she would have to obtain if she had to move. Diana's laser focus on luring Trenton into matrimony meant Jess didn't have time for frigid butt feelings or relaxation. And her jewelry was still missing.

She needed to get to Poppy's office.

Sighing, Jess pushed to her feet and walked toward the stepping-stone path. Just before she reached the first flagstone, her sneaker slipped on the gravel. She stumbled forward and it was all she could do not to yelp "Whoops!"

Which she figured would eventually be her last word before she died in some horrible accident . . . that she caused.

"Ooof." Jess caught herself before she face-planted directly into the stepping-stone path. She righted herself and looked around, grateful that no one was present to see that. She would never tell Dean. *Never.*

The good news was being so close to the ground made it a lot easier for her to spot the silver clasp of her necklace, which was a foot or so to her right. The pearls were wedged into the soft dirt surrounding one of the stepping stones. "Yes!"

Jess dug the necklace out of the dirt with her fingertips. It was pressed down into the cold earth, as if someone had stepped on it. She brushed the dirt off the gems and checked for her initials on the clasp, just to make sure it was her own. The little crack in her heart, one that she hadn't even realized had formed, healed over in a rush of relieved warmth.

Thick dirt stubbornly clung to the creamy surface of the pearls. She carefully moved over the thousands of tripping hazards near the water, thinking she might be able to wash it off. She'd take the necklace to a jeweler for a proper cleaning when she got home, but would this work for now?

As she got closer to the pool, she spotted long drag marks in the gravel, as if someone had stumbled through the hollow, disrupting its Zen simplicity. Someone had dropped a fork on one of the stepping stones.

"What the?"

Who would carry a fork all this way? Jess crouched to get a closer look. And that's when she noticed the red sandal floating in the meditation pool.

Jeremy from Harmony Villa was floating face down in the rounded basin of the meditation pool. And he wasn't moving.

"Hel—" She stopped herself. She had to stop calling "hello" when she was isolated in a dangerous location with ... she wasn't ready just yet to admit that it could be a dead body. "Sir?"

Between the obscuring greenery, the distance, and the dark clothes, Jess hadn't seen him floating like a lecherous leaf on the surface of the water. She'd been in this hollow for twenty minutes. And he hadn't made a sound.

Her jaw didn't seem to work the way it was supposed to. She could barely unclench it long enough to say, "Mr. Treadaway?"

Hands shaking, Jess looked around for a stick or something to roust him out of the water. But the place was kept so immaculate that there was nothing out of place. Well, other than the fork. And the dead guy.

Instead, Jess picked up a handful of pebbles. She tossed one at him and missed, but the second hit him right in his thick, wet hair. He didn't move. His ashen blue hands floated free near his head, listless. The cold-dread space where she suspected an emergency *might be happening,* split from the realization that it was *actually happening,* sort of crystallized in her head. And she realized she'd been "meditating" thirty feet from a dead body.

Jess had only seen one dead body in her life, and that had been her beloved Papa Burt, tucked away in a coffin in his best JCPenney Sunday suit. Tidy. Sanitized. Jeremy was a grim reminder that life could leave the body anytime, and what it left behind ...

Oh no, she'd been tossing rocks at what was left behind.

"Gah," she muttered, flinging the rest of her pebbles to the ground. Her fingertips felt numb, while her other hand gripped her necklace like it was a lifeline. She glanced down at the pearls in her hand. They'd been squashed down into the dirt when she found them. Had Jeremy stepped on them on his walk to the water? Her necklace could be considered evidence now.

She was glad she hadn't picked up the fork.

Had Jeremy Treadaway wandered down here after his late-night pasta? Jess had trouble with the incline in her snug, sensible shoes. How much more difficult would the path be in Jeremy's fancy flip-flops? And the fork . . . why would he carry a fork all this way? Where was his plate?

It had to be an accident. Murders weren't supposed to happen at places like this. Well, OK, Jeremy's wife seemed really frustrated with . . . well, everything about him. And Jeremy's interactions with other people seemed exclusively creepy and intrusive. Susan did mention he was ordering a lot of late-night room service. Maybe he'd pushed someone in the kitchen too far? Dean Osbourne did seem awfully high-strung.

No, Jess was being ridiculous. This was an accident caused by uneven surfaces and ill-advised footwear. One day it would be studied by occupational health and safety experts and used to prevent silly deaths in health spas.

Jess took a deep breath.

Right, OK. This was definitely *not* how she expected to start her day, but she needed to get to Poppy or Sis—anybody—*fast*, before a guest came down here and started screaming, starting a facility-wide panic. Jess was no branding expert, but "luxury death hollow" was *not* the vibe the Osbournes were going for here.

Hands shaking, Jess walked back up the path to the spa's calm, mostly-dead-body-free grounds. She took another deep breath, which seemed a lot more necessary after the climb up the hill. What was the fastest way to get someone to the scene of an "issue" without making a huge scene?

She had some experience at this. Like that time at the Taft-McMillan wedding when two of the groom's little cousins broke into the reception venue during the ceremony and gorged themselves on the bottom tier of the wedding cake. By the time Jess and the caterer were done, the bride had completely forgotten that her four-tier cake used to have five tiers.

Down the hill, she spotted a group of yoga-gear-clad people trooping past the golden ash, led by Sis. But Dean and his sous chef, the older man with the utensil tattoos, were closer, carrying big wicker baskets. Jess thought maybe the baskets were more decorative than useful.

"We never harvest herbs this late in the day," Dean was telling the other man. "We should be doing the lunch prep right now."

"I'm not the one who insisted on chimichurri two nights in a row," his companion replied. "You're taking all my parsley plants."

"It's a popular item," Dean said. "Give the people what they want."

"Oh, you could give a damn about people and what they want—" the other man started before spotting Jess. "Miss? Are you OK?"

Jess opened her mouth. How was she going to explain herself? *Hi, we're out of towels in Tranquility Villa and there's a dead guy in the meditation pool. You might want to take care of that?*

In the distance, Jess overheard Sis say something about "mindfulness." Sis was leading her group to a meditation class in the death hollow. Jess smiled sweetly, her expression one of false cheer, and nodded toward the approaching group. "You need to stop them."

"Stop who?" Dean asked, taking a step back.

Now that they were closer, Jess could see that the embroidery on the other man's jacket read "Jamie Ortega, Sous Chef." Jamie gently wrapped his large scarred hand around her arm. The little bit of warmth that seeped into her sleeve seemed to draw her back to earth. "Why is her face doing that? Honey, why is your face doing that?"

"He's right. It's a very creepy face," Dean agreed. "You look like an anxious mannequin."

"I'm trying to remain calm while I tell you to stop that group from going into the hollow before they see the dead person floating in the meditation pool," Jess told them quietly while she attempted to loosen up the "creepy" smile. "And I need you to go get someone."

"Who?" Dean asked, taking her other arm. His hand was just as big and warm as it had been the night before.

Jess shrugged, but to her surprise, she didn't shake off Dean's hand. It felt good on her arm, keeping her anchored to her thoughts. It connected her enough to the anxious dread in her belly that the calm mask slipped. "I don't know. Poppy, anybody who's important enough for a walkie-talkie."

"No, I mean, who's in the pool?" Dean whispered.

She frowned. "Oh, I'm pretty sure it's the guy from Harmony Villa."

Dean's mouth dropped open in shock, and without being asked, Jamie disappeared down the hollow path. Dean's hand stayed on her arm, and it helped her breathe, plan.

"I thought I told you not to go down there by yourself?" Dean said pointedly.

"Clearly, I ignored you. I needed to find my necklace," she said, holding up her dirtied pearls.

"Oh, well, obviously, that's what I meant, don't go down to the dangerous location alone unless there's jewelry involved," Dean retorted. "Are you all right?"

She shook her head. "Not really."

"You're holding up well," he murmured.

"It helps that I'm here for work and this isn't some vacation I'd saved up for years to enjoy. If I was a real guest, I would probably freak out," Jess said. When Dean shot her a confused look, she changed the subject. "I overheard Susan Treadaway say that Jeremy was trying to target you to work at some restaurant project of his? She thought Jeremy was bugging you about it . . . which, now that it's left my mouth, I understand that sort of sounds like I'm accusing you of something. Sorry, this is my first dead body."

Dean's eyebrows shot up. "So, just to clarify, you *don't* think I had anything to do with the dead body?"

"No. I mean, it has to be an accident, right?" she said. "Has anything like this ever happened before?"

"Not an accident necessarily," he said. "But it's not the first time someone's died on-site—heart attacks, strokes, that sort of thing. But we've been open for a long time. And when you think about how many people wait until their retirement years to travel, you'd be hard-pressed to find a tourist destination that hasn't suffered some sort of incident. The stories people in town could tell you would curl your hair."

"I know it seems too soon to blame the victim, but the guy did huff off into the dark, without a flashlight, so I guess this isn't a shock," she told him.

"You saw him?"

"It was right after you left me near the villas."

Dean shook his head. "How the hell did he end up all the way down there?"

"Do you keep the exterior lights on all night?" Jess asked.

"Some of them," Dean said. "The lampposts go out at midnight, but the footlights stay on. It's an energy-saving measure."

"Could he have gotten turned around in the dark?" Jess guessed. "I can imagine that, with only half the lights on. Maybe he followed one of those will-o'-the-wisps too close to the water and he lost his footing?"

"I'm pretty sure you're the only person I've met who would fol-low ghost lights into the woods," Dean told her.

"That can't be true if it's a legend your granny used to tell you," she snorted.

"Yeah, a legend about people who fell for shiny, dangerous lights hundreds of years ago," Dean shot back, making her snort. "Before standardized education was a thing."

"Don't make me laugh, there's a dead guy," Jess whispered. Dean looked like he was about to laugh, too. At least he did until Sous Chef Jamie returned, a grim expression on his face—which was replaced when he stared at the way Dean was touching Jess's arm. He said, "I'll go get Poppy."

Dean let go of Jess's arm to meet Sis's group before they got too close. The Yoni Egg Queen was amongst them, her sunburned face shiny-clean of makeup, save for lip stain in a magenta that matched her ruddy cheeks. Jess noted that she was limping. Weird.

Jess really had to learn this woman's name. Even in her head, the nickname was starting to feel unseemly.

"Jess, are you looking for your group?" Sis asked. "Miss Helston decided she'd rather move directly into the thermal suite this morn-ing, once she saw the various steam treatments available."

Jess nodded, struggling to keep her expression somewhere be-tween "neutral" and "anxious mannequin brought to life." Dean put on the most cheerful tone she'd ever heard him use to say, "Good morning, I'm afraid class is going to have to be relocated today. Jamie and I are handpicking herbs for a special treat for tonight's dinner, and I wouldn't want you to see how the magic happens."

Jess was impressed. Technically, it wasn't a lie. And there was no mention of the dead body or danger, so that worked. Sis tensed as if she was going to argue. But when she saw the look on her brother's face and the way Jess was standing there, with her brittle, unnatural smile, Sis grinned back brightly. "Oh, well, we wouldn't want to get in the way of creative genius, now would we?"

The group, guests Jess didn't recognize save for Yoni Egg Queen, nodded agreeably—probably because they thought the cooperation would result in some form of dessert.

"I'll just take the group to the yoga platform and we can work on some breathing exercises. I'm sure Dean wouldn't mind going to Poppy and booking y'all some extra vitamin C exfoliating facials for your trouble."

"Of course not," Dean replied through gritted teeth.

"And maybe later, you can explain to me"—Sis gave Dean a pointed look—"what is going on in . . . the kitchen."

"Thanks, Sis," Dean called after her as she led the group away. Jess worried her thumb over the clasp of her pearls.

"I guess we can be grateful that Mrs. Treadaway wasn't in that group," Dean said quietly. "I'm not sure how I would have handled that, ethically speaking. Better to let the authorities notify her, I think."

As Sis's group reached the trail to the yoga platform, Jess spotted the same dark-haired woman who'd made the paper bag delivery the night before. Jess's mouth dropped open to say something, but then the well-shod possible drug dealer gave Sis a hug and handed her a rather large tote bag. If there were drugs in that bag, there were a lot of them. So . . . that wasn't good.

Jess wondered exactly how she was supposed to tell Dean that there might be nefarious characters, possibly including his own sister, selling drugs right under his nose. That would go over well, right? Jess was going to disrupt spa operations, family relationships, and whatever was going on with Mr. Treadaway, all for the sake of appeasing her sense of right and wrong. And she had to admit, she tended toward the goody-goody side of things. Who was Jess to come crashing in and wrecking everything? The family had enough to deal with right now, what with the dead body and all.

Thinking over her options, Jess closed her mouth—physically and metaphorically.

Jess's Big Book of Life Plans: You didn't see anything. Mind your own damned business.

"Jess?" Dean said, breaking her from her thoughts. "Poppy's going to probably need to see you in her office. Blister's probably gonna want to talk to you."

Jess blinked at him. "I'm sorry, Blister?"

"The local sheriff. It's a childhood nickname," Dean said. "It will make sense once you meet him."

The wait for Blister took longer than expected, so Jamie loitered near the hollow pathway to keep people from wandering down to the scene. Dean prepared a simpler-than-usual lunch menu solo. And Jess was left waiting in Poppy's office, unattended. While her hands itched to call Mavis, she knew that she couldn't possibly muster the energy to remember the details of Diana's proposal right now. And if she called Mavis without work questions, she would have to explain why.

So instead, she studied the framed black-and-white photos on Poppy's office walls. She was mid-anxiety spiral the previous night, too keyed up to notice them. But now she could see that the featured landscape looked familiar, surrounding one huge white clapboard building marked "Osbourne Spring Hotel." The older pictures looked like they started right after the Great Depression, when the hotel was just a large family home. The Osbournes had clearly changed over the years, too, though Jess could sort of trace the cousins backward to their parents and grandparents.

Poppy walked in with the dark-haired lady, she of the cute shoes and questionable deliveries. Jess froze. This could be the moment Jess found out that Poppy was fully aware of the dubious bags.

"Jess, you OK?" Poppy asked, hugging her gently.

"I'm fine," Jess lied.

"Ms. Helston has demanded that Jonquil come up with a hypoallergenic, gluten-free facial mask that will make her look like she has no pores. While I was trying to deal with a dead body on the premises, without letting anyone know there was a body on the premises." Poppy sighed, pouring herself a large coffee. "I like to think my customer service tolerance is impeccable . . . but I was tested."

"That woman is something else," the other woman huffed.

"Pretty much full time," Jess agreed.

"That much coffee, huh?" the mysterious bag deliverer asked, pointing to Poppy's very large, very full mug. Poppy made aggressive eye contact with the woman while drinking deeply of her coffee.

"Wasn't someone from their group in the office last night when I stopped by?" the woman asked. "The taller of the two redheads. She was on the phone with someone who was yelling at her, sounded like a cranky older lady."

Jess frowned. The taller of the two redheads would be Kiki. Unless Kiki had used the spa's landline to call a superior at the lab, it sounded like she'd spent the previous evening being yelled at by her aunt Birdie. When had she even had time to sneak away and do that? The only time they were apart was when Jess was dressing for dinner. Was Kiki reporting Diana's activities back to their great-aunt?

That seemed so sneaky, and Jess wanted to believe the best of her roommate. So far, Kiki was the only person in their group who hadn't been awful to her.

Jess cleared her throat and awkwardly pointed to the photos. "You should put some of these in the main lodge or the dining room, where the guests can see them."

Poppy frowned. "It doesn't really match the feeling guests want to get when they're here—what was it your friend Aubrey said? Lavish, romantic, and innovative—"

"I'm going to be a professional here, so I'm just going to limit my comments to: Aubrey is also *not* my friend. She isn't a client, either, so I can talk bad about her. She's an acute and persistent pain in my ass."

Poppy snickered. The other woman flashed a grateful smile at Jess, as if she'd helped Poppy somehow. "Well, there you go. I'm Beth. Nice to meet you, Jess. Poppy says good things about you."

Beth's accent was flatter than that of a typical Tennessean, Jess noted, more nasal. New York? New Jersey, maybe?

"I've found that in times of crisis, you feel better when someone makes an inappropriate joke and gives you the excuse to laugh," Jess said.

"It provides the necessary emotional release." Beth grinned at her. "Let me guess, you're here to seek respite from your high-stress career in crisis management back in the real world?"

"No. Are you a therapist?" Jess countered.

That would make the bag delivery make sense. Some therapists prescribed psychotropics, right?

Poppy laughed again. "Beth is the spa's general counsel. And my cousin-in-law. She's married to Jonquil."

OK, lawyers didn't prescribe psychotropics. But Jess decided to continue her mouth-shut policy.

"Do most spas need a general counsel?" Jess asked.

"Absolutely," Beth replied. "Slick surfaces. Steep climbs. Potential asthmatic reactions to aromatherapy. And then, you know, bodies floating in the water features."

"Right." Jess frowned. "And as far as muted responses to crises go, I *was* a wedding planner. You don't know what panic is until your justice of the peace decides that his doctor is overexaggerating a late-in-life shellfish allergy and dives face-first into a shrimp ring five minutes before the ceremony."

Beth shuddered. "Yikes."

"I got him into an ambulance and then ordained the groom's uncle through an online church before anyone realized anything was amiss," Jess told her, preening just a little bit. "Anyway, I have a lot of experience handling crises in a really public way while trying to act like nothing is wrong. I think I can help."

They didn't need to know about the Pepperfield-Cooper wedding.

Beth's brow lifted. "What could you do?"

Jess shrugged. "Answer phones, make more coffee, deflect media requests."

"Media requests." Poppy groaned. "Wait, won't it upset Diana if you're distracted from, well, Diana?"

Jess shrugged. "Probably. I'll tell her I've had to change her custom eyelash supplier last minute and it's requiring a lot of calls."

"What even is your job?" Poppy shook her head.

"I'm not going to take that from someone who claims goat yoga expenses on their taxes," Jess shot back.

"Oh, no, don't even bring goat yoga up in front of Sis," Beth said, shaking her head. "She would never trust strangers around her babies. We're lucky she lets us use the milk in our spa treatments."

Poppy's frown deepened when an SUV marked "Chickenhawk

Valley County Sheriff's Department" rolled to a stop in front of the lodge, red and blue lights flashing. An ambulance rolled in behind it, in full siren. "I told Blister the lights and sirens weren't necessary. I'm trying to keep the guests from noticing."

That idea of an unhurried ambulance struck Jess as sad, but having seen the body . . . yeah, she got it.

Poppy rose and strode out of the building, her coffee fueling her ability to whisper-hiss "*Blister!*" loud enough that Jess could hear it through the windows.

"Poppy's not wrong," Beth told her, nodding at the photos. She busied her hands, making a cup of tea from an electric kettle next to the office coffeepot. It was some sweet-smelling herbal blend, kept in a Bybee Pottery jar. She handed the mug to Jess before making one for herself. "Our guests are looking for something special, to distance themselves from their everyday lives. The original hotel started off as a sort of sanitorium and resort in the early 1900s, promising the middle class some time away from the city grime. And the Osbournes had a famous spring."

When Jess laughed incredulously, Beth added, "I know, I had to learn about it when I moved here. Jonquil says families around here take particular pride in their water. They brag that their spring is the best, the cleanest, and all that. But somehow, the Osbourne family spring developed a reputation for being able to cure people of their ailments. I mean, they ran a *goat farm* at the time, and still. People started camping out on the edge of the property to get a chance at drinking the waters. Poppy said their great-great-grandpa decided that he might as well make some money off being harassed, so the family built the hotel. It was beautiful and cutting-edge for its time. But by the 1990s, it had deteriorated to the point that a location scout called Jonquil's dad because she wanted to use it as the exterior set of a horror movie. After that, the parents decided it was time to update things a little."

Jess sipped her tea—a fragrant blend of mint and chamomile. The tag was branded with the Golden Ash logo. "That must have been interesting, growing up on a . . . horror movie set."

"The old goat farm setup didn't help," she admitted. "I've seen the pictures. It kind of gave everything a threatening pastoral undercurrent. The family renovated and moved the goat pen to the far edge of the property just to keep the smell of actual mountain life from the guests' noses. Sis and the barn staff prefer it that way."

Through the window, they watched as Poppy quietly fussed at Blister—a small, slender man in his forties with a wispy brown moustache and wire-rimmed glasses. He had to look up at Poppy when he spoke, and Jess thought maybe by the set of his shoulders that annoyed him. Meanwhile, the paramedics marched down to the hollow, rescue backboard in hand, to retrieve Jeremy's body.

Fortunately, guests seemed to be engaged elsewhere. Maybe they could get Jeremy into the ambulance without being observed.

Beth checked her watch. "I was supposed to have a private guided meditation in Zephyr's villa in a few minutes. I'm kind of glad Jana said she would cover it for me while I wear my lawyer hat. The lawyer hat is preferable."

"Zephyr?"

Beth supplied the details, "The blond lady in Stillness Villa? That's her name—first name only. Just Zephyr, like Cher."

"Suddenly, me calling her the Yoni Egg Queen doesn't seem so bad," Jess muttered.

Beth stared at her for a second, then burst out laughing. Jess giggled, too, and clapped her hand over her mouth. "I'm sorry. I shouldn't be laughing. A man is dead."

"Is he going to be any less dead if you laugh?" the other woman asked.

"Nope." Jess pursed her lips. "Good point."

Beth paused to study Jess for a moment, and then laughed all over again. "Zephyr's had a difficult week, so if she comes across as . . . grumpy, give her a little grace."

Suddenly, all the little tumblers in Jess's head fell into place.

"You were giving her one of Jonquil's remedies," she said, feeling sheepish. "That's why I saw you at her villa last night."

"Yeah . . . why else do you think I would be there?" Beth grinned. "I'm sort of surprised you even saw me."

"I'd never seen you before, and you weren't wearing a spa uniform, so I didn't know," Jess replied quickly.

"Well, I wasn't there for the company," Beth said. "I really shouldn't be telling you this, for privacy's sake, but *someone* unidentified and unknown called Jonquil *screaming* because she has a rash on her . . ." Beth paused for a second to find the right words. "Lady area."

"Yikes," Jess cringed as they sank into the chairs in front of Poppy's desk. "That's rough."

"Apparently, this someone bought one of those herbal 'steaming' kits that some newly spiritually awakened actress just started selling online. Not sanctioned by the spa. And not something I would try— especially if I was already paying people a ridiculous amount of money to design treatments specifically for me," Beth noted. "But I would also avoid it if I was already sort of chafed from taking yoga classes and very mildly allergic to one of the steaming ingredients."

Jess's cringe became a full-body shudder. Steaming one's . . . lady area with an allergen had to be uncomfortable.

"Why would you travel to a spa with that?" Jess asked.

"I *know!*" Beth said, flinging her hands up. "I'm all for self-care and embracing homeopathic alternatives, but I also heartily endorse reading directions and ingredient lists. Anyway, I tried to explain that Jonquil was busy and if she was really hurting, it might be better for me to call Owen—Poppy's husband, who is a licensed medical doctor—over to see her. But this person insisted that she wanted natural remedies only—and she wanted them *right that minute*, or as soon as she got back to the real world, she would inform the *real* holistic healing community that we're a bunch of posers who refused to give real care to our guests while draining them for every last dollar. So, I took her some of Jonquil's miracle balm. Herbs, beeswax, a bunch of proprietary stuff Jonquil wouldn't want me to tell you about. Super effective against burns and skin irritation. And for good measure, I brought her an over-the-counter cream that Owen recommended."

"*Someone* still seemed to have a little hitch in her step when she was walking with Sis's group," Jess noted.

Beth's dark brows drew together. "I might have Owen check in on her. He runs a family practice here in town—"

Beth was interrupted by Poppy walking in with Sheriff Blister. Jess glanced outside, where the ambulance crew was loading a body bag on a gurney and into their rig. They didn't seem to be moving with any urgency and pulled away without lights or sirens.

"Poppy, I'm not here to cause you any trouble, you know that, but you also know I gotta follow through, even with accidents," the mustachioed lawman said. "It's not every day somebody drowns around here."

"It happened twice last summer, Blister," Poppy countered. Jess froze. She wasn't sure she was supposed to be here, listening to what felt like private business or a law enforcement chat. But getting up and running out seemed more disruptive, so Jess just watched while Blister flopped into the nearest chair, paying no heed to how the many metal attachments on his uniform belt dug into the leather seat.

"Well, that was a couple of flatlander tourists who didn't know any better than to try to swim rapids." Blister sighed. Up close, the glasses, combined with a slightly hooked nose and a head-to-toe brown uniform, gave him an overall owlish appearance. "Not a guest in a fancy spa tripping and smacking his head on a rock and rolling into a 'meditation pool.' What the hell is a meditation pool anyway?"

"Is that really what you think happened?" Jess asked. "Doesn't it seem weird that a grown man could drown in what is basically a decorative fountain?"

Blister stared at her as if she didn't have the right to ask these sorts of questions—which, she supposed, she didn't. He finally replied, "We're exploring all our options. Why wasn't anyone watching him?"

"Because he wasn't a small child?" Poppy replied.

"And you don't have a security camera on the whole damn property." Blister shot a guilty look at Jess. "Apologies for my language, ma'am. I'm Sheriff Turnbow. Wish we were meeting under better circumstances."

She raised her hand in a small wave. "Jess Bricker."

"Why does Jess get an apology?" Beth asked.

"'Cause I don't know her," Blister told her. "I apologized for cussing in front of you up until you'd been here a year."

Beth considered that. "Fair enough. Does that mean I'm local?"

Blister jerked his narrow shoulders. "Sure."

"We don't have cameras because people tend to get real tetchy when you sell them a luxurious, relaxing experience and then videotape them in a bathing suit or less," Poppy told him. "We have cameras at the front gate, but that's it."

"If it helps, I overheard Jeremy talking about local bars," Jess said. "Maybe he managed to get ahold of some alcohol? It can't be safe walking around in those shoes without all your faculties."

"If he had booze, he brought it with him," Beth said. "And if he was drunk on his personal stash, then walked into off-limits areas, ignoring caution signs, that strikes me as his own bad choices catching up with him, not the spa's responsibility."

Both Poppy and Jess shot inquisitive looks at Beth, who *was* laying on the lawyer-speak a little thick.

Blister was apparently tired of Beth's and Poppy's interjections, and asked Jess a series of questions about how and when she'd found the body, what she'd touched at the scene. Because she didn't want to admit she'd taken her own property from the scene, she blurted out, "Also, I heard his wife say that she could just kill him last night, after they argued. And he stomped off."

"What time was this?" Blister asked.

"Quarter 'til midnight," Jess said.

"You heard someone utter a death threat and you didn't report it?" Blister asked, clearly appalled.

"OK, but how many times have you told somebody you were going to kill them and not meant it?" Jess said.

"Look, Sis spent several hours with them in a couples' yoga class this week," Beth said. "Mr. Treadaway let his wife fall on her ass several times. Mrs. Treadaway probably said stuff like that all the time."

"Are you trying to help Mrs. Treadaway or build a case against her?" Jess whispered.

Beth shrugged. "I'm neutral."

"Well, hearsay issues aside for now, the coroner has to declare cause of death, whether it was an accident, all that. And you know Marty. The fish are biting this week, so it could take a while," Blister said, as if efficient police work and outdoorsmanship were somehow connected. "I'm gonna have to ask you to let Mrs. Treadaway stay here until we get everything settled. We don't want her running off."

"She's paid up for the week," Poppy noted.

"I'm gonna need to go talk to her," Blister said with a sigh. "Poppy, would you mind making the introduction?"

"I'd rather you move that marked car first, somewhere the guests can't see it," Poppy shot back. "I know it sounds terrible, but I'm trying to let the guests forget this as soon as they learn it happened. People are more than willing to let unpleasant things slip from their minds while they're on vacation, as long as something else comes along to distract them. It's like the twenty-four-hour news cycle, but with more room service involved. And as soon as you move the car and you've informed Mrs. Treadaway, I'll have Dean make you a late breakfast."

Blister thought about it for a second. "Is he still making those fancy French pancake things?"

"Maple pecan crepes," Poppy said, her smile warming slightly. "If you move the squad car now, I'll tell him to fire up a batch just for you."

"With the candied pecans?" Blister asked, his eyes narrowing. Poppy nodded.

"Deal." Blister hauled himself out of the chair and scooted out the door.

"The man eats like a horse, but I swear that's the same uniform he was wearing ten years ago," Poppy muttered, watching as Blister slowly rolled his squad car toward the service lot.

"Why don't you go join your party in the treatment suite, Jess?" Poppy suggested. "I know I promised you use of the phones, but I kind of have my hands full right now. Would tomorrow work?"

Jess watched the warring instincts on Poppy's face, the desire to please and help fighting the need for Poppy to protect her family, her business. And Jess felt like the source of that stress. She was fully aware that *she* hadn't put the dead guy in the meditation pool, but she was the messenger who'd delivered the news. She decided, then and there, to do anything she could to help the Osbournes handle this mess.

"Jess?"

"Tomorrow will be fine," she promised, pointing to the tree outside Poppy's window. "Sorry, I was, uh, just admiring the golden ash."

"Oh, that's not an ash, hon," Poppy confessed sheepishly. "That's a ginkgo. No one is sure how old it is, but we think it was a gift from an early sanatorium guest. We knew it was something special, that beautiful blaze of color, so we built the whole resort around it, the construction, the theme, everything."

Jess squinted at the tree and realized she'd been so awestruck by the fiery golden frenzy of leaves that she hadn't recognized the distinctive fan shape of ginkgo leaves.

"But . . . you named the spa the Golden *Ash*," Jess noted, letting herself be distracted by this tidbit of trivia.

"Well, most people don't know the difference," Poppy said.

Jess thought about it for a moment, pursing her lips. "My experience in customer service tells me that you're correct."

CHAPTER 6

Jess promised to keep anything she knew about the Treadaway situation to herself for the time being, and she managed to make it from Poppy's office to the treatment building without finding another dead guy. She considered that a promising sign.

She was greeted at the entrance by a scrubs-clad woman with close-cropped silver hair and flawless deep-umber skin. She was her own best advertisement for her position, which according to her name tag was "Lenore, Head Aesthetician."

In tiny print under her name, the tag read "Jonquil's Most Trusted Lieutenant," which made Jess smile. Lenore led Jess into a dreamscape delicately scented with lavender and citrus. From the blue-tinged lighting to the chime-based music, the treatment areas were built to take guests out of space, time, and their everyday worries.

Jess slipped into the sinfully soft spa-issued robe and slippers, making her all the more comfortable as she perched on a heated stone lounger outside the treatment rooms. The blue-green stone floors looked like they'd been hewn from the sea floor somewhere near Atlantis. Jess splayed back on the heated stone, finally feeling a little bit of that promised relaxation. Was it wrong, indulging like this after finding Mr. Treadaway? This trip couldn't be entirely composed of derailed work calls and meditation hollow deaths. Right?

Yeah, that probably wasn't a very nice thought to have right now.

And then Aubrey popped into her line of vision like something out of a jump-scare prank video.

"Hi! Are you finished up with your work from this morning? Diana and Kiki are having their treatments," Aubrey chirped from an adjacent stone area bench, sounding . . . oddly sincere. Her entire body language read differently. Her expression could even be interpreted as friendly and interested.

Weird.

"Uh, yeah . . ." Jess asked. "Did you fall and hit your head in yoga or anything?"

Aubrey didn't look like she had a concussion. She looked stunning. Somehow, she made the spa robe look like it was tailored to fit her. Jess was starting to wonder if Aubrey had access to some sort of fairy godmother—one of the mean ones, who cursed household objects to force regular girls like Jess into centuries-long naps.

Jess's Big Book of Life Plans: Stay away from spinning wheels, combs, and sharp objects in general.

"Well, I may have pulled a hamstring, overdoing a bird of paradise pose. It definitely added to today's difficulty rating, but you know how it is," Aubrey said. "Anything to get the job done."

"Such as . . . coming up here on this very odd 'work retreat'?" Jess asked. "It's a little outside of a wedding planner's usual scope, isn't it? The wedding's not even scheduled."

"It's a little outside of *your* scope," Aubrey retorted.

"I'm self-employed. I make my own scope."

"If I can spend a day helping a bride climb in and out of a bathroom stall because she decided to *triple* down on Spanx, I don't think serving in the bridal party is all that weird by comparison, do you?" While Jess was considering that, Aubrey added, "I'm just saying, for all Diana's pretensions—the ridiculous 'branding language' and the aspirational influencer stuff—this wedding is going to be *huge.* If I can give her half of what she wants, I will be a *legend.* Hell, I might be able to start my own firm. Build something of my own. I mean, you get it. You used to be something in this industry before—"

"Yeah, yeah, the Pepperfield-Cooper wedding," Jess told her. "I swear if you repeat that bullshit story—"

"Oh, honey, I know you didn't have anything to do with that," Aubrey scoffed. "I helped plan Cooper's wedding, when he married the usher the next year. The bride brought me photos of your work from his original wedding, and I was impressed. You showed real talent, before you left weddings for your unorthodox side hustle."

OK, first the Treadaway thing, and now this? Had *Jess* fallen and bumped her head? This could be some awful, prolonged hallucination.

When Jess's chin retreated in disbelief, Aubrey rolled her eyes. "What? It's an interesting spin on your training. You found a whole new market. I admire the innovation of it, and that you were willing to take a risk."

"Wha— Why are you being nice to me right now?" Jess asked. "You've been *awful* to me since we got here."

"Oh, that?" Aubrey scoffed. "That's just playing up to Diana. I'm playing it safe. I mean, yeah, you're a proposal planner *now.* But Diana isn't exactly a predictable personality. She might decide that you could do *both* jobs, to keep a consistent vision or keep control or whatever excuse she could come up with to fire me. So, I'm playing the advantages I've got. I mean, Diana *really* has a bone to pick with you, that's clear enough when you're not around. It's probably some leftover high school thing. You know too much, about her and her family. It puts her on edge."

Jess's brain was having genuine difficulty switching gears from being questioned by law enforcement to this overtly restful space. Later, she would blame this inner turmoil for telling Aubrey, "I barely knew her in high school. Nobody knew anything *real* about her in high school. She was too good at spinning different versions of herself, her life at home. You never knew if she was wearing real designer shoes or knockoffs."

Aubrey laughed and Jess added, "No, really. Diana knew things about etiquette and expectations that you only learned at the knees of people who'd lived through it. She always claimed to have spent holidays in Madrid or Paris. She knew all the names of the right restaurants and museums over there, and the Helston name had enough remaining weight to make it believable. We didn't know what was going on."

"Well, you know enough," Aubrey told her. "And she resents the hell out of it. She *really* doesn't like the fact that she needs you to make anything happen. So, if my pushing you around a little bit curries some favor with her? Prepare to be pushed. It's not personal. It's just gamesmanship."

Jess sat there, blinking rapidly at Aubrey. "There is something wrong with you."

"It's called 'being goal-oriented,'" Aubrey told her as Kiki and Diana walked toward them, ensconced in their own fluffy robes. Kiki veered left toward the far window. Diana made a beeline for the lovely Lenore to discuss cellulite elimination treatments. Aubrey climbed up from the lounger to hover nearby Diana's conversation. Jess swore if either Aubrey's or Diana's eyes landed on her or Kiki . . .

Nope, nope. Jess would not get kicked out of a classy joint like this for fighting. She would not repeat her brief but colorful Girl Scouting career.

Resolute, Jess got up and padded to where Kiki stretched across her own chaise. The extensive windows allowed an endless view of the surrounding trees.

"I am made of pudding," Kiki purred.

"Oh, man, was there a 'mud infused with weed' option?" Jess teased, sliding onto her own lounger. "Nobody told me!"

Kiki's grin was brilliant and fully sated. "No weed, just ylang-ylang massage oil administered by a technician with magic hands. Would it be weird to ask Olivia to marry me? I could give her hands an amazing life."

"I think that's going to come across as creepy no matter how nicely you phrase it," Jess said, moving her head back and forth.

"Fair enough. Also, they're going to make you drink a lot of that spring water," Kiki said as a male technician, whose name tag read "Mark," brought them tall glasses with apple slices floating in them.

"Hydrate, hydrate, hydrate," he told them, smiling so sweetly, Jess didn't have the heart to tell him that she hadn't enjoyed a treatment yet. "We're moving a bunch of nasty stuff through your lymphatic system and you need to chase it out. You ladies just sit back and think happy thoughts."

"It feels wrong that I feel this relaxed," Kiki suggested. "Like I should be working or something."

"Oh, I have a feeling you hustle plenty." Jess snorted into her glass, even if she did understand the sentiment on a professional and a "just found a dead guy" level. "What are you even working on right now? I probably should have asked sooner, but I've been distracted by, you know, everything. I can't ask educated questions, but I'm guessing it's related to 'cancer stuff.'"

"I am indeed working on 'cancer stuff,'" Kiki said with a chuckle. "In the lab, I'm trying to help my company find ways to synthesize rare organic compounds that we might be able to use in treatments, so we can produce them on a mass scale instead of tearing down an entire ecosystem to harvest them."

"Wow, that is . . . weirdly philanthropic? For a scary Big-Pharma-type company?" Jess suggested.

"Well, not all corporations are evil incarnate for no purpose," Kiki said, smiling wryly. "Just half of them."

"How do you even go about making something 'natural' out of chemicals?" Jess asked.

"I'd rather not get into it, because I am not in a 'work' headspace right now."

"Oh, right," Jess said, feeling a flush of guilt. "Sorry, I didn't think of that. Just because I think about work all the time doesn't mean you should have to."

"That's OK," Kiki said. "It's nice that you asked. Nobody asks. I think they're afraid I'm going to break out a dry erase board or something."

"I'd still like to hear about it sometime, if you ever feel like it," Jess said. "It sounds interesting. I know you said Diana is the family favorite, but I think you came out with the better end of the deal. Independent of the family politics, making your own path in the world."

And suddenly Jess remembered that Kiki had visited the office the night before to call her aunt Birdie. Was it Birdie's fussing that had Kiki staring out the window, all contemplative?

"We're never away from the family politics," Kiki told her. "I know it sounds ridiculous. Grown adults not being able to say no to their elders, but it's practically bred into us. The family is like a hive mind. They just overwhelm you with their absolute certainty that they have every right to demand what they want and you're a brat for even thinking of saying no. They just repeat themselves over and over, but they make it sound like they're giving ground or asking for something different. And it makes you think *you're* crazy. I mean, they basically ignored me for most of my childhood, but they think it's reasonable to tell me to drop everything at work and fly up here with no notice. And here I am."

"They're never going to be able to take your education away from you, or who you are when you're away from them," Jess told her. "You're *Doctor* Kiki. Not many Kikis can say that."

Kiki waggled her eyebrows, making Jess giggle. Just then, Aubrey and Diana came shuffling over to them. Diana frowned at the pair of them laughing. "What's so funny?"

"The fact that I'm ninety percent sure there were heavy amounts of THC in Kiki's massage treatment," Jess told Diana, making her giggle.

"Oh, no, Kiki doesn't get high. She would never disrespect chemical compounds like that," Diana informed her primly. "She had this whole 'science will save us all' speech she'd do when we were kids, made her sound like one of those guys from the nerd TV shows."

"Aunt Birdie was *not* a fan of that speech," Kiki said, shaking her head. "And I think you mean the Discovery Channel."

"She said you were ruining yourself with books and no man would ever want to marry you," Diana hooted.

Kiki hummed and gave a half smile. She didn't seem to find the memory nearly as funny as Diana did. "For someone who's single, Aunt Birdie spends a lot of time worrying about marrying us off."

"Aunt Birdie is the spinster aunt?" Aubrey guessed. "There's always a spinster auntie who makes the family gatherings awkward, under the protective umbrella of 'that's just the way she is.'" Jess stifled a laugh. If Aubrey was going to plan Diana's wedding, she was going to become very familiar with Birdie's protective umbrella.

"Well, technically, she's not a spinster," Diana noted. "She was married once."

Even Aubrey's curiosity was piqued by that. "And then?"

"Um, he died on the honeymoon," Kiki said, her lips contorting into a pained grimace. "My mom said she never understood why Thornton would go swimming in the ocean when he had so many health problems, especially when Birdie insisted on keeping his meds—allergy, asthma, heart murmur—in her purse. In their hotel room. Mom thought maybe he had an asthma attack or chest pains or something mid-swim and couldn't get back to shore. Birdie only talked about it with the family once. All she said was that she looked up from her book and couldn't see Thornton anymore. They didn't find his body until after she flew home."

Jess thought of Jeremy and was grateful that at least he hadn't had room to disappear in the tiny meditation pool. Jess couldn't imagine losing a husband so soon after marrying him. How had that affected how Birdie influenced Diana? Would Diana keep Trenton's meds in her purse? Did Jess have an obligation to warn Trenton? Where did Helston LuxeGram stand on suspicious honeymoon deaths?

"No one talked about it, especially in front of Birdie. It was 'family ugliness,' and the Helstons can't abide ugliness," Kiki said, shaking her head as if she could clear it of the memory. "It's next to godlessness and debauchery. And not the fun kind."

"Birdie took to her bed anytime anybody brought it up," Diana said, examining her manicure. "No one had the nerve to tell her to remarry. It created this power vacuum in the family after Grandma died. And she just sort of ran things after that."

"How have I never heard about this?" Jess asked. "I would think that's the kind of thing that would have gotten around a place like Wren Hill."

Diana raised her brows before repeating, "Family. Ugliness."

Before Jess could hear more Helston family legends, Lenore arrived to claim her for her appointment. It was finally time for her to enjoy these fancy-schmancy weed-mud treatments she'd heard so much about. She led Jess to a white subway-tiled room with a sort of morgue table in the middle, covered in a foil-lined blanket. Lenore instructed her on how to lie down comfortably and cover her private areas with the tiny towels provided.

(Jess knew it wasn't technically a morgue table, but honestly.)

"Just undress to your comfort level and I'll be right with you," Lenore told her in what Jess was coming to think of as the "spa voice"—soft, gentle, and meant to prevent disturbing other guests.

A few minutes later, Jess's ears perked up at the sound of soft footfalls. She turned her head back and saw a feminine shape silhouetted against the frosted-glass hallway door. A tiny brunette woman with a long ponytail poked her head through the door after a soft knock.

"Hi, I'm Jonquil," she said, a mischievous quirk to her lips. Her milk-pale face was almost elfin in its upturned features.

"Did your family ever worry about running out of flower names?" Jess asked, pulling at the towels to give herself a tiny bit more coverage.

"The last one working here that you haven't met," she replied. "Congratulations. You have caught us all."

"Is it normal for an owner of a spa to give body wraps?" Jess asked.

"Normally Lenore handles this sort of thing, but I took a special interest in your appointment," Jonquil told her. "I understand you've already had a very eventful visit—"

"I'm so sorry," Jess blurted out. "I know I shouldn't have been wandering around unsupervised. Twice. I see now that finding a dead man was the consequence of my choices . . . Also, I really hope you knew about the dead man and I didn't just tell you in the least sensitive way possible."

Jonquil's mouth dropped open. "Well, yes, I did. And yes, finding Mr. Treadaway has complicated things a little bit, but no one is upset with you. Sometimes people need to wander a little bit before they find what they need. And sometimes you find things you weren't expecting. It happens."

Jess was left wondering what Jeremy Treadaway had needed when he was wandering. But the final Osbourne was being so nice, Jess didn't want to disrupt the conversation with more dead-guy talk. Jonquil had a quieter presence about her than Poppy or Sis—a serenity that Jess suspected came from doing exactly what you wanted in life and being married to someone like Beth, who went all soft-eyed when she spoke of her wife.

"What *doesn't* happen is my stubborn-ass cousin interacting with guests."

OK, clearly there were hidden pockets of Osbourne in Jonquil.

"I'm sorry?" Jess frowned at her. This was a rather awkward position to have a conversation from, staring up at her, upside down and horizontal. But even from this angle, Jonquil's smile was amused as hell.

"Dean doesn't like people."

"He's a chef. He feeds people for a living," Jess countered.

"He likes food, not people," Jonquil told her. "We've had fancy travel magazines come up here to shoot big photo spreads and he won't let them take photos of anything but his hands. Really irked the guy from *Luxury Travel*. He's contrary. It's part of his charm."

Jess wrinkled her nose. "Would we call it 'charm'?"

"Dean stays in the kitchen. On the rare occasion he interacts with a guest, he keeps it as short as possible. He does not take walks in the woods with them while *talking*."

"So, I basically had an encounter with Kitchen Bigfoot?" Jess guessed.

It was only slightly less ridiculous than Strawberry Chef Guy, in terms of nicknames. Still, Jonquil nodded. Enthusiastically.

"We weren't so much talking as bickering," Jess confessed.

"It's still remarkable progress, considering," Jonquil said. "My cousin's a good man, one of the best, really. But he's got trauma, the big 'being processed but barely' kind relating to women, and if he's willing to utter more than a few words to you? While making eye contact? You have me intrigued, Jessamine Bricker."

"There were definitely more than a few words uttered," Jess conceded. "But the eye contact was more along the lines of glaring. Also, no using my old-lady full name just because you saw it on the intake forms. That's not playing fair."

"Accept my tacit approval and know that it comes with strings," Jonquil told her. "And that string is labeled, 'Don't hurt my cousin or there will be consequences.'"

"Well, you have me vulnerable in what feels like a murder room, so I don't feel like I can disappoint you," Jess replied.

"Right?" Jonquil chirped.

With this settled, Jonquil proceeded to scoop handfuls of a warmed paste that felt like sandy clay and smelled of cinnamon and oranges onto Jess's skin. She rubbed it down Jess's limbs with gloved hands, and Jess felt like she could sink through the table, she was so relaxed. She decided right then she was going to like Jonquil. Jess didn't care if the woman was a little pushy, she was *good* at her job.

By the time Jonquil enclosed Jess in the foil blanket like a burrito, Jess's skin felt like rose petals covered in morning dew and unicorn spit. "I'm going to let you marinate in this for a while and then I'll come back and rinse you off," she whispered softly, laying hands on Jess's towel-wrapped shoulders. Jess murmured something in the vicinity of "OK" as she heard the door open and then shut.

She closed her eyes and tried to let the events of the day melt away. She tried to concentrate on the pleasant warmth seeping into her skin, and the lovely, sweet scent in the air.

And just when she felt her toes unflex, deep within the foil wrap, a thought popped into her head. *What rock had Jeremy Treadaway hit his head on?*

More thoughts popped into her head unbidden. Blister said Jeremy had tripped and hit his head on a rock, then drowned in the meditation pool. Jess hadn't seen any drag marks surrounding the seating stones, just the ones near the water. And as far as she'd been able to see, there were no rocks *in* the meditation pool. It was a sort of rounded cup without any stalagmites he could have fallen against. Unless he'd hit his head *before* he'd entered the hollow . . . but wouldn't there be a blood trail leading to the water if he'd hit his head that hard?

Jess wasn't sure she was qualified to do gravel drag-mark analysis. But what about Zephyr and her late-night ointment delivery? Jess realized she had a little more consideration for staff than the average Golden Ash guest, but she couldn't imagine calling Beth to her door for a delivery at that hour, no matter how singed her . . . places were. It could be some sort of cover. Zephyr could have wanted Beth to see her at her villa so she had an alibi. Zephyr was pretty short. Did she have the height or strength to whack Jeremy over the head hard enough to take him out? But why would she do that in the first place?

It had to be Susan. Remembering the way that woman screamed from inside her villa sent a shiver down Jess's spine. The woman had deep wells of frustration and anger and hurt. She could see Susan tearing across the spa grounds, cracking Jeremy over the head, maybe even with his pasta plate, and dragging him to the pool.

No, Jess was a planner of other people's special life events, not a cop. She needed to let this go, reset her brain, and get back to work at her actual job. She intentionally shoved all thoughts of the various people who might want Jeremy Treadaway dead *out* of her mind.

For a few unspoiled seconds, Jess floated on a bubble of nonconcern. She was warm and comfortable and safe and . . . just as her mind began to ebb away, Jess's left thigh itched.

With her hands swaddled at stomach level, Jess was helpless against the agitation skittering over her skin. She tried to concentrate on something else, on floating on that beautiful cushion of nothingness without worry, without strain, without the ability to scratch her fucking thigh.

Jess tried to reposition her arms so she could reach down and scratch, but she couldn't find footing with her legs wrapped so tight. And it was fine, really, because she also couldn't move her hands to scratch in the first place. With the back of her head levered against the table, she arched her back and caught a glimpse of the frosted glass door behind her. The staff had lowered the hallway lights to maintain the mellow space, and yet Jess could still make out the silhouette of a person just on the other side of the glass.

Weird.

Jess assumed it was a staff member checking on her . . . but they were too curvy to be Mark and too tall to be Jonquil. She waited for them to speak, but they sort of hovered outside the door, their hand on the doorknob. Maybe it was a technician who was just headed to the wrong treatment room? Surely there had to be door mix-ups at a place like this.

"Lenore?" she called.

But there was no response from the shadow. Unease, cold and clammy, crept up Jess's belly. Why wouldn't they respond? They just stood there, as if they were thinking over their options.

And while these endless seconds ticked by, with no speech from this person, Jess realized how vulnerable she really was in this position, in an unlocked room, trapped in what was basically a straitjacket. There was no way she could run to safety if the person on the other side of the glass had bad intentions.

Why wasn't this person talking?

"This room is occupied," she said, louder.

Jess watched as the doorknob turned silently, and for reasons she couldn't explain, it filled her with dread. She was going to die, wrapped up like a baked potato, naked and covered in mud.

That was going to be an interesting obituary.

Despite all the spring water Jess had recently consumed, her mouth went dry. She couldn't seem to make another sound, just watched in mounting terror as the door pushed open a fraction. She wanted to scream. She wanted to growl. She wanted to tell this person to walk the *fuck* back down the hall and leave her alone. She managed to open her mouth to produce a pathetic, breathless "buh..." when the door stopped moving and gently closed. The shape moved away from the glass and disappeared.

Relief, warm and sweet, flooded Jess's chest. Suddenly, breathing became a possibility.

She stared at the door, unwilling to look away. Why had she been so scared? Why had her brain leaped right from cinnamon-clay-restfulness to potentially-being-murdered-while-wrapped-in-foil?

Was the Golden Ash messing with her head?

"Fuck this," Jess whispered, wriggling in her foil bonds, attempting to make some room. She wasn't going to be stuck in this position if the shadow person came back.

A soft knock sounded at the door. Jess froze. A shorter shape—probably Jonquil—appeared on the other side of the glass. "Jess? You OK?"

Jess swallowed heavily before finally managing to produce a squeaky "Come in."

Jonquil stuck her head in the door. "Are we feeling relaxed yet?"

Jess huffed out a shaky breath. As Jonquil released her from her foil cage, Jess tried not to let Jonquil see the relieved tears slide down her cheeks. Jonquil gently rinsed the mud from her skin, using a series of ceiling-mounted showerheads. As the warm water cascaded over her, Jess told herself the shadow person was probably just a confused technician heading into the wrong treatment room. They probably hadn't spoken because they didn't want to draw attention to their mistake. It probably had nothing to do with Jeremy Treadaway, but . . .

Susan Treadaway was around the right height to be the shadow person. Jess wondered if Susan was aware that Jess had been the one to find Jeremy's body. Was Jess safe at the Golden Ash? Was anyone?

Jess's Big Book of Life Plans: Stop asking yourself these questions while ninety percent naked and covered in dirt.

CHAPTER 7

As far as Diana was concerned, there was no reason for their party to leave the spa just because someone died.

A Daily D-Ash left on their kitchen counter announced "an unfortunate incident on the grounds" and the delay of certain services while promising a percentage taken off their bills for the inconvenience. Rather than being concerned about the nature of this "incident," Jess overheard Diana wonder if this would disrupt the reflexology treatments they had scheduled for the next day. And then she'd flounced into her room to change her clothes for dinner.

Jess shared a look with Kiki, who only pursed her lips and nodded, as if to say, *This is who we're dealing with.* Then Jess indulged in a particularly long hot shower to rinse off the remnants of orange-cinnamon mud. She wasn't sure why the word "incident" bothered her so much. It was probably the fear she'd felt, watching that person standing outside her treatment room. What was *happening* at the Golden Ash? Jess walked out of the bathroom to find Kiki scrambling over her bed.

"Just a second! I'm changing!" Kiki yelled as Jess opened a door that was already slightly ajar. She was clambering over her bed, trying to scoop loose papers into a thick five-subject notebook with a smiling narwhal on the cover.

"Um, changing into what?" Jess laughed as several sheets of loose-leaf paper fluttered to the floor.

"It's just some research I'm doing," Kiki said quickly. "Sort of a fun side project."

"On life before the cloud existed?" Jess asked, tossing her towel in the provided hamper.

"It's not for work, so I have to be sort of careful about where I save it, because I don't want it to belong to my employer," she said. "The thing about notebooks, they're untraceable. There's no search history."

"So even your fun side hobbies are more work?" Jess teased her.

"I have this idea." Kiki sighed. "Truffles can be grown in the root systems of pecan trees. Locally grown luxury ingredients are really trendy now, you know, 'homegrown delicacies.' Eat local, farm-to-table, and all that. The Tillards haven't tried it because the older generation, namely Trenton's grandfather, is very traditional. The company's arborists systematically root out the truffles and throw them away because they still think of them as a nuisance! Those things sell for hundreds of dollars a pound! I've done some research, and I've managed to hybridize several different types of truffles to create something that will be cheap to grow, difficult to kill, and carry a unique flavor. After the initial lab costs, it won't cost the Tillards anything extra to grow them."

"Can you hybridize truffles?"

Kiki grinned. "In my lab, I can do anything. I want to pitch the idea to Trenton, but I want to wait until after the wedding to do it.

They might be a little more likely to take a chance on an in-law than a not-quite-connected-to-them girl approaching them with an idea."

Jess offered Kiki a delighted grin, but she didn't want to be the one to tell her that Diana wouldn't stretch her neck out a single inch to help Kiki. Diana wouldn't risk that sort of "capital" with the Tillards. That wasn't Jess's job, to hurt Kiki. Diana would have to handle that on her own.

"Do me a favor, just don't tell Diana, OK?"

"I probably wouldn't be able to explain it anyway," Jess said, shrugging.

"True."

Jess tied her thick hair back and brushed on a little makeup. "But you're not going to accidentally create some sort of evil zombie pecan that will wipe out all known pie forever, right?"

Kiki pursed her lips. "Probably not."

While Kiki was occupied with her makeup, Jess threw on a cranberry long-sleeved dress and black flats. And while she itched for the comfort of her pearls, she knew it was a bad idea to wear them. They were dirty . . . and possibly evidence. She still wasn't sure about that. It would only look worse now, she was sure, to tell Blister she'd taken them from the scene. So, she shoved them in one of her socks and buried it at the bottom of her underwear drawer. Because it didn't feel like something she should leave lying around.

Rather than wait on Aubrey's usual outfit audit, Jess ducked out of the villa and headed up to the kitchen—which took a little while, even in flats. Outside the open kitchen door, she could see the older chef, Jamie, smoking. He dropped his cigarette as soon as he saw her, grinding the butt with his foot.

"Terrible habit," he said, ruffling a hand through his silver-streaked black crew cut. With his smile tilted at a guilty angle, he picked up the butt and dropped it into a nearby garbage can. "But a lot of people who work in kitchens pick it up. Something about high-stress work and break times. Do me a favor, don't tell anybody you saw that? Jonquil and Beth will try aromatherapy or meditation—again—to help me quit. *Again.* I love them, but no man can take smelling that much chamomile. It's just not right."

She burst out laughing. "Nobody will hear it from me. I wouldn't subject anyone to involuntary chamomile."

"You seem like a nice girl, not like—" He stopped himself. The unspoken "not like the people you're sharing villa space with" hung between them. He placed a large hand, covered in the sort of tiny kitchen scars she'd seen on caterers through the years, over his heart. "Jamie Ortega."

"Jess Bricker. Nice to meet you, officially."

"Jamie, you all right?" Dean called through the kitchen doorway as he poked his head out. He was using a much kinder tone than she'd ever heard from him. His face went from relaxed to tense at the sight of her.

Beyond Dean's shoulder, she could see the kitchen. His work-space was exactly what she'd expected—clean, organized, without frills. The white tile walls showed no sign the room was even used. She'd never seen so many sauté pans in one place. They were stacked neatly next to a massive stove range, surrounded by gleaming chrome counters. And knives. Little knives. Big knives. Cleavers. Serrated.

So many knives.

"So, are you here to ask me to take the carbs out of the bread?" Dean asked.

"No, that's Diana's thing. I would probably offer you lewd and licentious carnal favors in return for a cheeseburger right now."

Dean's mouth dropped open and Jess swore she could see his breath stutter.

Good.

A warm pink flush crept across Dean's cheeks for a second. She felt a little guilty, talking to him like that when he was trying to work…

Nah, it went away after a few seconds. She was fine. Dean, however, was still red-faced and he was visibly shaking off whatever state of shock she'd reeled him into.

"Can I ask you a weird question?" Jess asked.

"You only seem able to ask weird questions."

She rolled her eyes. "Did anybody find Jeremy Treadaway's room service plate?"

Dean frowned at her. "What?"

"After his fight with his wife, he came bursting out of his villa, grabbed his room service plate, and ran off into the night. Maybe he left it somewhere on the grounds?"

"Now that you mention it, Aaron said he found one of the cloches underneath the ginkgo tree early this morning. He found the plate on the yoga platform. I thought it was one of the weird things that rich people do just because they can," Jamie admitted.

"That sounds about right," Jess said.

"You know, there are law enforcement agencies looking into it, even if it is Blister," Dean told her. "You don't need to worry about this. I thought the whole point of y'all coming up here was to get away from stress."

"Well, I sort of brought my stress with me," Jess said. When Dean and Jamie merely stared at her, she added, "I'm a professional proposal planner, and the woman I'm here with—Diana? Her boyfriend messed his proposal up, and he's paying me to help him fix it."

Dean scowled. "You're a what now?"

"Really?" Jamie chuckled. "That's cool. Do you do proposals at basketball games?"

"Decidedly not," Jess said, making him laugh.

"That's a job?" Dean said, shaking his head. "I don't know whether to be sad for humanity, in general, or kind of impressed that you turned relationship incompetence into a full-time gig."

Jess waited for the insult, and when it didn't come, replied, "Thank . . . you?"

Dean turned to Jamie. "The dinner rush is starting and you're out here talking proposals at basketball games. Marianne would hate being up on a Jumbotron."

"He's not a romantic at heart," Jamie told her.

"Actually, my professional experience shows he's spot-on about the Jumbotron thing," she said, patting his muscled arm.

"Aw, man." Jamie pouted briefly.

"Back to the engagement drawing board," Dean told him. "As is the 'smoke break that we don't call a smoke break because you don't want Jonquil and Beth to hear about it.'"

"Bye, Jess!" Jamie exclaimed, ducking into the kitchen.

"No Jumbotrons, Jamie!" she called after him.

She heard him laughing, which only made her grin.

"Jess?"

She turned to find Diana, Aubrey, and Kiki frowning at her. It appeared that Jess's departure had left Kiki unguarded, because she'd been shoved into one of Aubrey's cast-off dresses, navy blue with a bow at the neckline. She looked like a desperate politician's wife, and she seemed pretty unhappy about it. Poor Kiki. Jess felt like a terrible roommate, particularly after Kiki had trusted her with the truffle information.

Diana, in particular, seemed very displeased to find Jess chatting with the kitchen staff. She was staring at Dean in a way that made Jess nervous. "What are you doing up here? I had some thoughts about fonts for the social media announcements. I would think you'd appreciate my input."

"We were worried when you left without saying anything," Kiki said quietly.

"And then we heard your horse laugh coming around the corner and followed it," Aubrey added.

Dean stared at them, hard. "Miss Bricker was just making some breakfast requests for your party for tomorrow morning."

"Fruit as far as the eye can see," Jess assured them. Diana's face relaxed ever so slightly. Jess supposed it was OK for her to go missing if she was missing in the course of doing something for Diana.

"Oh, and something with kale, if you have it," Diana told him. "Something like a smoothie."

"Something *like* a smoothie?" Dean replied. He cleared his throat, glancing at Jess. "Sure."

"Let's just go to dinner and see what the chef comes up with, OK?" Jess said, ushering them away from the kitchen door to the lodge's front porch.

"Since when do you talk to the kitchen staff?" Diana asked. She kept craning her neck, trying to get a look at Dean.

Jess turned on her sweetest "Wren Hill armor" smile, the one she wore when she heard the other girls whispering behind her back about her mom, about her shoes, about her lack of a vacation home. "I'm just trying to support your goals however I can."

Diana blinked at her. "I suppose that's all right, then."

Diana peppered Jess with questions about Dean, even as they were led to their table and seated. What was the chef's name? When did Jess meet him? Were they really just talking about breakfast? What else did they talk about? She supposed she shouldn't be surprised that Diana didn't know anything about the dining services at the spa. She didn't really know anything about the staff at most places, it seemed.

But passing the table that the Treadaways had occupied previously made Jess's mind wander back to that room service cloche. She could imagine how it ended up under the tree, but the plate was left on the yoga platform. Did Jeremy really wander that far? Did he leave the items in both places or had someone "helped" him?

Of course, it was entirely possible that the whole thing was an accident and she was obsessing over nothing.

"Jess?" Diana said, sounding annoyed. "Are you ignoring me?"

Jess realized she was holding that night's menu and staring off into space.

"Oh, sorry. Just having some thoughts about your big day," Jess lied—through her teeth. "And the chef's name is Dean. He's one of the Osbourne cousins."

"Dean Osbourne?" Diana repeated. "Why does that sound familiar?"

Aubrey gasped.

"Oh, wait, I've *heard* of him." She craned her neck to look into the kitchen. "There was a write-up in some culinary magazine. I think the title was something like 'Chef on Recluse Mountain.' He worked with all these big names right out of culinary school and was on the short list for a James Beard Award before he had some sort of breakdown. He moved out to the middle of nowhere . . . well, I guess it was here. But he won't do interviews. No social media. He's turned down multiple offers from the Food Network. Him being all withdrawn just makes everybody want him more. Smart, really. It will only create more demand."

Dean Osbourne was an onion, with many, many layers. Issues

with women? Rejection of success? Reclusive tendencies? Oh, no, Jess was halfway to having some ill-advised feelings toward this man. Mavis would have a *fit*.

Still, the look on Diana's face was the kind of expression that any wedding planner knew meant trouble with a capital "T," for "terminated contract." If she was looking at Dean like that, what did it say about Diana's feelings for Trenton? The youngest Tillard was burly and blond and, well, sort of . . . soft, like an overgrown Saint-Bernard-puppy-turned-human in a hilarious and heartwarming lab accident. And it looked like Diana was about to bolt for fear of missing out on swimmer builds and broody moods.

Jess didn't talk about Those Proposal Jobs. The rare occasions when a client overestimated their partner's interest in matrimony and left Jess with a heartbroken mess, dead flowers, unwanted jewelry, and, on one occasion, a custom message that needed to be chipped out of the surface of an ice rink. Trenton's legal people had been smart enough to write a refusal clause into her contract, meaning that if Diana said no, Jess didn't get paid. Diana had been so eager for her perfect proposal, Jess hadn't worried about it at the time . . . but seeing the look on Diana's face as she stared at Dean's ass as he walked away?

This was trouble.

Time to bring Diana's brain back to the point of their stay, and if that happened to distract her from Dean, all the better. Jess asked, "So, Diana, are you going to go for a custom gown for the wedding or do you have a designer in mind?"

Diana's face brightened as she waxed poetic about "this *adorable* little designer" she'd discovered on a recent trip to London with Trenton, and how she couldn't wait to make an appointment with him. This lyrical enthusiasm continued through their salads, the delicately seasoned salmon Diana insisted they order, and their dessert course (fruit), until they were ambling toward the front door. Not only was Dean forgotten, but Jess suspected Diana had forgotten that she, Kiki, and Aubrey were present, too.

Still, it had been nice to get a solid, uninterrupted meal.

"I see what you did there, redirecting her to the dress talk," Aubrey told Jess quietly as they walked out behind the still-yammering Diana.

"It's called 'being goal-oriented,'" Jess shot back, making Aubrey snort. Jess cleared her throat. She would not develop a friendship with Aubrey, who had proven herself to be a needlessly competitive pain in the ass. She had to draw the line somewhere.

Somehow, Diana seemed to register that they were having a conversation without her and turned. "What was that?"

"I was just telling Jess, I don't blame her for wanting a piece of the chef," Aubrey drawled as they walked around the front of the lodge. "But I think it's sort of tacky to go after him. Your attention should be focused on Diana right now, Jess."

Jess narrowed her eyes at Aubrey. Apparently, they weren't quite past the whole "gamesmanship" thing. But rather than make a scene, she simply said, "I'm not trying to get a piece of anything."

"Oh, leave Jess alone," Diana sighed. "Besides, she wouldn't go for Dean Osbourne. And he wouldn't go for her."

Jess blinked at Diana, wondering what *that* meant.

"I don't know. I could see Jess chasing hopelessly after the hot chef and then him filing a restraining order against her," Aubrey said, smiling slyly.

"I don't know why that was something that had to be said out loud," Jess muttered.

"It's normal, chasing after the shiny option, the one that *feels* good, instead of the one that's good for you. It's human nature,"

Diana said. "The trick is to be discreet. And Jess is way too strait-laced to do anything that would upset her orderly little life."

Jess tried not to side-eye Diana, she really did. But it didn't sound like Diana was talking about hypotheticals. These didn't seem like the words of a person ready for a lifetime commitment, and Jess had serious doubts about Diana's ability to be discreet. Had Diana thought about what would happen after the champagne went flat and the rose petals had been thrown? Diana was going to have to make a life with Trenton. Jess knew the right club privileges and cash flow could smooth the way toward contentment, but even that only extended so far.

What was Jess setting Trenton up for here? And did Jess have the financial wherewithal to question these things?

No. No, she did not.

Also, Jess didn't think she was *too* straitlaced. She was just the right amount of laced.

"Wait, so does that mean you previously *didn't* get caught or that you're *currently* not getting caught?" Kiki asked, frowning at her cousin.

The look Diana shot at Kiki could turn a lesser person to stone, but then Diana's face shifted to an expression of horror as they reached the front steps of the lodge. She stopped in her tracks at the sight of three rather large men climbing onto a golf cart at the base of the lodge steps.

"Trenton!" Diana squeaked.

"DeeDee!" Trenton Tillard the Fourth's boyish face lit up as he threw his arms wide. "Surprise!"

Jess's Big Book of Life Plans: Panic. Everybody, panic. Fuuuuuuuu—

CHAPTER 8

For once, Jess was sure that she and Aubrey were thinking the same thing.

What did Trenton hear?

For his part, Trenton seemed oblivious to any "getting caught" comments. He appeared to be absolutely thrilled to have pulled off this . . . prank? Surprise? Ambush? He held his arms aloft. "Didn't expect to see us here, did ya?"

Diana froze as he rushed up the stairs to hug her, her own arms stiff at her sides.

Kiki was staring at them, her brow slightly furrowed, which seemed normal, considering Trenton springing out of nowhere like a damned jack-in-the-box. Meanwhile, Poppy just sat there on the cart's driver seat, watching the growing awkwardness with a strangely blank expression. Was it the remaining stress of Jeremy Treadaway's death or the additional stress of unexpected guests arriving in *the wake* of Jeremy Treadaway's death? Did the Osbournes even have room available for Trenton's group? Sis had mentioned that this was the end of their season, but honestly, this felt like an imposition on the spa staff.

"Well, DeeDee made it sound so nice when she called." Trenton wrapped his thick arms around Diana's unyielding shoulders. "I didn't like the idea of you being out here all by yourself, so I thought we would join y'all."

Diana nodded, and Jess could see the effort it was taking to thaw her face. Aubrey, for once, was quiet, glancing between the prospective bride and groom with a calculating expression—as if she was trying to figure out how to best spin this development to her advantage. Jess stepped out of her line of sight, closer to Kiki.

"Oh, he brought Chad," Kiki sighed. "What joy is mine."

Jess sort of recognized Trenton's longtime best friend, Chad Hardcastle—blond, built, boorish. He'd attended Harrow with the rest of them and bumped the outskirts of the social circles that Jess orbited. He definitely seemed more Diana's type, but honestly, Jess couldn't remember seeing the two of them together at school. Then again, Jess had largely avoided Chad, who had all the personal charm of discarded Kleenex. And his eyes never seemed to stray above the neck of any woman unlucky enough to interact with him.

"Did Trenton and Diana start dating in college?" Jess asked quietly, watching as Diana ruffled Trenton's hair. Trenton ducked his head into her neck and hugged her tight.

Kiki shook her head. "The pair of them didn't really 'find each other' until years after graduation. Trenton found Diana scary and aggressive, which . . . wasn't entirely wrong. But a few years ago, right after Trenton's, well, 'starter marriage' fell apart, they met at some charity thing. Diana had learned to fawn a little more effectively by then, to hang off Trenton's arm and treat everything he said like it was a fascinating treatise on geopolitical polarization—like she's doing right now."

Jess glanced at the "happy couple." Trenton was leaning into Diana's hands as she stroked his hair, which really didn't help with the whole "man as a Saint Bernard" thing. Clearly, he was no longer afraid of Diana.

"Did you bring Bitsie, too?" Diana purred. She peered around as if Trenton's older cousin and her stamp of Tillard family approval were being concealed somehow behind Chad.

"No, she still couldn't make it," Trenton said glumly. "She had a nail appointment she just couldn't miss."

Ouch.

Diana frowned, her expression appropriately insulted. The Tillards were really making an effort to let it be known they didn't approve of Trenton's choice. Jess might have felt sorry for her, but she'd heard Diana speak aloud, so . . .

"Well, did you at least bring one of those fancy satellite phones that will get a signal up here?" Diana asked. "I could at least post the selfies from inside the villa."

"No." Trenton frowned. "Was I supposed to?"

"I told you it was impossible to get a signal up here and I was having to use the office landline," Diana said, pouting prettily. "What did you think I was trying to tell you?"

Trenton shrugged. "I kinda thought that was the whole point of coming up here, getting away from it all. Reduced screen time, mindfulness, and all that."

"Honey, part of marriage is recognizing each other's needs and meeting them before your partner can even make them known," Diana told him. "And I *need* to let my followers know that I'm OK. I'm just on a break to focus on our loving, luxe future. Remember?"

"External attentiveness and internal affirmation," Trenton assured her, kissing the tip of her nose. "I'll work on it, DeeDee, I promise."

Jess was willing to bet there were going to be even more flowers waiting in the villa when they got back. It did strike Jess as odd that Trenton didn't pick up on that rather enormous opportunity to meet one of Diana's demands . . . maybe Trenton wasn't as supportive of Diana's social media aspirations as advertised. Maybe Trenton wasn't as much of a clueless puppy as she thought. Maybe he was clueless like a fox.

None of this boded well for them long term, but . . . Jess didn't include a happiness guarantee in her contracts, so that was not her problem.

"Wait, our phones won't work?" Chad spluttered. "What the hell, Trent?"

"I texted you about it," Trenton insisted, sending Chad an imploring look as Diana wound her fingers through his.

Chad pulled his phone out of his pocket and searched for a signal. Finding none, he let loose a string of extremely creative, colorful curses.

"It's not so bad," Diana admitted, giving Chad her best sympathetic pouty-face. "I just miss being able to wake up and see how many people loved my posts while I was sleeping, you know? But I hardly think about it now, they keep us so busy here."

"Well, your typing thumbs probably need a break from your phone anyway, because pretty soon you're going to have some big news to share," he said, kissing her hands. Diana squealed with delight and Trenton beamed as she threw her arms around him and covered his cheeks in loud smacking kisses.

Somehow, he'd managed to redirect Diana from one of her favorite subjects—her followers—to her other favorite subject—their engagement. Jess's eyes narrowed as she watched Trenton gleefully accept Diana's affection. Well played, Trent. Well played.

The other newcomer, who bore a close resemblance to Chad, was loading bags into the rear luggage rack. Jess had met him in passing at a few of Trenton's family events. Seth or Shep. Something like that.

"Now, don't worry, ladies," Trenton told them, holding up hands that seemed the size of baseball mitts. "I'm not here to interrupt your sacred wedding planning time. Chad and Sev and I brought our golf clubs, so we're good. You won't even know we're here."

Jess glanced at the third man. Sev, that was it. Jess remembered now. Sev Hardcastle had the same athletic good looks as his . . . cousin maybe? But he lacked the cruel glint to the deep-set brown eyes, the smirking quirk to the thin lips. Jess's neck didn't immediately clench up in Sev's presence, so she considered that a positive sign.

Also, Jess was going to let Poppy be the one to break it to Trenton that the closest golf course was about an hour's drive away . . . and that none of the villas had TVs. But Poppy wasn't making eye contact, she was staring into space, probably imagining the number of guest-death-on-the-property-related chores she had to do.

"Jessie, Trenton says we all went to school together. I don't really remember you, but I probably should," Chad said, winking at her while he looked her up and down. He wasn't even subtle about it, like she should just expect it. Because Jess and her boobs were present in his eyeline. Also, was he trying to neg her with a lack of nostalgia? Jess shivered.

"But I'm looking forward to us getting"—he paused to grin at her—"reacquainted. Trenton told me they've got all kinds of hot tubs here."

Jess smiled without showing any teeth. She would *so* rather be imagining death-related chores at that moment. When Jess didn't add anything more, Chad turned to Trenton. "I'm not into foot rubs and facials and shit. Maybe we can find a place to rent ATVs or something."

Jess could see the conflict playing out on Trenton's face. Trenton

Tillard the Fourth desperately, *desperately* wanted to be the kind of guy who could just tear ass across a mountain trail on an ATV with his buddies. He wanted to be the guy who would skydive or bungee jump or even roller skate without a helmet. But Trenton's dad had never really invested that sort of time with him, preferring the company of his own college buddies and, well, various cocktail waitresses. Between an emotionally detached father and a mom who spent most of her time at Junior League meetings, Trenton turned out to be more of an "intense gaming sessions while the housekeeper brought him snacks" type of guy. Golfing was as physical as he got. He didn't enjoy being muddy or sweaty or covered in fish guts—all the traditional markers of Southern masculinity.

Fortunately, Diana was savvy enough to know Trenton would *never* voice that in front of Chad. Instead, she curved herself around Trenton's side and twined her fingers through his. "Oh, if you're here, I just won't *stand* for you going off and doing all that. I want you right here with me, where I can see you all the time," she purred into his ear. "Maybe we can find a hot tub for two."

Ooof. That was almost as well played as Trenton's anti-social-media maneuver. Maybe Diana and Trenton *were* equally matched.

Trenton beamed at her. "You heard the lady, Chad. She needs me right there with her."

"Whatever. We're gonna *kill* some balls on that back nine," Chad grumbled, throwing his golf bag into the cart's second row.

"Well, we're so pleased to have you!" Aubrey cooed, finally finding her spot in the conversation. She moved forward to shake Trenton's hand, only to have Trenton pull her into a bear hug. Aubrey didn't appear to enjoy it, which made Jess's day just a little bit better.

"All right, all right, I'm gonna need a beer before I'm decent company," Chad groused.

Jess wondered if he would be decent company after a whole six-pack.

Poppy seemed to snap out of the trance she was in. She huffed out a long breath, shoving the sleeves of her goldenrod-colored sweater up her long pale arms. "Oh, we don't serve alcohol here."

Chad suddenly straightened in his seat. "Wait, *what?*"

"Ladies, if you'd join us, I'll drive you down to the villa and get the newcomers settled," Poppy was saying.

"What do you mean there's no alcohol!" Chad demanded as the women climbed into their seats—everybody but Jess.

"Oh, uh, I don't think there's enough room," Trenton said, frowning at the golf cart.

"Oh, well, Jessie can walk down," Aubrey said. "You did say you liked to walk around the property, right? You're sturdy."

"Why. Is. There. No. Alcohol?" Chad ground out.

Poppy shot a glance at Jess, but Jess waved her off. Poppy then launched into her "booze, hot tubs, and heights" safety explanation, which seemed more poignant now, considering the Jeremy of it all.

"Oh, well, I don't feel right about that," Trenton protested over Poppy's speech. "I'll walk down with you."

"Don't be silly, Trenton," Aubrey said. "We can't have our host walking down a mountain!"

"Come on, man, just get on the cart, she'll be fine," Chad said with a groan. "We were in that car for an hour and I gotta take a piss!"

Sev pinched the bridge of his nose in a gesture that felt very familiar to Jess.

"I don't mind," Jess assured Trenton.

"That's right, Jess doesn't mind walking," Diana said, now fully transitioned into the mincing, sugar-sweet version of herself that seemed to emerge when Trenton was around. "In fact, Trenton, honey, you should walk Jess down. You know she gets a little clumsy."

Jess knew this wasn't a gesture of trust toward her. Giving Trenton and Jess time together meant they could talk about the impending proposal. Aubrey tried to speak up, "But—"

Poppy hit the gas pedal and the cart took off as Chad yelled, "You can't be serious!"

Jess assumed that someone had just told him about the lack of golf.

Trenton gave her his best sheepish smile. "Hey, Jess."

"Trenton." She took a deep breath. Even after all these years, it was still difficult to take this man seriously. How did he work for a major international corporation while looking like an overgrown teddy bear? Unfortunately, this also made it very difficult to be mad at him. "We weren't expecting you."

"I know!" he said, grinning and bumping her lightly with his shoulder. "That was the whole point."

"But how are you gonna meet us at the airport, ready to escort Diana to her dream proposal and surprise engagement party, when you're already here?" she asked him. "I don't want to be rude, but I think we both know that if you're not present at the botanical gardens to greet your family, they're going to claim there was some sort of misunderstanding about the date and slink off before we can get there."

He blinked at her as if he hadn't thought of that, and then frowned because he realized she was right. "Mama did say that she thought maybe she had theater tickets for that night."

If the extended Tillards thought they could get out of even the appearance of welcoming Diana into the family, they would cling to any excuse. Jess pressed her lips together and prayed for patience. He'd tossed all her botanical garden plans aside without a thought.

"Do you think you could arrange a new proposal up here?" he asked, his mood brightening suddenly. "It could be something quick, so we can just enjoy the rest of our week together. I know we set up the whole garden party thing, but I just don't think I want to spend another day *not* engaged to Diana."

Jess frowned at the almost frantic tone in Trenton's voice. Was he trying to rush things because he was afraid his family would try to stop him or because he was afraid Diana would say no? Or both? What had his parents said to him since Diana had departed for Chickenhawk Valley? There had to be more at work than his mother's bullshit explanation about *maybe* having theater tickets.

"It won't be the spectacle Diana's expecting," Jess reminded him. "And, as you mentioned, I will have to undo all the work I did to set up the party. You will lose deposits."

"Yeah, well, I was having trouble getting people from my side to RSVP to the party on such short notice in the first place. Diana would hate a barely attended party worse than having no party at all," he said, frowning. "Besides, she'd probably like this better any-way. *No one else* has ever posted a proposal story from this place. I asked her, and trust me, Diana would know."

Jess knew he was right. Diana would *love* to have the first proposal documented at the Golden Ash, particularly if it would help her ignore the Tillards' mass avoidance of her party. Jess could arrange for the proposal here, but it would be more difficult to keep it a secret from Diana. Jess would have to forgo any enjoyment of the amenities and make a lot of contact with the outside world, but ultimately, Trenton was the client and this was what he wanted.

Jess would just have to do a lot of sweet-talking to make it happen.

Or begging. She was going to have to do some begging.

"Do you have the ring with you?" she asked.

"Oh, yeah, I keep it in my pocket, just in case." He beamed at her, pulling the box out of his jacket. The man was walking around with a four-carat diamond in his pocket like it was loose change.

It was the first time Jess had seen the engagement ring in person and she knew that Diana was going to *love* it.

"It's not the Tillard family ring," Trenton said, his tone sheepish. "Mama didn't think it would suit Diana. She said that five generations of Tillards wearing it was probably enough and we should give Diana a fresh start."

Jess's eyebrows winged up. She knew a matriarchal rejection when she heard one. Bitsie's refusal of a bridesmaid role was one thing, but this was truly a dark portent of marital felicity. Diana had zero chance of ever *truly* being accepted by the Tillards, even if she married Trenton. She would spend her whole life as an accessory, posed at the edge of formal portraits, never really folded into the family. Jess wondered how deeply Diana would mourn that loss.

But . . . the ring in Trenton's hand was a perfect emerald-cut solitaire flanked by two smaller rectangular stones on a band studded with tiny round diamonds. It certainly fit the wedding's "branding language." It was lavish. It was romantic. It was definitely genuine.

"It's perfect." Jess patted his arm, and his smile grew even larger.

"I'm glad you think so," Trenton said. "You probably know Diana better than anybody."

Jess stared at him, wondering if Trenton had confused her with someone else. She knew what she could cull from Diana's social media. That didn't exactly equal emotional intimacy.

"I'm just going to need to talk to the Osbournes to set it up," she told Trenton. "And this is going to increase my fee, because you have effectively undone and then doubled my work on short notice."

This didn't faze Trenton in the slightest. "I'm sure it won't take any time at all to cancel all the botanical garden party plans."

Spoken like the guy who wasn't going to have to make all those phone calls.

Jess sighed. "Right."

"Oh, I knew you could do it, Jessie!" he exclaimed, hugging her tight.

"I haven't done anything yet," she reminded him after he released her. They began their descent down the hill, while a rapidly growing to-do list spooled through Jess's head.

"I know, I'm just so glad that you're here with DeeDee. Having one of her best school friends around at a time like this? It's just a huge weight off her shoulders," Trenton told her. "And to think you're pulling double duty as our proposal planner *and* her bridesmaid. That's just so sweet of you."

OK, this was getting weird.

"Oh, but I'm not a—" Jess started.

"It's going to be perfect," he gushed. "And Diana is just so thrilled to have one of her closest friends involved in her 'wedding journey.' I mean, I know you and I didn't spend a lot of time together back at Harrow, but I'm glad you two have stayed close over the years. And now we'll have the chance to get to know each other better."

Jess opened her mouth to respond. While Chad had said almost the same thing, it sounded infinitely more sincere and less creepy coming from Trenton. But she had to wonder what *exactly* Diana had told him about their "friendship." Did Trenton not realize that Jess and Diana hadn't spoken in years? What kind of narrative was Jess walking into here?

With Trenton's payment in mind, Jess chose the better part of getting paid and shut the fuck up.

"She's just so nervous about fitting in with my family," Trenton told her. "And that's fair, I guess. They're not super thrilled about her whole Instagram thing or her family. Especially her family. But she's just so . . . Diana, you know? You can't just ignore her. She'll win them over eventually."

Jess wasn't exactly a gambling expert, but she didn't like Diana's odds.

Trudging along the path gave Jess a chance to survey the grounds. The first rule of proposal planning was thinking about what the client wanted, not what you wanted. And Diana's priority was photos. Everywhere you looked here, there were solid locations for photos. Jess could arrange for them to have some sort of candlelit picnic down by the trees. She could create a luxury camping site out here—no, Diana wouldn't like that. Jess could try a light installation, using the thermal suite as a backdrop. No . . . she kept going back to the trees. That was the best asset at the Golden Ash, the forest.

Right, right. Diana wouldn't want to sit on the ground, but Jess could get a table arranged over on a flat area between their villas, surrounded by trees. She could ask Dean to make a special small menu just for them. Jess could beg and wheedle and bribe Andrew into flying up here to take just the right photos.

"I can do it," she told him. "But it's going to cost you."

"Oh, absolutely," he said, nodding quickly. "Do whatever it takes."

Wait.

"Do me a favor? Don't tell Aubrey about this," Jess asked.

Trenton frowned. "Why not?"

"Well, I'm not going to be around much, trying to set this up for you two, and Aubrey needs to be focused on wedding details, which will also distract Diana from my absence," she lied. Aubrey had proven she was willing to take over something Jess considered important, simply to prove she could do it better. That would be the ultimate work-related checkmate for that weirdo.

"Aw, that's a good point," he said, nodding. "You're such a thoughtful friend, Jess."

"Mm-hmm," Jess hummed, smiling sweetly. "So, you brought Chad?"

"Well, he's gonna be my best man," he said. "This is sort of our pre-engagement party, right? And you can't have a pre-engagement party without your best man. You know, I was thinking that you two would be good together. You could help him straighten out, calm him down a little."

Jess snorted. She would rather hook up with a rattlesnake . . . with chronic halitosis.

"Oh, I think you should probably talk to Aubrey about that," she said as they approached Tranquility. The golf cart was still parked out front. From a distance, she could see Aubrey and Diana standing on the porch, deep in discussion. Where was Poppy? Was she inside getting yelled at by Chad about the alcohol thing?

Jess tried to pick up the pace down the hill, but Trenton slowed to an all-out stop. He appeared to be watching Sev carrying their bags the considerable distance to the next villa, Serenity. He frowned. "Aw, I was kind of hoping Chad would help him with the bags. I don't want Sev to feel like he's working this week."

"Beg pardon?"

Trenton lowered his voice, like the squirrels nearby were eavesdropping. "Well, you know Sev works in the general counsel's office for my family's company."

Jess had no inkling of Sev's profession but nodded anyway. "Sure."

"His dad is friends with my granddad, which is how he got the interview. And Chad . . . well, Chad hates the fact that his own dad doesn't have that kind of pull with Tillard Pecans. My family holds Chad at arm's length because Granddad thinks Chad's whole branch of the Hardcastle family are a bunch of idiots. He's OK with us hanging out, but he doesn't want any one of them near our business." Trenton paused for what she assumed was an impersonation of his blustering grandfather. "'Wouldn't even let those dipshits water the orchards.'"

He grinned at Jess as if he expected applause. Meanwhile, she marveled at the extensive tangled mess of generational grudges and old-dude entitlement.

"But doesn't the 'whole branch' of the family cover Sev, too?"

"Not in my granddad's mind. You know, because Sev is technically Chad's uncle," Trenton said, pressing his lips together.

"But they're the same age."

"Sev's dad, Chadwick Upton Hardcastle the Fourth, is damn near ninety, married five times. He's also Chad's *granddad*. Married the nanny he hired for the children from his fourth marriage." Trenton paused to wave toward Sev. "Sev's mom was that nanny. I think Chad's dad, the Fifth, is from the second marriage. Anyway, Sev is about two months younger than Chad—who is Chadwick Upton Hardcastle the Sixth. And because Sev's mom is just a little bit petty and never liked Chad's parents, she decided Chad shouldn't be the *only* one to carry on the name for his generation. So Sev is Chadwick Upton Hardcastle the *Seventh*. And to keep things easier, he just goes by Seven. Sev for short. Sort of an inside joke."

Jess shuddered. "I think I'm gonna need a chart to keep up."

"Southern families," he said, shrugging. "Anyway, Sev kind of insisted on coming with us, last minute. He was in Savannah on business and flew here to meet us. I didn't even think about it. But Sev's a nice guy and I thought great, maybe this would be a chance for them to, I don't know, bond or something. I mean, weddings bring people together, right?"

In Jess's experience, weddings made people lash out over a venue's inability to magically create more tables and fight over whether shrimp cocktail could be considered a vegan option. But that wasn't what Jess's client needed to hear.

While they'd explored the complexity of Sev's family tree, their party's conversation groups had shifted. Diana and Chad were having a quiet conversation while Chad sucked down a tiny airplane bottle of vodka. To Jess's surprise, Poppy wasn't giving him the "you know your own body" speech. She hovered at the end of the porch, watching the group warily. When Poppy saw her, Jess could *see* the attempt to slide her customer service mask into place, like a ripple of cheerful, porcelain-perfect control settling over Poppy's face. But then her features sagged in exhaustion, giving up the fight. Poppy was simply too tired to continue the effort. Diana caught sight of Jess and Trenton, and a welcoming smile burst over her face.

"What do you think of this place, honey?" she cried, stretching her hands out toward Trenton. She gripped his hands and pulled them tight against her chest before giving him a loud smooch. "Isn't it beautiful?

"It's real nice," he agreed.

"I might as well go check out our minibar. I don't care what the lady said, there has to be more booze somewhere around here. My supply won't last me all week," Chad insisted, glaring at Poppy. He slumped off toward the other villa, tapping the last few drops from his mini-bottle into his mouth.

"Why don't I show you to your rooms?" Diana asked, all lovey-dovey chirrups. "You're too good to me, TrentyBear, really."

"You two go on," Jess told them. "I need to chat with Poppy for a second."

Trenton winked at Jess as Diana pulled him toward the men's villa. Kiki was apparently somewhere inside their own rooms. But where had Aubrey gone?

"Are you OK with these people?" Poppy asked her. "The energy of the group seems off."

"It's fine. Diana just wasn't expecting Trenton to make himself part of all this," Jess said, waving her hand at the general splendor. "But I'm going to need to talk to you about the combined group's stay and how Trenton just changed it."

"Yeah, well, I'm not thrilled with some of his add-ons," Poppy muttered. "Come by my office when you can, Jess. I'm an early riser, and mornings are best. We'll talk soon, OK?"

With that, Poppy practically scurried to her golf cart. Jess sighed, staring over the spa's landscape, trying to recall the peaceful feeling she'd had when she'd arrived. The view was still charming, but her week had gotten a lot more complicated. And well, there was the dead-guy pall hanging over everything.

Jess chose to savor these precious private minutes to herself. She wished she could be any one of the other guests in those little glowing bungalows. She wished she could move over to the Osbournes' side of the grounds, where there were people who liked her. She turned toward the door and noted the lights on inside the Serenity Villa. Through the window, she could see that Sev and Chad were arguing. Well, Sev was arguing. Chad was sitting on the couch, looking bored and chugging more tiny booze bottles.

Classy.

Jess turned to find Diana walking up the villa's steps. "Any idea why Trenton keeps talking about what 'close friends' we are?"

Diana scoffed as they moved inside their living area.

"Well, when he botched his own proposal, I told Trenton we

should call you. I may have made it sound like setting up a proposal for me was something you would *love* to do, as a dear old friend from school and someone who wants to see me happy. Otherwise, it would just look weird that I immediately thought to call some girl I haven't seen in years."

"I don't think you have an accurate gauge for what's weird," Jess noted, following her into the villa.

Diana frowned at her as she dropped gracefully onto the sofa. "Well, I haven't *ignored* the word-of-mouth about your little company. And I've seen the photos your clients have posted of your work. I *want* that for myself. Honestly, I didn't know you were the Bricker in Bricker Consultants until Lally Shoemaker told me. I'd kind of forgotten you existed."

"Well, the world makes a little more sense now," Jess told her. "So do you frequently fabricate relationships from thin air to impress your boyfriend?"

Diana plucked at the fringe of a soft coral throw over the couch's arm. It felt like an attempt to prevent making eye contact. "Look, I *implied* to Trenton that we've kept contact over the years . . . And that we were close when we were kids . . . and that's why I was able to get ahold of you so quickly when he messed up his proposal. Honestly, I didn't expect your grandmother's number to still be listed. Who even has a landline anymore? Anyway, it doesn't hurt for Trenton to think that I'm friends with a girl like you."

"What does *that* mean?"

"You know, a *nice* girl," Diana huffed. "Someone who's *grounded* and *real* and works hard—even though Trenton spends most of his work time on the golf course, 'developing contacts.' He barely remembered you from college, but when he looked into your background—after I insisted we should hire you—he was just *so* impressed with what you've done with your life, especially when you consider that you're 'self-made.' He says you have *substance*. He's never said that about any of my other fri— well, the girls I've introduced him to. I don't have that many people I would call 'friends.' Besides, isn't part of your job to put me in the best light possible, even with my own fiancé?"

Jess considered that and . . . yes, that was probably part of her job.

Diana heaved a put-upon sigh. "It's just so on-brand for him to come running up the mountain like a big, adorable, goofy cartoon bear, crashing into everything. I suppose he wants you to set up a proposal here?"

When Jess's brows arched, Diana responded with an eye roll. "I know a panic response from Trenton when I see it. I didn't expect him to travel here, but if he's going to make the effort to do that, he's going to want to seal the deal before we leave. I guess his parents are still giving him grief about me?"

"He didn't say exactly," Jess said, trying to be kind.

"That Penelope Tillard is such a—" Diana stopped herself before she said something unforgivable and sighed. "Of course it's them. They don't want him rushing into another 'mistake.' Trenton *only* rushes toward things, that's just how he is. It's sort of endearing, that enthusiasm. And Penelope will have to get over the fact that he doesn't want to marry one of her friends' daughters. He wants *me*."

Jess shook her head. "OK, I have to ask, why risk the second proposal? You had him and then you sort of spiked him like an unwanted volleyball."

"First, because the proposal was terrible. Not photogenic. Not memorable. Not personalized at all. Second, Trenton isn't used to being told no, and he is intrigued by chasing what he thinks he can't have. I'm getting him to double down." Diana shrugged. "He's way less likely to go back on the proposal if he's done it *twice*—he's invested. And if he does it in a big, showy, public way—like me posting our proposal story from such a high-profile location—there's no way his parents will make him break the engagement, as distasteful as they may find it. He'll be tied to me, and his parents will have to shut up about it.

"I'm playing the long game here, Jess. How do you think I was able to hold out this long to get married? *Patience.* You *don't know* what it's like," Diana said, seething. "There's a difference between growing up working for *more* and growing up twisting yourself inside out to try to get back what you *used to have.* You don't know what it's like to have family that sees you as an *investment* instead of a person. They never stop calling or texting or dropping by to remind me of what I owe every single one of them for making my life so *easy*—like my life is easy. They never *stop*, and I can't think or move or breathe without being reminded of how to do it better, sweeter, prettier. And I can't get away from them, because then, who would I be? Just a pretty girl, alone in a world full of pretty girls. Getting engaged to Trenton will make it easier for me to breathe—to build my *brand.* And when my numbers get big enough, I can launch a cosmetics line, perfume, hair extensions, home furnishings. It will give me a chance to make something of my own."

Jess had never expected to feel sorry for Diana. Jess's mom had been, well, awful, but at least she knew her grandparents loved her. Who did Diana have? Kiki seemed to be one of the nicer Helstons, but even she was only there for Diana to avoid criticism from their family. Jess wasn't sure if Trenton loved Diana or if he was just fascinated by her, as he seemed to be fascinated by many shiny objects. But securing long-term happiness for Diana wasn't Jess's job. She could only try to secure her own.

And seriously, where was Aubrey? This was the sort of emotionally vulnerable moment she'd probably been hoping for—to trauma bond them and secure Diana's loyalty. As it was, Jess felt like she was listening to a supervillain monologue. Calming a supervillain couldn't possibly be *her* job.

"OK, so there's no reason to be upset," Jess replied. "I'll arrange a beautiful, memorable, *personalized* proposal right here at the spa. We'll get you two engaged—with lots of photos and tasteful public exposure. Trenton will pay my fee. But after that, I will not be wearing any sort of bridesmaid's dress. I don't care what color it is."

Diana looked confused for a moment. "Oh, right, I told Trenton you were going to be one of my bridesmaids."

"He mentioned it," Jess replied, sounding very tired, even to her own ears.

"Well, I still want Trenton's cousin Bitsie to be my maid of honor. I think that would help me cement those connections with Trenton's family, you know? But like I said, she hasn't gotten back to me."

"I do appreciate that, Diana, but that's not how any of this works," Jess said.

"Oh, don't fuss, it's only temporary until Trenton finally pins his cousins down, but honestly, two bridesmaids and a maid of honor is a nice conservative bridal party. I'll probably ask Aubrey to fill in as well. She's ambitious enough to say yes. Of course, if Trenton's cousins fall through and you have to walk down the aisle, we might have to do something about your hair."

Diana was talking in a stream-of-consciousness rant, staring off into space. Jess wouldn't have been able to make eye contact while shoveling that bullshit, either. She was starting to see why Diana didn't have any friends.

"Yeah, I'm not agreeing to that. Not even temporarily," Jess told her.

"You don't want to be part of my wedding?" Diana asked, sounding oddly insulted.

"Decidedly not. It's a super weird blurring of professional boundaries. It's possible I blurred those boundaries myself, agreeing to this 'work retreat' in such a remote location. But I'm here now, and I'll deliver the best proposal I can for you. And, with respect, once Trenton's payment clears, that's where our relationship will end—personal, professional, or otherwise."

"Well, for now, I think you should play nice and keep Trenton thinking that we're dear old friends," Diana replied, her lips curving upward, which was downright unnerving. "Otherwise, I might have to ask him to cancel your contract, maybe even get him to demand the deposit back. I would hate to do that, since that would hurt our relationship. Especially since I'm not asking that much, Jess, really. So, I think it's in your best interests to keep me happy."

There it was. The threat. Go along with this incredibly weird charade or Jess wouldn't get paid. Her dreams of buying the bakery building would be smoke in the wind. Hell, Diana might use Aubrey to spread rumors about her incompetence in her target demographic. She'd be a laughingstock with no apartment and no office. She would have to start over from almost nothing.

Again.

Any semblance of sympathy Jess might have felt for Diana disintegrated. Jess slid right back into a wary desire for distance.

"I will deliver the best proposal possible, Diana, and that's where the relationship ends," Jess told her again.

Diana shrugged and walked toward the bridal suite. "We'll see."

"What does that mean?" Jess called after her. Diana ignored her and shut the bedroom door. Jess stared after her. How was it so difficult to set boundaries with these people? Was it a money thing or an "attractive people with confidence" thing? Either way, Jess seemed to be really bad at it.

She whispered to herself, "What the hell does that *mean?*"

CHAPTER 9

Even with the unsettling presence of Chad Hardcastle next door, Jess slept like a rock, only getting up to go to the bathroom once. Jess could swear she saw lights bobbing in the woods again, like overgrown fireflies, but it was probably the stress getting to her.

She woke before the rest of her party and set off for Poppy's office. As she climbed the hill, a flash of red caught her attention in the distance, close to the trees, near a sign that read "Private—Staff Only." It was Sev, walking out of the woods like he was strolling out of a boardroom. He was wearing workout gear that looked like it had never seen the inside of a gym. There were folding creases in the basketball shorts, for goodness' sake. Was he secretly searching for a phone signal?

Absently, Jess wondered if Aubrey would have the nerve to chastise Sev for underdressing. Jess doubted it. A lot.

It didn't surprise her to see the lights on in Poppy's office long before normal working hours. The lodge's entrance was unlocked, but Poppy's office door was closed. She could hear muffled voices on the other side. They sounded strained and upset.

Jess was pretty sure she heard Dean say, "Don't we have the right to refuse service to assholes? The Hardcastles definitely count as—" only for Poppy to cut him off with something like, "This isn't a damn gas station, Dean! We're a five-star resort! I have enough on my plate right now without you—"

Jess took a step back. She hadn't heard Poppy speak to even Sheriff Blister in that tone, and it was clear how much Blister annoyed her. Another voice, male, was calmer, in professional mode as he said something like, "The best thing to do is just act like they're any other guests. Let them finish out their party's stay and send them home happy and healthy."

Dean replied, "I don't like it. You know how he was around Emma Lee, how he was around all of you. He's a—" But then the sound of the staff dragging tables and chairs into place for breakfast interfered with Jess hearing the rest until Poppy said, "Over stupid kid stuff— creepy, stupid kid stuff, but kid stuff all the same. And we're not kids now, Dean. We have a lot more to lose."

Which of the Hardcastles had prompted this response from Dean? It had to be Chad. She could see him being creepy as a kid. He was certainly creepy as an adult, almost exclusively.

"Fine," Dean grumbled. "But he's not getting any of the special flourishes. No molecular gastronomy or alginate sphere garnishes or any of that shit. I won't even cook anything with Tillard's damn pecans. I will have Jamie make a special trip to the store just to buy another brand."

"Your perfectionist nature will not allow you to do a half-assed job," Poppy said.

"OK, but I'm only going to do a whole-ass job. He will not get additional ass," Dean told her. And that was the moment he opened the office door to find Jess standing there. His eyes went wide.

Unable to think of any other response, Jess told him, "I am not expecting additional ass."

Behind Dean, Poppy cackled. A tall, barrel-chested man with a thick, dark beard stood at Poppy's side, grinning at Jess.

"OK, fine, in terms of embarrassing things said out loud, you win this round," Dean admitted.

Jess pinched her lips together to keep from laughing, but a giggle burst out. He shook his head and joined her in it.

"You're all right?" he asked.

"I'm fine," she told him. "And don't worry about, um, the Hard-castles. I've dealt with *so* many creeps through work. Drunk, handsy, asshole groomsmen. Drunk, handsy, asshole uncles of the bride. Drunk, handsy, asshole uncles of the groom. I can handle myself."

"Some people are their own brand of drunk, handsy asshole," Dean told her, his fingers wrapping around her wrist. "Please be careful."

"I'll be fine," she promised. A pained expression crossed his face, one of loss and regret, making Jess turn her hand to grasp his. He just squeezed it and walked away.

Jess was left staring after him.

Walking into the office, Jess felt like she was seeing behind the Wizard of Oz's curtain. This was Poppy at her least glamorous—a red Chickenhawk Valley High sweatshirt, hair pulled back in a po-nytail, no makeup. She was sitting behind her desk, slurping a face-sized coffee as if her life depended on it—and maybe it did. Jess couldn't imagine that Poppy had gotten a lot of sleep the night before.

"I really don't think that amount of caffeine is a good idea all at once," the bearded man told her. "Just in terms of your cardiac health."

Poppy's full unlacquered lips pursed as she swallowed one last gulp of coffee. "Baby, I love you. I respect your opinion as my spouse and as a medical professional. But if you try to separate me from my precious, life-giving coffee, I will lock all the streaming services on ToddlerToonTV and walk away. You don't know how to change the settings back."

The man's responding frown was visible, even through the beard.

"OK, I wouldn't, but I would think about it real hard," Poppy muttered, sipping more coffee. Poppy waved Jess into her office. "Is everything all right at your villa, Jess? In terms of, well, everything?"

As she moved closer, Jess noted that there were several legal-type papers on the desk, including a document labeled FARM SHIELD INSURANCE—UMBRELLA LIABILITY POLICY across the top. Poppy moved them into a file folder and looked up, giving her an awkward smile.

"This is my husband, Owen," Poppy said. "He worries."

"Almost professionally," Owen told Jess, shaking her hand.

"Is it time for the planning calls to begin?" Poppy asked cheerfully. Clearly, the coffee was kicking in. "Would you like coffee or tea?"

"Tea, please. And yeah, we'll definitely need to talk about the planning."

There was a casual intimacy here, letting Jess into the secret behind-the-scenes club. She'd established herself as one of them, people like the Osbournes who kept things running, while the Dianas and Trentons of the world carelessly chased the next new fascination. Honestly, Kiki aside, Jess was a lot more comfortable on this side of the curtain.

Jess took a sip of the fragrant tea Poppy had poured for her, lavender and mint with the slight honey-sweetness of chamomile. "But first, is there any news about Mr. Treadaway?"

To her surprise, Owen gave Poppy a meaningful glance. Poppy nodded. "Jess found the body. She's invested."

"For now, the police are still trying to determine whether Mr. Treadaway's death was accidental or something else, but honestly, something here isn't right," Owen told her. "I'm calling every contact I have in the law enforcement community to try to get the state to move on this with some urgency. With all due respect to Marty and Blister, this is a bit beyond them."

"Owen, like Beth, is a beloved transplant from the outside world," Poppy said, grinning up at her husband, her eyes all googly and warm. "He used to be a medical examiner in Chattanooga."

"I came to the valley for a fishing getaway." Owen bent down and kissed his wife's forehead. "Poppy convinced me to take an open position at the clinic, and I just never left.

"Anyway, I made contact with the medical examiner handling the case, got a look at the preliminary reports, the photos," Owen said. "There are some things that don't make sense."

"Isn't it sort of a conflict of interest? Letting you look at the autopsy results when you're married to Poppy?"

Owen nodded. "It is, which is why I wasn't allowed to touch anything. I could only use my connections to push it up the chain for further testing."

"Isn't it in your best interest, as a family, to keep this quiet?" Jess asked.

"We want to make sure the investigation is handled correctly and resolved quickly, no matter the results," Owen said. "Otherwise, it can drag out for years with the case closing, reopening, new leads, et cetera. Rumors start, news media starts making suppositions. So-cial media campaigns start. Netflix documentaries get made. It's better to be proactive and deliberate."

Jess raised her hand, as if she were attending an extremely un-comfortable science class. "Is it OK to ask what about the case doesn't seem right?"

Owen gave Poppy another pointed look. Poppy nodded again. Owen sighed. "I'd really rather not say more than that until we know something official."

Poppy rolled her eyes, but Jess understood. This was an actual criminal matter, and she was basically a stranger. Even though Jess desperately wanted to know what was happening, she understood not trusting her with more.

"I'm off to work." Owen slid into his jacket and kissed Poppy again. "Let's just say I prefer treating small-town living-people problems more than big-city dead-people problems. Nice to meet you, Jess."

"Owen is overcautious," Poppy said as Owen quietly closed the door behind him. "He knows how much it bothers me, the idea that someone came onto my property and hurt someone under my pro-tection. He's actually trying to rule out something suspicious, not find it."

"I hope there's nothing to find," Jess said. "I hope Jeremy Tread-away was just a tragically clumsy creep."

"You said you needed to talk to me about Trenton and how his 'surprise' affects your group?" Poppy asked.

"I had a proposal arranged for when we arrived back home, but Trenton has decided he wants me to plan a new one on your grounds, on the fly. It's impulsive and kind of ridiculous, but so is Trenton. Instead of gleaning the little details that make a proposal special by observing Diana, I'm going to be scrambling to put something together at the last minute. So basically, I need your permission to do that. Because I don't want to alienate the few reasonable people on this mountain."

Jess splayed her hands out in front of her. "I'm saying all this in the hopes that you will take my personal and professional distress into account when Diana asks to bring a professional photographer onto the grounds, post her engagement content to social media, whilst tagging the Golden Ash. I know that you guys have concerns with client privacy and exclusivity, but I think that if you post a small number of *highly curated* images from within the spa, it will drive even more interest from potential guests."

"Eh, don't worry about it." Poppy waved her concerns off. "To a certain extent, the phone policy is about relaxation and safety, but really, we ask people not to post on social media from the Golden Ash because we want them focused on their experience. I care way more that those jerks don't really deserve the work you're going to put into making something special for them."

"Thank you." Jess sighed. "I'm just sorry about all the trouble on top of all the Treadaway stuff. Trenton must have had you scrambling, making all those last-minute villa reservations."

"Not really; he booked the Serenity Villa weeks ago," Poppy said, chewing her lip. "He showed up a day earlier than I expected, and with guests he didn't have listed on his contract, but these things happen."

Jess's mouth fell open. "What?"

"He booked both villas at the same time," Poppy said carefully. "I thought you knew."

For a few seconds, Jess could only pinch her lips together as she forced air through her nose.

Rage.

Did that mean that Trenton was never going to use the proposal he was paying her to plan? He was always going to come up here and disrupt the very thing he supposedly wanted Jess to spend a *week* away from her office to do. And she was just expected to go along and clean up his mess while he plied her with his weaponized helplessness and aw-shucks-who-me-I'm-just-an-adorable-human-sized-puppy bullshit—and she was going to run behind him with a mop because his money was standing between her and losing the home that she'd made for herself.

"He—he . . . Selfish, inconsiderate, intentionally clueless mother-*fucker*!" Jess yelled, just as Jonquil walked into the room.

"Well, good morning to you, too, sweetheart," Jonquil snorted. "Y'all doing OK?"

"No, no, I am not." Jess set her tea aside, put her head down, breathed deeply. When she looked up, Poppy was pouring clear liquid from a jar marked "Chickenhawk Valley Moonshine Distill-ery" into Jess's teacup. "It's eight in the morning."

"Trust me," Poppy told her.

"I'm sorry." Jess sighed. "You've got so much other stuff to deal with—"

Poppy finished topping off Jess's tea. "No, no, this is really a pleasant distraction."

Jess paused to sip from her cup. She gasped as she swallowed what tasted like lightning-infused gasoline. "Poison."

"It's not for everybody." Jonquil passed her a glass bottle of spring water, which she used to wash the moonshine taste from her mouth. Jess's entire body shuddered.

"I thought you didn't serve alcohol here at the Golden Ash," Jess wheezed.

"Well, exceptions for every rule. And you're not exactly a guest,"

Poppy said. "And in response to Trenton's fuckery, I'm going to have Jonquil upsell their whole party on the most expensive spa treatments we have. The stuff with ground moonstone and saffron in it. And fourteen-carat-gold flake. And I'm adding a ten percent service fee to his total bill, out of principle. I'll put it in the staff Christmas bonus fund, but still. It will hit his wallet."

Jess laughed. "Thank you."

"Just let me review any social media posts before you click 'Send,'" Poppy said, as if she hadn't just done Jess a huge favor. "What can we do to make this easier for you?"

"Build a time machine and go back to convince me not to take this job?" Jess suggested.

"Why don't you come to family dinner tonight? All the key players will be there in one place, except Dean, of course," Jonquil said. "He's got dinner service here. Even if you don't accomplish much planning-wise, I get the feeling you could use the break from your roommates."

"Is that allowed?" Jess asked.

"Just treat it like a fight club. Don't talk about it," Poppy replied. "Beth is going to make her famous meatballs. That alone is worth the price of admission, which is that you'll have to listen to my family try to wheedle the recipe out of Beth, without success."

"The super chef can't figure the secret recipe out for himself?" Jess asked.

Poppy shrugged. "Dean probably could, but he considers that to be bad sportsmanship."

"I will agree to the meatballs, but what I need is continued access to a reliable phone line and a computer, because I'm going to need to contact a bunch of contractors and vendors as soon as possible."

"Would you mind if I worked with you on that? I'd kind of like to know who you're asking onto spa property," Poppy said. "And I know all the locals anyway."

"Yeah, that seems reasonable given . . . everything." Jess nodded. "Does the fourteen-carat-gold flake really do anything for the skin?"

Jonquil shook her head. "Not really. Makes people feel fancy."

"Sell the hell out of it to Trenton," Jess told her, standing up.

Chuckling, Poppy paused and said, "And I'm sure the on-call spa florist would be more than willing to help you with whatever you need to make Diana's vision all floral and fancy. She does all the flowers for the villas, so we know she's dependable. And she's real discreet."

Jess's brow furrowed.

"Beth," Poppy added. "The florist is Beth."

"I thought Beth was your general counsel and spa concoction mixer," Jess said.

"She is. She and Jonquil met a few years ago on some forum for botanical nuts. She was completely burned out practicing corporate law in Hackensack. Jonquil invited her here, and Beth found a life she liked much better. Dabbling in almost everything she loves without being bogged down by the stuff she doesn't." Poppy beamed at her. "Now, go enjoy a nutritious breakfast, and come back to use my phone for your business dealings. I should be dressed like a professional business lady by then."

Jess took one last sip of her tea and let loose a rasping wheeze. "Gah! I forgot about the moonshine."

Still trying to rid her mouth of moonshine taste, Jess walked out of Poppy's office and almost ran *into* Mrs. Treadaway. The newly minted widow was clad in a long flowing caftan in aqua and cobalt linen over what appeared to be a wet swimsuit. Jess wondered how she was tolerating that in the mountain's autumn chill.

But Susan seemed to be in a pretty breezy mood for someone who, by rights, should be planning a funeral. On seeing Jess, she hitched her sunglasses into her dark hair and offered Jess a brief smile. "Oh, good, I've called three times to ask for a brow-threading technician to be sent to my villa, but I've been told that isn't a service you offer here." She sniffed. "That can't possibly be correct, can it?"

"Oh, I'm sorry. I don't work here," Jess replied.

Susan blinked at her as if she didn't understand that there might be people at the Golden Ash who were not present for the specific purpose of doing her bidding. "But I've seen you walking in and out of the manager's office all week."

"Yes, but I'm not an employee. I have no authority to book any sort of treatment for you."

"But I've seen you talking to the owner," Susan said.

"Ma'am, I'm sorry, I don't—"

"I just need my brows threaded," Susan insisted, her voice growing louder by the syllable. "This isn't the level of service I've come to expect, considering the loss I've suffered at this facility!"

Jess stared at her. Was this one of those situations where someone going through a crisis fixated on some tiny detail so they didn't have to process their misery and anxiety? Jess knew a little something about that, personally and professionally. But that didn't seem to be what was happening with Susan Treadaway. Her eyes were clear and dry. She'd taken the time to apply lip liner that morning. She smelled like Jonquil's orange-cinnamon mud concoction.

Suddenly, Poppy appeared in the doorway to her office. "Mrs. Treadaway, can I help you?"

"This rude girl refuses to schedule my treatment!" Susan exclaimed, pointing an accusatory finger at Jess. Poppy's brows raised. Jess shrugged.

"Well, let me see if I can take care of that for you," Poppy said, ushering Susan into her office.

Jess mouthed the word "Sorry."

Jess stood staring as Poppy closed the door. Unless she was planning on showing her grief through perfectly groomed funeral eyebrows, Susan didn't appear to be mourning her husband that hard. Between that and Jeremy's apparent need for validation from every woman he saw, Jess was struck with the distinctly uncomfortable sensation of feeling a little sorry for Jeremy Treadaway.

As most of the guests were having breakfast in their villas, the main dining room had been reconfigured so their larger-than-average group table was positioned central to the huge back window. The table was spread with the same sort of fruit-and-healthy-options array from the day before. But clearly, a benefit of Trenton's arrival was that Aubrey wasn't about to tell the Pecan Prince that he couldn't have carbs. Their menu had expanded to include multiple sauces, bacon, and *fried chicken*—which Jess planned to *drown* in hollandaise sauce on principle. Like the well-raised young man he was, Sev stood and pulled out Jess's chair for her. Unfortunately, he chose the chair between himself and Chad . . . which meant she had to sit next to Chad. Sev slid into his own seat as she began her enthusiastic and unnecessary saucing. He muttered, "Well, this is going to be interesting."

She looked up at him and quirked her lips twice in quick succession, making him laugh. She noted that he patted his pockets as he sat again, probably looking for the cell phone that wasn't there.

Chad didn't look all that pleased by the arrangement, but it didn't stop him from putting his hand on the back of Jess's chair, no matter how many times Jess pressed back against his fingers to pinch him out of the gesture.

"Oh, come on, *Jessie*, don't be a drag," Chad said on a sigh, making a sad puppy face at her. It was not nearly as effective as Trenton's. Jess wondered if Aubrey had told him to call her that. It was definitely an Aubrey move. Chad reeked of barely processed booze and hangover sweat, and it was all Jess could do not to visibly recoil. "Trenton told me you're all mine this week. You should take advantage, live a little. We could have a lot of fun, you and me."

Chad seemed to think a casual hookup with him would bring some meaning to Jess's life.

Yikes.

"No," she told him, keeping a pleasant if distant expression on her face while she dragged bacon through the hollandaise. "No, thank you."

"Boring." Chad huffed out an annoyed breath and moved his hand when she gave his thumb one last press of her shoulder blade. "So, are we really supposed to just sit round, stare at plants, and think about the oneness of the universe and shit?"

"It's not a bad thing to relax a little bit," Trenton told him, shrugging amiably.

"That's the problem with this place—there's nothing to do except for this one great rock-climbing spot, not even two miles away from here," Chad told him. "We could go there right now, blow off some steam."

Trenton glanced toward the entrance, as if he could summon his fiancée by the power of will. There was no way Trenton would climb a rock wall unless there was a bear underneath him. "Oh, I'd hate to leave DeeDee all alone."

"Come on, man. You promised me a good time." Chad sighed, sliding his hand back across Jess's chair. Trenton ignored him and focused on his plate. Chad grumbled to himself, "I'm going to have to make my own good time."

Jess heard a commotion by the door and saw Diana strutting toward them, with Aubrey in her wake. Kiki was nowhere to be seen. Diana's hair billowed behind her like she was starring in her own personalized shampoo commercial. Trenton was mesmerized, the bacon practically falling out of his mouth as Diana approached.

Chad's hand snaked up Jess's shoulder and squeezed tight. With everyone else at the table distracted, she reached up with her fork and poked it into his hand. *Hard*. Chad hissed and snatched his hand away, causing her to drop the fork.

Diana slid into the chair next to Trenton, where there was, in fact, a green juice waiting for her. She kissed Trenton's cheek because, well, half-chewed bacon. "Morning."

"Morning, DeeDee. How'd you sleep?" Trenton asked.

"Well, it was pretty hard drifting off without my honey bunny," Diana cooed. Aubrey sat across from Jess, frowning at the amount of hollandaise on her plate.

Just then, Dean stepped out of the kitchen with a huge platter of pastries. There was a sort of hesitation in his step when he saw their party. His eyes seemed particularly focused on Chad's proximity to Jess. His lip curled back.

"Chad, Sev, Poppy mentioned you were staying with us this week. It's interesting to see you again," Dean said in an icily polite tone.

Sev, however, was all warmth and sincerity. "Dean! Good to see you. I hardly recognized the place."

Jess glanced back and forth between Dean and Sev. How did Dean know the Hardcastles? The Hardcastles hailed from Virginia before they'd moved to Nashville a few generations back, looking to diversify their newspaper empire into radio stations, retail development, and restaurants. How did they have any connection to middle-of-nowhere Tennessee? This wasn't even Pigeon Forge. It was Chickenhawk Valley.

But dropping her fork gave her the excuse of not using it after she'd poked it into Chad's hand, so she was counting it as a win. A server, bearing a name tag that read "Tracy," seemed to appear out of nowhere and replaced it. Jess whispered, "Thank you."

Dean looked at Jess with a concerned brow but said nothing as he disappeared into the kitchen.

"I didn't realize you knew anyone around here," Diana said, her fingers entwined with Trenton's. How was he still managing to shovel food into his mouth with one hand?

Sev smiled blithely. "The family has a little retreat, up the mountain a little bit. We used to spend summers hanging out with the Osbournes."

Jess had seen a magazine pictorial of the Hardcastles' "little retreat" in Bimini. There were twelve bedrooms and a separate residence for the staff. She hadn't noticed a palatial mansion on the way into town, but she had been distracted by Aubrey's "maneuverings."

"Would have thought they'd have added a golf course by now," Chad grumbled. "Cheap-ass place."

"Well, since you're sticking close to us, we have Pilates after breakfast," Diana said, clapping her hands like a cruise director. "Trenton, I'll help you find something you can move around in."

Trenton rubbed at the back of his neck. "Oh, I don't know, DeeDee, maybe I'll just join you later."

For the next half hour, Jess discreetly shoved breakfast into her face while Trenton continued to attempt Pilates evasion, encouraged by Chad's cries of "stretching isn't a *sport*."

"Oh, Chad, don't be a sourpuss," Diana told him, pouting prettily. "Join us for Pilates, pleeeeease? For me?"

Chad stared at her for a long moment and finally grumbled, "Fine."

Something sour solidified in Jess's belly.

Chad's complaints about the "lack of amenities" at the Golden Ash—no booze, no extreme sports, no TV—continued until the group finished breakfast and Diana practically herded Trenton and Chad out of the dining room. Sev shrugged and followed them at an amiable pace.

"Diana is in rare form this morning," Jess observed after they'd gone.

"I think Kiki's conserving her strength," Aubrey told her. "Said she wanted to hang back and pumice her heels instead of coming to breakfast."

Jess thought maybe Kiki just wanted some time to herself so she could get some peace and quiet. Jess wished they'd stretched out the meal a little longer for her.

"What did Diana say?"

"That Kiki should do her elbows, too," Aubrey said, shrugging.

"Charming," Jess sighed.

"I'm hoping that this week doesn't convince Kiki to back out of the bridal party because you and I are going to look sort of silly walking up that aisle without a Helston cousin to, you know, anchor things," Aubrey said. "Of course, best-case scenario, Trenton manages to persuade his cousins to take our spots and we don't have to worry about it."

"And this seems normal to you?"

"Oh, no, not at all, but I've never told a client that I refuse to accommodate them, so I'm going to figure it out," Aubrey replied, pushing up from the table. "Which is why I'll probably be maid of honor."

Jess called after Aubrey: "That's not something to brag about!"

Jess looked up at Tracy, who had been silently observing these conversations with an impressively passive expression. "I'm surrounded by insane people."

"I'm not allowed to have an opinion on these things," Tracy said, even while she nodded.

"Thank you, I feel validated."

CHAPTER 10

J ess was starting to get the feeling she was just the latest in a long line of people responsible for untangling Trenton's messes.

Poppy made Jess comfortable at the little table, where she was treated to a comfy armchair and a cordless phone with plenty of signal. She dialed Mavis's number with relatively little difficulty and was pleased that her assistant picked up on the second ring.

Instead of greeting her, Jess said, "You know when you forced me to memorize yours and Nana Blanche's numbers to the tune of that 'Jenny' song? And I said it was silly, but you asked me 'What are you gonna do if you lose your precious phone and you have to call me?'"

On the other end of the line, Jess heard a deep exhalation, as if Mavis had been holding her breath since they last spoke. "Well, you were right. This is your official phone call to notify you that you did, indeed, tell me so. Your 'I told you so' trophy is in the mail."

"Honey, we both know there's no trophy for 'I told you so.' There's a ceremonial 'I told you so' dance. With jazz hands. I'm so glad it's you," Mavis sighed. "When I saw the spa come up on caller ID, I assumed the worst."

Relief at hearing the voice of someone who loved her warmed Jess's chest. "Mavis, I'm at a spa. It's not exactly hazardous duty."

It was for the best, Jess told herself, not to mention the dead body. The "I told you so" trophy would only increase in size. Jess's trophy budget was limited. Also, Mavis would worry. She might even call Nana Blanche home from her trip.

"With those girls? I have my doubts," Mavis countered. "The more I hear about this Helston family, the more they come across as a low-rent country-club crime family."

"That's not nice," Jess chided her while wondering if she'd made the right decision, calling before checking with Poppy whether outgoing calls were recorded. "You're not wrong, but . . . not nice, either."

"'Nice' is for bad dates and Christmas sweaters from elderly aunts," Mavis retorted. "How's it going? You feeling relaxed yet?"

Jess took too long to find an answer. From the other end of the line, Mavis sighed. "Uh-oh."

That was the thing about Mavis, she was quietly supportive . . . until she felt Jess was being a dumbass, and then she pointed it out to her in full Technicolor detail. Sometimes there were PowerPoint slides involved, showing bullet points explaining her dumbass-ery. Sometimes she had research to back up her bullet points. Sometimes the slides had special sound effects when Mavis highlighted the bullet points.

Mavis showed considerably more technical skills than the average not-quite-retiree.

"It's a long story, one that begins with me starting a whole new proposal for Trenton here at the spa and will probably end with me wearing a bridesmaid's dress." Jess sighed. Poppy's head swiveled toward her, expression awash in confusion before she stood and walked to a table in the corner, where she turned on an electric kettle.

Jess outlined her preliminary thoughts on Trenton's Proposal, version 2.0, while Mavis made notes. While she had Mavis on the phone, Jess asked for updates on several other clients whose plans were still in the initial stages. (A moonlit gourmet picnic with a backup rain plan. A scavenger hunt. A private blacksmithing lesson to forge the happy couple's wedding rings post-proposal.) The guilt that Jess felt leaving Mavis to handle her work ran deep, but Mavis assured her that she had everything under control.

"Now, let's go back to the bridesmaid thing. Don't think I'm going to let you distract me from that," Mavis insisted. "I don't know what Diana Helston is trying to talk you into, but it's not worth it. We don't need fancy downstairs office money that bad."

"'Fancy downstairs money' sounds like it's for something else entirely," Jess said and snorted. Poppy burst out laughing, covering her mouth with her hands.

"This is not a reasonable expectation," Mavis said, ignoring her. "This is not—you don't have to stay. I looked up flights to Nashville for every day this week! I can book you home in five minutes."

Jess closed her eyes. "I can't do that, and you know why. It's not just the office. I don't want to lose my apartment, either."

"We can figure something else out," Mavis swore.

"Not fast enough," Jess reminded her.

"At least tell me this is some long con where you just keep adding extra hot-stone massages to your tab until you bankrupt Tillard Pecans."

"That would be a Mavis move." Jess snickered while Mavis crowed in the affirmative.

"Call me when you can!" Mavis commanded. "If nothing else, I want to know you're OK. And the gossip. I want the gossip. I am not proud."

"You're a terrible influence," she told her.

"But a fantastic assistant!" was Mavis's final shot before Jess hung up.

The rest of Jess's day was very productive. She and Mavis worked in tandem to cancel the botanical garden party. Deposits were lost all over Nashville. The butterfly provider, in particular, was disappointed. Andrew could not come up in time to take Diana's engagement photos, but Poppy helped Jess find a very nice local photographer who would know how to handle the lighting and terrain. Dean agreed to create the menu, and Beth was more than happy to arrange an extensive (also, expensive) floralscape to surround the "rustic sweethearts' table." She happened to have plenty of flowers in Cameo Coral from setting up their villa. Hell, Poppy even helped Jess find someone who could build them a tiny wooden platform, so Trenton wouldn't have to kneel in the grass. And Diana's expensive shoes wouldn't have to touch actual nature. All in all, she'd set up a pretty nice proposal in less than eight hours, and in two days, Diana would be engaged and Jess wouldn't have to worry about this bullshit anymore.

Jess's Big Book of Life Plans: Finish proposal, celebrate with copious amounts of forbidden alcohol. Close self in apartment for a week. Speak to no one.

Jess supposed she shouldn't resent Trenton's thoughtlessness too much. Without his fickle decision-making skills, she might not have had the opportunity to spend so much time with the Osbournes. Kiki aside, they were certainly the preferable group.

Sev seemed Kiki-level reasonable, but Jess hadn't made up her mind about him yet. So, she approached him slowly when she found him hunched over a bench near the meditation path, going over some papers in a manila folder.

"Hi, Sev. Fresh from a facial?" Jess asked.

"Sadly, no." Sev chuckled, shutting the folder and gesturing to his face. "I thought you'd be able to tell from my lack of an exfoliated glow."

"It's a compliment, really, when you think about it," she said, provoking a rather glorious grin from him. And unlike when Chad smiled, Jess was filled with a warm sense of, if not affection, at least regard.

"I spent the day at the family place, Hardcastle Pines. It's on the other side of the bluff there." Sev pointed to a ridge in the distance. "I wanted to make sure everything was all buttoned up. We have caretakers, of course, who live on the property, but there's nothing like seeing to the job yourself."

Clearly, Chad had never received that particular Hardcastle lesson.

"It's so weird that y'all grew up around here," Jess said.

"Eh, I wouldn't go that far," Sev told her. "We spent some *summers* here. Chad did more socializing than I did because I was usually cooped up in the house, doing extra summer coursework or working with a tutor. *Hardcastles don't just survive, son. Hardcastles surpass.*"

"Wow, that sounds . . . intense."

"Well, they don't call us Softcastles," Sev replied.

She wrinkled her nose. "That was terrible."

He grinned. "I got to spend some time with the Osbournes and their friends. It's just that we weren't that close, you know? We would see them at their beer bashes, July Fourth fireworks, the Flannel

Days Festival, that sort of thing." When Jess frowned at him, Sev added, "Flannel Days—It's sort of like Founder's Day in most towns. It's the first Saturday in September and the official end of summer around here. Craft booths. Cakewalks. Moonshine tasting. The whole town dresses up in red flannel underwear with the button-up flaps in the back. They used to make them at a factory down the mountain. It was the first industry in the town. It's a whole thing."

"I am familiar with the concept of a Founder's Day Festival," she huffed, shivering at the memory of grain alcohol burning her throat. "Without the moonshine."

"We all fell out of touch over the years, when my half siblings started insisting on their own vacation spots," Sev said. "But I was happy to hear the Osbournes were doing so well with this place."

Sev sounded like he meant it, and she liked him just a little better for it.

As they negotiated the steps down to the next level, Jess's foot slipped on a loose stone and Sev grabbed her arm to steady her. While it did restore her faith in chivalry, it also meant that Sev's papers spilled out onto the gravel.

"Sorry!" she exclaimed, stooping to pick up the paperwork. The letterhead was marked with the Tillard Pecans logo. The first sheet looked like a fax cover sheet with the subject line **Last Round of Adjustments** and the second had **PRENUPTIAL AGREEMENT** written in bold letters across the top. Diana's and Trenton's names were all over the text in all caps.

"What's this?" she asked as they stood. She handed him the papers, and she appreciated that despite being considerably taller than her, he wasn't looming. And she'd just grabbed at his legal papers, so that was another check in the "good" column, as far as Jess was concerned.

"Sev, is that a prenup in your folder?" she asked, finally processing what she had seen.

He chuckled awkwardly. "Maybe I'm just happy to see you."

She glared up at him. "No, Sev. Please be better than that joke."

"Yeah, sorry, that was bad," he conceded. "Please, Jess, I can't answer any questions about what you just saw. Attorney-client privilege and all that."

"OK, I'll try a different angle," she said. "Sev, are you here to prevent Trenton and Diana's engagement? Because that is really going to mess with my week."

Briefly, Jess wondered if she should warn Diana and ask Beth to intervene on her behalf—arrange a sort of lawyer versus lawyer battle on the mountain. Like the legends of old.

Probably not. That wouldn't be very nice to Beth, to give her a client like Diana.

He held up his large hands, as if in surrender. "Look, I can't say— The family is . . . I wouldn't describe them as 'happy' about the engagement, but when they saw that Trenton was joining Diana at such a picturesque location with Aubrey, a professional wedding planner, in tow . . ."

"They think this is an elopement," she guessed, nodding. "And they wanted you to have the prenup papers on hand, just in case."

His face lit up. "You understand."

"Trenton can be very easily led," she agreed. "Will-o'-the-wisp bait."

Sev stared at her. "What?"

"Uh, apparently, in these parts, there are ghost lights that lure travelers off safe paths. I've been seeing them all week. Anyway, I think Trenton would be particularly easy to lure."

"Truer words," he said, and sighed. "It's nothing personal. But

Trenton's first marriage ended after eleven months. After the pictures with the . . . dancers surfaced on social media. Because Chad thought it would be funny to post them. An ironclad prenup protected Trenton and the family's interests."

Jess's shoulders sagged a bit in relief. "OK, but just so you know, Diana wouldn't be happy with a quaint little justice-of-the-peace thing up here in the middle of nowhere. She wants a full bridal coronation. Her family demands it."

"That's part of the problem, her family," he grumbled.

"I can't help you there. Just be warned, 'No prenup to our disadvantage' is practically carved under the Helston family crest," Jess told him. "You're up for a fight."

"Well, the company's entire legal department had a hand in drafting this, so good luck to her," Sev replied. "Honestly, I don't usually handle this sort of thing. I like the minutia of business law. But my dad, he wants me to help protect his friend's kid. I don't want to let the Tillards down."

They walked over the last rise before their villas and stopped in their tracks. Diana was standing on the grass between the two villas, talking to Chad . . . and it didn't look like a particularly friendly conversation. Chad had his hands clenched around her upper arms while she was pulling away from him, a derisive scowl on her face. Diana was shaking her head, occasionally glancing over her shoulder, as if to check for anyone who might be nearby, listening. Chad's jaw was tense, his head bent low, and it looked like whatever he was saying, it wasn't *Gee, Diana, I sure am glad you're marrying my best buddy in the world. I look forward to years of Friendsgiving celebrations and weekend barbecues.*

Was Chad trying to talk Diana out of marrying Trenton? Jess could see him demanding that Diana back off, if he thought he wouldn't have Trenton to rely on for "bro time" anymore. Worse, Diana might stop letting Trenton pay for things for Chad, who seemed to enjoy a free ride despite having his own money. Maybe Chad was just trying to establish the pecking order of "people who benefit from Trenton's cheerful obliviousness." Chad clearly expected to remain at the front of the line.

With one last hissed reply, Diana shrugged him off and tried to walk away. Chad had size and strength on his side and dragged her back, but Diana did exactly what years of watching reality television had trained her to do—she reared her right hand back and delivered a loud stinging slap to Chad's cheek.

Reality Housewife Chanterelle would have been proud.

Sev's mouth dropped open in shock. Diana stomped off to her villa and slammed the door.

Jess asked, "Any idea what that's about?"

Sev shook his head. "Not a clue."

Jess asked, "Do Chad and Diana usually get along?"

"I wasn't aware that they talked," Sev said. "I thought they just sort of orbited around Trenton while he tries to orchestrate awkward conversations at parties."

"Are you going to do anything about Diana assaulting your nephew?"

"Buy her a fruit basket?" Sev suggested. When Jess laughed, he added, "I have also dreamed of one day smacking Chad's stupid face."

Sev grinned at her. While that was lovely to look at, Jess caught sight of Susan Treadaway's caftan (red and orange this time) blowing in the breeze, and her brain leaped at the chance for a distraction. Susan was walking over the hill from the treatment suite, but to Jess's surprise, the woman veered toward the meditation hollow. She ducked under the yellow caution tape stretched across the entrance to the path, which the Osbournes had tried to dress up with a sign stating: **THIS SPA FEATURE IS CLOSED. PLEASE SEE THE FRONT OFFICE FOR ALTERNATE SERVICES.**

"Would you excuse me?" she asked Sev.

"Sure, see you at dinner."

Jess turned and followed Susan toward the hollow. She would think Susan would want to avoid the scene of her husband's death . . . unless she was trying to find something? Something that Jeremy had dropped, besides the fork? Or was she looking for something that *she* dropped when she shoved Jeremy into the pool? Wasn't there something that killers had about returning to the scene of the crime?

The police had left caution tape across the cave. Susan was standing in front of the tape, peering down into the water. Jess listened for the sound of crying and heard nothing but the splashing of the water. Susan's shoulders were stone-still.

Maybe she shouldn't have followed someone she suspected was capable of murder into this isolated location? Jess turned to leave but—

"Can I help you?" Susan called.

Well, no turning back now.

Careful to stay on the path and not set foot on the slippery gravel, Jess moved toward her. She had no idea what to say—*Hi, just wanted to check in to see if you're a murderer?*

Susan filled the silence with, "I know I'm not supposed to be down here. And I also know that I owe you an apology. It's been made clear to me that no matter how tragic my circumstances, it's unacceptable to speak like that to anyone here at the Golden Ash, staff or not. Ms. Osbourne is right. I was terribly rude to you. I've been rude to everyone I've spoken to since I got here, and I can't even blame Jeremy for my misery anymore. I think I'm just so accustomed to it that I don't know any other way to be."

"My condolences," Jess replied, sounding uncertain.

"I hear the question mark in your voice and it's entirely appropriate. He wasn't always . . . that way." Susan sighed. "When we got married, I was the wild one, if you can believe that. I was the one who wanted to try new things, vacation in places without a *Forbes Travel* rating, stay out salsa dancing until two. Jeremy was the calming influence, the sensible one. I resented him, I think, for pushing me to grow up, to take my job at my family's company. And it got worse when things didn't turn out so well for him at the bank. He is—he *was* an assistant regional manager of a branch, and that's as high as he was ever going to rise. His brothers took money from their father's life insurance settlement and invested it in some start-up app to help people find the right glasses for their facial shape. They asked Jeremy if he wanted in, and of course sensible, cautious Jeremy said no. But it took off and his brothers got rich. Not as well-off as my family, but very comfortable.

"It turns out that the boys had a knack for finding unlikely-but-somehow-successful investments. But after Jeremy had turned them down the first time, they never offered to bring him in again. I think that was as much fun for them as any luxury item they bought, rubbing the fact that Jeremy hadn't believed in them right in his face."

Jess stood absolutely still, because if she moved, Susan might stop talking. She had the weirdest feeling that she was about to hear a murder confession. Was she about to have some sort of *Jinx* moment? Should she call somebody? Surely Blister was more qualified to handle this sort of thing. Well, maybe not Blister, but *somebody*.

"Jeremy became obsessed with the idea that he could be just as successful as his brothers. He threw his money into any idea that he thought might take off. We turned forty and he got more frustrated—it was like my husband was replaced by an entirely different person. He decided his best chance at 'hitting it big' was this innovative restaurant concept. Because the only thing his brothers couldn't make work was a high-end steakhouse. But even with that, they made a profit off selling the location. So, Jeremy's big idea was a restaurant ... in a decommissioned lighthouse in middle-of-nowhere Maine, with no parking. No matter what I said about what an absolutely *stupid* idea this was, he insisted he was going to make it work. He said he just needed investors and the right team. He started dressing flashier, using obnoxious hipster lingo, insisting on going to expensive restaurants to 'scout talent.' And worse, he flirted with women right in front of me. He'd never been that guy, the guy that needed so much validation."

Susan's eyes welled up with tears. "My promotion only made things worse. I understand that it's not fair, that nepotism exists, but what was I supposed to do? *Not* take over my family's company, just because it made Jeremy unhappy? When he announced this trip, I thought that it was an attempt at a fresh start, you know? I've been asking for this sort of trip for *years*, to help us reconnect, to focus on each other. But he's been—was, he *was* being so awful. From the minute we got here, he was hitting on every woman he saw and trying to ingratiate himself with poor Dean Osbourne, who was just trying to do his job. He had to throw Jeremy out of the kitchen on our first night here. Chef Osbourne was too polite to do it physically, but the 'fuck off out of my kitchen' was obvious to everyone. Except Jeremy."

Susan dropped to a seated position on one of the meditation boulders. Jess gingerly sat down next to her.

"When I realized he'd only brought me up here to try to recruit Dean for his 'project,' I think I actually felt something in my chest break. It was so desperate and hopeless and deranged. And it was *so* humiliating that he dragged me along for it. He didn't care about our marriage anymore. He didn't care about me. He only cared about this dream that was going to suck the life out of him. He didn't even want the restaurant, really. He was just obsessed with not being less than his brothers. He didn't even know that much about food! He ordered red wine with fish. He expected the tagliatelle ai funghi to come with *clams*. He ordered his steaks well done, and he was always confused as to why they were so tough." Susan sniffled, even as she smiled. "And he covered them in ketchup."

Jess awkwardly patted Susan's shoulder, unsure of what to say.

"It makes sense that he died down here, in such a stupid, preventable accident. Such a waste." She sighed. "A wasted marriage. A wasted life."

The tears were flowing freely now, and in them, Jess saw the years of hurt. The scream Jess heard that night outside Harmony Villa was Susan mourning the marriage she thought she had. Jess imagined that Susan knew then it was over. Even if Jeremy had lived, the marriage was dead. And Susan had loved him, even if he was a bit of an ass.

"So, you think that Jeremy's death was an accident?" Jess asked carefully.

"Of course I do." Susan sniffed. "If I didn't kill him, no one else could have."

"Well, that logic is airtight," Jess mused. She realized she was still patting Susan's shoulder and withdrew her hand.

It was not Jess's job to tell Susan that the authorities were investigating Jeremy's death as something else. So instead, she asked, "Any idea *why* he might have come down here?"

"Honestly, no," Susan admitted. "He didn't want to come to the meditation classes. He thought they sounded 'stupid' and 'pointless.'"

Jess pursed her lips, wondering if this was a smart question to put to Susan, finally asking, "Could he have been meeting someone?"

Susan shook her head. "I don't know. I really don't want to think about it. But I don't think that any of the ladies on staff had been receptive to his attentions. He probably came down here because he wanted to be away from me, which, I admit, isn't entirely unreasonable. Being an awful bitch has really been the only way I've gotten a response from him in years. It's almost second nature at this point."

The space between them was filled with the sound of splashing water and rustling trees. After a long moment, Susan dabbed at her eyes, careful not to smudge her makeup. "This isn't how I wanted my marriage to turn out. This isn't the life I wanted. I don't want to go home and face my empty house. I don't want to plan a funeral for his awful family, knowing how they helped drive him over the edge. I just want to stay here."

"OK," Jess replied, patting her on the shoulder again. "We can just sit here for a while, picking apart the lighthouse restaurant idea."

Susan sniffled. "All right."

"Would the tables at the lighthouse restaurant go at the top?" Jess asked. Susan nodded. "Wouldn't the food get cold by the time the waitstaff got it up there?"

"Yes!" Susan cried. "Which was why he wanted to focus on a menu of 'fragrant salads.' There were almost two hundred steps from the bottom to the top of the lighthouse, where the seating area would be. And there was only room for four tables! Jeremy said scarcity would drive reservations."

"That is the stupidest idea for a restaurant I've ever heard," Jess said, nodding.

"I know!" Susan wiped at her eyes, careful not to smudge her makeup. "The decor was going to be Tuscan inspired."

"What? Why?!" Jess gasped. "It was a *lighthouse*. The theme was *right there*!"

Susan Treadaway seemed to feel a little better by the time they'd left the meditation hollow. She'd rambled for at least another twenty minutes about the stupidity of Jeremy's restaurant plans. The ridiculous sixteen-page menu, which intentionally omitted desserts for health-conscious patrons. The plan to take out the internal workings of the lighthouse lamp and replace it with a rotating sushi bar. The fact that there was no room for bathroom facilities . . . or a kitchen. It was a veritable buffet of bad ideas.

While venting her troubles seemed to ease Susan's mind, Jess was more confused than ever. She realized she wasn't exactly an expert on these matters, but the grief on Susan's face seemed so genuine. Jess just didn't think that Susan had it in her to kill Jeremy.

Susan thought Jeremy's death was an accident. But Owen didn't . . . so, where did that leave them?

Jess looked up when she heard goats bleating in the distance, which only added to the pastoral coziness of the Osbournes' "model village." If the spa campus was the Shire, the Osbournes' compound was Brigadoon, a row of neat little homes practically hidden away in the hills where no one could see. Jess thought if she changed positions, viewing the little valley from the wrong angle would make it disappear. She respected the Osbournes for using the mountain's natural topography to their advantage when laying out the facilities.

Each house had a plaque on the front that reminded newcomers which branch of the Osbournes lived where—Poppy's plaque denoted that she lived with Owen in the largest farmhouse-style house with the big wraparound porch. Sis lived alone in a tidy cottage with white carved wooden goats placed in herdlike groupings around the porch. By comparison, Dean's cabin looked like he'd ordered it off a farm catalogue's shed section.

Jonquil and Beth's porch was overflowing with planters full of blooms in every color, surrounding huge picture windows. Nana Blanche's home training had Jess chafing at the idea of showing up at their door without a hostess gift, but what was she supposed to bring them?

Before she could even knock, Beth opened the door and greeted her with a long hug. "Hi! I hear you've had a long day."

As expected, the interior of Jonquil and Beth's home was a greenhouse that happened to have a few white walls. Every available surface had a potted plant on it, their vines trailing along shelves and spindles to form their own sort of decorative borders around the room. The few nonorganic items were framed photos from Beth and Jonquil's wedding—just as outdoorsy and floral focused as Jess had secretly pictured it—and the Osbournes in happier times. Or at least, times when there had been more Osbournes at Chickenhawk Valley. And there appeared to be entire shelves filled with scrapbooks—so *many* scrapbooks.

Wow. For someone Jess had once suspected of being a drug dealer, Beth kept a really cheerful home.

Jess waved awkwardly to Sis as she slid onto a barstool, industrial metal painted a cheerful emerald. Sis was puttering around the spring-green kitchen, while Jonquil was clearly in charge of assembling the final touches of the meal. Sis slid a glass of deep red wine across the counter with a wink. "Don't tell your roommates."

Jess noted a cell phone on the counter. The wallpaper was a picture of Jonquil and Beth, grinning at the camera with their faces pressed together at the temple. Multiple notifications were popping up on that screen. Apparently, Jess's confusion showed on her face.

"It's a mountain, not the moon. We have a private Wi-Fi network here for family devices," Jonquil told her, holding out a small chunk of crusty country bread soaked in barbecue sauce. Jess popped the bread into her mouth and closed her eyes to revel in the sweet-tangy-smoky taste. She thanked the universe for the healing power of carbs.

Beth told her, "The network shows up as 'Sauna Temperature Controls.'"

"I thought there was no Wi-Fi at the Golden Ash," Jess replied around a mouthful of saucy-bread.

"This isn't the Golden Ash," Sis told her, making a wide gesture with a wooden spoon. "This is Osbourne family property. Streaming TV can exist on the Osbourne family property. In fact, it must, to fuel my awful reality show fix."

"Ah," Jess said, nodding and sipping her wine. It was a rich burgundy, earthy and heavy on the berry notes.

"More often than not, an emergency at Owen's practice keeps him in town. Poppy's at her office wrapping up some last-minute things. She'll be along any minute," Jonquil said as Beth spooned thick barbecue sauce over meatballs in an oversized trencher-shaped ceramic casserole dish with "The Meatballs" hand-painted in green letters on its side.

It occurred to Jess that Poppy had chosen someone who had the same instinct to help, to serve, that she had. As someone with those same tendencies, Jess recognized her own. Jess wondered how much that wore on them as a couple, whether the rest of the family was able to balance that out, to help them recharge the batteries that would inevitably run down.

"So, I have a question," Jess said, sipping her wine.

"I'm sorry, Jess. We don't have any more information about the Treadaway thing. Blister is still looking into it," Beth told her. And even though that wasn't the question that Jess was going to press, it did hurt a little bit to have it preemptively blocked.

"Oh, no—I mean, yes, I would like to know as much about Mr. Treadaway's death as you'll tell me, but I figured you weren't going to tell me anything yet," Jess assured them. "I get it. It's family."

Sis shot her a surprised but grateful smile.

"My question was, how did you go from scary goat farm to a luxury spot in the middle of Appalachia?" Jess asked, making Sis laugh.

"Trust me, it was not what I expected when I first landed at the Chickenhawk Valley airport," Beth assured her. "The town gives a . . . different vibe."

"Our family, with the exception of my mom, was . . . indulgent, I guess, is the right way to put it," Sis said. "Trying to make sure that we enjoyed life at the hotel. They gave us room to explore our interests, which is why they were so open to offering spa treatments after Jonquil went through her super-hippie phase."

"I'm sort of sorry I didn't get to see that," Jess told her.

"Me, too," Beth agreed, only to have Jonquil smack her with a dish towel.

"Everything that *could* be treated with arnica *was* treated with arnica," Sis said, shuddering. "*So much* arnica."

Jonquil rolled her eyes. "Our parents have retired to Florida or moved closer to town because as a group we agreed that living that close and working together was just a little too much togetherness. And I think after we changed over to the spa format, they felt a little . . . lost? They were used to having ownership of the business, but they didn't know how to run a spa, and there was still this parental urge to correct what we were doing, even though they didn't understand it, and it got a little tense there for a bit. You know how it is with parents—they never see you as a grown-up, not even when you're fifty."

Sis muttered something under her breath that Jess didn't catch. Her own smile was forced. Jess didn't know any such thing about parents, but she wasn't about to bring that up. Her mother would never see her as an adult because she probably wouldn't recognize her in a lineup. It was one of the reasons that Jess largely avoided social media. She didn't want Hadley tracking her down.

Poppy bustled into the cabin. "I know, I know, I'm late. I'm sorry. Owen sends his love, but unnamed twins in town have chicken pox. Twice the itching, twice the dangerously high fevers."

"Well, that stinks," Sis replied, hugging Poppy to her side.

"Welcome, Jess," Poppy said, accepting wine from her cousin.

Jess waved awkwardly from her seat on the barstool, chin balanced on the palm of her hand. She was used to quiet, orderly family gatherings with Nana Blanche. This was chaos—loud and bright and hectic. It was interesting watching each member of the family slide into their spot, serving their purpose within the group without even asking. The Osbournes belonged here, with one another, and they knew it. Jess wondered what it would be like growing up like that.

"Thank you for including me in Meatball Night Fight Club," Jess told her, making Poppy snicker. She turned to Beth. "I get that you won't give me the meatball recipe, but can you tell me what's in the mud that smells like cinnamon and oranges?"

"I'd sooner tell you what's in Nonna's meatballs," Beth told her as Jonquil shooed everybody toward the dinner table. "But I'm not going to do that, either. To be fair, most of the herbal recipes are Jonquil's. I'm just mixing it together to save her time, but only because I enjoy the quiet irony of the one person in the bunch without a flower name stirring up the botanical compounds."

"And she's really good at it," Poppy noted.

Jess nodded. "I guess you and Dean and Owen, kind of even things out, in terms of name averageness."

"Isn't your full name 'Jessamine'?" Jonquil asked, smirking at her. "A flower name, by the way. Sort of jasmine-y and sweet-smelling."

"Oh, right, I kind of forgot about that." Jess waggled her head. "Jessamine was such an old lady name that I swore off it in elementary school."

"Aw, you fit right in with the other blossoms. That's nice," Beth said, grinning at her. "Besides, Dean does have a flower name. Technically."

Jess gasped, clapping her hands together and hopping up and down. "Is it Chrysanthemum? Please tell me it's Chrysanthemum and he refused to go by Chrys. Please please *pleasepleasepleaseplease*!"

"I don't know if we should be telling her this," Poppy said, her chin retreating toward her chest. "There's an unholy gleam in her eyes right now."

"My brother's name is Hemlock," Sis told her.

"OK, that's meaner than Narcissus," Jess cried. "That's an actual poison."

"Our mom is an interesting person, and we don't talk to her much," Sis said dryly. "There's a reason for that."

"And what was he supposed to do?" Jess asked. "Go by Hemlock at school? Did she call him Lock?"

"Our. Mom. Is. An. Interesting. Person," Sis said again, emphasizing each word.

"I identify very heavily with that. Change of subject: I've heard things about these meatballs," Jess said, as Sis heaped six of them onto toasted garlic bread on Jess's plate.

Beth waggled her fingers like a stage magician. "I put them in the smoker and slow cook them until they're so tender and tasty that they're practically meat marshmallows, and then I put them in a homemade barbecue sauce using a recipe that I got from a college roommate raised in Memphis—the very heart of good barbecue—which I will also not share with you."

"Or me. I would like to point out that she will not share the meatball recipe with me," Jonquil noted. "Despite the fact that we're married and she knows all my herbal treatment recipes."

"A girl has to maintain some mystery about her," Beth replied. "Nonna would support that, even if she is deeply upset at the idea of her meatballs in barbecue sauce."

"She handwrote a letter detailing her disappointment with the barbecue sauce treatment," Jonquil mused, dishing up her own plate. "The whole family threatened to disown us."

"I always thought it would be the lesbian thing that set them off, but really, it's the barbecue sauce that got me nearly excommunicated," Beth said. She shrugged and added, "Anyway, Jonquil's told me all about your wedding group! Those girls you're with sound *awful.*"

"Yeah, I don't think we have the time or energy to deal with that can of worms tonight," Jess said with a sigh, shutting herself up by shoving food in her mouth. Her fork paused midway back to her plate. She needed a minute to just *be* with this food experience. This was a symphony in her mouth. Bright, tangy sauce on soft, yielding savory-and-smoky meat. It shouldn't have gone with the taste of a sophisticated burgundy, but it did. After swallowing, she reached across the table and squeezed Beth's hands. "I know you're taken, but can I marry these meatballs?"

The rest of the women cackled.

"I mean, Dean's food is good, but this is . . ." Jess paused to eat another bite. "You can't tell him I said that."

"He accepts that I surpass him in this one area," Beth said. "He's pretty gracious about it, honestly."

Sis picked up her own wineglass and said, "So, Jess, about Dean . . ."

"There's no way for me to get out of this, is there?" Jess sighed as Poppy pointedly refilled Jess's wineglass.

"I'm just saying, he talks to you. We like that he talks to you," Sis replied. "But I have concerns."

"He's your brother," Jess told Sis. "I don't need you to give me the 'if you hurt him, I will bury you in a shallow grave so the scavengers will turn your femurs into chew toys' speech."

Sis blanched. "Well, that was more graphic than I expected."

Jess took another sip of wine. "I'm saying, I understand that if this flirtation goes wrong, there's a lot of woodland acreage available to you."

Sis looked vaguely uncomfortable. She looked to her cousins. "She's threatening herself. It sort of takes the fun out of it."

Meanwhile, Jonquil's eyes narrowed. "So, you admit there's a flirtation."

"You forgot to say 'Aha,' babe," Beth whispered.

Jonquil rolled her eyes, pointed her finger at the ceiling, and added, "Aha!"

"I'm not going to pretend Dean is *unattractive*," Jess said. "I can't help but notice that he's all . . ."

"Mysterious and broody?" Beth affected a falsetto.

Jess frowned. "I was going to say 'unpredictably cranky.'"

"In my brother's defense, he has his reasons," Sis assured her.

"We're just gonna drop all of this on Jess on Meatball Night? Really?" Jonquil asked, glancing around at her cousins. "Meatball Night is supposed to be a safe place."

"I don't want his first attempt since *it* happened to go wrong," Sis said, gesturing toward Jess. "If they're gonna become a thing, it would be nice if she wasn't walking into it blind."

Poppy raised her hands. "Sis is right. Forewarned is forearmed."

"Why do I need to be warned or armed?" Jess whispered. "Is Dean secretly a bank robber? Is that why he never leaves the kitchen?"

"Bank robbery would actually be a little simpler," Jonquil said. "Readily available cash. The opportunity for fun disguises."

"Jonquil, focus," Beth reminded her gently.

"Right," Jonquil agreed. She cleared her throat and made a more "serious" face.

"OK, no more coy preamble," Sis said, turning to Jess. "Dean's girlfriend disappeared about fifteen years ago."

"I think I liked the coy phase," Jess told her.

"Dean and Emma Lee were childhood sweethearts," Poppy added. "Emma Lee was super smart. Like, 'we kept waiting for the government to show up to recruit her for secret evil military projects' smart. When we were still in high school, she made extra cash tutoring *college students*—including Sev Hardcastle, who was one of the few kids she said nice things about."

When Jess's brows rose in question, Poppy added, "Because Sev was always cooperative and paid on time. Anyway, Dean was good for Emma Lee. He softened her edges."

"Really?"

"Dean was different back then. He was loud, spontaneous, and fun. But that faded away when Emma—well, we still don't know if she left or something else happened," Sis told Jess. "The last time we saw her, we were having a party down where we used to have a fire-pit. It was where the thermal suite stands now. Our shenanigans were just youthful stupidity. And by that, I don't mean the youthful stupidity that leads to a *Law & Order* episode. Just a bunch of dumb kids sitting around a fire, drinking cheap beer, and telling stories about things that may or may not have happened. It was only about twenty of us. We didn't even make a lot of noise."

"But something happened at this party?" Jess prompted her.

"No, not really, which the police did *not* believe," Poppy said. "Nobody fought, nobody argued. Emma Lee was there, and she was her usual snarky self. Everybody just sort of had their last beer and drifted off home. We woke up the next morning, thinking everything was fine, other than the fact that we needed to hide all the beer bottles before our parents saw. We started cleaning up and Blister, who was a deputy then, showed up, saying that Emma Lee's mother had called, hysterical, because she never came home."

"We never heard from Emma Lee again. Dean blamed himself, couldn't eat, couldn't sleep. He'd been exhausted that night, worked a long shift in the kitchen and had a few beers. He kissed Emma Lee good night and turned in before the rest of us," Sis said, staring out the window into the shadows. "And none of us noticed when Emma Lee headed home. You know how loud kids can be when they're all together. If someone just peels off from the group quietly, you don't even see it. And Emma Lee always walked home, so it's not like we saw her drive off."

Jess blurted out, "She walked? From here?"

Sis smiled sadly. "Emma Lee had this special shortcut that she used to take across the valley. She loved it, her own special secret path to us. She managed to accomplish that in a family—hell, in a town—where having a secret isn't exactly easy."

"She wouldn't show any of us where it started, where it ended," Poppy said. "She said she liked having one thing that was just for herself. And when she went missing, Dean wandered all over the woods trying to find it, find her. He was so angry with himself for going to sleep that night without making sure Emma Lee was home safe. The weeks went on, then months. Blister was no help. Dean sort of went dead inside. Emma Lee's dad made some noises about suing our parents, saying they were negligent, letting us have parties. They said *we let* Emma Lee go missing."

"It was the not knowing that was the worst part," Sis said. "He didn't know if she ran away. He didn't know if she was taken by some psycho. He didn't know if she was living or dead. And the police couldn't help, really. They didn't even know where to start."

Jess thought of Susan Treadaway and her certainty that Jeremy's death was an accident, how she seemed to take comfort in the fact that if *her* anguish hadn't driven her to kill him, nothing else he did could provoke murderous rage. Even if she was wrong, according to Owen, what would it be like not to have that certainty—not to know what happened to someone you loved? For more than a decade?

"Emma Lee's house was always such a damn mess that her parents couldn't tell if anything was missing," Jonquil added. "But if she ran away, I like to think she would have at least let Dean know she was OK—called or sent a postcard or something."

"When he started making money, Dean hired a private detective to see if he could find her through tax records, legal name changes, what have you," Sis said. "But . . . nothing."

"Did people around here suspect Dean or something? Is that why he's so reclusive?" Jess asked.

"Not really," Poppy said. "You'd think in a town like this, that it would be something that hung over us for years, inspired a podcast or something, but people just kind of forgot Emma Lee was ever here. She wasn't exactly beloved, and people were sort of relieved when her parents faded out of the community. And I think that made it worse on Dean, that nobody gave her that kind of attention. People assumed she'd run away, that she wanted to get away from her family, wanted that more than she wanted Dean. And if not, if it was something more sinister, well, the Redferns were always unstable, and who would expect anything else?"

"Even when he moved home, he hid away in the kitchen, and we just let him because who were we to tell him that was wrong?" Sis said. "Jamie was the only one who could even talk to him regularly."

Jess sat back in her chair, blowing out a breath. Dean wasn't prickly. He was in pain. Well, both things could be true. He was prickly *because* he was in pain. And she knew what that was like. A handful of years was just scratching the surface in terms of recovering from the uncertainty of a loved one disappearing.

Plus, it felt a little icky lusting after Dean when he was still pining for a lost love. Frankly, Emma Lee's personality reminded her a lot of Kiki—smart, independent, ambitious, all without getting support from a family who didn't give a damn about her.

"Well . . . fuck," Jess huffed out.

Poppy nodded, lips pursed. "That just about sums it up."

"Is he going to be upset with you for sharing all this with me?" Jess asked.

"Probably," Sis said, jerking her shoulders. "But again, he's talked to you more than he's talked to anybody outside the spa family in years, so we'd like to encourage that."

After a long, silent moment of contemplation, Beth slapped the table lightly. "To salvage Meatball Night, on to more cheerful subjects. Let's talk shit about the mean girls you're hanging out with."

Jess laughed. "Oh, I don't think that's safe for me after three glasses of wine."

"OK, we won't get too hateful and detailed, but I have to ask—I know about Tillard Pecans, but how did the Helstons make their money?" Poppy asked. "Because that girl acts like her family is the backwoods Kennedys or something."

Jess mulled this over. Did her "no shit-talking the client" policy apply to talking badly about the client's family?

The three glasses of wine she'd consumed said no.

"I think there was only one generation of Helstons that had any money sense," Jess said. "And that was Diana's great-great-grandfather. Back in the forties, he started a company that made parts for rotary phones. It was really profitable for a time. The family settled into wealth pretty quickly, bought a lot of property and built big houses, but none of the generations since have had grandpa's entrepreneurial vision. And they figured everybody loved rotary phones just as they were. After all, you didn't have to crank it like the original version."

Jess paused to mime turning the hand crank on the sort of phone that required you to shout into a horn while you held a cup-shaped receiver to your ear. "They thought it would stay that way forever. But another faction of the family persuaded the stodgier relatives to diversify . . . into phone books."

While the other women groaned, Beth hissed in mock pain. "Ouch, sort of a postmillennial one-two punch to the generational wealth."

"Yup. And phone technology evolved over time, without the Helstons adapting their strategies. The family coffers all but emptied. By the time Diana was born, the Helston Regional White Pages had pretty much died off. And the family was convinced that the only way to maintain the appearance of wealth was to marry it."

"And the Tillards have the wealth," Poppy said, nodding.

"In spades," Jess agreed. "The Tillards are old money enough not to splash it around on big boats and cars or . . . basically all the things that make Diana happy, which is sort of what's putting her on edge. I think she's afraid that Trenton's parents will change his mind before she gets down the aisle."

"Wouldn't it be—" Jonquil's question was interrupted by Owen walking in.

"I know, I'm late again, but I was healing sick, adorable children," Owen announced. His voice boomed so loudly that Jess thought maybe he had a career as a Santa ahead of him, once his beard went more silver than dark brown. "Can I please have forgiveness in the form of meatballs?"

Dean appeared in the door behind him. "I was not healing sick children, but I was making last-minute, late-night room service orders for whiny guests. Does that qualify me for forgiveness meatballs?"

Jess could only hope that the whiny guests weren't part of her own group. But she was sure she was wrong.

Jess glanced at the clock on Jonquil's wall. "I better get back. It's getting late."

How long had they been talking? She scrambled to pick up her dirty dishes, only to have Beth take them out of her hands.

"Put those down," Beth told her. "Jonquil will take care of them tomorrow morning, Meatball Night rules. I cook, she cleans."

Jonquil nodded. "It's harsh, but fair."

"Well, some of us have to be up early," Dean said. "So I'm gonna take my meatballs and run. But I can walk you back to your villa, Jess, if you'd like."

Jess nodded. "I will accept your offer, but only because the last guy who wandered around unattended—well, you know."

She immediately felt bad for mentioning Jeremy Treadaway when they were having such a nice time. Dammit, three-drink Jess.

But Poppy merely shrugged. "I'd feel better knowing you're safe."

Dean accepted his to-go container from Jonquil. He grinned at Jess. "Well, at least this time you're not trying to lure me into isolated places in the dark."

"I lured you into *one* isolated place in the dark," she retorted.

"What?" Sis asked, stopping in her tracks as she carried the meatball dish to the sink.

"Technically, he followed me with very little luring required," Jess scoffed.

Dean said, "When I surprised her, she threw a glass water bottle at me and hit me square in the chest. If it was a sharp object, I could have died. It was weirdly alluring."

Jess watched the Osbourne cousins' faces shift in delight, disbelief, hope. It was a little weird how happy Dean's family seemed that she'd hurled a glass projectile at him—but it felt like a stamp of approval. And she wasn't sure if she was quite ready for that yet.

"And on that note, let's go," Jess said, slipping out the front door and dragging Dean with her.

Poppy yelled after her, "Spoilsport!"

"You are the worst," she told Dean as they left the porch, making him snort.

"Ah, I was messing with them more than you," Dean told her. "They're shifting into their meddling auntie phase much earlier in life than I expected them to."

Jess stayed mostly quiet on their walk back to the villa. With all the information that the cousins had dumped into her head, she didn't know what to say or how to say it. If she opened her mouth, more than likely she would blurt out something horrible, or embarrassing, or horrible *and* embarrassing. But it wasn't uncomfortable, sharing companionable silence like this.

"You OK?" he asked. "They weren't too rough on you, were they? Sometimes they forget that boundaries are, you know, real."

"Oh, no, they've been great," Jess assured him. "It's just been a long couple of days."

He nodded. "So, between us, Owen was not in town curing sick, itchy children."

"Was he in town curing sick, itchy adults?" Jess asked.

"He was videoconferencing the medical examiner in charge of Treadaway's case," Dean said. "He didn't want to worry Poppy. She's under a lot of pressure."

"What did the medical examiner have to say?" She didn't mean to pounce on that so quickly, but again, three-drink Jess.

Dean hesitated for a moment. "I understand that my family wants to keep you in the dark about this because we don't know you very well. I'm telling you because I saw the look on your face when you found Treadaway's body. We owe you this much. And I'm trusting you not to repeat it. Not to the people in your party. Not to anyone."

Jess asked, "Has Poppy made it clear that I have basically no loyalty to anybody in my party beyond the financial?"

"Yes, and that doesn't make me feel better about you spending time with them," he replied.

"I promise not to repeat this to anybody," she said, holding up her right hand in a mock oath. "Unless Poppy asks me directly—I won't lie to anybody in your family."

"Oh, no, Owen will find a way to tell her without worrying her. He just wanted to give her time to process away from everybody," Dean said. "So, there was no alcohol or drugs in Jeremy's system. He didn't have any head wounds. I think Blister just assumed that. There was no obvious reason a fully grown adult man should have fallen face-first into that water and not been able to get himself out."

"So what does that mean?"

"More tests," he said. "Owen said the stomach contents didn't look right, even in the photos. He said the mushrooms in Treadaway's gut look like morel mushrooms. But I don't use morel mushrooms. Never have."

"Why not?"

Dean shrugged. "Personal preference? I grew up eating chicken of the woods mushrooms and like to work with them. They're this beautiful orange color that looks really nice on a plate. I have a good local supplier. And my granny thought morels were bad luck or something."

Jess frowned. "Do you think Jeremy picked mushrooms on his own and . . . snacked on them?"

She'd heard of people from the more rural areas of Tennessee foraging for food in the woods. Hell, one of Nana Blanche's friends used to brag about earning her Christmas budget by digging ginseng every autumn on a cousin's hunting tract. But in general, people didn't mess with mushrooms unless they were experts. Was Jeremy Treadaway foolhardy enough to think himself an expert?

Jess mentally reviewed what she knew of Jeremy.

OK, yeah, that tracked.

"I would say only an idiot would do that, but it feels rude to speak ill of the dead," Dean said.

"At least it's being taken seriousl—" Jess paused as they passed the thermal suite. She tilted her head at a curious angle, watching a strange single light bounce in the trees far beyond Tranquility and Serenity.

Was she really seeing this?

Jess's Big Book of Life Plans: Schedule optometrist exam when you get back to town. Maybe a CAT scan.

"Will-o'-the-wisps again." She rubbed at her eyes.

"I don't see anything." Dean got quiet for a moment and her gaze returned to the trees. If she'd seen a light, ghostly or otherwise, it was gone now.

"So, you went to the same school as those girls?" Dean asked.

"Just Diana."

"How did the fancy school translate into 'proposal planning'?" Dean asked. "Don't most people who go to that sort of place end up in . . . what's a nice way to say 'fancier jobs'?"

"I got a scholarship to Harrow based on my 'fancy' Wren Hill transcripts and a nice recommendation from the headmistress," Jess said. "The wedding planning thing was one of the few paid internships I could find. My grandmother needed help with the bills. A professor helped me get it through a friend of a friend. I liked it more than I thought I could, watching an event that started as this faint idea come together into this beautiful complex thing that made people smile—even if people acted like absolute lunatics to get there. When Angenette offered me a job, the money was too good to walk away from, even as a junior planner. And then I was able to start my own business."

"I get it. I mean, I never really wanted my own restaurant," he confessed. "I know that's the dream for most chefs, but it's *so* much work that has nothing to do with cooking—paperwork, staffing, paperwork."

"You said 'paperwork' twice," Jess noted.

"Yes, I did," he told her. "I really hate paperwork. This place is sort of the best of both worlds, because Poppy does most of that for us. And I get to control the kitchen and concentrate on what I enjoy."

"Is paperwork the part that Poppy enjoys?" Jess asked.

"Weirdly, yes."

They moved toward her villa but paused as they heard Trenton's voice singing some college football fight song inside Serenity Villa at the top of his lungs. It wasn't easily identifiable, but having attended the same college, Jess knew it wasn't their alma mater's. And the sad thing was, he sounded sober, just loud.

"Are you sure you're all right with those guys around?" Dean asked, his fingers slipping around her wrist. Jess was distracted for a second by a flash of yellow in the trees behind their villa. She shook her head and squinted, but whatever it was, if it had been there in the first place, was gone. "Look, I don't know Trenton, but the Hardcastles, they're not good people. They think money can buy them out of anything. And the scary thing is, they're not all wrong."

"Sev's all right," Jess said, shaking her head. "Trenton's harmless. Chad's just an emotionally impervious man-child mess."

Dean seemed unconvinced, and didn't let go of her hand, even when they climbed the steps of her villa. He didn't seem very happy when she opened the *unlocked* door. "Just lock up behind yourself, OK?"

Jess wanted to protest that he was being overprotective of someone he barely knew, but then she remembered, his girlfriend had disappeared. And Jess had recently found a dead body nearby. Asking her to lock up wasn't a stretch.

"You're very sweet," she told him. "Sometimes, when the mood hits you. And the stars are aligned just right and the wind blows from the north—"

"Oh my God." He snorted out a laugh, set the meatballs aside, and moved his hands lightning-quick to cup her face. He pressed his mouth to hers, tasting of spice and a special warmth that was just Dean. She melted against him and pulled him closer. She hoped no one was watching from either villa, because this was something she wanted just for herself. His hands, rough and warm, moved from her jawline to her hair and she wanted to stay there, on this porch, until the mountain fell away.

But then a noise from inside her villa startled her and she pulled back. Dean's hold tightened on her, but when no one came barreling out of the villa, calling her a traitorous hussy, they relaxed. Over Dean's shoulder, she noticed motion at Zephyr's villa. The door opened and Chad crept out, shoes and pants in hand.

"Oh, ew," Jess whispered.

Jess supposed that Chad's late-night visit meant that Beth's ointment had resolved Zephyr's "injury." Or maybe it hadn't, Jess really didn't want to know. She crooked her finger at Dean and they moved quietly around the corner of the villa, out of Chad's line of sight. As they moved, Jess heard the clinking of an empty glass bottle rolling across the deck, followed by Chad cursing.

From the shadows, they watched Chad tiptoe like a cartoon villain back to Serenity Villa. He stopped, dropping his shoes and bending over into the bushes. The sounds of him piteously retching echoed across the mountain. Dean and Jess shared an anguished glance.

She sighed, "This is consistent with the rest of my stay here."

"I don't feel like you're experiencing the Golden Ash at its best," Dean whispered.

"It's not your fault," Jess told him. "Good night."

"Good night. Lock up tight," he said, giving her one last kiss that stretched a little longer than she was comfortable with, given the proximity to one of Chad's hookups. She pulled back.

"Because of the pantsless wonder?" Dean guessed. "And the puke?"

She nodded. "Yep."

"Fair enough." He laughed and she edged away, waving. She opened the door, wincing at every little noise as she closed it behind her.

Touching her fingers to her lips, she wondered how long it would take Dean to get back to his house. She wasn't sure if it was the tragedy of Emma Lee or drunken Chad's proximity, but something felt unsafe, knowing Dean was out there alone.

As she drifted off to sleep, she thought of the will-o'-the-wisp, and wondered if Dean would stay on the safe path if he saw one in the woods.

CHAPTER 11

J ess rolled out of bed early, quiet as a sigh, but she still managed to wake up Kiki. Because her grace didn't extend to avoiding tripping over her own shoes, which she left in the middle of the floor.

"Sorry," Jess whispered. Kiki slid her glasses on as she followed Jess into the darkened room. "I guess my stealth mode isn't stealthing."

"It's OK," Kiki grumbled. "Where are you heading?"

"Up to the kitchen to finalize the dinner details for Trenton and Diana's big day," she whispered as she walked into the kitchenette and reached for the custom-blended Golden Ash breakfast tea. The kettle, normally situated next to the mini-coffeepot, was nowhere to be found. "I'm trying to get out before Diana wakes up. Don't want to ruin the surprise."

"So we're still pretending it's a surprise." Kiki yawned.

"Have you seen the electric kettle?" Jess asked, turning around to inspect the pristine counters. "It was here before . . ."

"I'll be honest." Kiki blinked at her. "Up until now, I wasn't aware that we had a kettle."

"Weird," Jess muttered. "Maybe housekeeping took it?"

Kiki shrugged. "Either way, could you order us coffee service while you're up at the lodge?"

"Sure, and some of those mini chocolate croissant things. I'll have Dean hide them under the fruit."

"Oh, that's why you're my favorite." Kiki sighed.

"Yeah, but consider my competition," Jess said, jerking her head toward Diana and Aubrey's door. Through the back window, Jess saw Sev loping across the lawn, dressed as if he'd gotten up for some early morning hike. That reminded her.

Jess cleared her throat. "So, I was talking to Sev. He seems really nice—"

"Oh, please don't try to set me up with the spare cousin," Kiki said with a groan. "It's a little too matchy-matchy, don't you think?"

"Actually, they're not cousins. Sev is Chad's uncle."

Kiki stared at her. "Weird."

"Yeah, but I'm not trying to set you up with him. I'm wondering if you should pitch your truffle idea to Sev instead of Trenton? He might have the connections to the right people within the company— the people who make decisions, as opposed to the people who humor Trenton. And he'll see past the family baggage for the great idea it is."

"It's not a bad idea, but honestly, I find him so intimidating," Kiki said, shuddering.

"I'm just saying, Sev seems to enjoy discussing work more than he enjoys spending time with any of us," Jess told her. "He might jump at the chance to talk about anything other than . . . whatever it is Chad and Trenton want to talk about . . . golf, cars, probably something involving illegal underground gambling. You could make an opportunity out of that."

And if Kiki could distract Sev from approaching Diana with the prenup, maybe Jess would have one less blowup to try to defuse. And it would make Jess very happy to help Kiki, which went without saying.

Kiki beamed at Jess. "That's a good idea. Thanks, Jess."

"Good ideas are what I do." Jess grabbed her tote bag from its spot beside the couch and backed out of the door.

Jess hiked up the hill, marveling at the thick gray clouds gathering overhead. The forecast had been clear the day before, but Jess supposed the weather changed faster in the mountains. She only hoped it didn't interfere with her plans for the outdoor picnic proposal the next day. Fortunately, she had a rain plan mapped out for a gazebo behind Harmony Villa. Maybe she could persuade Diana that a candlelit scene surrounded by raindrops in the background would be romantic and dreamy.

"Jessie!" She startled at the sound of her name. She hoped it was Sev, but no, Chad was sort of stumbling up the hill, looking like freeze-dried hell. His face was sallow, sort of clammy-looking, with dark circles under his eyes.

"You feeling all right?" Jess asked, taking a step back as he approached.

He waved her off. "Sure, sure. I'm heading up to the thermal suite, try to sweat out some of the booze."

Frankly, Jess was surprised there was any booze left in his system, considering how much she'd seen him vomit the night before. But it seemed to be radiating out of his pores.

"Oof," Jess said, fluttering her hand in front of her face. "I can smell your choices on you."

"Grow up." He scoffed, pulling a pack of Marlboros out of his hoodie pocket and a book of matches. When her brows lifted, he shrugged and waved a green paper matchbook. "I keep losing my damn lighter. That's why I keep cheap shit like this around."

"Really, you're gonna light up a cigarette at a wellness retreat?" Jess asked, hitching the tote bag on her shoulder. "OK, sure. Of course you are."

It was different when Jamie did it. He wasn't there to get well. Also, Jess liked Jamie, so there. Chad plucked the last little cardboard match out of the book, lit the cigarette, and tossed the lit match over his shoulder. She glared at him, circled behind his back, and ground it under her foot.

Leaning closer, Chad said, "You know, Trenton's been saying what a nice girl you are, how *helpful.*"

"Please breathe away from me," Jess wheezed, trying not to inhale through her nose. She wondered if she should tell Jonquil all about Chad's smoking. It would be worth the tattling, to see him subjected to involuntary chamomile.

"You really think you're better than us, don't you?" he asked with a smirk.

She took a deep breath of non-Chad-polluted air, telling herself she would not respond, but she'd stopped moving. Which gave Chad the chance to say, "Sometimes people who don't have anything see us as not having any real values. You think you're better than us, deep down where it counts, but really it's just something you tell yourself at night so you can sleep."

She smiled at him, lips stretched so thin she thought they might crack and bleed. "You know, if you could remember what happened before you fell asleep last night, I would probably take your moral philosophy a little more seriously. Go sweat it out, Chad."

She walked off as quickly as possible so she couldn't hear his response.

When she reached the kitchen, Dean was near the stove, sharpening a rather large butcher knife. Why was he always holding a weapon?

"Hey, you OK?" Dean stood in the kitchen door. Behind him on the kitchen counter, there were large piles of chopped mushrooms, onions, peppers—probably omelet ingredients. He had multiple burners going on the massive stove. She could see cinnamon rolls cooling on the counter.

Would it be weird to move her blankets in and sleep here? Probably.

"You know, I hope that we've moved to a phase in our relationship where you waving a knife around isn't considered a threat," she told Dean, smiling wryly.

"Be nice." He rolled his eyes and pointed, with the knife, at a stool near a big metal worktable. "I'll make you breakfast."

Sliding a plate across the worktable, he dropped two toasted English muffins on it, then turned to a pot of simmering water. He deftly scooped out two poached eggs and slid them onto the muffins. The perfectly golden yolks were still jiggling as he practically drowned the plate in hollandaise sauce.

"If this is your attempt to flirt with me . . . you're off to an amazing start," she told him.

He smirked. "I noticed your passive-aggressive saucing yesterday."

"The saucing was a passive-aggressive statement, yes, but it was also delicious," she replied around a large bite of just-right eggs. He dropped two slices of thick-cut bacon on the rim of the plate. "Well, now you're just showing off."

"I'm only sorry it's not a cheeseburger." He turned back to his pile of chopped vegetables. She shook her head and flashed him a thumbs-up. Her mouth was too full of deliciousness to talk politely. "The cinnamon rolls are for the staff, but I'll let you have one if you promise not to find any more dead bodies on the property."

"I mean, I didn't find the first one on purpose, but I'll try to avoid it in the future," she said, her mouth still half-full.

"I was hoping we could talk about the tasting menu while I work," he said.

"Where's Jamie?" she asked. "I didn't realize I would be bothering you while you were working through the breakfast shift alone."

"Farmer's market, picking up some fruit," he said. "Breakfast is a little easier to manage, as long as you keep the menu to a few specials. Otherwise, gluten-free, keto-friendly avocado chaos reigns. And on that note, I think we can keep your friend's 'tasting menu' pretty simple, considering the lady only wants to eat fruit and her boyfriend favors mashed potatoes and chicken wings."

"Can you make chicken wings sound fancy?" she wondered aloud. "What's French for 'chicken wing'?"

"Do you try this hard for all of your clients?" he asked, shaking his head. "Are you sure they deserve it?"

She chewed thoughtfully. "When I help people arrange their proposals, I'm a part of their story. Even if they don't mention me when they tell it, I was there. I'm helping people build their lives."

"But then they leave you, just like the people who eat here leave my table. And you're left alone." Something about the way he said "alone"—the depth of the grief one could feel with one word—had her looking up, her expression stricken.

He rolled his eyes heavenward and groaned. "They told you, didn't they?"

"They did," she said, nodding slowly. "As long as you're asking if they told me about Emma Lee."

"Please don't tell me that you're sorry," he said, shaking his head. "Or that you know how I feel, because you don't."

"I acknowledge that," she said. "But I'm glad that they told me, so I didn't shove my foot in my mouth."

Overwhelming guilt for having forced him out of his comfort zone, for indulging in that kiss with him when he was still so torn up, boiled up through her gut, turning the divine egg in her mouth to ash.

"I was in a daze, that last semester of culinary school, a cooking robot. I never really wanted to go away to college anyway. I could have lived my whole life on the mountain, but Em insisted, saying we needed to experience the outside world if we were going to be sure about each other. After she was . . . gone, I buried myself in work, wherever I could get it. Moved all over. It kept me from feeling, and to be honest, I needed that. I needed to be numb, and I knew every single one of my family members would kick my ass if I tried to get that with booze or drugs. But the more I worked, the better I got in the kitchen—I know it sounds like an asshole thing to say, but it's true—and I got more attention. My bosses were happy and I got left alone. The problem was, the more attention I got, the more people wanted to talk to me. I was expected to do interviews and schmooze. I *hated it*. You can't hide if you're expected to do interviews and social media and all that crap. And the girls, they were coming up with their big business plan to change the hotel. I ran home to be part of it. I was lucky they made room for me."

"They don't strike me as the 'excluding' type," Jess noted.

"No, but I felt bad, horning in on this plan they'd been perfecting forever," he said. "The girls had wanted to run this place from the time they were in high school. I just wanted to marry my girlfriend and have some kids. But when Emma Lee disappeared, that all sort of fell away."

"The not knowing, it burns," she said. "It's like a poisonous fog that just sucks the oxygen out of your lungs. People watch as you suffocate from the inside out because you can't explain it."

He stared at her for a long silent moment, then added, "And after a while, it hurt less, but I was angry. I want more in my life now, but it scares me. I don't want to get hurt like that again."

"No one can promise you that you won't get hurt again. That would be really patronizing," she said. "But I spend my whole life seeing couples in love, seeing it work. There's hope out there."

"God, that optimism is annoying," he huffed.

"Yep." She picked at her remaining breakfast. He set about checking his order system, starting several omelets, dropping bread in the massive toasters.

Without looking up, Dean said, "So, uh, the suffocating fog thing . . . that seems very accurate. And specific."

"So, what I learned in therapy is that sometimes, even if you don't want a person who is missing to come back, your body can't process the 'not knowing' any differently. You still get all the same stress responses. The anxiety. The sleeplessness. Nightmares when you do sleep." Jess poked her fork at the brilliant yellow yolk film drying on her plate. When Dean's face drained of color, she added quickly, "My grandparents had full legal custody of me by the time I was three. My mom—Hadley—had me young, and well, she took off. I don't think she liked sharing my grandparents with me. She came back every year or so, usually around my birthday, loud and chaotic and kind of mean. Calling me *Jessie*, which I hated. Picking fights with me, and it was always over stupid things. She was mad that I was sleeping in her old bedroom. She was mad I was using her old tire swing. But later, it wasn't silly anymore. She was honestly angry with me just for living in a house she'd left years ago. When I was nine, she insisted on driving me over state lines to some diner for pancakes in the middle of the night. The roads were slick and we crashed into a ditch. She left me, just wandered off from the scene and left me trapped in the car until some good Samaritan drove up and called nine-one-one. She didn't come home until after I had surgery on a broken ankle. I don't think my grandparents forgave her for leaving me there at the accident scene, because after that, she didn't come back. Ever."

"But you don't know where she is now?" he asked.

She shook her head. "At my college graduation, my grandmother gave me the set of pearls that belonged to the original Jessamine, my great-grandmother. If Nana Blanche had any hope that the breach *could be* healed, she never would have given them to me. I think I knew then that I would never see her again."

"I told you that you didn't know how it felt," he said, wincing.

"Yeah, but I don't, really," she reasoned. "I knew *why* Hadley left. You don't know why Emma Lee is gone. Or if she left under her own power, which is so much worse."

"It's not a contest," he reminded her. "Your story doesn't have to be worse to be worth telling. And really, I'm glad for you; your grandparents sound pretty awesome."

"They were. Nana Blanche still is. They got me into therapy, helped me cope with the sleep issues and nightmares resulting from being trapped in a car for what felt like hours. I think it was part of the reason they were so desperate for me to go to Wren Hill. They knew they weren't going to be around forever, and they wanted to make sure they set me up for security later . . . Oh, God, were they trying to match me up with boys from good families? Oh, ew, how did this thought just occur to me?"

She opened her mouth to lament the possibility of being "matched" with somebody like Chad, but Dean crossed around the worktable and stopped her mouth with a kiss. He leaned forward and brushed those lips across hers, lips that should not have been nearly as soft as they were. She wanted to melt against him, to scrabble up his body and attach herself so he couldn't let her go. She had never felt this sort of desire to be held by someone, to be kept close. She wanted to be claimed by him, to belong in this world built by his family, even if she knew it wouldn't work long term. Maybe a little taste of it was better than never knowing it at all?

Just then, Jamie walked into the kitchen holding a crate of apples.

"Oh, sorry. I will . . . walk out now. Please keep doing what you're doing," he said, backing out of the room.

Dean burst out laughing and said, "Jamie likes you."

She squinted at him. "Just Jamie?"

He pursed his lips. "I am not indifferent to you."

Reluctantly, Jamie brought in the crate when Dean called him in. By the time they'd worked up a tasting menu that would fit Diana's preferences and Trenton's lack thereof, it was nearing lunch. Jess's group was scheduled to be in Sis's Pilates class.

"You know, you can just walk in at the thermal suite and use a sauna or something. You don't have to wait for an appointment or anything," Dean suggested, sliding a paper-packaged turkey wrap across the counter to her. "It doesn't get busy until the afternoons."

"It's just such a shame that you couldn't catch up to your group in time to join Sis's class, which just started," Jamie added cheerfully. "They have robes and stuff in the suite, so you don't even have to go change back at your cabin."

"Particularly if someone happened to take their bathing suit with them when they left the villa this morning," Jess said, lifting the little tote bag where she'd stashed her pool gear. "Because this is the only time I'm going to have free today."

"You really do plan for everything, don't you?" Dean said, marveling.

"If that was said with even the tiniest bit of sarcasm, it would have hurt my feelings," she told him, dashing out the door. "Good luck with lunch!"

Fueled by a lunch she could eat while sneaking across the grounds, she felt like she was leading some sort of clandestine mission centered on the strange near-Olympian thermal suite. Susan Treadaway was walking across the grounds near the lodge building. And while Jess felt some inclination to check in with her, following their cathartic late-husband-and-restaurant-bashing session . . . Jess really needed a little time to herself.

The front desk was manned by one of the spa's younger staff members, Hannah, who was flipping through a magazine focused on not health or healing but the five key components to a better blow job. The olive-skinned brunette barely acknowledged Jess as she walked into the women's locker room and slipped out of her clothes and into her sensible one-piece suit and robe.

For the next hour, Jess lost herself in a grown-up playground, the tiled warren of little alcoves and pools dedicated to helping people separate themselves from their racing thoughts and connect with their bodies for a little bit. The Polar Shower that sprayed you with a mist of peppermint-scented water so fine it felt like being hit with tiny snowflakes. The Persephone's Garden Shower, warmed by amber and red lights and featuring clouds of flower-scented water that felt like kisses. And the Bliss Pool, tiled and surrounded in the perfect shade of tranquil sky blue and keyed in at exactly room temperature, which made her feel like she was gliding on air.

Jess's Big Book of Life Plans: Just float.

Jess was able to tolerate just a few minutes of not thinking until Dean, of course, eventually drifted into her head.

It wasn't as if they had any chance of long-term anything. He lived hours away, and neither of them was likely to move. But now, away from the noise and other people, where she could just think . . . she didn't know. Could she really walk away from someone she felt this connected to? She wasn't really built for that unfinished relationship business. And she didn't even know how Dean felt, if he could feel something for her from under the fog of his past.

And there was the whole Jeremy Treadaway thing hanging over them. That seemed ominous in terms of dating. Could *Dean* have given Jeremy something that made him sick? Why? The man was obnoxious, but that wasn't reason enough to kill him. Dean dealt with obnoxious guests all the time, and . . . he just didn't seem the type. The worst she could imagine him doing to someone was serving them something made with margarine.

Climbing out of the Bliss Pool, Jess decided on one more round in the Polar Shower. Shivering and smelling of peppermint, she squeezed the excess water from her hair. Maybe a round in one of the saunas would help warm her up? Or maybe she was just trying to avoid going back to the villa and preparing for this evening and listening to Aubrey pick at her until she wanted to scream.

Probably the second one.

Wrapping herself in an oversized towel, Jess padded into the long tiled corridor, set with cedarwood doors that almost looked like vaults. Most of them were propped open ever so slightly—maybe for safety purposes? The humid air was thick with the scents of eucalyptus and peppermint and, well, wet wood. But as she passed the Alpine Steam Room, she detected a fouler, sour smell . . . like expired cheese.

It smelled like overgrown frat boy.

The door to the Alpine Steam Room was shut tight, the window in the middle dark and fogged over. A combination of dread and curiosity had her wrapping her hand around the handle. Jess opened the door and steam came billowing out, rushing over her like an unwelcome embrace from a clingy aunt. Waving her hand in front of her face, Jess's eyes landed on a dark shape that seemed out of place on the green stone floor.

Is that who I think it is?

She'd thought she was alone in the thermal suite, but a mass of a person—she could see now, as the steam cleared, it was Chad—was slumped face down on the floor. His arm was thrown over his own body at an odd angle, just short of the door. It looked like he'd been trying to crawl toward it and passed out. There was a thin brownish puddle surrounding his head, with odd white chunks drying in the glaze of it. It absolutely reeked, and Jess had to pull back to the door to keep herself from throwing up on him.

Maybe he'd been more hungover than she thought?

"OK, get up," Jess sighed. "This party-till-you-pass-out nonsense was embarrassing when you were twenty. Now it's just sad."

Jess knelt to shake his shoulder. When she rolled him over on his back, his eyes were open and vacant, staring up at the ceiling with no life behind them.

No. No no no. Nononononononoonononono.

Chad wasn't hungover. Chad was dead.

No pulse. Cool skin. Not breathing. *Dead.*

This couldn't be happening to her *again*.

Jess let loose a strangled shriek, falling back over the lip of the door. She lost her towel, scrambling back against the far wall. She could feel it against her back, hard and warm, but there didn't seem to be much else tethering her to this earth.

She couldn't seem to produce any sound. How was she even breathing? How was this so much worse than finding Jeremy Tread-away's body? Chad had been alive just this morning. He'd been his awful, creepy self, but he was *alive*.

Jess's face felt cold. How was her face cold when there was steam pouring out of the saunas? Her hands scrabbled, numb and useless, against the tiles as she tried to stand up.

She tore herself away from the sight of Chad's chalky-gray face and felt dizzy as her eyes seemed to zip about the room like a hummingbird. She couldn't get them to focus on anything, and then something caught her attention.

She forced her eyes to focus and saw that it was a big red plastic circle inside a plastic case that read **PRESS IN CASE OF EMERGENCY**.

Grunting with the effort, she hoisted herself to her feet and slapped at the button. In the distance, she could hear a shrieking sort of alarm bell. It was as if the effort sucked all the energy out of her, and she sank back down to the floor. When she heard the footsteps coming, she was still staring at the husk of the person she'd never really cared for—and she was heartbroken for Chad that she was the first person to know he was gone.

CHAPTER 12

She knew that someone had helped her into a robe and out of the thermal suite building, then seated her in an ironwork chair overlooking the cloud-shrouded mountainside. But she didn't know who did it or what they said to her. She wasn't even sure how long she'd been sitting there.

Why was this so much worse than finding Jeremy? His face. Jess had seen Chad's face, the blank, slack mask of it, while Jeremy's had been obscured from her. She'd known him a little better than Jeremy, but it wasn't as if she liked Chad. Maybe she felt guilty because she'd been so rude to him that morning? Or maybe finding Chad felt worse because she hadn't had a chance to process the first dead body she'd found?

A hand closed around her numbed fingers, willing warmth into them with firm squeezes. It was Sis, telling her firmly, "Take a deep breath for me, OK?"

"It's Chad," she whispered. "He was on the floor and I told him he was embarrassing. Oh, God, he's . . ."

It was all she could do not to vomit right there.

Nope, she *was* vomiting.

"We know. We've got it. You're going to be OK." Sis held Jess's hair back as she expelled the contents of her stomach onto the grass. She rubbed Jess's back and told her, "All right, OK, that'll help. Good girl."

Lenore jogged up, water bottle in hand. She wrapped one of the spa's oversized robes around Jess's shoulders. "Here. We don't want her going into shock."

"I'm sorry, I don't know why I'm acting this way," Jess mumbled, wiping at her mouth with the back of her hand. She took a drink of water and swished it around her mouth. "I didn't even like him."

Lenore shushed her. "It's all right. Seeing a dead body is pretty upsetting, even if you weren't particularly close to the person."

"This is my second one," Jess whispered. "I promised Dean I wouldn't see any more dead bodies on the property."

"I'm sure Dean will understand," Lenore told her.

"Am I the Golden Ash jinx or something?"

"I'm sure you're not a jinx." But Jess saw the little quirk of Lenore's mouth that showed even she didn't fully believe that. Poppy stepped out of the thermal building. When had she gotten there?

"Honey, I've called the sheriff's office and you're going to have to talk to them. But how about we go get you changed into clean, dry clothes?" Poppy told her, helping her stand up. "Deep breaths, OK?"

"Someone needs to find Sev," Jess said. "Sev is his family."

"We'll take care of it, Jess," Sis assured her.

And yet Jess was still talking: "He might not seem upset at first, but neither did Susan, and it turns out she was pretty torn up about

Jeremy. So, if Sev is all stoic and stony, we should try not to judge him too much."

"When did you have a chance to talk to Susan Treadaway?" Poppy asked.

Sis shook her head. "That's not important right now. We just need to get you warm. Blister's on his way."

"Great." She sighed. Jess did not want to be wearing a damp bathrobe while talking to the police. That was not an enviable position in life.

"Jess!"

She heard a voice yelling for her and turned, only to be hit by a freight train disguised as a person. Dean threw his arms around Jess and lifted her off her feet. Over his shoulder, she could see Jamie jogging up behind them, out of breath. He waved at Jess and bent at the waist, panting. Jonquil approached him with Sis, helping him to a nearby Adirondack chair.

"Goddamn smoking," Jamie grumbled, holding up one finger in a "just a minute" gesture.

Dean set her on her feet, cupping her face in his hands. "You OK?"

She nodded. She was still upset, still unsure, but she was so glad to have his arms around her. "I swear, I wasn't looking for another body."

"You're coming back to my cabin with me," Dean told her.

"I can't," Jess insisted. "I need my clothes. I need my toothbrush. I need my great-grandmother's pearls before Diana finds them and claims they're a Helston family heirloom."

"Look, Dean, I need to get Jess back to her cabin, get her stuff, and talk to her group about what's happened," Poppy said. "You can go with us, but you're gonna have to actually be civil to people. I love you, but I don't have the time or the patience to deal with you setting people off with your special brand of surly."

Poppy and Dean loaded Jess into a nearby golf cart, leaving Sis to deal with the chaos of the treatment suite. Jamie assured Dean he could handle dinner service, but Dean barely nodded. His arm was warm and heavy around her shoulders, in a way that kept Jess from floating away inside her own head.

When they arrived at Tranquility Villa, everybody in their group was lounging on the front porch, chatting and drinking their spring water, looking relaxed. It looked like an ad for what the Golden Ash was supposed to be—an escape from the stresses of the outside world. Not a "finding a douche-bro's dead body in a sauna that stank of cheese booze sweat and ass" place.

Jess's Big Book of Life Plans: Be less mean about the dead man.

"Jess?" Diana frowned, taking in Jess's disheveled appearance from head to toe.

If Diana said one thing about preserving her brand, Jess was going to end up in jail.

Sev got a wary look on his face when he saw the state of Jess, like his lawyer's spidey-senses were going off. And Jess didn't know how to feel about it. She knew Sev and Chad weren't exactly close, but that didn't mean it was going to be any easier on Sev to call Chad's father and tell him that Chad was dead.

"Jess?" Trenton rose to his feet. "Everything OK? Have you seen Chad around?"

"I'm sorry to tell you this, but there's been an incident," Poppy said as Dean took Jess's elbow.

Every nerve in Jess's body told her to just walk past them, to let Poppy be the one to deliver the bad news. But she'd spent too much time around people who dropped the emotional payload on others while they swanned off to something more convenient, less arduous. And she wasn't about to do that to Poppy.

"Another one?" Kiki asked.

Aubrey shook her head. "Oh, Jessie, what did you do?"

"Not the time." Jess shook her head at Aubrey.

"Jess, I've got this," Poppy assured her. "I have a feeling you're gonna need to conserve your energy for the next few days."

"What are you talking about?" Diana demanded. "Jess? What happened?"

Dean gently pulled Jess into the house and closed the door behind her, leaving the rest of the party outside.

"Jess, honey, you need a break from these people, because I'm starting to worry about you," Dean said, sliding his arms around her. "Well, that's not true, I worried about you from the minute I saw the Hardcastles . . . and now I feel bad that I'm shit-talking a guy who died today. Wait, no, he was an asshole. I'm OK with my choices."

She leaned close and groaned into his collarbone and was grateful for the spicy smell of him chasing the smell of death from her lungs. "And I really hate that you just called me a sweet name for the first time and it's connected to Chad."

Dean snorted and kissed her forehead. "Go shower."

By the time she emerged from the shower, her hair damp and dressed in her comfiest jogger pants and a soft purple sweatshirt that hung off her shoulder, the group had moved off the porch into the living area, where Trenton sat on the couch, looking like a lost puppy. Poppy and Sev appeared to be out on the porch, where Sev was doing a lot of nodding. Dean was standing by the door, watching all of them with his arms crossed and his mouth thinned into an unimpressed line.

Through the windows, Jess could see red and blue lights flashing at the top of the hill. Apparently, Blister and his police force had arrived. And this time, Poppy couldn't hide the squad car from the guests.

Diana was sitting on Trenton's right, her arms around him. Her face was paper-pale and her eyes oddly hollow. She was making soft shushing noises as his eyes filmed over with tears. He covered his face with his hands. "How could something like this happen? People don't die at places like this."

Jess frowned. Had Trenton already forgotten about Jeremy Treadaway, or had he never paid attention to other people talking about it in the first place?

Aubrey was standing by the kitchen counter, like Diana's cornerman, poised to support Diana's next move. And Diana . . . those were real tears coursing down her cheeks. Her eyes were red-rimmed, surrounded by smears of sooty gray. Was she crying heartfelt tears for Chad?

Maybe it was for Trenton's benefit?

"I'm so sorry, Trenton," Jess began, and she found herself crushed to his chest.

Unlike Dean's sudden embrace, this was unwelcome and . . . damp, like hugging a moist teddy bear. "He used to scuba dive in caves. He went bungee jumping off a bridge in Peru. He was supposed to drive ATVs through the Sahara next year."

Jess patted his back awkwardly. "I'm sorry."

"I'm glad it was you that found him," Trenton was saying into her hair. "I'm glad the last thing he saw was a friendly face."

"I didn't—" Jess took a step back from him. Trenton tried to hold her arms, but she managed to slip out of it. "I wasn't with him when he died, Trenton."

"Oh, well, that's too bad," he said. "It would have been better if you'd been with him."

Jess blinked at him. Trenton was grieving his friend, and it was too much to ask him to recognize the shittiness of trying to lay the emotional labor of being Chad's death witness at her feet. "Sure."

Dean's cousins entered with Sev on their heels. Sev looked . . . conflicted, like he couldn't decide what expression to wear. Sadness. Weariness. Anger. Relief.

"You OK?" Sev asked.

"Nope," Jess answered honestly.

"She's fine," Diana huffed, looking more than a little annoyed.

"Blister said he'd rather take your statement at the lodge, away from your friends, so your memory of finding Chad doesn't get . . . influenced," Poppy said.

"Blister?" Trenton asked. "Who's Blister?"

"What do you mean, 'influenced'?" Diana demanded. She kept glancing back and forth between Jess and Poppy, as if she couldn't decide who she wanted to glare at.

"He'll come by to take your statements later," Poppy told Trenton.

"Why don't you come stay at my place, Jess?" Sis suggested. "You've been through a lot, and I don't like the idea of leaving you with those people."

"What do you mean, 'those people'?" Aubrey demanded.

"I would feel better if you stayed with Sis," Dean told her.

"Wait, so you want to escort Jess to talk to the police as the only witness to a damaging, potentially criminal liability that occurred on your property? And then isolate her in one of your homes?" Sev asked, frowning at her.

So Sev's lawyer brain *was* engaged.

"I don't know how I feel about Jess staying with you," Diana protested. "Jess has things to do! She works for me."

Jess's jaw dropped. Did Diana still think her proposal was happening the next day? Trenton was a wreck. And Chad was fucking *dead*.

Slowly, it felt like Jess's brain was starting to fire again, like it was a rebooting computer catching up with the new dead-body-based programming.

"I need to make some calls," Sev told Poppy. "I assume I can use your office?"

Poppy nodded. "I'll meet you there shortly."

"I hate to be insensitive here, but this is probably going to end up on the news," Jess said, rubbing her arms to try to generate some warmth. "Particularly so soon after Jeremy Treadaway's accident. Networks love stories like this, death in the places that rich people hide away. It's like a postmillennial Agatha Christie story."

"What? No! This can't get out," Trenton cried. He rubbed his hand over his hair, leaving the thick gold strands sticking up at all angles. For once, Jess's hand didn't itch to reach out and smooth it for him. Her smoothing-out resources were exhausted. "My family's gonna shit. They warned me about spending time with Chad, that he could get me into trouble. Aw, man, my dad's gonna *kill* me."

Jess didn't know whether she felt bad for him or felt like smacking him. Chad was dead. He was *dead* and all Trenton could think about was how bad it was for *him*. And it wasn't like Jess was in deep mourning for the guy, but *geez*.

Poppy's expression was grim. "I don't see how we can prevent news coverage, Mr. Tillard. We can only issue a press release sincerely expressing our sympathy for the Hardcastle family and hope the court of public opinion isn't too harsh."

"Well, I think we know how that's going to go," Sis muttered.

"Sweetie, this is why we have PR people," Jonquil reminded her. "Call Chandra. Tell her we need a whole containment strategy, OK?"

Clearly, Jonquil was one of those people who became extremely rational in a pinch.

"I think I need to be included in that conversation," Diana insisted, suddenly tearless. "I have an online presence to protect. My brand is focused on luxe positivity, not sauna death!"

Jonquil's eyes nearly rolled, but she managed to stop herself mid-iris-rise. Jess jumped in to remind Diana, "No one even knows you're here right now. Remember? You haven't been able to post anything."

"And rest assured, we won't tell anyone," Poppy told her. "The good news is that we only have a handful of guests right now. There's generally a lag between weekends."

"I can promise that I will not talk about this to the press," Jess told Trenton. "I barely want to relive it while talking to a cop. Named Blister. Which I have to go do now."

"Jess, you can't be serious!" Diana cried. "You can't just go! *I need you!*"

"Did you miss the part about the police?" Jess demanded. "They tend not to accept, 'Diana needs me to reschedule' as an excuse."

Trenton patted Diana's shoulder as she buried her face in his shirt. "Um, Jess, DeeDee could really use a friend right now."

"Jess found the body," Kiki reminded her. "She probably needs a minute to herself."

Diana barely lifted her face from Trenton's shirt monogram, where she was leaving a distinct mascara streak, to yell, "Well, it's *my* pre-engagement week that's ruined, not hers!"

Wow.

Even Aubrey's expression faltered at that.

Sensing that she was losing the crowd, Diana blinked rapidly. A strange current of emotion seemed to ripple over her face, like she was trying to remember how to cry. "It's all ruined! The wedding is ruined before it's even started!"

"No, honey, of course the wedding isn't ruined," Aubrey told her. She knelt in front of Diana and Trenton, patting their joined hands. "I'm sure one of Trenton's cousins or friends can step in as best man!"

"But it won't be the same!" Diana wailed.

"Um, I couldn't replace Chad," Trenton told her, pulling his hand away from Aubrey. "I just couldn't."

"Jess, I need you and Aubrey to put your heads together and find a way to fix this!" Diana shrieked. When Trenton recoiled slightly, she glanced at him and changed her pitch from strident to pitiful. "Please!"

"Yeah, I'm just gonna . . . go. Yeah, I'm gonna go," Jess said as Dean hoisted Jess's yoga tote bag onto his shoulder.

"I'll walk you out," Trenton told her. He basically handed Diana over to Aubrey, who seemed to be at a loss as to what was expected of her, like an alligator given care of a toddler.

Dean put a protective arm around Jess, even as Trenton tried to stand to be the one to "escort" her out of the villa. Jess waved him away, so he sank back onto the couch. She appreciated Trenton's attempt to reassure her, but she couldn't help but feel that eventually that support would somehow turn into Jess comforting Trenton.

The walk up the hill seemed to draw oxygen into her blood, helping her to focus—something that was probably important when one was talking to the police. As they passed the gate entrance, Jess noted several guests standing with their luggage.

"People are checking out?" Jess asked. Dean nodded grimly.

By the time they reached the main lodge, Jess felt connected to her body again, less like she was caught up in an awful dream. Jamie was waiting in Poppy's office with a carafe of strong coffee and a crème brûlée with a particularly thick sugar crust. He had even taken time to put little edible flowers in a decorative crescent on top.

"You're gonna need the sugar once the adrenaline wears off, hon, trust me," Jamie said, giving her a fatherly kiss on the forehead.

Jess felt weird, indulging in a sugary treat while Dean just sat there, watching her. He, however, looked pointedly at her spoon every time she stopped eating. Poppy joined them shortly, guzzling the coffee Jamie handed her. The smell of the decorative flowers hit Jess's nostrils and she was reminded of the steaming Persephone's Garden Shower, heavy with the smell of jasmine. Suddenly, she remembered the disinterested spa employee at the thermal suite.

"Wait, wasn't there a clerk at the front desk?" Jess asked. "Why didn't she find Chad?"

"Hannah," Poppy sighed, rubbing at her temples. "Chad slipped Hannah cash to pretend he wasn't there so he could sit in the sauna as long as he wanted. No recording his time of arrival, no keeping his Bliss Key at the front desk. He also made some pretty disgusting offers of a personal nature, so Hannah wasn't real inclined to follow our safety procedures and check on him regularly. Don't worry about it. We have insurance agents and lawyers to deal with that. I mean, Jonquil may seem like she's away with the fairies, but she got a risk assessment expert to review our policies before we even opened."

A loud knock startled Jess, prompting Dean to take her hand. Dean yelled for the person to enter.

"I need to talk to her," Sheriff Blister said, taking off his round campaign-style hat at the door. Beth came in at Blister's heels, giving Jess a nod and a smile. Dean seemed immediately tense at the sight of the man. Given how little help Dean seemed to receive after Emma Lee's disappearance, that wasn't particularly surprising.

"Jess, give me a dollar," Beth told her.

Jess just stared at her.

Beth said, "Give me a dollar, so you're officially my client and Blister doesn't question you without an attorney present."

"Do I need an attorney present?" Jess asked, as Poppy handed her a bill from her own pocket.

"Well, it feels like it's not in my best interest to say so, but this is the second dead body you've 'stumbled upon' in a week," Blister told her. "Couldn't hurt."

The shock of finding Chad made way to fear. Did the sheriff think she killed Chad? How? It wasn't like she could overpower the guy. He was huge. But she'd been in the treatment suite building for who knows how long, unsupervised, alone . . . Oh, shit. Given the Jeremy of it all, this did look pretty bad.

"How did Chad die?" Jess asked.

"We don't know yet," Blister replied, watching her carefully. "The case is headed straight to the state medical examiner's office. This time."

Dean glared and stood, making room for Blister to sit near Jess. Beth stood behind Jess, a hand on her shoulder. Jess's stomach rolled as the image of Chad, dead and still on the floor, popped into her mind. And that bled into an image of Jeremy floating face down in the hollow. Who was next? Should she just leave the Golden Ash before anyone else got hurt? Poppy slid a bottle of spring water across the desk to her. Jess sipped it until her bile was no longer crawling up her throat.

With a gentler tone, Blister asked, "Can you tell me what happened?"

Jess recounted the unpleasant cheese aroma, the puddle of vomit, Chad's cold skin, finishing with, "I don't remember much after slapping the panic button. Oh, no, I need to cancel the arrangements for Trenton's proposal. I can call the vendors."

She stood on wobbly legs, but Poppy pushed her gently back into her seat.

"It's done. I had your list. I had Sis make the calls, telling them not to come. It came in handy, being so involved in the planning process." Poppy gave her a glum smile.

Blister tapped a hand lightly on Poppy's desk, trying to bring Jess's attention back to him. Dean glared, but Jess appreciated the gentle attempt to keep her jumbled brain from spinning out of orbit.

"Did you see anyone else in the building?" Blister asked.

Jess shook her head. "Just the front desk attendant."

"What about the swipe security thing?" Blister asked Poppy. "Whose keys were swiped in at the thermal place at the time of Mr. Hardcastle's death?"

"Hannah, the front desk clerk," Poppy told him, sliding him a piece of paper labeled BLISS KEY ACCESS LOG—THERMAL SUITE, which appeared to list all the key swipes for the day. She shot a guilty look at Jess. "And Jess. They were the only ones in the building with him. Jess arrived four hours after Chad checked in."

"That's helpful, thanks. Miss Jess, did the deceased seem agitated or stressed when you last saw him alive?"

Jess wanted to laugh, but that seemed *so* inappropriate. "Chad didn't get stressed. He had no reason to. Everything was taken care of for him by his family. But from what I know of him? If he was told he could only sit in the sauna for fifteen minutes, he'd sit in there for three hours. Just out of spite."

"Are you sure you're not just saying that because you're trying to protect the Osbournes?" Blister asked. "You seem awfully chummy for someone who just got here a few days ago."

"Some people have a little more personal appeal than you do, Blister," Dean retorted.

Blister frowned at Dean. "How would you classify your relationship with the deceased?"

Jess glanced at Beth, who nodded. "I didn't have one?"

"I was given to understand that you were classmates at college," Blister replied.

"Barely."

Blister shrugged. "Well, sometimes that's worse, being ignored. Hurt feelings can fester. You see someone years later, when you least expect it—"

"Wait, are you accusing Jess of trying to protect our family from claims of negligence or accusing her of having intentions of harming Chad Hardcastle?" Beth asked. "Pick a lane."

Blister raised his hands. "I'm just trying to clarify the situation, explore every possibility."

"Well, explore the ones that don't lead you to stupid conclusions," Dean shot back.

Blister stood, and he seemed to realize how much shorter he was when standing next to Dean. He moved away, which honestly helped Jess breathe a little better. "Well, we're gonna have to wait for the medical examiner to make an official report in terms of cause of death. It's not professional for me to speculate now."

"Yeah, I would hate for you to be unprofessional," Dean muttered.

Blister stood there, fidgeting with his hat. He ignored Dean pointedly as he backed toward the door.

"Is this one of those 'don't leave town because we're suspects' scenarios?" Jess asked.

"Why do you think you would be suspects?" Blister asked as Dean pinched his nose.

"Because I found a young, otherwise healthy guy dead in a sauna?" Jess suggested.

"Stop trying to get your 'aha' moment, Blister," Beth told him.

"Miss Poppy says you're paid up for the week," Blister said. "And most of the other guests seem to be leaving anyway, so you might as well stay until we get confirmation that this was just an accident."

Poppy shrugged. "We told the guests there was a problem with the gas heating that renders the thermal spa and treatment suites unusable."

Dean asked, "So they think the emergency vehicles are here because of a gas leak?"

"Pretty much," Poppy said, pursing her lips. "And they were more than willing to leave now in exchange for deep discounts on future stays."

"You are fiendishly brilliant," Jess told her.

"Most of them were scheduled to leave in the next day or two anyway. It's not a huge loss," Poppy said. Her gaze shot to Blister. "Except for the loss of Chad, of course—I just meant financially. Oh, don't get all wound up, Blister."

"I'll follow up with any questions," Blister said, patting her hand. "Thank you for your cooperation."

Dean was right. Blister's name made sense now. He was rubbing her nerves raw.

"I think we should let Ms. Bricker get some rest," Beth said, escorting Blister out the door. "You're welcome to come back or call with any follow-ups at any time. We will all cooperate fully."

Poppy closed the door behind them and flopped into her desk chair, her head tipping back. "Fuck."

"I'm so sorry," Jess said.

Poppy's head snapped up again. "Why are you sorry?"

"I honestly don't know," Jess replied.

"It's going to be OK," Dean assured Poppy. "We didn't do anything wrong."

"I know. And I know I need to call Chandra and do all the logistical things," she sighed. "One accident, we could explain away and people would forget. But twice in a week? This is a disaster. It's just . . . it fucking sucks."

"It really does," Jess agreed. Just then, Owen burst into the room and pulled Poppy into his arms. Jess smiled as Poppy just melted against him. For the first time, Poppy's facade cracked and Jess heard her sniffle.

"We should go," Dean said as Jess stood.

They quietly exited as Owen let Poppy cry out the loss in their little sanctuary.

The grounds were eerily silent save for the wind whipping through the trees, rattling the yellow crime-scene tape around the thermal suite building. The emergency vehicles had pulled away. The guests had been whisked off into the dusk by the shuttles.

Jess didn't feel entirely safe walking across the grounds. Even with Dean holding her hand, there was a sense of menace, like some monster could come running out of the trees with a chainsaw at any second.

"Are you going to be able to sleep tonight, do you think?" Dean asked her, giving her hand a squeeze.

"I have no idea," she said. "And it's probably better that I'm staying at Sis's because I don't want to keep you from being able to get up for breakfast tomorrow morning." She blinked. "That sounded way dirtier than I intended it to be. It's just that the potential for me having nightmares is pretty high here, and you have to get up early."

"The disrupted sleep will come," he promised as they approached the family houses. "Which also sounds dirtier than I intended . . . But I will be happy to have my sleep disrupted on another night. Right now, I think we're both a little too traumatized to make responsible choices."

"I wish you weren't so smart." She nodded as he wrapped her tight against his chest. Sis opened her door.

"Clear out, bud, we're gonna have the world's weirdest slumber party," Sis told him, making Jess laugh.

"I'm going to bed," Dean called. "I'm a loud yell away if you need anything."

Jess waved as Sis put her arm around her.

"We're getting drunk," Sis informed her, pulling an icy bottle of vodka from behind her back, its frost creeping all the way up the neck.

Jess's head dropped forward as the full weight of the day seemed to drag her entire body down. "Yay for us."

Inside, Sis's place was just as orderly and neat as the outside. Jess's shoes almost echoed on the hardwood floors because there was very little hanging on the sky-blue walls besides little framed photos of what Jess assumed were Sis's goats. Jess half expected to see the couch made up for her, but Sis carried her bag into a tidy little guest room. The sight of the neatly made bed with its white-and-purple wedding ring quilt—complete with a little stack of towels at the foot—shouldn't have warmed Jess's heart, but it did.

"I like goats. I like time to myself. I don't like knickknacks," Sis told her. "Plus, when I'm stumbling around at four in the morning to get out to the farm patch, I don't need extra things to trip on or knock over."

"That's very sensible. I appreciate you letting me stay here. You don't even know me."

Sis shrugged, sliding a molded-ice shot glass full of vodka across the counter to her. "Eh, Poppy ran a background check on you before you got here."

"What?" Jess exclaimed as Sis sliced a block of white cheese mixed with herbs and arranged it on a plate with some crackers dusted with red flakes.

"I'm kidding. But I have a good feeling about you. My cousins like you. Dean more than likes you. Jamie let you into the kitchen, which is always a good sign," Sis told her. "I think you're having a hard time, and I want to help you out. But if you murder me in my sleep, my cousins will make sure the true-crime documentary makes you look like a total asshole."

Jess raised her shot glass in a mockery of a toast. "Understood. My nana and her friends will do the same to you."

"Mutually assured destruction, then," Sis said, clinking her glass against Jess's.

Jess tossed the vodka back and winced at the cold burn in her throat. "Yep. Still better than moonshine."

Grabbing their provisions, Sis nodded toward a comfy-looking couch covered in white canvas material. Jess collapsed onto the seat and sighed, pulling one of the sea blue cushions to her chest. She was starting to see what Jamie meant about the adrenaline crash.

"Probably need to wait a bit on my next shot," she said. She and Sis put their ice shot glasses on little blue-and-white tile coasters featuring leaping goats. "Drinking makes my nightmares worse. Also, I have nightmares. And sometimes I shout absolute nonsense in my sleep, so . . . that's what you've welcomed into your home. Good luck."

"It's going to be fine. I was raised with a big family. Sleeping alone in a silent house freaks me out sometimes," Sis assured her.

"How are you doing?" Jess asked. "This place is your home. You're stuck taking care of me when you're probably, I don't know, at least a little discombobulated. And you knew Chad since you were a kid. Are you OK?"

Sis blew out a long breath, taking another shot. "I mean, it sucks, and it's going to leave an unpleasant mark on the end of this season. But as far as this place goes? We've had some form of hotel on this mountain for the last hundred years, so yeah, guests have died here. We're probably haunted as hell."

"Wish I didn't have to think about it in terms of guests dying being 'not that big of a deal,'" Jess muttered.

"But over the years, I've come to understand rich people. They will forget about this by the spring and come back clamoring for body wraps and yoga. After all, nothing like that could ever happen to *them*," Sis said. "And the fact that I knew Chad? Eh."

Sis took a long drink from a glass bottle of spring water. "When we were teenagers, Sev and Chad would drift around to some of the townie bonfire parties. We knew them, but we didn't *know* them, you know? We didn't spend enough time around them to really learn anything deep about them. Sev was mostly OK, but Chad . . ."

"I'm sure teenage Chad was a delight," Jess commented dryly.

Sis chewed on a cracker, considering. "You know what I kept thinking about, like, since you got here? The fact that Chad got really creepy with Emma Lee when we were kids. He wouldn't take no for an answer, not even when Dean kicked his ass."

"I know it's wrong, but I sort of wish I could have seen that," Jess said, cringing.

"Emma Lee was my friend before she was my brother's soul mate. She was tough as hell but never cruel—even though she had every right to be. Her dad thought nothing of stealing every dollar in the house to take on one of his 'casino trips,' like calling it something that sounded fancy would make it something other than dragging his family into hell. And we told ourselves it was going to be OK, because we knew that one day, Emma Lee was going to go on to invent something that saved the world. Or blew it up."

Again, Jess thought of Kiki, of the similarities of greatness growing in such unlikely soil. She poured herself another shot and said a silent apology to her former roommate for leaving her alone with Diana.

Sis plucked a slice of garlic cheddar from the tray. "When the time came for us to go to college, I thought schools would fall all over themselves to hand her scholarship money. And they gave her some scholarships, but not nearly enough to pay for everything. She should have qualified for more financial aid, but her parents never filed taxes. Didn't see the point. I thought maybe once she was there, she would earn more, like 'The National Fund to Support Brilliant Brunettes from Terrible Families' or something. But there were some questions . . . about her academic performance."

"They thought she was cheating?" Jess asked, downing her shot. "But you said she was scary smart."

"She *was*, that's how she managed to get away with cheating *for other students* without getting caught all through high school," Sis said. "I'm pretty sure she took the SAT for a girl over in Draffenville. Her own college suspected her multiple times, over the years, of 'helping' other kids, but the administration could never prove anything. So, they couldn't kick her out, but they weren't about to make it easier for her to stick around.

"Anyway, because of the lack of scholarship money, Emma Lee had to work even harder to scrape together what she could to get her through the school year," Sis said. "That last summer, I hardly saw her because she was spending all her time waiting tables at two restaurants in town. I mean, I saw more of Chad and Sev than I did her, which I still find depressing. But she came to that last party and it was great, because she was in such a good mood. She'd been so stressed out that week, and she wouldn't tell me what was going on, but suddenly, she was almost giddy. Everything was going to be OK. And then, she was gone."

"She couldn't have been pregnant, could she?" Jess asked. "I mean, if I was a college kid with big plans, trying to pull myself out of the poverty cycle, an unexpected pregnancy would stress me out."

"Not with Dean's baby," Sis said, scoffing. "Unless you can get pregnant by text message. They never saw each other. They were always working."

Jess's mouth dropped open. "You don't think *Chad* got her pregnant, do you?"

"Ew, no," Sis said, blanching as if she'd been slapped.

"Well, you said he wouldn't take no for an answer, and Chad was a fucking creep. God . . . rest . . . his soul. Oh, Jesus, I'm a terrible person." Jess sighed, pouring herself another shot. "Is it possible her dad hurt her? You said she had that special secret path through the woods. What if her dad caught up to her on the secret path and tried to shake her down for money?"

"And killed her when she said no?" Sis guessed. "It's something I thought about. Anything's possible. And after Emma Lee disappeared, it came out that someone wrote a check for cash, clearing her entire savings account."

"When?"

Sis shook her head. "A week or so before she disappeared? It could have been Emma Lee, getting ready to run. It could have been her parents, forging her signature on the check. Rumor was, their house was about to be foreclosed on—and it was, almost a year later."

"What happened to her parents?"

Sis frowned. "Her dad ran off a few months after Emma Lee disappeared. Never saw him again. Her mom moved away to Kentucky to be with family, and then she passed away of cancer a few years later. We were the only ones who really looked for her. We were the family that wanted her."

Sis poured a final shot for both of them. "Why are you asking all these questions about Emma Lee?"

"Well, for one thing, it's keeping me from seeing Chad's face, over and over again, every time I close my eyes. And, I don't know, I just heard about the Emma Lee thing last night and Chad happened today. In my brain, I guess, the two things are linked. It's probably nothing." Jess scrubbed her hand across her face. "Augh. I'm exhausted."

"Right." Sis stood and pulled Jess to her feet. "Bedtime for both of us. I'll clean this up in the morning. I put out the fancy guest towels and soaps. Help yourself to anything in the fridge. There won't be any more deaths between now and sunrise. I'm almost eighty percent sure."

"Too soon," Jess told her, slumping toward the guest room.

"Eh, inappropriate humor. It's my chief defense mechanism."

In the tidy little guest room, Jess climbed into the bed and pulled the covers up to her chin. She could hear Sis settling into her bedroom on the other side of the wall. For an hour, she tried to focus on her breathing, on intentionally relaxing her body into sleep. She was warm. And she was safe under Sis's roof.

But it wasn't enough.

She considered the vodka bottle in the kitchen, but that seemed like an unhealthy sleep aid. She crept out of bed, listening for the sound of Sis breathing. Jess didn't want to wake her host, but she also didn't want to worry her. She slipped on her shoes and padded into the kitchen, grateful for the lack of clutter for her to trip over in the dark. She grabbed a spare key from the hook near the door and scribbled an explanation on a Post-It, leaving it where Sis was sure to see it. She was careful to lock the door behind her, and walked over to the smallest of the Osbourne cottages.

Dean was waiting up, like he knew that she wouldn't be able to sleep, and answered the door within seconds of her knock. Without words, he took her hand and led her through the tiny living room to the bedroom. It certainly wasn't as organized and Zen as Sis's place, but for a man living alone—it wasn't terrible.

They crawled into the bed, and Dean pulled the covers over them both. She burrowed into his arms, her nose buried into the warm, spice-scented crook of his neck. Her breathing evened out as he stroked her back. Her mind drifted, and for the first time in a long time, she didn't worry.

Jess's Big Book of Life Plans: There is no plan for this. Jessamine Bricker has no plan.

CHAPTER 13

In the morning, Dean didn't mention her tornado hair or her post-drinking morning breath. He just kissed her soundly and ran out the door for the breakfast shift. He also didn't mention nightmares, which she considered a good sign. In fact, she didn't remember dreaming at all, just deep and endless sleep that left her feeling less tattered.

It was a feeling she didn't want to lose. Jess wondered if she could just stay on this side of the property until Blister decided he'd asked her enough questions. She could tell Trenton she didn't need his money. She could fly back to Nashville without any guilt whatsoever—but if she did that, she would have to live with knowing she lied to Trenton, because she did need his money.

She'd tried. She really had. But this whole week was starting to feel like a fever dream. From the start, Jess had been chasing the idea that she could make this last-minute, half-assed job into some sort of life-preserving miracle, but now . . . two people were dead. That seemed like a bad sign, in terms of miracles.

Outside, the wind was whipping leaves off the trees, stripping them bare as fat, cold raindrops spattered against the windows. She saw a bright yellow rain jacket through the haze on the glass, walking toward the door. She rose to open it, but her hand drew back from the knob.

Given all the weird deaths, maybe she shouldn't open the door to this unknown yellow blur.

"Open the door, Bricker!" a familiar voice called from the other side of the glass. "You brother-seducing hussy."

Jess opened the door to find Sis standing there under an umbrella with an amused look on her face. "I woke up before dawn to find your bed empty. Clearly, I should have put some sort of bell on the door to alert me to you sneaking out like a hormonal teenager."

"I couldn't sleep," Jess said. "And Dean and I didn't do . . . anything, we just—"

"I don't need details. I'm just happy for you," Sis said. "Though it goes without saying that if you hurt my brother when he's opening up for the first time in decades, I will murder you. I might be able to make it look like a spa-related accident, considering the week we've had."

"Too soon," Jess told her. "But understood. I won't do anything to hurt Dean. At least not on purpose."

Sis held up Jess's bag. "I brought your clothes. Poppy says your group is having breakfast at the main lodge, if you're up for it."

Jess groaned loudly. She was not proud of it.

"You don't have to go," Sis assured her. "Dean said you have complete access to his fridge or he will make something for you, if you don't want to see them."

Jess thought of Kiki, left behind with that den of snakes. Not to mention poor Sev, who was going to have to deal with the logistics of getting Chad home to his family. She hadn't liked Chad, but Sev seemed like a decent guy. Jess could be of some use to him, as opposed to just sitting around an Osbourne's house twisting herself into knots. And desperately resisting the urge to go through Dean's stuff.

"I'll go," Jess sighed. She went to Dean's bathroom and pulled on her most comfortable joggers and claimed a faded blue hoodie of Dean's.

"I see we've given up on 'lavish, romantic, and innovative,'" Sis said dryly as Jess walked out.

"Don't forget 'genuine'!" Jess chirped, pulling her shoulder in front of her chin in a mockery of a pouty pose.

"Don't get me wrong. You look cute as a button," Sis told her. "But I saw Diana when Jonquil and Poppy were driving the group up the hill for breakfast. The girl was wearing what looked like a church dress—in that weird tampon package pink color she's always wearing. What is with the pink?"

"It's her signature color." Jess cringed. "I'm pretty sure that was the dress she wants to wear for the proposal, which I think she believes is still happening today, despite the best man having died in a sauna accident yesterday. I imagine she's wearing it as a reminder to me. I haven't gotten the job done."

"Oh, fuck her," Sis said as they locked Dean's front door behind them. "It's not like you planned to find Chad's body just to interrupt her precious social media posts—unless, of course, you murdered Chad just to interrupt her precious social media posts, in which case, you were the last person I would have suspected. Good for you."

Jess shook her head. "Again, too soon."

The yellow crime-scene tape flapped violently in the cold wind as they trudged around the thermal suite. The rain clouds seemed to be passing over them with all the speed of an angry mob. The spa felt more than empty; it felt abandoned, and brought to mind the story Beth told her about location scouts and horror movies. Jess supposed the Osbournes never felt this weird isolation, having one another around.

As they passed the "Y" in the path that led to the main lodge, a piece of litter fluttered across the ground, an anomaly on the pristine Golden Ash campus. Jess bent to pick up the matchbook that Chad must have dropped on the ground the day before when he'd lit his cigarette. Jess turned it over in her hands. The bright green logo was damaged from the rain but it was still there—a leaping bass breaking through the surface of a lake near the Sportsman's Lodge Motor Inn. Just off Route 9.

Fuck.

Well, that explained why Diana seemed to be taking Chad's death a little harder than was appropriate. Chad and Diana hadn't just been arguing that afternoon Jess and Sev had spotted them. That was a *lovers' quarrel*. Diana had been sleeping with Chad.

At a fishing motel.

Not exactly lavish, innovative, or romantic.

"You OK?" Sis asked.

Jess nodded, shoving the tattered matchbook in her pocket. They entered the main lodge to find Poppy answering questions with a calm authority usually reserved for press conferences post–natural disaster. Meanwhile, Jess's party sat like some Renaissance painting celebrating a feast of displeased dickheads.

Dean waved to her from inside the kitchen, but without a weapon this time, so that was nice. Jess idly wondered about the location of Susan Treadaway or Zephyr, but thought she was better off not knowing.

"Yes, but I don't understand why we have to talk to the police," Aubrey was saying. "We didn't see anything. It was Jess—"

Aubrey paused as her eyes bulged, taking in Jess's extremely casual outfit. "Jessie, what are you *wearing*?"

"Clothes," Jess shot back as Poppy handed her a cup of coffee. Kiki offered her an awkward little wave. Diana was so focused on stroking Trenton's shoulder that she didn't even look up as Jess approached. Trenton looked miserable, sallow and drawn, his eyes red-rimmed.

Sev was . . . where was Sev?

"Never mind Jess's unfortunate choices, fashion or otherwise," Aubrey sniffed. "Please tell me that you have some plan to accommodate our party in whatever facilities are still open. I would hope that we're not expected to just sit around, staring at the walls, while we wait for the police to release us."

Poppy appeared to be dumbstruck by this.

"You really want to use the thermal suite after this?" Jess marveled at her, shaking her head.

"Well, obviously the thermal suite is closed, but that doesn't mean that we can't get our money's worth," Diana huffed, turning her attention from Trenton. "You can still do facials and manicures, right?"

Of course, it wasn't Diana's money, but Trenton had the good grace not to bring that up. He was too busy staring into his plate, picking at his eggs, while Diana rubbed his arm.

Jess simply stared. Did Diana really expect the Osbournes to continue to provide mani-pedis and facials when someone had just died in their facility?

"I'm sure we can arrange something," Poppy said, through gritted teeth. "Let me talk to the staff."

"I was going to help Sev with the logistics of dealing with . . . everything," Jess said. "Can you tell me where I can find him?"

"I think he's still back at the villa. Something about packing up Ch—" Trenton swallowed heavily. "Chad's stuff."

"Well, then, I think I'll just take this delicious coffee and a pastry and go down to the villa to help him," Jess said, backing toward the door.

"Aw, that's sweet, Jess," Trenton said, beaming at her and then turning to Diana. "Isn't she sweet?"

"Jessie, what could you possibly *do?*" Diana asked, following as Jess backed toward the door.

"Something useful," Jess replied, walking out of the lodge and toward the villas. Dean stepped out of the kitchen as though he was going to follow her.

Poppy cleared her throat. "Jess, why don't you let me walk you down?"

"I can go with you," Dean offered. Behind him, Jess could see Jamie working three different pans on the stove.

"You both have your hands full here," Jess said, looking toward her table.

"At least take this. The rain is picking up," Dean said, handing her his dark green rain jacket. She took it and slipped it on. Had he been listening to her table's conversation the whole time? Weirdly, that made Jess feel better, that he was looking out for her. "I don't love you spending time with Sev, but I also don't love telling you what to do. So just be careful."

"I will, I promise," she told him and then kissed his cheek. Over his shoulder, Jess could see Diana's brown eyes narrowing, her lip curled back. Jess walked away and, not for the first time, wondered if she was a fool to turn her back on Diana Helston.

It took quite a few knocks before Sev answered. He looked . . . well, perfectly handsome because he was Sev, but tired enough that he had dark shadows underneath his eyes.

The Serenity Villa was anything but. The poor housekeeping staff couldn't possibly keep up with the amount of filthy clothes and wet towels three grown men had dropped and walked away from. Dirty room service dishes were strewn across the kitchen countertop. And the living area, while just as tastefully decorated as the Tranquility Villa, had a familiar distinct bad Parmesan smell that made Jess gag.

What in the frat-house fuck?

"Come on in, Jess," he said, sounding very tired.

Would it be rude to ask him to come outside? Into a gathering storm? Just to avoid the odor of his cabin, which vaguely smelled of Chad's death scene? Probably. She swallowed heavily, stepping into the fray. The dirty, disgusting fray.

"Somehow, *I'm* Chad's next of kin," Sev said, his voice small and helpless. He cleared debris off the couch so Jess could sit. She noticed an empty full-sized vodka bottle amongst the garbage—a midrange brand called Steel Hills. "I didn't even like the guy, but right now, I'm the closest one in the family who can handle all the details of death. My brother asked me to take care of things until they can get here. They're at the Bimini house right now, and I guess there's weather coming up that's messing with flights all the way up the Eastern Seaboard."

He nodded out the window to the swirling gray sky.

"The family is sending someone to pick him up, but the sheriff said they can't release him until the coroner is done with his body," Sev said. "And then we take him to Algren and Marris in Richmond. They've always handled our people."

"It's probably pretty routine to do an autopsy on a thirty-two-year-old no matter how they die," Jess told him.

A tray full of room service domes on the kitchenette counter caught Jess's eye . . . and her nose. It seemed to be the source of the smell in the room—in particular, a plate with bits of wide, flat noodles dried to the surface in the gluey remains of cream sauce. Was this the pasta dish Jeremy was raving about? Susan Treadaway was right. It did smell like feet.

"I want to move over to the family place," he said. "I figured I'd wait there for my brother and my dad, but I don't want to leave Trenton alone here with Diana."

"Yeah, that seems pretty sensible," Jess admitted. Meanwhile, her conscience and her sense of self-preservation battled it out, and only her financial self-awareness kept her from blurting out *Hey, the prospective bride you're here to protect your employer from? Yeah, she was sleeping with your dead nephew. Small world, huh?*

So instead, she said, "I guess you haven't had time to talk to Trenton or Diana about the prenup?"

Sev shook his head, dark gold hair falling into his eyes. "It didn't seem like the right time before, and now? Trenton's just taking this so hard. And part of it is not wanting to bother him with something that seems so far off, you know, and unimportant. And the other part is the guilt. I mean, Trenton is mourning . . . and it's *Chad*. He obviously saw something in him that I didn't, and I'm the guy's family."

Sev thanked her quietly while she poured him a cup of coffee from a carafe on the counter. Jess noted that the electric kettle was sitting right next to it . . . so where was the one from their kitchen? "It sounds like a dick thing to say, but I was the golden child. And I never missed a chance to prove I was smarter, faster, better—because it made my old man happy. For Hardcastles, that kind of thing matters. Something about Chad's whole being provoked my need to dunk on him. And now that he's gone, that makes me feel just fucking awful."

Jess reached out and patted his arm, careful to keep her fingers over his sweater sleeve because she didn't want to touch him with hands that had touched Chad's dead body. That seemed . . . wrong. "I spent some time with Chad this week. I get it."

"I just never understood the guy," Sev said, standing up and unzipping a leather weekend bag with Chad's initials stamped on the side. He pulled out reams of loose paperwork, legal pad pages, and glossy brochure mock-ups. They showed 3D renderings of what looked like an amusement park superimposed over the nearby mountains—and that amusement park catered exclusively to douchebags. Little fake 3D people were riding ATVs on a maze of dirt tracks, wingsuit flying from an obnoxiously orange platform, and bungee jumping from an entirely different obnoxiously orange platform. It looked like Chad had been planning an outdoor sports complex right next to the spa. Frankly, a lot of these mock-up images looked like they were captured *from* the spa property, and a lot of the proposed changes involved cutting down huge swaths of trees visible from the Golden Ash.

"Hardcastle Pines *Extreme?*" Jess said, holding it up for Sev's inspection. "Ew. On several levels."

"I found this stuff in Chad's room," Sev said, sitting next to her on the couch. "Honestly, it looks like he was trying to come up with a proposal to develop the family property into some sports mecca that only we could use. And unlike most of his dumbass ideas, there was some chance my dad might actually fund this one because he desperately wants the family to spend more time together at Hardcastle Pines. Which means Chad would have spent months, possibly years, dicking around with construction crews while siphoning cash off the budget my dad gave him. Honestly, the cash siphoning might have been the whole point. Other than fucking with the Osbournes, which he also enjoys. Enjoyed, ugh. I haven't adjusted to past tense yet."

"Wait, what?"

Sev spread the papers out on the nearby coffee table. "I think he'd been sneaking around here at night, like, scouting the property? It makes no damn sense, but I saw him walking out the first night we got here with a flashlight."

"Probably not, Sev," she said, frowning as she looked over the half-assed prospectus. "I never saw Chad go near the woods. He bitched about having to walk to the main lodge."

Well, she did see Chad walk to the Stillness Villa to hook up with the Yoni Egg Queen, but Jess didn't think that was a productive thing to add to the conversation. Hell, as far as Jess knew, Chad had snuck over to Hardcastle Pines to raid their liquor supply. That might explain the empty vodka bottle.

"Jess, I was staying with him and even I couldn't say where he was every minute of the day," Sev insisted. "And if one of the Osbournes saw him . . . Well, really, they wouldn't have had to see him themselves. Chad was just the sort of dickhead to just walk into Poppy Osbourne's office and announce that he was going to build a loud, intrusive sports playground right next door that was going to ruin her views and disrupt her guests' tranquility with loud engines."

Jess's thoughts strayed to the lights she'd seen bobbing around in the woods all week. Could it have been Chad out there? Wait, no, she'd seen those lights before Trenton's group had shown up. "What are you getting at here, Sev?"

"I wonder if the Osbournes had anything to do with . . . all of this. You know, one of them could have messed with the controls on the sauna, locked Chad in. Left him for you to find. And no one would suspect you."

Jess burst out laughing. "What? No!"

"Why? Because they've been nice to *you*? I know they seem all sweet and hippie-dippie, Jess. But I've known these people since we were kids, and there's things you don't know about them. There was a girl who disappeared when we were in college. She broke up with Dean, and the next thing you know, she was never seen again."

"Wait, you mean Emma Lee Redfern?" Jess laughed, incredulous. "The Osbournes loved her. *Dean* loved her. They dated for years."

"Yeah, and the two of them fought *all of the time*," Sev said. "About everything—where to go, what to do, whether to spend time with his cousins. She wanted to move to some big city far away and take Dean with her. Away from the family, and trust me, those girls didn't like that. Sis especially."

"Are you sure you read the situation right?" Jess asked. "Sis said she and Emma Lee were close. That the whole family was worried when she disappeared. You were the one who said that you were cooped up doing schoolwork most summers."

"I don't know." Sev groaned, rubbing his hand over his eyes. "Maybe I just got a bad impression when we were kids. I'm just tired and overwhelmed with the bullshit that my nephew left behind for me to deal with. As usual."

After a long moment, she said, "Neither one of us should be involved in Chad's eulogy."

Pursing his lips, Sev shook his head. "Nope."

Jess thought it was probably a sign she was spending too much time in Poppy's office when Poppy welcomed Sev and Jess inside to use her phone and set out Jess's "usual mug" for tea—blue Bybee Pottery with hand-painted red poppies scrolling over the sides.

They needed Sev's contact list to reach his family. There was no way he would remember all the phone numbers necessary to notify the Hardcastles of Chad's passing and Jess thought they might be more willing to answer a call from a known number. To make things easier, Poppy gave Sev access to the secret private internet connection with a one-time guest password. He swore that he would never breathe a word to Diana. Poppy wasn't going to push back too much, considering the "death on the property" liability of it all.

Sev created a call list and split it with Jess. The Hardcastles' reactions ranged from outright disinterest to mistaking Jess for a prying member of the press to Chad's great-uncle Carl trying to order Jess to pick up his dry cleaning. It wasn't even a shirt he needed for the funeral. He just knew he had a shirt waiting on him somewhere.

The weather got progressively worse as the storm system keeping Chad's parents island-bound moved north. While Sev returned to the villa to search for Chad's ID and other items that Blister had requested, he asked Jess to get a start on Chad's obituary using an online form.

She muttered while clicking around on the funeral home's website. "It's going to be really hard to concoct an obituary from 'never *convicted* of a felony' and 'his dad building a library wasn't enough to get him into his legacy college.'"

An unexpected voice sounded from the door. "This sounds like a 'name, date of birth, date of death' situation. Keep it short and simple."

She looked up to see Dean standing over her, holding a silver room-service cloche. "Yeah, I'm kind of glad *you* heard me say that and not one of Chad's family members."

"Don't get in the habit of not saying true stuff. That would make you less interesting," he said, giving her a peck on the lips. She liked that he'd become comfortable with casual gestures of affection so quickly. Yes, they were far from progressing into a sexual relationship or even a relationship, really. But this was . . . good.

"If that is a cheeseburger under that dome, you'll get a lot more than a kiss," she told him.

"I am aware of your cheeseburger barter system," he said, waggling his eyebrows. He lifted the cloche to reveal the most beautiful cheeseburger she'd ever seen, on a perfectly grilled, butter-soaked brioche bun. Thick-cut bacon peeked flirtatiously from under the lettuce and tomato, and Jess could just make out the golden edges of a fried egg. And Lord help her, there were hand-cut, homemade potato chips piled high on the plate.

"Well, now I am in serious danger of offering you the worst proposal of my career," she told him. "Clumsy and based entirely on grease-soaked carbs, and sure to be rejected."

He laughed. "Let me make you a few more cheeseburgers before we start talking long-term . . . sandwich-based commitment."

"Fair enough," she said, biting into the most delicious fucking cheeseburger her lips had ever touched. All she wanted to do was eat this burger, crawl into his lap, and maybe stay there forever.

"So, how are things in the kitchen?"

"Eh, less stressful than usual. Most of the other guests are gone, except for your group, that Zephyr lady, and Mrs. Treadaway, so it's pretty quiet. I think Diana managed to talk Poppy into a round of hot-oil rose quartz scalp massages or something."

"I guess I'm glad they're occupied?" she said, chewing thoughtfully. "I have a question for you."

"You should have that tattooed somewhere. I have location suggestions."

"Ha ha," she snarked back, still chewing. "So Susan Treadaway complained that your signature pasta dish smelled like feet. Is that normal?"

Dean blinked at her. "That is not the question I expected."

"You thought it was going to be some filthy burger proposal, didn't you?"

"Yes, and I am weirdly disappointed," he confessed. "And a little offended."

"I will proposition you over a cheeseburger in the near future," she promised him.

"Thank you," he said, hitching his hip up on Poppy's desk. "And yeah, it's not shocking that she said that. Real imported Italian cheeses can smell pretty sharp for people who are used to the Parmesan dust available in the grocery store . . . and OK, Taleggio and fontina cheeses are known for their smells, but that's half the reason I use them, to offset the nutty sweetness of the mushrooms."

"And Chad and Jeremy both ordered the same pasta dish and . . . and now they're dead," she said. "Any chance that the cheese has gone bad since it was imported? Don't some cheeses have problems with listeria and such?"

"I doubt it. I've used one provider for years. They're reputable importers, and they would have notified me of a recall. Plus, multiple guests have eaten that dish in the last few weeks, using cheese from that order, and they haven't had any problems," Dean said, frowning.

"But now that you mention it, Chad and Jeremy didn't eat *exactly* the same pasta dish. Jeremy's dish included mushrooms. Chad hated mushrooms, even when we were kids. He pitched a fit when somebody brought his favorite super meaty pizzas to one of the bonfires because it had mushrooms on it. He actually threw half a pizza on the ground and whined about how the mushrooms ruined it. He couldn't just pick them off. So when he ordered the pasta, he put a note on the order insisting that no mushrooms touch it. I mean, it's right there in the name—tagliatelle ai funghi. But since Chad is a known pain in the ass, I used allergy protocols. Separate pans, separate utensils, separate plates."

"So . . . not the cheese . . . and not the mushrooms. Damn," she muttered. "I thought maybe I was onto something there."

"Sorry, Sherlock, you're just going to have to settle for being really good at this one job," he told her. "Speaking of which, take a break from Sev's dirty work and finish your lunch."

She took a big bite of cheeseburger. "I'm fine, really. Sev's not asking a lot. And it's good for me to keep busy. It keeps my mind off things."

"I still don't like him, never have. But I will deny my caveman instincts and respect your right to autonomy," Dean said, holding up his hands. "Also, it's no Meatball Night, but we're having family dinner. Your group is getting a selection of frittatas, which I can make ahead. For us, I'm making a standing rib roast, wrapped in bacon. And Jonquil's making our aunt Rosemary's bourbon cream pie for dessert."

"Are you trying to seduce me, Chef Osbourne?"

"Is it working?" Dean asked, cocking his brow.

"I'm ashamed to admit that it is," she said, as he kissed her cheek.

Behind him, they heard someone clear their throat. Poppy was leaning against the door frame, smirking. "Oh, no, please feel free to use my office as your hookup spot."

Jess blushed while Dean snickered. For some reason, Poppy had hauled a heavy-duty garbage bag into her office. The thick black plastic didn't quite go with her stylish eggplant-colored sweaterdress.

"You know we pay a very competent maintenance staff, right?" Dean said, nodding at the trash bag.

Poppy rolled her eyes and dropped the bag to the floor with a *clank* of broken glass.

"Terry Lynn just carried this up the hill, to bring it to my attention," Poppy said. "I asked the housekeeping staff to keep an eye out for anything weird in the guest villas."

"Who's collecting glass shards in their villa?" Dean asked.

"Zephyr," Poppy said. "Terry Lynn said she went from 'nothing weird' to hiding broken bottles under the rest of her garbage."

Poppy lifted one of the bottle remnants from the bag. Jess saw the broken remnants of several Steel Hills bottles, the same brand as the bottle Sev had whisked off their couch earlier. How much vodka had Zephyr consumed this week? She was so petite . . .

Oh, wait.

"I think she was sharing her stash with Chad," Jess said. "We saw him leaving her villa the night before he died. Maybe she's worried that counted as 'impacting the other guests'? She could be hiding them so she doesn't lose her reservation."

"Huh, that is something to consider." Poppy shook her head. "It seems like a bad idea for a guest to drink that much, but it seems like a worse idea to provoke Zephyr right now by asking her about bottle hoarding."

"This seems like a Beth conversation," Dean agreed.

Poppy sighed. "I don't want to bother Beth, but I could also use a bit of a walk over to our side of the compound. Can I help you with anything?"

Jess shook her head. "I just need to call Mavis."

"I'll come with you," Dean told Poppy. He stood and patted Jess's shoulder. "And we can see if maybe Beth has vodka in *her* house."

"I would like to know that myself," Poppy replied as they ambled out.

Jess shook her head, wondering how she'd missed Zephyr drinking heavily all week. She'd seemed steady on her feet, clear eyed; she'd attended yoga classes. So much for Jess's pride in her observational skills.

Jess dialed Mavis's number. It struck her that Poppy was showing a considerable amount of trust, leaving Jess alone in her office like this. Mavis picked up on the *first* ring this time. As usual, she was on top of her game.

"Jess, you haven't touched base with me in more than twenty-four hours. You can't do that when you're isolated in the middle of nowhere with questionable characters. I start to panic!" Mavis practically yelled in her ear. "I almost called Blanche!"

"Mavis," she sighed, her voice shaking slightly with relief. Mavis's protective anxiety was, at least, dependable. "I'm fine."

"You don't sound fine."

"I can't tell you much. Just don't believe everything that you see on the news, *if* you see anything on the news," Jess said, distracting herself by stacking the papers she'd scattered around Poppy's desk. She picked up a file folder and saw that Sev had left his cell phone behind. Jess supposed that after nearly a week without his phone, Sev had simply stopped thinking about it.

The latest model, protected by a sleek matte-silver "destruction-proof" case, it was just like Sev—low-key, professional, and easy to miss. The most exciting thing on his all-black lock screen was a Memories preview from the Photos feature, where there were streaks of red across the picture. The thumbnail was too small for Jess to see what it was, but honestly, it looked like the photo had been taken accidentally while Sev was standing in a crowd. And in the center of the photo, the only thing that was sort of in focus was a red square with white buttons on both top corners. Jess supposed this updated Memory was a response to Sev's connection to the spa's Wi-Fi.

"Jess?" Mavis prompted, bringing her back to the conversation. "How in the hell are you not freaking out from the Tillard proposal not going forward 'for now'? That was your whole plan to keep the building."

"I'm juggling a lot of stuff right now that's keeping me distracted," Jess said. "And I know that sounds cryptic and unhelpful. It's just a mess up here, and I need you to be ready for me to unload the mother of all 'whine and wine' sessions when I come home."

"And when would that be?" Mavis asked pointedly.

"I don't know. I'm just trying to salvage what I can."

"Well, then you're sticking your neck out for Diana, who would *not* do the same for you. And I say this, knowing that you're my boss, but smarten the hell up. Jess, the business is *you*. It's not some building, no matter how much you love this place. We're going to figure it out."

"Understood," Jess grumbled as Kiki appeared outside the window, waving. Jess waved back awkwardly. "I have to go. Just know that I'm safe. I'm not alone."

"Don't you hang up on me, Jessamine Laverne Bricker!"

"You know that's not my middle name!" she whispered back, gathering her stuff. Sev's phone, she left on Poppy's desk. She was unwilling to take responsibility for anything else for her group for the day.

"Yeah, but it's the worst one I could come up with!" Mavis shouted as Jess hung up. She rose and moved out to the front porch to give her former roommate a weirdly stiff hug. It was difficult, considering Kiki was holding two of the spa's spring water bottles in her hands, thumping them lightly against Jess's back.

Jess found that she'd missed her. Like the Osbournes, she felt that maybe Kiki was someone she could continue some sort of friendship with after they all finished this "vacation." It felt like forever since she'd spoken to the most tolerable Helston.

"Hey," Kiki said, handing her one of the bottles. "I thought you might need a break. The staff keep telling us hydration is a solution for grief and stress."

"I'm sure it's *a* solution, but I'm not sure it's *the* solution," Jess replied, opening her bottle. Her throat was awfully dry, considering all the talking she'd been doing. "How are you holding up?"

Kiki dragged a hand through her penny-bright hair. "This whole thing is so weird. Chad dying in the middle of a stupid spa trip. I just came up here to keep my mom off my back about being in the wedding, and now this? It's such a mess."

"Are you hearing anything from the family back home?" Jess asked.

"From our family?" Kiki shook her head. "Our phones still have no signal and Diana seems . . . weirdly OK with that? I asked her if she wanted me to call home on the office phone last night, and she said no. I think maybe she's afraid of what Aunt Birdie is going to say if she hears that Di's not engaged yet *and* we're embroiled in a double-dead-guy scandal here. I didn't have the nerve to call Birdie myself. You know how my family is. I hate how quickly I fold when I'm around them. It feels impossible to stand up to them, and they use this certain *tone* on me and I just panic."

"I get it. I guess. I mean, I haven't exactly been the picture of strength against peer pressure myself," Jess muttered. "Remind me to block your aunt from my phone when I get back."

"I already have her blocked in mine," Kiki said, opening her bottle of water and taking a long gulping drink.

"So, have you talked to the sheriff yet?" Jess asked.

"The weird guy with the creeper moustache?" Kiki replied,

shuddering. "Yeah, but once he realized I really didn't spend time with either of the dead guys, he lost interest. I mean, he had some questions about you, but that's about it."

Jess tried not to spit out the water she was drinking and mostly succeeded—but there *was* dribbling. "What kind of questions about me?"

"Just about . . . how long you and Chad had known each other, how well you and Chad got along, that sort of thing."

Jess wiped at her mouth with the back of her hand, "Well, shit. That doesn't sound good."

Kiki's whole body tensed and she held up her hands, sloshing her water. "I wouldn't worry about it. I mean, he's investigating this whole thing as an accident, right?"

"As far as I know, but it sounds a little bit like they think I'm a suspect," Jess grumbled. She thought of Sev's suspicions of the Osbournes, of how many people at the Golden Ash had a reason to want Chad gone—even Trenton, if he'd somehow found out about Chad and Diana.

A shiver ran down Jess's spine that had nothing to do with the chilling breeze ripping over the grounds or the extended conversations with Chad's somewhat sucky family. Jess realized she was probably the last one to talk to him. And the conversation hadn't been very nice. What if the police thought she had something to do with it? If anybody in the Tillard-Helston party thought it meant getting away without inconvenience, they wouldn't just throw her under the bus, they would park the bus *on* her. What if the Hardcastles thought she had something to do with it? Unlike the Tillards and the Helstons, the Hardcastles managed to combine wealth *and* competence. That wasn't fair. Jess was probably letting her bias against Trenton show.

If they decided that she did have something to do with Chad's death, they could ruin her. They could tank her tiny business. They could rezone Nana Blanche's house and surround her grandmother with mini-malls and vape stores with a freeway running through the front yard. And Mavis—hell, they might try to deport Mavis. No one in their circle seemed to understand that coming from Jamaica, Queens, didn't make her "foreign."

OK, maybe she was spiraling a little bit.

Jess hadn't done anything wrong. She wasn't even sure anything wrong had been done. But if it had, she doubted very much that anyone in the wedding party would go down for it. Did she need a lawyer?

Meanwhile, Kiki was staring at Jess while she very quickly lost her mind.

"Dammit, I gotta go," Jess told her, just in time to hear Diana yell across the hilltop.

"*Jessie!*"

Jess turned to see Diana marching up the steps toward her. Diana looked incredibly *not* relaxed, considering she'd spent the afternoon getting her scalp massaged. And she was still wearing her stupid church dress.

"Well," Jess huffed. "Double dammit."

Suddenly, Kiki cried out in indignation, as if Jess had stomped on her toes. "Really, Jess, you thought this was an appropriate time to take a water break? There's no time for you to 'take a breather.' You're here to do a job!"

Jess gasped. "What the fuck, Kiki?"

"I'm sorry!" Kiki whispered, backing away from Jess as if she were radioactive. "I have to show loyalty. If Diana kicks me out of the wedding party, my mother will never let me hear the end of it."

Kiki disappeared down the hill as fast as she'd appeared. Jess had to admire the fleetness of Kiki's total abandonment, even if it did piss her the hell off.

"I'm sorry to interrupt your precious *downtime,* Jess, but I'd like to know what you've done today to earn your place here?" Diana threw her arm back to gesture at the spa grounds at large. "What have you done to convince Trenton to propose to me?"

"I'm sorry, Diana. I've spent my day calling the Hardcastle family members because *Chad is dead*," Jess reminded her. "And I've been too busy helping Sev handle that to salvage anything. Trenton is in mourning. What exactly do you expect me to do?"

"Convince Trenton to move forward with the proposal!" Diana insisted, her eyes watering at the mention of Chad.

Jess gaped at her. "His best friend just died."

"So we should focus on something positive," Diana insisted, wringing her hands. "Give him something to look forward to. Find a way to make Trenton think that proposing is the best way to memorialize his friend."

"That borders on the pathologically insensitive," Jess told her.

"Oh, get off it. You need this just as much as I do! And I'm *so close* to getting everything I ever wanted!" Diana cried. "Everything my family wants. It's all right here, at the tips of my fingers. All you have to do is help me grab it, like you promised!"

"Diana, in my professional opinion, this is a bad idea."

"I'm not saying we do it now, but maybe you could talk him into taking the engagement photos later today," Diana said, her tone edging on wheedling. "Just so he feels invested."

"It's been raining all day," Jess said, pointing up to the clouds overhead. "And you're going to try to ask him to smile in anticipation of nuptial bliss when—just trying to remind you—His. Best. Friend. Just. Died."

"Is this how you always speak to your clients?" Diana demanded.

"Technically, you're not my client. Trenton is," she shot back.

"You are some former classmate who didn't speak to me for years until she needed something from me."

Diana scoffed. "I'm just trying to help *you*, Jess. I'm trying to bolster your little business—"

"How would working my ass off to cover for whatever personal drama you have going on help *me*?" Jess demanded. "This is insane, Diana. Your family's plan to hitch onto Trenton's gravy train is no way to build your life."

"Well, it's not like I'm the only one getting something out of it. Do you think Trenton wants to be with me because I have a beautiful soul?" she said, rolling her eyes. "He's just like any other guy I've dated. He wants me because he thinks the fact that I chose him makes him a big strong man, more impressive than all the Trenton Tillards before him. So, I'll let him call me 'DeeDee' despite the fact that I *hate* it. I'm gonna get married and secure my life and do enough for my family to get *them* off my back before Trenton finds a sidepiece that he gives a ridiculous nickname to that makes her feel like she's being stabbed in the ears."

"Well, that's bleak," Jess commented. Diana didn't reply, so Jess pressed ahead. "Do you want to tell me what this rush to get the proposal over with is really about? Because I have my suspicions, and I'd really like to not have to say them aloud."

"It's not what you're thinking." Diana carefully climbed down the steps in her heels. She took Dean's jacket from Jess's arm and draped it over her own shoulders—without asking.

Something visceral and mean rose up in Jess's chest at the sight of her wearing Dean's clothes. It gave her the stones to dig the matchbook out of her pocket and quietly say, "I think you were meeting Chad at the Sportsman's Lodge every time Trenton's daddy made him go on a business trip."

Diana's perfectly glossed mouth dropped open.

"So maybe it was what I was thinking?" Jess replied.

"Yes, I was sleeping with Chad, OK?" Diana whispered, glancing back at the lodge. "Only a few times. It was purely physical and I couldn't help myself. We hooked up a couple of times at college, and Trenton's sweet, but there's just not a lot of *heat* there, and you saw how Chad liked to flirt. He wasn't marriage material—he was too unpredictable. He was self-destructive. Trenton is *predictable*. He's biddable. I can handle him. I knew it wasn't gonna go anywhere with Chad. It was just . . . fun."

Jess stared at her, shaking her head.

"You know, I kind of feel better, telling you about this," Diana said. "It was really weighing on me. And you're not going to tell anybody because, again, you need Trenton to propose just as much as I do. We're going to cross this finish line together."

Dammit. Diana was right. While it might give Jess immense satisfaction to watch Trenton collide with a clue, that collision would cost Jess a lot of money. It would cost her a home. It would cost Mavis a workplace. Maybe she could leave Trenton an anonymous note after he and Diana left the spa engaged. She inhaled deeply, bunching her hands into fists she *knew* she wouldn't use, and asked, "What were you going to do once you were married? Have Sunday barbecues with your husband and the guy you used to bang on the side?"

Diana dragged her fingers through her damp hair. In the misting rain, it was darkening to a color that reminded Jess of blood. "Well, don't put it like that—you make it sound so cheap."

"You were meeting him at a bass-themed motel."

"Yes, and I need your help to get Trenton all tied up before he finds out," Diana hissed, wrapping her coral-tipped fingers around Jess's wrist. Jess jerked her arm out of the hold. She didn't want to admit—again—that Diana was right. If she was going to orchestrate this proposal, she was going to have to do it before Trenton caught on. But Jess didn't have the energy for it at the moment. She just needed to be somewhere else, away from Diana.

"I am *very* distressed by your lack of effort today."

Jess threw up her hands, her water sloshing in the bottle. "OK."

"And you're not concerned about that?" Diana demanded.

Jess thought about it. Diana was distressed and the proposal hadn't been cemented. And here Jess was, heading to a friend's house for dinner. With other friends. And she was probably going to spend the night with a man who enjoyed kissing her. And when she went home, she would have people in Nashville who loved her, work that needed to be done. The Helston-Tillard job had not worked out as she'd hoped, but Jess Bricker was doing just fine.

"Nope." She grinned at Diana as she took Dean's jacket back from around the woman. "You seem to forget that you need me just as much as I need you. *I'm* the one who has developed relationships with the Osbournes. *I'm* the one who has secured permission for you to have strangers and vendors trooping onto the spa property for your proposal—if you manage to talk him into doing it before we leave. And *I'm* the one who has secured permission for you to post professional photos of that 'lavish, innovative, romantic' proposal you want so badly. And I swear to God, if you mention the word 'genuine' to me right now, I will walk off. If I quit, you're left with nothing, and who knows if Trenton will want to make a third run at this, especially with Chad gone. If you stop dicking me around, I'll press forward with the planned engagement when and if Trenton is ready. And you can bet your ass I won't be wearing a bridesmaid's dress afterward. Now, if you'll excuse me. I'm late for a previous engagement."

CHAPTER 14

The Osbournes were *howling* by the time Jess got to the point of the story where she'd refused bridesmaid duties.

"You used the word 'engagement' just to mess with her, didn't you?" Jonquil hooted while she turned the potatoes roasting in the oven.

"I did a little bit," Jess admitted, sipping on her bottled water as she sat at Beth and Jonquil's kitchen counter. While she was riding emotionally high, physically . . . she wasn't feeling great. She felt sort of floaty and disconnected. Maybe she was dehydrated? It didn't feel possible, given all the water she was drinking, but she had spent an awful lot of time doing Sev's errands that day, only pausing to eat Dean's cheeseburger. It had been a delicious burger, but it didn't equal a day's worth of nutrition.

Jonquil threw an arm over her eyes while still holding the wooden spoon. In her best Southern belle accent, she asked, "You could have really ramped up the drama and said you had a gentleman caller waiting on the veranda."

"Trust me. There was enough drama. I was just trying to get out of smacking range," Jess said.

"You're not really going to put anything special together for that awful girl and that . . . well, Tillard's not awful, really, just sort of a doofus," Beth said, gluing down a decorative edge on a scrapbook page, securing a photo on a sky-blue background.

"I don't think so, at least not now," Jess said, leaning against the counter and balancing her cheek on her palm. "She's pushing for it, but it just feels ghoulish."

"It is ghoulish," Poppy agreed, clicking on the keyboard of her laptop from her perch on the couch. "Just like all the calls I'm getting from media outlets—legitimate and not-quite-so—about the rumors they're hearing about 'accidents' at our facility. It's only a matter of time before they start camping at the gate like a bunch of turkey vultures."

"This is why our PR rep has a job," Sis reminded Poppy. "Forward the calls to her."

"And if that doesn't work, have them call me," Beth said, attaching a sparkly crescent-moon-shaped accent to the page.

"Poppy," Jess began, "I'm so s—"

"If you say you're sorry, I'm going to take away your potatoes," Sis informed her.

Jess clamped her lips shut.

"You were gonna say it," Sis said, squinting at her. "Weren't you?"

"You don't know that," Jess retorted, even as Sis gave her a look that could only be interpreted as *Bitch, please.*

"Look!" Beth said, holding up her finished page. It was a veritable phantasmagoria of decorative borders and sparkly quote stickers. "All done."

"I love you, but you have a scrapbooking *problem*," Jonquil informed her, kissing her soundly.

"Everybody has their outlets," Beth informed her primly. "*This* is how I process interacting with multiple law enforcement officials in one day."

"Wow," Jess said, cringing.

Jonquil shot Jess a pointed look.

"I wasn't going to say anything." Jess sipped her water. Eager to change the subject, she asked, "What's the page about, Beth?"

Beth grinned, tapping her finger against the photo of the Osbournes standing by a bannered table full of little jars. "It's the most recent Chickenhawk Valley Flannel Days Festival. We gave away little jars of body scrub and raffled a chance for a free day of treatments here. It went over really big!"

"Yeah, Sev mentioned something about going to the festival when you were kids," Jess said. "He said something about a moonshine tasting, which I have to say would be a big no from me."

Poppy frowned. "Huh."

"What?" Jess lifted her hand and it felt weirdly disconnected from her body, like it would just float away if she let it. She pulled her arm close to her stomach and pressed it there.

"They wouldn't have had the moonshine tasting when Sev was around. It was a new thing they added this year," Beth said. "Moonshine is trendy right now, and the festival committee is trying to connect with the younger-but-still-drinking-age crowd. Trust me, I was there for the discussions of permits. It was protracted . . . and involved, even for a discussion about offering free samples of pure grain alcohol to the general public."

Jess snickered, even if she was bothered by the comment for some reason. Something was nagging at the edge of her mind, like a pulled thread in a sweater. But before she could pin it down, Owen opened the door, making way for Dean as he carried an enormous silver roasting pan, covered in foil.

"We have arrived with roast beast!" Owen announced grandly in his big sonorous voice. "Much like a Whovian feast from the Grinch story, it is so comically large Dean had to roast it in the industrial kitchen, but it's sure to be delicious."

"I think that's a compliment, but I'm not sure," Dean said, shaking his head. He grinned at Jess. "I'm glad you're here. I was afraid I was going to have to drag you out of the villa as Sev and What's-Her-Face barked orders at you."

"It's a vivid image, and not entirely inaccurate," Jess admitted.

Dean placed the pan on the counter and peeled back the foil to reveal a perfectly lovely beef roast encased in crispy bacon.

"I mentioned something about a marriage proposal in exchange for a cheeseburger?" Jess said, ignoring the way Poppy, Jonquil, and even Sis went all soft and googly-eyed. "This is so much better than a cheeseburger."

Dean merely grinned at her. "Slow-paced, long-term, sandwich-based commitment. Besides, Owen here has news even more dramatic than his whole 'roast beast' entrance."

"It was a little dramatic," Poppy told Owen, just as he kissed her. Behind them, the rest of the family sat around the table while Dean carved the roast. Beth and Owen piled the plates high with hearty servings of meat and potatoes. Jess's mouth watered, and she took a long drink from her bottle before anyone noticed the gathering drool.

"Oh, right, in this family, *I'm* the dramatic one." Owen snorted. As they took their seats, Owen said, "And on that note, I feel it's now safe to say that Chad's death wasn't a tragic sauna accident—I mean, those things happen, but I used what chips I have left within the forensics community to ask 'hypothetical questions' of my contacts in the state bureau of investigation. Blister, believe it or not, was downplaying the seriousness of the case—or cases, as it turns out. Given the general absence of deaths *this* weird in our area, my contacts pulled Chad's test results. He didn't die of heatstroke, or at least not *just* heatstroke. Chad had high levels of a chemical called coprine in his system, really high levels. That led to his overall cause of death, which was sort of total-body 'blue screen of death.'"

"Is 'total-body blue screen of death' a medical term?" Sis asked.

"So they're saying he was poisoned?" The blood drained from Dean's face. "From something out of my kitchen?

Owen shrugged. "It could have come from anywhere, but most of the time, poisons are introduced through food and drink. The fact that no one else at the spa has gotten sick is a good sign, I think, in terms of your kitchen safety."

"So . . . Chad's death wasn't an accident?" Jess asked, around a mouthful of heavenly potatoes.

Sis raised an eyebrow at her. "Um, yeah, honey, we covered that."

"Coprine." Jonquil got a pensive look on her face. "I know that word."

"But what about Jeremy's test results? If Chad's death wasn't an accident, that means Jeremy's death probably wasn't an accident, either. And Dean, didn't you say there were weird mushrooms in Jeremy's gut?" Jess demanded.

The rest of the family turned to her, their expressions confused.

Oh, shit. She wasn't supposed to let on that she knew that.

Why had she blurted that out? It was like a bubble that popped out of her mouth, without any effort from Jess. She put her water bottle aside. She felt like she was drunk, but she hadn't had a drop of liquor all day. Maybe it was low blood sugar? She scooped more potatoes into her mouth.

"I told her about the morels," Dean sighed, putting his arm around her. "Considering that she found the body, it was the least she deserved."

"I didn't tell anybody," Jess promised. "I don't trust anybody in my villa with my favorite lipstick, much less autopsy secrets."

"So, that confirms it—unless Chad accidentally poisoned himself somehow, this was intentional, meaning there was a murder, here at the Golden Ash. I feel weirdly violated," Poppy said, sagging against the chair. "And that means Jeremy . . . ugh."

Jonquil pursed her lips. "Who would want to kill Chad?"

"Who *wouldn't* want to kill Chad? He was a dick," Sis said. When the rest of the table responded with various levels of facial cringe, she added, "OK, I know that sounds bad now, but I don't think any of you are going to report me to Blister, are you?"

"As your attorney, I would like to remind all of you not to say any of these things outside of these four walls." Beth sighed, and then drained half of her wineglass.

Jess propped her chin on both hands, trying to process the information. A lot of people here at the Golden Ash had a motive to go after Chad. Maybe Diana tried to end things with him and he got "insistent" about keeping their thing going? Sev was clearly annoyed with every breath Chad took. For that matter, any of the Osbournes could have poisoned Chad, considering their knowledge and access to plants. And given some of the history between the Hardcastle and Osbourne families—and some of the things people on both sides said about Emma Lee's disappearance . . .

Wait.

"What about the Yoni Egg Queen?" Jess asked.

"Never going to stop calling her that, huh?" Beth asked.

After a long moment of consideration, Jess said, "No. She and Chad hooked up right before he died. Or at least, he was leaving her villa in the middle of the night when Dean was walking me back to mine. Maybe Zephyr gave him something? They were drinking together, I think. Hell, maybe *she* took something, too, trying to get high? Has anybody checked on Zephyr lately? Or Mrs. Treadaway?"

Jess realized she seemed to be talking a lot . . . like . . . a *lot*. That didn't feel right. *Hmm.*

"Could Trenton have done this?" Dean asked. "Or maybe Sev? They were the ones who had the closest access to Chad. Would they have had any reason to hurt Jeremy Treadaway? I don't think they knew each other."

Jess chewed on her lip considering. "Trenton has never been aggressive. He gets what he wants by wheedling, and he's the kind of guy who sticks with what works for him."

"Poisoning isn't exactly a confrontational way to hurt someone," Beth noted.

"As for Sev . . . Well, he's spent more time around Chad than anyone, so yeah, he probably had the most motive. But Trenton might have caught on to the fact that . . . something was going on between Chad and Diana. But he wouldn't have a reason to hurt Jeremy Treadaway," Jess noted, scrubbing a hand over her face, suddenly feeling very tired. "That I'm aware of."

"You mentioning coprine is bothering me," Jonquil said. "I've heard it somewhere before."

"And we are all very impressed," Dean promised her.

Jonquil rolled her eyes and got up to retrieve a book from the shelf. "This is why you buy books on a variety of subjects. It saves you from questionable internet searches."

She went through the bookshelf before she finally selected a volume called *Fascinating Fungi from around the World*. Jonquil put it down on the table and started flipping through the pages until she found what she wanted. She showed the group a photo of a puffy white dome growing out of the ground. It sort of looked like a cross between a dinosaur egg and an evil pope's hat. "This is an inky cap mushroom. There's this chemical in it, coprine, that reacts badly when combined with alcohol. It's nicknamed 'tippler's bane.' Eat enough of them and combine them with alcohol, they can be fatal."

"I've never had anything that looks like that in my kitchen," Dean insisted.

"Do those grow around here?" Jess asked.

"I've never seen them, but I'm not exactly an expert. Um, symptoms after eating include dizziness, nausea, general unwellness. Symptoms can appear within a few hours of eating them," Jonquil continued. "And if he was putting his body through dehydration in the sauna and booze and who knows what else, they might act even faster."

"I think Chad was drinking pretty much from the moment he got here," Jess mused, her mouth suddenly very dry. She swallowed down more water, but it couldn't seem to make the thirst go away. "Tiny airplane bottles."

"Yeah, but Chad hated mushrooms," Dean replied. He took a bite of potatoes and added salt and pepper, even as Jonquil glared at him. The implied seasoning battle made Jess snicker. Dean gave her an amused glance before adding, "He ordered the pasta without it. Jeremy Treadaway, on the other hand, ordered room service almost aggressively, every damn night, the mushroom pasta. Maybe *he* was poisoned with mushrooms?"

Owen shrugged and pulled out his phone. "Well, Jeremy Tread-away's death was already being investigated because it was a little suspicious that a grown man drowned in a wading pool." Owen scrolled through some images on his phone and showed them what looked like a close-up of a jar of beef stew. "Anyway, when I looked at the stomach contents, I noticed that some of the mushroom chunks—"

"Ew!" Beth cried. "Owen, we're eating."

Jess put her hands over her eyes. That was an image she would never get out of her head.

"Sometimes *someone* forgets that their family members have never seen the inside of a human being," Poppy said kindly. When Jess took her hands off her eyes, Poppy was patting her husband's back. Under his beard, Owen had flushed bright red.

"Looked wrong," Owen said, putting his phone away. "OK, sorry, so I don't want to go into how I know, I guess, but in my opinion, when I looked at the photos from the autopsy, it looked like there were two types of mushrooms. The orange ones, which I see Dean use all the time, and these darker brown ones—which to me, look like morel mushrooms."

"Dean doesn't use morel mushrooms," Sis scoffed.

"Dean said it was possible that Jeremy had picked his own mush-rooms and eaten them, because that's what an idiot would do," Jess said, nodding. Beth just pinched the bridge of her nose and seemed to pray. Jess figured Beth was asking for legal patience.

"I did say that," Dean said. "Because in general, amateurs shouldn't pick wild mushroom and snack on them. And I don't use morel mushrooms because Granny always said they were bad luck or dirty or something, which, given the situation, kind of makes sense."

Jonquil shook her head. "Granny said morels were bad luck because you might pick the wrong ones. False morels look like real morels and they're poisonous. I mean, the person would probably have to eat a lot of them, but poisoning someone's dinner is pretty bad, karmically speaking."

Even at the look of alarm on Dean's face, Jess's attention slipped into some weird molasses-like state for a second, like she'd nodded off midsentence, but her eyes were still open. She blinked, clearing her throat and taking a deep drink of her water.

"So someone got into your kitchen and mixed poisonous mushrooms into your pasta dish?" Owen was saying when her brain snapped back into focus. "Or do you think Aaron the room service porter is up to no good?"

"People don't just walk into my kitchen. Ask Jess," Dean said.

"Nope, I was highly supervised every time I stopped by to flirt with Dean," Jess said, nodding. "Sometimes Jamie was there and he supervised me, too. He thought it was funny when I made Dean uncomfortable."

Dean's brows lifted, but he continued, "And Aaron wouldn't do that. If he had a problem with Jeremy, he would just beat the shit out of him and be done with it." Dean flicked through the tabs on his phone, in what Jess assumed was some sort of kitchen auditing app. "Look, Aaron even left notes on the order in the system. He said on several nights he attempted to deliver their food, but no one answered. Quote, 'It sounded like they were arguing pretty loudly in there.' He would knock, leave the cart outside the door, and run like . . ."

Jess's hearing seemed to go fuzzy and blank, like cotton had been stuffed in her ears. She wasn't sure how long she stared into space, trying to get her ears to work again, but it felt like a while.

Molasses brain again. This is becoming a problem.

Jess gripped the edge of the table. Something was nagging at her brain. She was missing something, something important. She was having an important thought.

"Chad and Diana were having sex at a low-rent, fish-themed motel," she blurted out.

Everybody stopped talking. She really had to get this "blurting out things" under control.

"Well, that's good to know," Sis told her, patting Jess's shoulder. "You're sounding awful tired, hon."

Jess nodded. *Right, time to be quiet. Until the molasses brain goes away.*

"I should probably call Blister about the mushroom stuff," Poppy sighed, standing up. "This seems like important information to the investigation . . . that's not going to look great for us as a facility."

Poppy stepped into the dining room to make her call. Jess stared out the window, watching the tree branches dance in the wind, feeling a weird dread in the pit of her stomach. They reminded her of skeleton fingers, scratching at the sky. They made her think of her mother and the way her hands had grabbed Jess's arms when she was little. And thinking of her mother was never a good idea.

She blinked up at Dean, who was shaking her shoulder gently. "Hey, I need to go over some things in the kitchen, make sure nothing's been tampered with. You'll be safe here, OK? Get some rest."

"Yep. Be careful." She inhaled sharply through her nose, like someone woken from a nap. "'Cause you know, potential poisoner?"

"She makes a good point," Owen said. "Maybe I should go to the kitchen with you, look some stuff over?"

"I would feel better if you did," Poppy said.

Jess glanced around the room. The table had been cleared and Dean and Owen were gone. How long had she been staring out the window? She wanted to talk to Nana Blanche. Desperately. Nana would help her bring her molasses thoughts back into order. She would help her sort through all these *very* inconvenient feelings, just as she had when Jess was a kid. But Nana was on a riverboat rolling . . . *rollin'* . . . *rollin' down the river.* And Jess's phone was still in her room.

A lock of dark hair fell in Jess's face and she pushed it back, wincing at how her fingers tangled into it. She wasn't going to be able to brush it at this rate and that would add a fun new level to her self-confidence. Nana Blanche had been the only one who could brush her hair when she was a kid. Thick curly hair was hard to manage without special brushes and detangler and—

Confidence.

Shit.

In her haste to pack, Jess had left her pearls stuffed in a sock drawer at Tranquility Villa.

Shit. Shit. Shit.

The Osbourne ladies were distracted with dinner cleanup. Jess could probably make it to her villa, grab her necklace, and sneak back so fast that they wouldn't even notice her slipping out the front door. The wind was still playing havoc with the trees, but the rain had stopped, and she managed to grab a flashlight as she left.

Right.

Jess jogged down the path toward the guest villas. At least it felt like a jog, but given the way her flashlight beam was bouncing around, she thought that she probably looked like Frankenstein's monster lumbering across the moors. She didn't want to be Frankenstein's monster. Dean wouldn't think she was cute if she were green.

What was she thinking about again? Pearls. She wasn't about to leave her great-grandmother's necklace down there with that villa of vipers. She'd be lucky if they weren't already packed away in Aubrey's suitcase as some weird victory trophy.

"Thieving bi-atch," Jess muttered to no one in particular. The tree branches seemed to shake their arms in sympathy.

Jess sped along the path from the family houses, hoping that she could get to Tranquility Villa without seeing anybody. Maybe they were having dinner in the men's villa tonight . . . to keep Trenton company and persuade him that getting engaged would make him feel better. Because that would work, hitching his wagon to a star that didn't. . . . something.

As she passed the thermal suite, she could see Sev on the hill, sort of . . . pacing back and forth. He was nowhere near the villas, but she wasn't sure that she could pass him without being seen.

She froze, chewing her lip.

Sev . . . something about Sev was pecking at the corner of Jess's brain. Something she was supposed to talk to Sev about.

And suddenly, she felt very vulnerable, out here in the open where Sev could see her.

Why would she be afraid of Sev?

Something was wrong.

Jess looked, back and forth, between the villas and the Osbournes' compound, promising whatever deities might be listening that if she could just get one place or the other, she would never be stupid enough to end up in this *Choose Your Own Adventure for Dummies* again.

"No, no, this is stupid," Jess said, shaking her head and backing up toward the safety of the Osbournes. "I'm not going to go running across a dark abandoned spa facility toward people I don't trust. Leaving behind the only allies I have. I'm not that high."

Something sloshed in her hand. Jess looked down at the water bottle. She hadn't even realized she was holding it.

"Oh, God, I am *high*," she whispered, clapping her hands over her mouth. "I'm super, super, suuuuper high. How did that happen?"

Jess hadn't smoked weed in ten years . . . probably. Maybe. She'd never trusted pills, given Hadley's . . . history. And she hadn't had anything to drink today but water.

"Weird," she muttered.

She turned, stopping midcircle when her eye landed on something glowing white on the ground. Or at least, it looked like it was glowing in the beam of her flashlight.

Mushrooms.

She slipped her flashlight back into her pocket.

Truffles were a mushroom.

That was what she was trying to remember.

Jess's Big Book of Life Plans: Wrench Gloss . . . Hemlock . . . Sprite—Try not to be so high when you're—Ow.

And that was the *last* thing she remembered before the world went dark.

CHAPTER 15

Jess woke up to the sensation of wet grass running across her cheek. It felt like she was being dragged across the forest floor by her feet.

Oh, God, had she been kidnapped by a Sasquatch? She was not in fighting form to face off against a Sasquatch. She blinked up at the sky, and everything was sort of shimmery and fuzzy. She was pretty sure she was still super high.

"Hey!" she yelled. "*Hey!* Let go of me, you big-footed motherfucker!"

And that was as far as she got before she drifted back into the darkness.

When Jess came to again, her head hurt like hell and someone was spilling water into her mouth.

"Poison," Jess spluttered and rolled to spit the foul stuff onto the ground. The taste of it was enough to make her gag, which brought more nasty liquid up her throat and onto the grass. Ugh, it tasted like she was French-kissing death.

"Good guess." A soft voice, one that had always sounded so reasonable and normal, filtered through the darkness. "Jeremy Treadaway was an experiment. And Chad? I wanted to hurt him. But you? Well, I was getting frustrated with the mushrooms. So many variables. And Jess, you didn't do anything to me, really. And I like you, so I gave you something entirely experimental. Think of it as a sort of potpourri of synthesized botanical intoxicants—a little bit of this, a little bit of that, enough to make you loopy and incapacitated but not kill you. Honestly, I thought it would be a lot harder to pull you around at your size, but you're pretty easy to drag."

"Kiki, what the fuck? You can't just go around poisoning people. Use your words! Also, fuck you, I'm statuesque!"

"Ugh, I had no idea you would be so annoying when you were this high." Kiki was cradling Jess in her arms, holding a metal Hydro Flask over her face. It tasted like it was piped straight from the gutter.

"Well, if you don't like high Jess, you only have yourself to blame," Jess said, fighting the hands holding the bottle to her lips.

Kiki had killed Chad. Jess's addled brain was finally catching up to the situation, and she could feel the warning signs lining up in her head like penguins on a glacier.

It had been more comfortable suspecting Sev or even Diana than it was to think that the person she'd slept three feet away from had hurt Chad. But everything made sense now. In her head, she could see the gray plastic case she'd spotted in Kiki's purse that first day— it was a sample case from Helix BioResearch Lab. A sample case containing . . . probably poison stuff.

Wait, no . . .

What possible reason could Kiki have to hurt Chad? Other than his general personality.

Kiki and Chad barely knew each other. But Sev . . . there was a history between those men, animosity. *Generational* animosity. Sev made more sense as a murderer. And Jess thought she and Kiki were becoming friends.

"Well, not friends, but definitely not 'poisoning each other' candidates," Jess muttered.

"Drink the tea, Jess," Kiki commanded her. "The water was just the appetizer, this is . . . let's call it 'dessert.'"

"No," Jess growled, even as she found herself unable to move her legs when her brain was *clearly* commanding them to help her stand up and run away.

"Look, I know the good little 'final girl' in you wants to fight, but trust me, the end is inevitable," Kiki said. And while Jess recognized that her senses were not exactly reliable at the moment, she thought Kiki looked genuinely remorseful. Or she could be smiling. Jess couldn't really tell. Damn, she was tired. And there was a lump under her side. Ow. It was probably a rock. "You're going to die. The only choice you have is how much elegance I allow you when you're found."

"Not a lot of elegance in smacking me over the head with a rock, Kiki," Jess grumbled.

"Well, you haven't been around very much since you started taking up with the Osbournes. It's limited my options. And it wasn't a rock, it was my water bottle . . . You hit your head on a rock when you landed."

"Bitch," Jess huffed.

"Now, Jess, there's no reason to be rude."

"Oh sure, let me up for a second and I'll apologize," Jess said. Kiki frowned at her and then pulled her up into a sitting position. When she let go, Jess flopped over on her side. The sudden change in head altitude made her throw up everything she'd ingested in . . . quite some time. And a lot of it splashed into her hair. Ew.

Kiki sighed. "Well, that's frustrating."

"Sorry to complicate your evening," Jess slurred.

"Jess," Kiki sighed. She crouched, brushing Jess's fouled hair out of her face. Her lip curled in disgust as she wiped her hands on her jeans. "I wanted to make this easy on you. I wanted you to see some pretty colors, and maybe stumble and drown in a puddle without a care in the world, like good old Jeremy. Your precious Dean could find you floating in the meditation hollow tomorrow. Very dramatic, poetic even. Very 'Lady of Shalott.'"

"No need. I'm good," Jess said, waving her off. Oh, that was nice. She was able to control her arms. "Also, I don't think you're using that reference right."

Throwing up had made her feel better than she expected. That bizarre heavy-floating sensation was starting to ebb away.

"Well, pardon me for not attending some elitist girls' school where we specialized in mascara and poetry," Kiki said, holding the bottle to Jess's mouth while she cradled her head. "I went to a real college. Where they taught us stuff like how to secretly grow poisonous plants on your boss's dime and doctor them up so some dumbass doesn't even notice when they're drinking them."

"Well, yeah, that school was probably a much better fit for you." Jess shook her head. "Wait. Is that what this is about? Wren Hill? Fuck Wren Hill. You're *Doctor* Kiki, for God's sake. You were much better off going to that college for supervillains you were talking about."

"Trenton was looking at you, talking about how *nice* you are, how easy it is to talk to you," Kiki said, seething.

"Yeah, because he wants me to solve all his problems and feel all his bad feelings for him, so he doesn't have to be a grown-ass man. It's not *romantic*. I'm a utility, like a wheelbarrow. He wants Diana."

"Bullshit. Being with Diana is *work*," Kiki scoffed. "Men might find it intriguing at first, but it's exhausting in the long term, and I think Trenton was starting to pick up on that. If you were around much longer, who knows what he would have done."

"What the hell are you talking about? I'm not interested in Trenton!"

"Everybody's interested in *money*, Jess. Pretending that you're not is just a fucking lie! We're the same, you and me!"

"Well, *I've* never murdered anybody, Kiki," Jess countered. "So we're not exactly the same."

Ha.

"Oh, fuck you, Jess, you don't know how hard it was for me, growing up. Do you know what it's like to have people look at you with a little smirk on their face?"

Jess nodded. "Every damn day. That's what Wren Hill was like for me, Kiki."

Kiki stood, letting Jess's head flop to the ground.

Ow.

"But it's *different* when your family used to have something," Kiki insisted. "When you used to *be* something. People look at you like *you* couldn't hold on to it, like it's your personal failure, your fault, when you didn't have anything to do with losing it. They look at you like you're less than because *they* were born into a family that happened to be a little luckier than yours. A little smarter."

Jess propped herself on her hands and managed to push herself a whole three inches off the damp ground. It turned out it was her flashlight, not a rock, poking into her side. "Yeah, I don't know about that, and you know what? I don't care. Yeah, your family's super dysfunctional and you've struggled a bit, but who the fuck cares? You're a successful person. You have an advanced degree in a STEM field. You have a good job. You have an idea that could make you a lot of money. The whole non-murder-y truffle thing? That was your golden opportunity!"

This was good. The more she talked, the more she could focus. *Words, words, words.* Fuck, she was still high. But was she still talking?

Yep.

"You made that for *yourself.* And now it's all over because you *murdered people,*" Jess exclaimed, yelling the last two words. Maybe if someone heard her yelling, they would come looking for her. "And I've seen enough true-crime shows to know you're not going to get away with it. So, fuck you, Kiki. I thought we were building a friendship. And you were just waiting around for the opportunity to murder me? Rude!"

Would people miss her if she was murdered? Nana Blanche and Mavis, for sure. Maybe Dean. She missed Dean. He was nice, and Jess wanted to see him again. So, she would just let Kiki rant. That's what final girls did, right? Let the murderers rant, giving the police time to show up. But no one knew where Jess was. It's not like she had time to leave a note before Kiki knocked her over the head.

How would anybody find her?

And would she be eaten by a bear before they got to her body?

They never found Emma Lee.

"I saw it as soon as I landed in Nashville for this stupid fucking trip. Diana was *wasting* my opportunity so she could fuck around with that idiot Chad. I had to pretend I didn't know, which is just so *annoying.* She's had so many chances, wasted them all, and she was *ruining* mine! Chad was in my *way*! It's not wrong for me to want something for myself," Kiki was saying. "It's not wrong to want something of my own! She could do something for me for once—all she had to do was not cheat on Trenton!"

"So . . . you murdered Chad? Seems like a weird solution."

"It was too easy, getting everybody here." Kiki laughed, and she sounded more than a little bit crazy-pants. "I'll bet if you asked Trenton, he'd tell you it was *his* idea to crash Diana's retreat week. Nobody remembers talking to me when they're looking for someone else more important. All it took was a couple of comments about the big, strong, handsome massage therapists on the spa's website, and how awkward it was going to be, having a strange man rub you down when you're not wearing anything but an itty-bitty towel. I knew Trenton wouldn't be able to handle that, that he would make some excuse to 'surprise' her. I knew he would book himself into the villa right next to her. And he never goes anywhere without Chad.

"I knew the effects the mushrooms were *supposed* to have on someone roughly Chad's size, but I needed a control sample," she said. "I'm a scientist. I needed a test subject. Our first night, I slipped false morels into Treadaway's late-night room service order before you even got back to the villa. I'd told Diana I had to call Aunt Birdie to check in, but it was an excuse to get the lay of the land, so I could sneak out later."

"Did Birdie know anything about this?" Jess asked. "Is she your murder mentor or something?"

Kiki scoffed. "Birdie doesn't know nearly as much as she thinks she does. If she did, she would have seen me for what I am—the real hope of the Helston family. This was all me, Jess. It was a risk, poisoning Jeremy. I mean, anybody could have seen me tampering with their food, but scientific advancement always comes at a cost. And the cart was just sitting there, like a gift. He and his wife spent so much time arguing, I could have mixed a *pound* of false morels into his stupid pasta and I don't think they would have heard me."

"How did you know Jeremy was going to eat the pasta and not Susan?"

"In my experience, women like Susan don't eat late-night pasta. And obviously he didn't know enough about the dish to notice I'd messed with it. I mean, they weren't even the right color. False morel mushrooms, they have this nasty little carcinogen called gyromitrin that attacks the central nervous system. Given how quickly he was found, I deduced the nausea, the confusion, the dizziness, set in almost immediately. Ultimately, Jeremy didn't die because of poisoning. He died because he tripped and drowned. He was probably so sick, he couldn't have rolled over to lift his head out of the water if he wanted to. And yes, it was helpful, in terms of concealing his cause of death, but I realized false morels just weren't predictable enough. Jeremy could have wandered around for *days* in that state. He could have secured medical treatment or even worse, *lived*."

"But Chad didn't eat mushrooms in his pasta," Jess said. "He just ate enough fancy cheeses to make it come out of his pores and smell like feet."

Kiki sighed. "I know, it was a real pain in the ass. I heard him bitching about smelling mushrooms in *Trenton's* omelet, so that wouldn't work. The tippler's bane was a last resort. I knew Chad was going to drink because that's what he does. And he was gonna go to the thermal suite because that's all he was talking about the night before. And because of Chad's irrational hatred of mushrooms, I had to switch delivery systems, change my methods—boiling them in the kettle to extract and concentrate the poison—but I knew it would work."

"You *did* know we had an electric kettle," Jess said.

"Of course I did, but I couldn't let one of you idiots use it after I boiled poisonous mushrooms in it, especially Diana," Kiki scoffed. "I needed her happy and healthy and engaged to Trenton. So, I smashed the kettle and threw it in Zephyr's garbage when I was done. Nobody noticed one more broken glass object in that mess. The woman never locked her doors. Bad karma, I guess. She was weirdly helpful this week, even if she didn't realize it."

Jess realized how often she'd separated from the rest of the group, working, spending time with the Osbournes. As Kiki's roommate and lone friend on this trip, Jess was really the only one who would have noticed if Kiki slipped away from yoga or the treatment suite. Diana ignoring her "add-on cousin" had made it so much easier for Kiki to get away with her murderous sneaking.

Keep her talking. If Jess could keep her talking, maybe someone would find them. Jess's fingers slipped into her pocket and closed around the flashlight. Maybe she could signal to someone if they passed by. She'd seen flashlights in the woods all week, clearly it was effective. Wait . . . That seemed important, too.

Dammit, she wished she could grab on to some of these thoughts.

"While I was there, I stole some vodka from Zephyr's stash," Kiki explained. "I doctored the vodka with the tippler's bane extract. I told Chad I'd stolen it from the kitchen. He was just enough of a douche to enjoy the idea of taking something from the Osbournes, and he was just thrilled to have a full-size bottle—so much that he didn't blink at the seal on the bottle being already broken."

"I'm assuming my super poison was clear, so I didn't even see it in my bottled water," Jess grumbled, feeling very thirsty. She almost picked up the discarded bottle to wash the acrid taste out of her mouth, but that seemed . . . counterproductive.

"And, unlike this particularly gross brew, odorless and tasteless. I'm getting better, I think," Kiki said, grinning cheekily.

"Why do I get the experimental gentle hippie super-poison treatment?"

Kiki leaned over and tucked Jess's hair behind her ear and then seemed to remember that Jess had puked in said hair. "I don't know, hon. I just don't like the idea of hurting you. You've been so sweet to me since we got here. I like you. And I don't make friends easily."

"Kiki, I mean this, from the very bottom of my heart. Please . . . fuck right off."

"You know, this feels good," Kiki said, huffing out a laugh as if Jess hadn't said anything. "I mean, nobody tells you how *lonely* it is, planning all this murder stuff out. I've wanted to talk to someone about it for *days*. This has been very therapeutic. Almost as therapeutic as the little thrill I got knowing Chad was pouring poison down his own throat."

"But why?" Jess asked. "Other than . . . you know, he was being Chad."

"I wanted to remove the distraction, shake Diana up so she would recognize how close she'd come to messing everything up for the family," Kiki huffed. "And if losing his best friend drove Trenton into Diana's arms, that would be even *better*. I didn't realize that *you* would get in the way of that, that stupid fucking Trenton would come to you every time he wanted to be propped up. Not that I blame him, because Diana has all the emotional warmth of a damned potato, but why couldn't *you* just stay out of the way? Why do you have to be so *helpful*? I mean, honestly Jess, people are gonna suck you dry if you keep offering yourself up like that. Well, I mean, they would, but I'm going to take care of that for you, so no worries there."

Jess could hear voices somewhere in the distance, see lights bobbing in the trees. Will-o'-the-wisps sparkling like lowborn stars. Jess smiled and wondered if they would have time to lure her anywhere before Kiki killed her. Wait, no, maybe it was bears. Did bears carry flashlights? That didn't sound right. Bears didn't have thumbs. Did bears have thumbs?

No. If bears had thumbs, they would be unstoppable.

Jess blinked into the darkness. Something about the way the lights were moving reminded her of something, but the panic and the drugs were too thick in her head to let her think.

"You're just an employee, even if she has pulled you into her bridal party. No one is really going to be that upset that you died. Not even Trenton." Jess glanced at Kiki, who had her back turned to her.

Given the way Kiki was rattling on, Jess wasn't entirely sure that she was speaking to her. "And then, when everything calms down, and Trenton and Diana are married, and Trenton realizes that he's given everybody in the family cushy jobs or gifts but me . . . I can pitch him my truffle idea. I don't think it will be that hard to talk him into something. I mean, I talked him into coming up here. It's going to be *perfect*."

Jess focused all her energy on a small series of tasks that on any other day wouldn't have taken any thought at all. She closed her fingers around a nearby rock, digging it out of the loamy earth that clung to it. She flung her hand out. The rock landed against something with a satisfying *thwack*!

Kiki's head whipped toward the noise. "What the?"

Jess pulled the flashlight out of her pocket and concentrated on moving her thumb over the power switch. The light flicked on and, at first, focused on the trunk of a nearby tree. She moved it so the light shone toward the dancing lights. She waved it around, just in case they didn't see her. And suddenly, the distant voices seemed to get louder and the lights moved faster. Faster *toward* her. Oh, that was good.

Jess focused hard on turning the flashlight off and letting it drop to her side before Kiki turned around.

"Hey, Kiki, Kiki. Kiki. Hey, Kiki," Jess said as Kiki turned to her. "I just want you to know that if you hadn't left bodies all over the spa, and you hadn't tried to poison me . . . I think we could have been good friends."

Kiki sighed. "I know. That's what makes this so difficult for me, Jess."

"You're still a nicer person than Aubrey."

"That's a real low bar, babe," Kiki said, tilting her head to squint into the distance. "What's that?"

"Well, I hope that's four people with embarrassing flower names. We have our own club," Jess said. "And I *really* hope that they brought a man named Blister. And his gun."

"Shit," Kiki hissed. "And you fucking tricked me into confessing like an *idiot*. What *is it with you?*"

"You like talking about your work," Jess told her. "And people like laying their emotional labor at my feet. It's a gift and a curse."

Growling, Kiki dropped to her knees next to Jess. She grabbed the water bottle by the neck and reached up as if to hit her with it, but Jess had the strength born of desperation and having no acute control of her arms. She flung her right arm up, holding the flashlight like a club, and smacked Kiki's temple with it. Fortunately, the flashlight was one of those heavy, metal-type jobs, so it had a lot of impact when colliding with Kiki's temple.

Jess slumped back down to the ground, giggling, as Kiki collapsed next to her. "Heavy metal."

Blister was running toward her. She never thought she'd ever be so happy to see a guy named Blister. And he *was* carrying a gun. And he was holding it on Kiki, even though she was unconscious. Oh, good. That was definitely good.

"Oh, my head is going to hurt so bad when this is all over," she groaned as Dean sprinted across the forest floor. He practically baseball slid next to her, pulling her into his lap as Sis, Jonquil, and Poppy caught up, breathing heavily. Owen was there, too, holding a medical bag. Where was Beth?

"Beth's back at the house," Jonquil told her. "We wanted someone near a landline, in case anybody else in your group got all murder-y."

"Did I say that out loud?" Jess asked. "Aw, man, I'm still all drugged up."

"Are you OK?" Dean asked, his face almost gray.

"I puked," Jess confessed as Owen knelt next to Kiki. "A lot. In my hair. But Owen is here, hey, Owen! Hey, Owen, I don't wanna tell you your business, but I'm gonna need my stomach pumped."

Owen grinned at her and patted her head. "Whatever you want. Charcoal. Saline. The works."

"Oh, that's nice," Jess said, snuggling into Dean's shoulder. "Did I tell you I puked? You may not want to get too close to my face."

"Yeah, you did, but I don't care." Dean chuckled, tucking his hands under her chin to pull her close. "That's how we found you. We found a bloody rock next to a water bottle on the path, and followed a trail of drag marks through the woods."

"Not as smart as you thought you were, were you, *bitch*?" Jess hollered toward Kiki's prone form. "Ow, my head. I'm sorry, apparently head injuries and drug potpourri make me use foul and misogynist language. And they make me super-duper sleepy."

Dean's face shuttered out of sight, and as she drifted off, she swore she could hear Dean say, "Don't close your eyes, Jess."

"Jess?" Owen called firmly as he shone a penlight into her eyes. "Look at me, Jess."

She closed her eyes. She couldn't help it. That fucking penlight *hurt*.

CHAPTER 16

When Jess woke up again, her head hurt considerably less, which was great. But everything around her head was really fucking bright, which wasn't.

Jess was lying in a hospital bed with multiple IV bags hanging over her. Dean was sitting on her right, slumped against the side of her bed, clutching her hand like it was *his* lifeline. She was *surrounded* by flowers of every color and scent. With the curtain closed to cut her off from the other side of the tiny room, it was almost overwhelming.

She threaded her fingers through Dean's hair as her eyes trailed over the different bouquets in every color but Cameo Coral. She supposed she had Jonquil and Beth to thank for them—because each one of them had a tiny card that said "Get Well Soon, Love, Owen and Poppy" or "You lit her ass up. (Get it? Because of the flashlight?)—Sis." Jess sincerely hoped whoever was in the other hospital bed didn't have hay fever.

Dean had apparently smuggled a silver service cloche into her room and left it on a little rolling table poised over her bed. Jess picked up the lid and saw a perfectly golden grilled brioche bun. Dean stirred beneath her fingers, raising his head to blink blearily at her.

"Hi," she rasped, her throat throbbing with the effort to speak. "Did you make me a cheeseburger?"

"It's probably cold," he told her, kissing her fingers. "I've been here a few hours. Owen said you're going to be here for a bit longer, but you're looking pretty good for someone who's been concussed and dosed with hard-core synthetic psychotropics."

"Am I allowed to eat this?"

"Probably not," he said. "But I hear the food policies at two-bed rural clinics are way less stringent than at big metro-area hospitals."

She tore into it. "I don't care. I've told you what cheeseburgers mean to me."

"I am willing to discuss long-term sandwich-based commitments as soon as your pupils are the same size again," he said. "Otherwise, I don't think it counts, legally speaking. We'd have to ask Beth."

Jess nodded. "OK, that makes sense. My decision-making impairment could be the drugs or the head injury, dealer's choice."

"That is just the worst, in terms of things your special lady friend could say in response to commitment discussions," he replied against her free hand.

"I have seen worse," she told him. "One day, I'll explain the origins of the no-Jumbotron policy."

There was a light knocking at the door. Blister was standing there, campaign hat in hand and a scraggly bunch of yellow daisies he'd probably bought at a gas station.

"Well, I can see I'm outmatched here," he said, looking around at her floral wealth—particularly the almost funereal spray with the card that said "We really, really love you—Beth and Jonquil." Blister rubbed a hand at the back of his head. "But I felt like I owed you an apology, since I sort of accused you of murder and all."

"It's very sweet of you, Blister, thank you," Jess said. "I appreciate it. Wait, did you *accuse me* of murder or just imply I was a murderer? I only remember you implying."

"Well, I said some things behind your back. And now I feel bad, having missed all the signs that Kiki was, you know . . ."

"A stark raving looney-pants poisoner?" she suggested. "Don't feel bad, Blister. I was with her all week, and I'm not sure there were any signs."

Blister bit his lip and waggled his head. Jess liked to think it was to keep from laughing in an unprofessional manner. "Miss Kiki said she wanted to 'control her own narrative,' so she gave a full confession, even while Sev Hardcastle *and* Beth begged her not to."

"Et tu, Beth?" Jess gasped.

"Beth just wanted to make sure Kiki got a fair, *final* trial," Dean explained. "No mistrials or barred evidence or any of that bullshit, but Kiki could not be contained."

"Kiki said she appreciated being able to talk about it. Being a murderer has been lonely for her," Jess told them. "Kind of sad, really. Maybe she can make some friends in prison. Dean, my throat is killing me. Can I have something warm to drink? Something that Owen can be sure hasn't been drugged?"

"I'll go talk to him," Dean said, squeezing her hand.

"Miss Kiki's confession is going to save us a lot of time and trouble," Blister said after Dean left the room. "But I'm still going to need to take your statement."

"I'm more than happy to give one," Jess agreed. "And then we can talk about what else was happening in the woods."

"Great," Blister said, nodding as he took his pen out of his pocket. "Wait, what?"

Hours later, Jess was sipping water, which Owen had guaranteed was poison-free, and reading Jonquil's copy of *Fascinating Fungi from around the World*. Owen had been in communication with Helix BioResearch Lab, which claimed to have no idea what Kiki had been working on. But her coworkers had some helpful suggestions on how to flush the drugs from Jess's system. Poppy and the girls had shown up to see Jess with their own eyes and then drag Dean back to "a place where he could shower and sleep."

Jess still had a lot of things to figure out, like how she and Dean were going to build something together, where they were going to build it, and whether she had a chance in hell of buying her bakery building. But she wanted that life. She would find a way to make that happen, be it commute, telecommute, or teleport.

Jess's TV was playing a game show in the background that she wasn't paying attention to. She was glad the other bed in the room was unoccupied because she hadn't watched anything in a week and found the cheerful noise comforting.

Sev appeared in the doorway, offering her that shy smile of his. He held up a box of fudge—not purchased from a gas station.

"I thought your inner chocoholic could use this," he said, setting the box on her bed table. "And I heard you were overrun with flowers."

"Thanks," she said, squeezing his hand as he kissed her cheek.

"You're a very thoughtful person." Sev had closed her door when he'd walked in, Jess noted. But she was willing to write it off as unintentional. She was just grateful that he'd decided to visit when Dean wasn't around.

He sat in the chair next to the right side of her bed, continuing to hold her hand. He leveled her with a sad, pensive look. "It's the least I could do for the person who got justice for Chad."

"Oh, Sev, don't," she said, shaking her head. He squeezed her hand again, and she curved her fingers around his. And it seemed to relax him. "All I did was get drugged and dragged into the woods. By my feet."

"No, really," Sev said. "I didn't know that was something I would even want or need. But you've given my family a lot of peace. It certainly doesn't make Trenton's situation with Diana any easier, but that's her problem, not mine."

"Still haven't talked to her about that prenup, huh?"

"You know, I don't think that's going to be an issue," he said, the corners of his mouth pulling back. "Trenton seems to have lost the urge to merge."

"Ew," she laughed.

"That was awful," he admitted. "Sorry. You seem to bring the dad jokes out in me."

"It's completely unintentional," she said, the corner of her mouth lifting. "Well, I guess that means my part in this whole fiasco is over. There was no 'it's OK not to deliver a proposal if there's a murder' clause in my contract. Got to remember to add that to the next one."

"We can talk about that later, Jess. None of this has been your fault," he told her. "And it's been good, having someone *normal* to talk to this week. I want to make sure you're protected."

"I wouldn't go that far," she teased him. "A normal person would probably be thrilled that a handsome, charming, professional gentle-man came to call while she convalesced."

"And you're not?" he asked, his smiled faltering.

"It just leaves me with a lot of questions, Sev. And keep in mind," she paused and pointed at her head. "Drugged and concussed, so my brain isn't really firing on all the levels it should, or maybe it ex-panded my mind and it's firing on more, I don't know—but I would have thought that as part of the Tillard Pecans legal team, you would have wanted to stick around the spa, to be close to Trenton in this latest crisis, or even wait for your family to arrive. Or hell, I would think you'd visit the police station to discuss the most recent devel-opments in Chad's case," she said carefully. "But instead, you came here, to make sure that your narrative stuck."

Sev scoffed. "What narrative? What are you talking about, Jess? Do I need to go get the doctor? Maybe Kiki hit your head harder than we thought."

Jess swallowed heavily, seriously rethinking the wisdom in send-ing Dean home. She just couldn't bear to tell him about her suspi-cions, and not because he'd already been through the emotional wringer over the last few days. He might insist on being out here in the hospital room with them. And that could be dangerous, consid-ering what she was about to say to Sev.

"After Chad died, you said he was sneaking around in the woods, taking pictures for his stupid project. That was a lie and an obvious one. Chad was at least partially drunk from the moment he got here," she said, noting that he hadn't moved his hand from hers. At his wrist, his pulse was jumping. And she wasn't an expert in these things, but that didn't seem to be a good sign. "He was chugging vodka like there was no tomorrow, which, it turns out, was poisoned by Kiki. He wouldn't have been stumbling around the woods in that state. He knew what kind of risks there were out there, heights and bears and stuff. Plus, Chad wasn't stupid, but he was pretty lazy.

"And I couldn't figure out *why* you would make up such a weird lie," she said. "And you had mentioned the moonshine tasting at the Flannel Days Festival, which also didn't make any sense. The organizers just added that event recently. And the picture that popped up on your phone from your Memories album? You accidentally selfied a photo while handling your phone at this year's Flannel Days parade."

She could almost see Sev processing each possible response— denial, realization, cost-benefit analysis of lying further, resignation. "OK. I drove through town during the festival and saw it, big deal. I think I need to call the doctor. I think you're really sick, Jess."

"It's the little details that get you. I mean, I can't tell you how many times I've been planning a wedding or a proposal and something that seems so insignificant comes back and bites you on the ass when you least expect it," she sighed. "I've seen it happen so many times when I was planning weddings—food allergies, scent allergies, pollen allergies. It's a lot of allergies. But you? I feel bad for you. How were you supposed to keep track of the timeline? When you were actually here in town, when you were *supposed* to be in town— at least the last three weeks hiding out at Hardcastle Pines, by my guess—what you knew, what you were *supposed* to know. It's a lot to juggle, and you were under so much stress. It had to be stressful, being back here, where it all began."

His pulse jumped against her fingers. When he saw her glancing down at their joined hands, he shook off her grip. "I'm gonna go," he insisted. "You've been drugged. You've been hit over the head. You're not making any sense. I'll come back when you're feeling better."

He moved toward the door, his shoulders hunched in a way she'd never seen in Sev. She plunged ahead.

"You're right," she said. "I'm probably confused. That would be really *stupid*, for you to slip up like that when you spent so much time weaving this story for me. And you're not *stupid*, are you? I mean, you're the pride of the Hardcastles, the best of the lot. Poor Chad never even stood a chance against you."

Sev's hand hovered over the doorknob, poised on the edge of leaving her in his wake. Sev was clever. He'd spent his entire life proving how smart he was, how much better he was than Chad. Poking at that particular soft spot was probably cruel, and part of Jess wondered whether it would be smarter just to let him walk out. But she figured she wasn't going to get this chance again, and she wanted this for Emma Lee, for Dean, for peace in her own head.

"What are you talking about?"

"I mean, I like to think you were just trying to get to know me this week, but most of the things you've said to me were calculated attempts to control how I saw people," she said, shaking her head—which hurt, so she stopped immediately. "Trying to make Dean and Emma Lee sound like the teenage Sid and Nancy. Telling me the Osbournes hold grudges. Telling me to be so careful. You were trying to keep me from trusting the family, spending time with them. You wanted me to take your word over theirs, so when I started to wonder what I was really seeing out in the woods, I would believe you. And now, you're here to make sure that if I told Blister about the lights in the woods, I'd mention Chad was probably the one behind it."

"You don't know what you're talking about, Jess. *I* don't know what you're talking about," Sev cried from the foot of her bed. "This is crazy."

"It *is* crazy," she agreed. "It doesn't mean I'm wrong. You're the only person, besides the Osbournes, to bring up Emma Lee to me, and you did it without me saying a word about her. Must mean she's been on your mind."

Sev glared, but it felt like a helpless gesture.

"I think you've been holding on to something for a long time, Sev. Kiki told me that it helped to talk to me about what happened with Jeremy and Chad. Maybe you'd feel better if you talked to me, too."

His eyes darted toward the door. If Sev ran out of the room, she would have been fine with that. She didn't know what she was doing. And she'd trusted her safety to a man named *Blister*. And yet here she was.

"It was just an argument," Sev whispered, sagging against her bed. He sat at her feet, staring down at her, like he was looking for absolution. She smiled softly, even as her stomach curdled.

"It was just *kid stuff*," he insisted, his voice hoarse as the pink drained from his cheeks. "It was right before my senior year of college. I just had so much going on at school. I was taking these extra summer courses online because my dad loved telling people how his son was doing a double major, taking on extra work, becoming a real Hardcastle. But I was just so far behind. I spent the whole summer locked up doing history courses, chemistry, literature, biology. Emma Lee offered to help, like . . . tutoring. Everybody knew how smart she was, and she was nice like that. I mean, she was tough, but nice. And pretty soon, tutoring became her just doing the assignments for me because I was so far behind, I couldn't catch up even *with* her help. She wrote essays for me and emailed them to my professors and took some online tests. I felt terrible about it, but she needed the money. It made everything so much easier . . . I didn't stress out about it anymore because she was getting paid, right? It was just like having an assistant or something. My dad had assistants who did almost everything for him."

He swallowed heavily. "But at the end of the summer, Emma Lee's tuition bill was due. She came to me, telling me that she'd been robbed. Something about her trashy parents and her bank account. I don't know. She needed me to replace everything I'd paid her over the summer, and she needed it *now* or she was going to go to my dad, to the school, and tell them she'd been doing my coursework all along. She had proof of all those emails! She could show that the IP addresses matched her internet service, not mine. But I couldn't pay her! It was *thousands of dollars*. My dad set limits on my accounts or he would get these alerts. And I couldn't have her telling him or telling the school. It wasn't *my* fault her dad stole the money! I'd done *my* part!"

He was yelling now, breathing hard, a blank expression spreading over his face. "At the party that last night with the Osbournes, she said, 'You have a few days to think about it, but then I'm calling your daddy.' The way she said it, with this sneer, like I was some stupid loser who needed his family to bail him out."

"Did she?" Jess blew out a shaky breath. His eyes darted up to hers, like he'd forgotten she was there. "Call your dad?"

"No. She was going to go home by that shortcut of hers, like she always did. I pretended to drive home, but I followed her to her secret path. I tried to explain I just needed some more time before I could get the money, and she *laughed* at me, told me to cry her a river. Poor little rich boy. She tried to walk past me, and I grabbed her arm. She yelled and slapped me, right across my face. And she didn't hit like a girl, either. She ran off and I chased her. I lost track of how long she ran or where we were, but when I caught up to her, she shoved me and I shoved her back and ... and I picked up a rock. I just wanted her to stop so I could talk to her."

Jess gaped at him. "And the rock was going to shut her up?"

Sev shook his head. "She fell and she was just gone. I didn't know what to do, so I just left her there, covered up with branches."

Jess couldn't help but notice the passive, helpless language Sev was using. He didn't kill Emma Lee. *She fell.* She didn't die. *She was gone.* Even after all these years, he couldn't take any responsibility for what he'd done.

What an asshole.

Fortunately, he was an asshole who was still talking. "It was dark. I didn't realize how far off the path we'd wandered. I went back to school and all year, I thought for sure someone would find her, but I guess we were so far off the path that they didn't ... After a while, it got to the point where I didn't think about it every day. And then, it was like it never happened."

"And when you heard that Trenton was coming here for Diana's girls' trip," she prompted him.

"My stupid fucking nephew and his stupid fucking sports complex," Sev growled. "He told me about it weeks ago, bragging that he was going to get my dad to build his stupid douche-playground because he *knew* my dad misses the family spending time up here together. And that meant people and machines, digging around where Emma Lee died. It was only a matter of time before they found her. I watch the true-crime stuff. You see those documentaries where they track down murderers from DNA evidence that's decades old. I don't know what kind of evidence I could have left on her body, what they could find that could tie me to her. I can't leave her out there, like a bomb waiting to blow up my life."

"So, it was you, out in the woods with the flashlight, trying to find Emma Lee's body," Jess said. "You're the will-o'-the-wisp."

"Chad and Trenton didn't pay that much attention to how I spent my evenings." He nodded. "I would have settled for the secret path. I think I could have found her if I could have found the path as a starting point."

Sev sat back in his chair, breathing deeply.

"You feel better?" Jess asked.

"Yeah." He scrubbed a hand over his face, smiling weakly. "You know, in a way, Kiki did me a favor, taking care of Chad for me. But I just don't know if I can take a chance, leaving Emma Lee out there. I wouldn't let her ruin my life then. I'm not going to let it happen now. And I'm sorry about this, Jess, but that applies to you, too."

Sev rose, rubbing his hands on his jeans. He pulled a capped syringe out of his pocket.

"It's just air, I promise. It'll be quick and it won't hurt. But I can't take the chance of you leaving this hospital room," Sev said. "Kiki pushed so much shit into your system. Nobody really knows what she gave you, and this tiny clinic wasn't prepared to deal with such a complicated pharmacological disaster happening in your body. Nobody is going to be surprised when you slip away."

"Sure." She waved off his apologies as much as she could, considering the tubes attached to her arm. "I get it. This is really my own fault for not just letting you walk out of here."

Jess's Big Book of Life Plans: Find a safer way to extract confessions from murderers.

"I like you, Jess. It hurts me to do this, but you know, loose ends." He tapped at her biggest IV bag, preparing to inject the air in the syringe into her line. Jess was mentally cataloging everything in the room that a person with diminished physical capacity could use as an anti-IV-tampering weapon when a small, sun-freckled hand reached through the curtain and clapped a handcuff around Sev's wrist.

"Cutting it a little close, Blister, shit!" Jess exclaimed as Blister grabbed Sev's other hand.

"Language," Blister warned her.

"What the fuck!" Sev shouted, jerking away from the tiny lawman. The uncapped hypodermic needle swung dangerously close to Jess's face. Sev looked down at her and, for reasons Jess couldn't fathom, looked hurt. "Jess!"

"Not my fault you didn't check behind the curtain before you started whining all over me," she told him. "Not my fault that everybody in this weird wedding party circle seems to think it's OK to dump their emotional baggage on me. And then confess to murder while telling me how much they like me. It's a little my fault I used that to my advantage. I'm a work in progress."

Blister began informing Sev of his rights when Jess noted, "Uh, he's a lawyer, he's aware."

"He's a lawyer who didn't think to check behind a hospital curtain while confessing to one murder and attempting another. I'm covering my ass," Blister retorted. "It's the law."

Jess nodded. "I see your point."

Dean opened Jess's hospital door. He gaped at Jess. "What is happening?"

"Your girlfriend managed to entrap a lawyer into a semi-sort-of murder confession," Blister groused at him.

"Blister likes me," Jess told Dean. "He's just cranky 'cause I cursed in front of him. He's very proper. I think I need to go home. Nobody tries to kill me or confess to murder around me at home."

"I don't think you need to be left alone just yet," Dean told her, touching her cheek. Jess grumbled.

"I'm gonna need to make some calls," Blister said, shoving Sev toward the door. "A lot of calls. Your woods are going to be crawling with search and rescue squads. And then I'll be back for your statement, Miss Jess, *again*."

Dean asked, "Are you OK?"

"No. You know, that's the second person who only admitted to crimes in front of me because they planned to kill me," Jess mused, feeling suddenly tired. "It's starting to hurt my feelings a little bit."

The Osbournes agreed that it was no longer a reasonable option to leave Jess under her own supervision. Owen cleared her to leave the clinic that night as long as he was right next door to check on her, and she agreed not to try to extract any more confessions from suspected criminals.

Though she was sleeping at Dean's, she spent most of the first night "home" at Jonquil and Beth's. Now she was being force-fed Beth's homemade chicken noodle soup on the front porch while giving the Osbournes a heavily edited version of Sev's story. She'd already talked to Dean, but he wanted to be with his family when they heard of Emma Lee's fate.

"So, he just . . . left her there?" Sis said, the color leached from her face. "He didn't even try to get her help?"

"He was young and scared," Jess replied from her place on the porch swing. She was sitting next to Dean, covered in a throw so soft she could barely feel it over her feet. The rest of the family was perched on various outdoor items as she revealed Sev's involvement in Emma Lee's fate. "It's not an excuse. It's just . . . the reason Sev gave. He couldn't remember where he'd left her. I think he kind of told himself he couldn't help anyway, so he might as well protect himself."

"I don't know if Emma Lee would have done that," Poppy said from her place on the wicker sofa, under Owen's arm. "Would she really blackmail Sev for college money?"

"To get away from her parents?" Dean nodded. "Yeah."

"Blister checked with the bank manager, and he looked into Emma Lee's accounts," Jess told them. She'd earned a little "informational grace" with the grumpy lawman, as long as she agreed to leave town. "Two days before she disappeared, Emma Lee's mama came into the downtown branch and cleared out her savings account. The manager remembered because it just so happened to be a week before the bank was going to be foreclosing on the Redferns' house. And, miracles of miracles, right around the same time, Mrs. Redfern managed to come up with just enough to hold the bank off."

"Wait, so Emma Lee's mom stole all of her college tuition money to keep a roof over her own head?" Jonquil said, marveling.

"Tina Redfern was a survivor," Sis said. "She would have kept her head above water even if it meant stepping on her daughter's back."

"The manager remembered Emma Lee coming into the bank and making quite the scene over her balance, or lack of it," Jess said.

"And he didn't think to mention that to the police when she disappeared?" Dean asked, his voice quavering.

Jess shrugged. "He thought it was a family matter, wanted to keep it private."

"In other words, they didn't want it getting out that they'd let the parent of one of their account holders drain their money without permission," Poppy guessed.

"I think we can trust Sev's version of events," Jess told Dean, taking his hand. She hated that it was the same hand that was holding Sev's just before he confessed to hurting Emma Lee, but she wasn't going to miss the opportunity to comfort Dean. "He had no reason to lie, and he thought he was about to eliminate the person hearing his version of those events. Kind of a double-blind study, in terms of confessions."

"I don't think that's what that means," Sis told her.

Dean's expression was heartbreaking. "I wish she would have told me. I don't know if we could have helped her, but she wouldn't have gotten hurt."

"Emma Lee always did things her own way," Sis reminded him gently. "She wanted her independence."

"She didn't leave me," Dean sighed, sinking against Jess's side. "I don't know if that makes me feel better or not. It's awful, no matter how you look at it. She was taken from us, and that's worse, in a way, but also, at least she didn't just walk away and pretend we were never part of her life."

"I think that's a good way to look at it," Sis assured him. "And now you can bring her home."

Dean squeezed Jess to his side and pressed a kiss to her hair. She hissed at the pain radiating through her head, even though it hurt a bit less than this morning.

"We'll leave you two to it," Poppy said, pulling Sis and Jonquil up from their seats on the porch steps.

"Ibuprofen and plenty of fluids," Owen told her, even as he checked the saline bag they'd hung on a planter hook as an impromptu IV pole.

"And no more tricking confessions out of murderers without backup," Beth told her. "Or at least, legal counsel."

"I'm sure it was just a one-time thing," Jess told them.

"Happened twice," Jonquil called over her shoulder as Beth led her into the house.

Dean kissed her, soft and sweet, and tilted his forehead against hers. "I'm gonna need more time. I'm gonna need to work through a lot of stuff. But when I come out on the other side of it, I hope you'll be there to talk about long-term sandwich-based commitments."

"I'm going to negotiate for at least one cheeseburger per week."

He chuckled. "I can manage that."

CHAPTER 17

The packing of the Tillard-Helston party became a thing of legend at the Golden Ash. Never had the staff moved so swiftly or so decisively, scouring through Tranquility and Serenity Villas like an army of ants, removing any trace that either group had spent time there. Now that the authorities had cleared the party to leave, the staff wanted them *gone*. Before Poppy could even arrive to supervise, with alacrity the bags were packed, the sheets stripped, and the windows left open as if to rid the place of the stink of Diana's bullshit.

There was no hope of a tip. The staff had nothing left to lose.

It was a strange juxtaposition, seeing the porters lugging Diana's matching luggage up the hill while the uniformed forensics teams from several counties trooped into the woods beyond them, looking for further evidence. Even with Sev's help, it would take search and rescue teams, drones, and cadaver dogs some time to find Emma Lee's remains.

It chilled Jess's blood to picture Sev chasing Emma Lee from the trail. She would have torn through the trees like her life depended on it. Because it did. Had Emma Lee known that she would never make it out of the woods? That she would never see her home again, such as it was, and that she'd never see Dean again?

Emma Lee had been a complicated girl who had done things that she shouldn't have—shouldn't have *had* to do—to survive in a world stacked against her. While Jess didn't have it nearly as hard, she could certainly understand the choices Emma Lee made.

There was some talk of a memorial, organized by the Osbournes, to give people who had known and loved Emma Lee some closure. But there would be time to plan later. When they were found, the remains would be evidence. No one seemed to know who would be in control of them once they were released by the state. Emma Lee's father hadn't been seen in years. She had no family left, no next of kin.

Between the remains and the accidental confession—recorded by Blister, which Sev's legal team were fighting like demons to get thrown out—Sev was denied bail. His family had proven themselves more than capable of providing the means for flight.

Dean had been heartbroken, of course. Jess wasn't sure if it was an invasion to go anywhere near him when he was mourning all over again, but Sis had shoved her through his cabin door and told her, "Stop being an idiot."

The Osbournes made her part of their circle as it enclosed Dean. And while Poppy and Jonquil's parents were confused by her presence, they'd accepted it without question. It helped that Dean and Sis's parents were still in Florida, so that emotional hurdle was somewhat delayed.

According to the elder Osbournes, the people of Chickenhawk Valley were not thrilled with the attention that the murders were bringing to their sleepy little town. Between the lure of old-money dysfunction, bizarre poisons, and the link to a decades-old cold case, the press and the true-crime podcast community had descended, and they weren't very polite about it.

While the hospitality community begrudgingly accepted money from news crews and celebrity legal analysts, Sev's legal team, sent by his father, had been rejected openly. The associates of Benson, Morton, & Rhyne were welcome to dine and stay in establishments one town over in Blue Patch, but not in Chickenhawk. Locals weren't going to hinder Sev's defense, but they weren't going to make it easy for some spoiled rich boy to explain away hurting one of their own. And that was Sev's mess to handle.

Jess stood with the Osbournes on the porch of the main lodge, watching the sheer pageantry of Aubrey trying to corral the members of the Tillard-Helston party into a stretch limo near the guest gate. Trenton had ordered another tank-like monstrosity that would be difficult to maneuver around the winding roads. Diana was griping at the porters about how her bags were handled. Now that he was allowed to use his phone openly, Trenton was wandering around, barely missing walking face-first into a tree, trying to find a phone signal near the gate.

"Are you sure you're OK watching this?" Jess asked Dean. "I mean, do they really deserve your attention?"

"In a way, they've done me a favor, even if they were absolute dicks about it," Dean said. "Without them, I never would have known what happened to Emma Lee. And they brought you to me, so in a way, I guess I owe them."

"That's very generous of you," Poppy said.

"Oh, no, they can go fuck themselves," Dean said. "I'm just saying, their stay hasn't brought exclusively bad things."

"Shouldn't we be a little more polite, at least while some of them are within earshot?" Jess whispered. She didn't know about mountain acoustics and how far they would carry Dean's exasperated words. Trenton might be able to hear.

"Nope, the payment agreement Trenton signed when he completed the reservation is pretty much an unbreakable route into his bank account. He and his guests used services, and now he has to pay for them. As for the tip . . ." Poppy grimaced. "I don't expect much beyond the requisite fifteen percent . . . which is maybe why the kids aren't being particularly careful with the party's belongings."

"The thin veneer of polite service has been shattered, got it," Jess observed.

"Pretty much," Jonquil agreed. "I'm not even giving them their complimentary sugar scrubs before they leave."

"Jonquil gets burns in, in her own way," Sis said, patting her shoulder.

Diana waved to Jess frantically behind Trenton's back. Jess threw up her hands in the internationally known gesture for *What do you want?* This only made Diana gesture even more wildly.

"You don't have to go down there," Poppy reminded her. "You don't owe them anything."

"Well, it ought to be entertaining," Jess said, rolling her eyes.

"Just be careful—she hangs out with a lot of criminal types," Dean called after her.

Diana led her a good twenty feet away from the limo, and after the week she'd had, Jess checked their surroundings for convenient drowning hazards. Diana was looking worse for wear. Her eyeliner was minimal. Her lip gloss had been chewed off. And her hair was pulled back into a simple ponytail. Diana had never worn her hair in a ponytail, not even for Sis's grueling yoga classes.

"What?" Jess asked. "What could you possibly want from me right now? I'm pretty sure proposing is the last thing on Trenton's mind."

"I don't know what to do," Diana sniffled. "The whole story is going to come out. Kiki is running her mouth to the cops about why she killed Chad."

Jess tilted her head and stared at Diana. Did she not think Trenton knew about her sleeping with Chad? Jess was nearly certain that she heard some porters talking about it outside the main lodge that morning. Everybody knew. Also, Kiki just confessed to double homicide, and Diana had somehow made it about her. "Well, yeah, that was sort of inevitable."

Diana's doe eyes were endlessly glassy with tears. "You've got to help me. If I lock him down with an engagement now, it will make it that much harder for him to break it off with me."

"You're delusional," Jess told her. "Your cousin killed Trenton's best friend because you were sleeping *with that best friend*!"

"*Shhh!*" Diana hissed at her, looking frantically toward Trenton. "I know he's going to find out eventually, but as long as I tell him in the right way, he'll know it didn't mean anything! And I know I'm what he wants! It was just a slipup! People have indiscretions! He knows that. Trenton the Third is a hound, but you never hear his mama complaining about his cocktail waitresses. Marriages have run for decades on worse."

"If you think that Trenton will tolerate the behavior that his mama tolerates from his dad, you have failed to grasp anything about traditional Southern gender politics," Jess told her. "I can't do this anymore. I don't want any part of it."

"If you walk away from me right now, you're out—" Diana swore. "I'll make sure Trenton doesn't pay you a dime!"

After the last few days, Jess had processed the fact that she probably wasn't going to be paid for this job. Trenton's legal team was probably going to figure out a way to get out of compensating her for her role in this debacle. She understood that her chance to buy the TonyCakes building was gone and that she was going to have to find a new place to make her life. But when compared to poison-y death in the deep, dark woods, losing a building was just . . . losing a building. Jess would figure it out.

Jess took Diana's hand in hers and squeezed it gently. "Diana, do me a favor. The next time you convince a man that you kinda-sorta want to marry him—even if you're not fucking his best friend—*don't call me.*"

"*Jessie!*"

But Jess had already walked away. She'd tried. But it turned out there *were* limits to what she could and would do for her clients.

Trenton and Aubrey were waiting at the base of the lodge stairs when Jess reapproached the Osbournes. She returned to Dean's side, giving Trenton a lukewarm smile. Trenton appeared to be pretending that he hadn't heard Jess yelling about Diana sleeping with Chad. And that was his choice. Jess was more than happy to let someone else protect him from himself.

"Obviously, I didn't deliver on the contract," Jess said. "And I'm sorry about that. Given what I just said to Diana, I would appreciate it if you don't mention my name to any of your friends."

"Oh, no, Jess, don't say that. You did your best." Trenton gave her a confused frown. "And even before he was arrested, Sev said it would be a good idea to award you a financial settlement, considering that we sort of emotionally traumatized you with Chad's body and all. And then, you know, Kiki tried to kill you, which probably wouldn't have happened if I hadn't insisted you come up here."

"Of course, Sev gave you that advice before *he* tried to kill me," she noted.

"Yeah, that's why my dad gave me permission to add a bit more to Sev's number," Trenton said. "Dad said you almost being murdered by one of our executives doesn't look good for Tillard Pecans. Bad for business."

He showed her a piece of scrap Golden Ash villa stationery with a big red circle drawn around a big red number.

"Oh," Jess said, nodding slowly. "That is quite a figure."

"You deserve it, for all this mess," Trenton assured her.

The collection of numerals would be just enough for Jess to make a very nice offer for the TonyCakes building, without a loan.

"Don't sign anything before Beth reads it!" Jonquil shouted from the porch.

Even Trenton smiled slightly at that. "I'll have one of our legal guys drop by your office to have you sign the papers."

"Maybe just have him email them to me," Jess said. "I'll do a digital signature. I haven't enjoyed my interactions with your legal team so far."

"Fair enough." Trenton nodded. "Jess, when we get back to town, how about we meet up for lunch? I'd like to talk a little bit about what got Sev so wound up."

Trenton was looking at her with that hopeful puppy expression, the "take care of me" stare. This was the stare that got Jess dosed with experimental drugs—the official face of Trenton and his need to be managed. He really needed to cut that out. Jess didn't think it was a coincidence that at that very moment, Diana decided to join them and wind herself around Trenton's arm.

"We have the family jet waiting for us at the airport," he said when she didn't respond. "You sure you don't want to come home with us?"

"I'm more comfortable here," Jess told him, taking Dean's hand. "Have a good flight."

Trenton shrugged, smiling amiably. "All right, then, call me when you get back to town."

Oh, Trenton Tillard the Fourth. He didn't get it, and probably never would. And that was fine. As soon as the Tillard check cleared, it wouldn't be Jess's problem anymore.

There was a prolonged awkward moment during which the two groups just stared at one another. Jess wondered if Trenton thought he was owed an apology somehow, for two members of their party being arrested during their stay. And suddenly, the headline of Trenton's potential Yelp review—"0 Stars, I found out my girlfriend is a cheater and my lawyer is a murderer, would not go again"—made Jess start giggling. And she couldn't stop. The laughter went on and on until Jess had tears rolling down her cheeks and she was leaning against Dean—who was only too happy to let her snicker-snort her way through the awkwardness.

"You done?" Poppy asked, grinning wryly.

Jess nodded, wiping at her wet cheeks. "Yeah, and I'm not sorry, I swear."

"Good. Never apologize for emotional honesty here," Jonquil told her, looking right at Diana. "It's a quality that's all too rare in today's world."

Jonquil *did* indeed get her burns in, in her own way.

"We hope you enjoyed your stay at the Golden Ash," Poppy said. "Please leave with our wishes."

"Isn't it supposed to be 'our best wishes'?" Trenton asked, his brow furrowed.

"No." Poppy continued smiling as she pointed at the limo.

"We hope you get exactly what you deserve in life," Sis said, smiling with a saccharine edge that sent a shiver down Jess's spine.

Ouch.

Apparently, this was too much for Diana. She took a stomping step toward Jess. Dean pulled her behind him, making Diana roll her eyes.

"This is ridiculous. I won't let poor sweet Trenton put himself out like this. You're being so *dramatic*, Jessie. I'm going to give you this one last chance to apologize and make things right," Diana hissed. "For the awful service we've received, the lack of attention, and your *terrible* attitude. And *then*, Trent will pay half of your original contract fee, after you've delivered the proposal I deserve. We couldn't let you fly home with us on the jet, of course. It wouldn't look right. But we don't want to leave you stranded. *I* was raised better than that."

Jess gaped at her.

Apologize.

The fucking gall of it, the absolute lack of self-awareness or accountability. It was as if, in the last few minutes, Diana had mentally edited every single thing that had happened since they arrived at the Golden Ash until she was just a poor innocent victim who sat still and had facials while Jess ran amok and ruined Diana's life. Jess couldn't help but laugh again, her head dropping until her chin almost rested on her chest. She felt Dean's hand on her shoulder, keeping her connected to the earthly plane so her scalp didn't pop right off. "I'm not going to apologize for any of that. I don't owe you anything, much less an apology. You need to go."

Bold words from a woman who was basing that on a scrap-paper promise, but Diana had referenced her upbringing. The gloves were off.

"Diana, that's enough," Trenton told her in the sternest tone Jess had heard him use, well, ever. "I would still like to pay for your ticket. It's the least I can do for you, financially speaking, because I don't think we're gonna be needing help with a proposal."

"Trenton!" Diana whimpered, gripping his arm like a panicky sea creature.

He patted Diana's hand absently. "I'm not saying it's off forever, Di, I just think we need to do something quiet, if we're gonna do it. It would be in poor taste otherwise, with everything that's happened. I mean, if you think my family was iffy about you before . . . Come on, let's just get to the airport. We can talk about it on the plane."

Jess could see the two factions of Diana's ambitions at war behind her lovely face. Her dreams of comfort and the need for her family's approval versus her desire for social media clout and life-affirming clicks. She'd been rendered immobile while Trenton ambled off to talk to their driver. Then she tottered over the gravel driveway without looking back, and Jess was fine with that.

Jess turned to Aubrey, who was face-deep in her phone. "You win. She is all yours."

Aubrey slipped her sunglasses on and flashed Jess an unapologetic smile. "I think we both know this wedding isn't ever going to happen now. And even if it does, any contacts I get—not worth living in this trashy drama-tornado. But call me when you get back to Nashville. Maybe we can do lunch."

"You—wha— After the bullshit of the last week?" Jess cried.

Aubrey waved airily. "I told you. It's not personal. This business is a gladiator pit and you're my new favorite opponent, even if I'm punching down a bit."

"Aubrey, I feel very comfortable telling you that you are the fucking worst."

Aubrey shrugged, unflappable, and slipped into the limo. When Trenton climbed in, the doors slammed shut and the car practically peeled out. Soon, the only thing left of Trenton and Diana at the Golden Ash was a puff of road dust.

Jess turned back to Dean, frowning. "So . . . everybody I know is insane."

"That's OK, I come with my own insane people," he said, gesturing behind him. "Might even call them a package deal."

"I resent that," Jonquil gasped.

"No, you don't, you don't resent anything. It's not in your nature," Sis told her.

"I resent that you're right," Jonquil retorted, now pouting thoroughly.

Almost a week later, Jess was still delaying the inevitable, avoiding her flight back, keeping her cell phone turned off to avoid the messages of industrious reporters who tracked her from her business's social media. She knew that she would have to go back home eventually. Nana Blanche's riverboat was docking soon. Jess could only abandon Mavis to the phones for so long. And she had to have an earnest discussion with the Anellos about the TonyCakes building.

But for now, she needed this quiet.

The Osbournes had moved up the spa's autumn closing routine while the media attention died down. Fortunately, Chandra, the handsomely paid Nashville PR guru, had managed to focus cable news outlets' attention on Kiki's method of murder and her history with botany and chemistry to downplay the *location* of Jeremy's and Chad's deaths. She tried to recast it as a *Snapped* episode rather than Agatha Christie.

Meanwhile, Jess was enjoying the hands-on work of shutting down the thermal spa, cataloguing and storing any body products that would still be usable come spring. She spent her evenings with the Osbournes, watching Dean and Beth battle it out for culinary domination. Occasionally she slept over at Dean's, but they were taking things slow.

Jess wasn't ready to uproot her entire life yet, but maybe there were people in this part of Tennessee who needed help planning out the most important question of their lives. For right now, she was happy to be deadheading flowers that needed it, under the close supervision of Jonquil. Sis was helping because she figured there was a sixty percent chance of Jess hurting herself with the gardening shears.

That seemed fair.

The autumn sun beat down on her shoulders. Poppy was working away in her office, the sound of Dolly Parton's "Jolene" barely audible through the windows. Jess could hear Jamie and Dean arguing good-naturedly in the kitchen while the delicious scent of baking bread drifted toward her. She couldn't remember a time she was this content.

It was probably a sign that she needed to use some vacation days.

Jess's Big Book of Life Plans: Make having a real life a priority.

Behind her, Jess could hear a car rolling up the long drive, crunching over the gravel.

"I thought the gate was closed," Jonquil commented, putting her gardening shears aside.

"If it's another reporter, you might have to break out some bail money for Sis," Jess commented dryly, without looking up from her flowerbed.

"You know, it shouldn't take almost being murdered by a mad

scientist to get you gardening. That's just sort of sad," a familiar voice said behind her. "I feel like I've failed you a little bit."

Jess stood, damn near tripping over her own feet as she turned around to find two small elderly ladies staring down at her. Fortunately, she dropped her shears as she gasped, "Nana! You cut your trip short?"

"I hopped off the boat a few stops early," Nana said, as Jess threw herself into her grandmother's arms. Nana Blanche was resplendent in a pale-yellow twinset and dark blue slacks, even if her tote bag was a casino giveaway proclaiming Tunica the "Las Vegas of the South." Jess was starting to wonder if Nana Blanche really spent her time playing bridge.

Mavis was looking around the property as if trying to absorb every detail. As usual, she had matched her sensible navy-blue bag to her even more sensible shoes and pantsuit.

But instead of questioning aloud, Jess simply launched herself at them and threw her arms around both. "I'm so happy to see you!"

"I've been worried," Nana Blanche told her sternly, her bobbed silver-white hair falling back as she looked up at Jess. "Particularly when I started seeing news coverage of a grisly murder at the 'perfectly safe' and 'world-renowned' spa I'd sent my grandbaby up to. Poor Mavis had to talk me down from chartering a helicopter."

"I told you, she's fine," Mavis said, waiting her turn for a full hug.

Nana Blanche squeezed Jess tight and leaned back, her dark brown eyes made to look even larger by her thick glasses. She placed her hands on either side of Jess's cheeks. "No more remote jobs, all right, sweetie?"

Jess nodded as Nana passed her over to Mavis, who hugged her tight. "Agreed."

"It sounded like you needed some backup," Mavis whispered into her hair. "I don't want to say 'I told you so' about isolating yourself out here with questionable characters. I'm willing to sing 'I told you so.'"

"She's absolutely serious," Nana told Jess. "She even has a shuffle-step dance routine to go along with it."

"That's hurtful, Mavis," Jess said.

Mavis shrugged. "Life is nothing without celebrating the little moments of victory. At your expense. Because I was right. And Diana Helston is a spoiled, awful bit—"

"All right, let's keep it clean," Nana Blanche protested. "Jess learns by bitter experience, and she just had to experience this particular lesson up close and personal, and under extreme circumstances."

"I know, Nana, you don't have to talk about me like I'm not here." Jess sighed. The Osbournes and Jamie had drifted out of their respective spaces to gather on the porch of the main lodge and watch the proceedings. "I get it. You told me so."

"We told you sooooooo!" her family chorused together.

Fortunately, they loved her enough not to add the little dance.

"Fine," Jess said, hugging Nana to her side. "You were right, I was wrong. I love you."

"We love you, too," Mavis said. "Even if we did tell you so."

"You were right," Jess sighed, turning them toward Jonquil and Sis. "And I want y'all to meet some of my new favorite people."

EPILOGUE

ONE YEAR LATER

tepping carefully through her bedroom door, Jess plucked at the scarf tied tightly around her face. "You know, I don't know if it's necessary to cut off the circulation to my eyes."

"How else are we supposed to know you're not peeking?" Jonquil asked from behind her, hands gentle at Jess's elbows.

"That's hurtful," Jess replied. "I like to think I've built some level of trust, considering the amount of time I've spent with you. The long hours working. The holidays—also, there was no reason to put duct tape across my door."

"Honey, we saw what you did during the Easter egg hunt." Sis's voice was to her left.

"You shouldn't have put tiny booze bottles in the comically over-sized eggs. It added incentive!" Jess exclaimed. Sis was there, just beside her, to keep her from tripping. She hadn't quite memorized the layout of her newly renovated office-slash-living-space for Bricker Consultants. The second floor had been completely reconfigured so that the storage room that used to be her shared office was now a bedroom. It was nice having more than one room to her apartment.

"Well, we didn't know you would take the tradition quite so seriously," Poppy said, her voice dry and amused in the distance.

"Can I take this off now?" Jess asked a few steps later.

"I suppose," Sis replied, though her voice was much farther away.

Jess pulled the scarf away from her face and blinked rapidly, squinting against what seemed like a thousand blinding stars in her apartment. Someone had covered the newly painted walls of her living room with strands of fairy lights. She hoped they'd used the no-harm picture hooks, but she wasn't about to bring that up.

There was a distinct lack of Osbournes in the apartment. Even Jonquil and Sis had disappeared. Instead, Jess found a chalkboard on her coffee table that read Start Here. Another chalkboard just a few steps beyond it read The Many Reasons I Love You.

Hanging over the sign was a little note card that read The way your first instinct is to help people. Or if you can't help, to be kind. She picked up the card and found it was threaded through with a little turquoise ribbon. The ribbon stretched out her open door. She followed it down her stairs, wrapping it around her hand as she walked, and saw that it led to a web of ribbons, in a rainbow of shades, strung across her office space.

The construction crews had done a great job stripping most of the evidence that the building had once housed a bakery. The consulting area looked like a cozy living room done in creams and yellows. They'd repurposed the kitchen so caterers could provide sample meals for potential proposal plans. Mavis spent her workdays in one of two fancy private offices she got to design herself. Her favorite part was the fact that she got to close the door to separate herself from other people.

It still smelled like cake. Mavis suspected that over time, the vanilla smell had soaked into the walls. Jess didn't have the heart to tell her about the scented candle she'd been burning. It would be like telling her assistant there was no Santa Claus.

All these changes were courtesy of Tillard Pecan money, which had been paid with an enthusiasm and swiftness Jess had not expected.

"What is this?" Jess asked, laughing as she turned around, searching for the others. Even a few months ago, this probably would have triggered a wee bit of PTSD, but over the last year, time spent at the spa had helped Jess move past Sev's and Kiki's attempts on her life. "I'm not going to be responsible for cleaning up all the ribbons."

"Don't worry about ribbon cleanup!" Dean called from Mavis's office. "I'm trying to be romantic here, woman!"

Dean had been spending more time in the city. Nashville's fine-dining restaurants had fallen all over themselves to get the reclusive chef into their kitchens, even on a part-time basis. Jamie had taken on more duties at the Golden Ash, and Dean was learning what it was like not to be in complete control *all* the time. They spent their free nights ensconced in her cozy apartment.

People still wandered in, trying to buy cannoli, but that was something Jess was willing to live with. It was a good life, one that Jess had carefully constructed for herself, and she was taking the time to revel in it.

The turquoise ribbon was tied to a lilac-colored ribbon, which led to a display of potential floralscapes. There she found a note card that read The way you never teased me about being named Hemlock.

Holding the card in her hand, she glanced around the room. There had to be twenty or thirty cards hanging at random on the ribbon web.

"Am I supposed to collect all the cards for the end?" she wondered aloud.

"No! Just drop them as you find them!" she heard Poppy yell, probably from the kitchen.

"Am I being watched?" she called.

Jonquil answered . . . from the bathrooms? "A little bit."

"After the murder of it all?" she asked.

"That's a good point," Jamie conceded from the supply room. "Didn't think that through!"

Jess swore she could hear Beth whisper, "I told you!"

"Just follow the damn ribbons, Jess!" Sis yelled. "You are the official proposal planner for the Golden Ash! Take a hint!"

Jess snorted. Yes, there was a small petty part of her that enjoyed organizing the spa's new Proposal Package offerings for no other reason than knowing that while Jess was planning dozens of adorable, personalized, *highly photogenic* proposals for Golden Ash guests, somewhere out there Diana had accepted a quiet private proposal that had looked very boring in the photos posted on Helston Luxe-Gram. Diana had managed to *lose* followers, despite multiple posts devoted to her four-carat sparkler. Months had gone by without a peep about the Tillard-Helston wedding plans, so . . . Jess wasn't sure how to interpret that, and she wasn't going to spend too much energy thinking about it.

Aubrey still texted occasionally, trying to plan a lunch together. Jess never replied.

Jess dropped the card and followed a peach ribbon to a card that read The way you vehemently defend your right to eat pancakes for dinner. She giggled and followed different-colored ribbons to a series of cards that read The way you managed to talk Sis into offering goat yoga.

And then The way you helped us keep the spa on track after a super-weird year while acting like it wasn't a big deal. *It was a huge deal.*

Yeah, he really emphasized that one.

The way you've learned to put your own needs first and stop apologizing for it.

The way you managed to talk Jamie out of the Jumbotron.

The way you're infuriatingly competent at ninety-nine percent of everything. The remaining one percent probably doesn't matter.

And on and on. She crisscrossed the office over and over to find the cards Dean had left behind for her. Some of the cards made her laugh. Some of them made her tear up. Some of them—The way you wear socks to sleep, even when you're not wearing anything else.—made her grateful that the Osbournes had such an open sense of humor.

When she reached the end of the last ribbon—cerulean and The way you've accepted my weird-ass family for who they are.—she found Dean on one knee with his bottomless heart in his eyes. And he was holding a cheeseburger. The cousins, Jamie, Lenore, Beth, Nana Blanche, and Mavis—all the people she'd come to love so much—had gathered around him, holding little white electric candles. Her photographer friend, Andrew, was documenting everything with his camera, no one had their phones out, and that was just how she wanted it.

"Jess, nothing about our relationship has been normal or expected or boring. I admire you so much for everything you are, and I just don't think I can go another day without knowing that you'll marry me. I really, really want to spend the rest of my life just watching what you become and what you do. I can't guarantee you perfect happiness. But I can guarantee that I will get somewhere near there or sprain something trying. I love you with everything in me. Will you please agree to long-term sandwich-based commitments and marry me?"

It wasn't social-media perfect, but it was heartfelt. And she saw that he meant every word. She nodded.

"Yes, Dean, I would very much like to marry you."

The family hooted as Dean slipped the ring onto her finger. She realized she hadn't even looked at it. It was a cushion-cut emerald flanked by rectangular diamonds. She grinned at this man who knew her so well. She didn't love diamonds, but she loved the color of other stones. And suddenly, it made sense that she'd woken up a few months before to a twist tie around her finger and a startled expression on Dean's face. He'd been sizing her.

"Get up," she told him just before he wrapped her in his arms. She loved this man. And life with him wouldn't be easy, but it would be interesting as all hell.

"Did I live up to the Jess Bricker standard?"

"Far, far exceeded it," she told him. "This was perfect."

"So, what about marrying me sometime next summer?"

Jess kissed him and gave him a grin. "I don't have any plans."

ACKNOWLEDGMENTS

Having a writer for a wife and/or mom is not easy. When that writer decides to write a proper murder mystery, it can get infinitely more awkward. To my family, you have been very patient, and did not act weirded out when I walked into a room and announced something like, "I think I've come up with a really interesting way to kill a person." You didn't make me feel self-conscious about it once. I love you for that, and so much more. To my husband—you, in particular, watched numerous books on botanical poisons arrive in the mail with considerable grace. Additionally, I can't thank my agent, Natanya Wheeler, and my editor, Esi Sogah, enough for sticking with me as I figured out this genre. I know it's been a lot of work, and I am so very grateful for your patience and fortitude. Thank you to Jeanette Battista, Lish McBride, Kristen Simmons, and Chelsea Mueller for listening to my endless anxious meanderings. And thank you to Caroline Johnson, who is always there, through all the shenanigans. My gratitude also goes to the authors of *The Pocket Guide to Wild Mushrooms*, Pelle Holmberg and Hans Marklund, for saving me from some very questionable internet searches. And yes, Flannel Days is an homage to the Red Flannel Festival in Cedar Springs, MI. It's one of the longest-running festivals in my new home state.

Author photo: J Photography of Grand Rapids, LLC

Molly Harper is the author of more than forty paranormal romance, contemporary romance, women's fiction, and young adult titles. A lifelong romance reader, she graduated with a master of fine arts from Seton Hill University, focusing on writing popular fiction. She lived in Kentucky for most of her life before recently moving to Michigan with her family . . . and she's still figuring out how to choose outerwear and play complicated winter card games.

VISIT MOLLY HARPER ONLINE

MollyHarper.com

⊙ MollyHarperAuth

𝕏 MollyHarperAuth

♪ MollyHarperAuthor

Ready to find
your next great read?

Let us help.

Visit prh.com/nextread

Penguin
Random
House